Donna Baker was born in Hampshire and is the youngest of four children. She began writing magazine and newspaper articles in 1973, moved on to short stories and has written a number of romantic novels under a pseudonym. She has two children, is married and now lives in the Lake District.

. . . .

Also by Donna Baker

Crystal
Black Cameo
Chalice
The Weaver's Daughter
The Weaver's Dream
The Weaver's Glory
Bid Time Return

M.H.Kelly

An Endless Song

Donna Baker

HEADLINE

First published in 1994
by HEADLINE BOOK PUBLISHING

First published in paperback in 1995
by HEADLINE BOOK PUBLISHING

10 9 8 7 6 5 4 3 2 1

ISBN 0 7472 4728 5

Printed and bound in Great Britain by
Cox & Wyman Ltd, Reading, Berks

HEADLINE BOOK PUBLISHING
A division of Hodder Headline PLC
338 Euston Road
London NW1 3BH

ACKNOWLEDGEMENTS

For much of the information on papermaking in the north of England, I am grateful to the museum of the Henry Cooke Makin papermill at Milnthorpe, Cumbria, and to the librarian and archivist at Bowater, who sent me the book *Bowater: a history*. My research into the Canadian logging industry was much aided by a visit to an excellent logging museum in the Algonquin Provincial Park, Ontario, and three books were especially useful: *Early Loggers and the Sawmill*, by Peter Adams, *Parry Sound Logging Days* by John Macfie, and *The Lumberjacks* by Donald Mackay. I have also drawn on information from C. F. Coons's book *The John R. Booth Story*, and others too numerous to mention. The Indian lore came from a book produced by my husband from his own childhood library, *Rolf in the Woods* by Ernest Thompson Seton.

My thanks also go to those in Canada who made our journey there such a pleasure – to Bob and Nancy Moodie, who spent an evening in reminiscence, to Monty Newman, who put his office and library at our disposal, to Ron and Margaret Collier, whose bed and breakfast was like no other, and, lastly but most importantly, to Jack and Mary-Jane Dyment, friends of many years' standing, who gave us a wonderful few days at their lakeside cottage and their home in Ottawa.

For Pauline, with love

Part One

Part One

Chapter One

A blustery March day in the year 1885, with the meadows a glory of dancing daffodils and sunlight glancing off the tumbling river with the flashing colour of new-cut diamonds. A misting of green over the winter-bare hedgerows and a flurry of small birds – tits, chaffinches, wrens and robins – searching out new nesting sites. A beginning everywhere.

Yet there were endings too. All over England, the day was set aside in mourning for General Gordon, the brave soldier who had been murdered in Khartoum after a bitter siege of over three hundred days. And in St Oswald's church at Burneside, beneath the fells which rose gently above to stretch the length and breadth of the Lake District, there was an ending for another man, whose life had scarcely begun and whose name was scarcely known other than by his friends.

For Rowenna Mellor, watching as the first shovelful of earth was scattered over the coffin to hide her brother from her for ever, it threatened a lifelong winter.

Wrapped in a heavy black cloak, she stood very still, her eyes fixed on the fresh-dug earth. Was Haddon really inside that box, so soon to be buried with no more than a gravestone to mark that he ever lived? Wasn't it all a bad dream, a nightmare from which she surely must soon wake? But the dream had been too long, too clear. The cheerful good-byes at the little railway station as he set off for his journey to London. The postcard to say he had arrived safely. The long letters describing his adventures there and the business he was conducting for his father. And then, quite suddenly, the telegrams which announced first his illness and then his death.

Diphtheria. A scourge that could take a man by the throat and kill him, so swiftly that those he loved could reach him only in his last gasping moments.

Rowenna lifted her eyes and looked around at the rest of the mourners, gathered about the churchyard. There were no relatives, for Warren Mellor had no close family and their mother had come from Canada. Most of them were local people, her father's business associates and friends from Kendal, together with the families they had known, the friends she and Haddon had made. The Somervells, the Wilsons, the Croppers. And Alfred Boothroyd, whose mill stood on the opposite bank of the river and shared the power of the tumbling water.

As if her thoughts had called him, Alfred Boothroyd turned suddenly and caught her eye. He was about forty years old, a tall, thin man of almost cadaverous appearance, with black hair that looked as if it were painted on his skull and eyes like black marbles. His lips were thin and wet-looking. He stared for a moment at Rowenna, and she stared back, feeling the creeping sensation up her spine that she always experienced when she met those cold, marble eyes. Quickly, she turned away.

For the first time in her life, Rowenna was thankful that their mother had died ten years ago, when Haddon was fifteen and she not quite ten. For Dorothy had adored her son more than any other living being, and to lose him from such a cruel disease would have broken her heart.

At the edge of the little crowd were the mill workers. They had all known Haddon well and Warren had allowed them an hour to walk down the road from the mill and attend the funeral. They stood sombrely amongst the graves, their eyes cast down, and did not look up as the coffin was carried from the church to its last resting place. But there was a heartfelt 'Amen' as the last prayer was spoken and the earth scattered on the wood.

Rowenna's eyes moved slowly over their faces. She too knew most of them. Haddon had often taken her to the mill with him, explaining the processes so that she knew almost as much as he about the making of paper. He had shown her the vats in which the pulp swirled, beaten into a porridge before the water was squeezed from it. He had shown her the fourdriniers, the great drying machines through which the mash passed, each stage bringing it closer to its transformation into paper, and she had stood beside him and watched as the huge sheet passed the length of the drying room and over the rollers. He had shown her the different kinds of paper made – from wrapping paper and tissue to wallpaper rolled into 'long elephants'. Some firms' catalogues, he said, contained over six hundred different samples.

He had explained to her the history of paper, from the days of parchment to the times only a few years ago when rags were used as the raw material. And he had told her how, when the demand for paper began to outstrip the supply of rags only twenty years ago, papermakers had searched desperately for a new source.

'They tried all kinds of things,' he said, lying back on the grassy riverbank near the mill. 'Grass – esparto was a favourite. Straw. Even rhubarb!'

'But finally they decided woodpulp was the best,' she said, feeding him with plums.

Haddon nodded. 'The world's covered with trees. It's just a question of discovering which produce the best pulp and harvesting them. New ones can be planted in their place. Of course, there have been problems. Until sulphite pulp was invented a few years ago, the wood was only ground mechanically and although the paper is good, it's not right for newsprint. But now, by combining the two, we can make just the right consistency for newspapers. And that's where the biggest market lies. More and more people can read and they want information. They want news. They want to see for themselves what's happening and what people are saying and doing about it.'

His words echoed in Rowenna's brain as she watched the mourners. He had been so alive that day, so interested, so eager to explain. He had talked about Canada, their mother's country. There were forests there, he said, that stretched for thousands of miles. Trees for the taking. One day he would go there to find out for himself, to meet their mother's family, to go into the 'bush' as they called it and see how they harvested the great white pine, the balsam and the hemlock.

'They float the trees down the rivers,' he said, sitting up and folding his arms around his knees. He looked young and boyish, enthusiasm shining from his flushed face. 'They actually *ride* them downstream to the ports. Can you imagine it, Sis? Huge rivers, broader than a road, filled with logs and men riding them as though they were horses. No, not horses. Standing on them – *running* on them. Oh, I'd like to do that!'

'So would I!' Rowenna felt the flame of his excitement sear her veins. 'Haddie – when you go, take me with you. Please.' She looked restlessly about her, at the tumbling river and the brown fells above. 'I want to see these places too. I can't stay in Burneside all my life.'

'Well, I don't suppose you will. You'll get married. You could go anywhere.'

Rowenna gave him a scathing glance. 'Like Kendal! Or perhaps even Lancaster. Who am I going to marry, who's likely to take me any further than that? We never meet anyone else, you know that. Besides, I don't know that I want to marry and have to spend my life doing what my husband tells me. I'd rather be free.' She looked at him again, envying his easy clothes, the way he could move without restriction, running and jumping without heavy skirts to hamper him, envying the freedom that was endowed him simply because he was a man. 'Please, Haddie. Take me with you, when you go to Canada.'

He looked at her and grinned, then stretched out his hand and covered hers.

'Of course I will, Sis. Provided you still want to come.'

But now Haddie lay in the cold ground and would never go to Canada, nor even sit on the riverbank beside her, his face aflame with excitement as he talked of his dreams. And how could she go without him?

Her eyes, moving almost unseeingly over the people clustered in the churchyard, suddenly paused in their movement, arrested by a face that stood out from the others. A dark, gypsy face with eyes that were almost black, sombre under straight brows. A firm mouth and a high forehead under tossing black curls. An uncompromising face, yet with a candour in the glance and a hint of sensitivity about the lips that caught her attention.

And it was at her that the gaze was directed. Despite her veil, she had the impression that the dark eyes saw straight through to her heart. She felt a quiver, as though his glance were an arrow that had pierced her breast.

She knew his name. It was Kester – Kester Matthews, who had worked occasionally for the last two or three years in the gardens of Ashbank. She had met him with Haddon in the grove that Haddie had been planting, for it was in the little wild woodland that he had been mostly employed. Together, the three of them had tended the rare seedlings that Haddie had sown in the little bed near the greenhouses, and talked about the mystery of their germination – a few weeks for the eucalyptus, ten years or more for the giant redwoods and sequoias.

'Such patience,' Rowenna had marvelled. 'And we'll never see them in their full growth. What makes you care so much about them, Haddie?'

But it was Kester Matthews who had answered, looking with his dark gypsy eyes deep into hers, and for a moment she had felt as if he looked straight into her soul.

'A man will always have patience to wait for what he most wants,' he had said, and his voice was deep and measured. 'And it's worth waiting for what's most worthwhile.'

Rowenna stared at him, and felt a quiver deep inside, as if something momentous had taken place. But the next second he had turned away, and when she next went into the garden with Haddon, Kester Matthews was no longer there.

He was looking at her now as if he had something to ask of her. Or perhaps something to offer. Yet what could either of them have to give the other? They lived in separate worlds and could never come together.

Haddon had been able to bridge the divide between those worlds, she thought sadly. But Haddon had gone, and a chasm lay between her and those who had worked with him and loved him, the chasm that lay between all those who worked and those who ordered the work. Only a fortunate few could bridge that divide. She might have been one herself, had she not been a woman, but her sex stood in the way, as it stood between her and so many desires.

The mourners were beginning to move away from the graveside. Rowenna felt a touch on her arm and turned to look into her father's face. It was still and shuttered, his pain hidden behind the stony mask he had worn ever since the news first came. If only he could let himself feel it, she thought, if only he could let it break free. But she knew that to Warren Mellor, such a release of emotion would be as horrific as the crashing of a great wave over his head, a wave that would bring with it the pent-up despair of his whole life. A wave he could not hope to control.

She glanced again at the open grave. Haddon had been everything to Warren, as he had been to Dorothy and to Rowenna herself. And now he was gone, snatched away as if by the blustery March wind, and the glory of the daffodils and the sparkle of the river were dimmed because he was no longer there to see them.

Slowly, she followed her father down the path to the churchyard gate. The mourners stepped back respectfully to let them pass, to allow them to reach their carriage first and lead the way back to Ashbank Hall for the funeral meats. Rowenna passed them with bent head, the heavy black veil hiding her tears.

But as she reached the gate some instinct made her raise her eyes. And there, standing apart from the others and still watching her with that sombre gaze, stood Kester Matthews, the man dark as a gypsy who lived somewhere on the fell and had been her brother's friend.

Once again she felt the quivering sensation that he had something to tell her.

'*You're* my companion now.'

The words hung in the air. Rowenna turned from the drawing-room window to stare at her father. He sat in an armchair by the fire gazing into its flames, but as she moved he lifted his head and their eyes met across the big room. She felt a small shiver of unease as she caught the expression that burned in his eyes.

The funeral guests had gone leaving behind them a house that felt empty and cold, filled though it was with furniture and servants and bright glowing fires. The afternoon light was still in the sky and the bubbling call of the curlew sounded through the windows. It had a cold, lonely tone to it, and it struck an echo in her heart.

'I? But you've never—'

'I've lost the son I had.' It was as if he had not heard her speak. He turned back to the fire and seemed to address his remarks to the flames. 'I can't be without one. That boy was everything to me, Rowenna. I needed him. But now he's gone – and you're all that's left to me.' He got up suddenly, crossing the room with long strides, and she shrank back against the window, lifting her hands as though to ward him off. His hands were hard as he laid them on her shoulders and his eyes burned with the torment of grief. 'Why couldn't you have been a boy too?' he demanded in a low, throbbing voice. 'Why couldn't you have taken his place, worked beside me, been my heir? Why did all the others have to die, and you survive?' His gaze scoured her face, as if by stripping it of its soft and feminine cast he could reveal a man, concealed beneath. 'But no matter. You're all I have left now, you and the mill. You'll be to me what he was. You'll be the companion I need.'

Rowenna stared at him. The iron control she had seen in him during the funeral was faltering. His face was ravaged, his dark eyes haunted, and she felt a surge of compassion, together with relief that at last he was allowing himself to feel his emotions.

But with the compassion came fear, for his emotion now seemed too intense, too overwhelming, and she shrank again, frightened by the passion in his eyes and voice. His huge body loomed over her, his fingers tightening on her shoulders, and his bushy beard brushed against her cheek. She could feel the heat of his agitation, see the shudders that racked his big frame, hear the rasping of his breath. She remembered her impression in the churchyard, of a man holding back a huge flood of grief and despair. Was his strength giving out at last? Was the wave about to break?

A groan burst from his throat and his face twisted. He's having a fit, she thought, some kind of apoplexy, and she wondered what would happen if he should fall. Would he take her with him? Would he crush her?

'Father!' she said, laying her palms against the wall of his chest and pushing with all her strength. 'Father, let me go. Come and sit down – you're not well. I'll ring for Ackroyd, he'll bring something to make you feel better.'

He shook his head. 'Nothing will make me feel better. Only seeing Haddon walk in at the door would make me feel better.' But he allowed her to lead him back to his chair, and sank into it like a man exhausted from heavy toil.

'Father, you know he won't do that,' she said gently, settling him with a cushion behind his head. 'He'll never come in again.' And she felt her own pain, like a white-hot knife twisting in her breast. 'But I'm here, Father. You still have me.'

He turned his head and she felt again that tiny shiver of unease. But it was too late now, and what else could she have said? He was her father, he had just lost his only son, he had no one but her. What else could a daughter do?

Warren reached out a hand and gripped hers. He dragged her closer, so close that their faces almost touched, and stared into her eyes.

'That's right,' he said. 'I still have you. And you won't leave me, will you? You'll always be here. You'll be a son to me, just as your brother was, and you'll stay with me always.'

'Always is a long time, Father,' Rowenna said uneasily, and he gripped her hand yet more tightly, so that she was sure the bones must crack.

'Always, Rowenna,' he said, and again that disturbing intensity throbbed in his voice. '*Always.*'

For a long moment, he held her there. And then, still fixing her with that burning look, he slackened his grip and released her.

Rowenna straightened, rubbing her wrist with her other hand. She looked down at him and saw, with a tremor of fear, a strange look of satisfaction upon his face.

What have I done? she asked herself. And then – oh, Haddon, what have *you* done? Why did you have to die and leave me alone – with *him*?

It was late that night when Rowenna finally went to her bed. Exhausted, she sank down on the chair by her dressing table and gazed into the mirror.

Dark blue eyes, smudged with black, stared back at her from a face almost as white as the paper made in her father's mill. Lifting her hands, she unpinned her hair and it fell in a cloud, the colour of honey blended with cream, to her shoulders. Listlessly, she picked up a brush and began to drag it through the drifting waves.

The evening had seemed endless. Her father had required her to sit by him all the time, silent as he stared at the day's newspaper – without, she was certain, having read a word of it – yet ready to entertain him with talk when he grew restless. And, as she had known he would, he soon tired of her talk – and what else was to be expected, when she had nothing to discuss other than the the affairs of the household and the doings of the villagers, both of which bored her as much as him?

With Haddon, there had always been plenty to talk about. But Warren had never expected her to take an interest in the mill, any more than he had taken any interest in her own affairs. And to find now that she had almost as much knowledge as her brother might serve only to remind him of what he had lost.

Desperate, she had suggested a game of backgammon, but her father had shaken his head. Instead, he rang for Ackroyd and the butler had brought him a tray with a decanter of whisky and a single glass of Madeira for Rowenna. They had sat together, she sipping her wine, he drinking steadily until at last he fell into a heavy slumber and she called Ackroyd again to help him to bed.

Now, assured that he would sleep the night through and that Ackroyd would remain within call should he awake, she was able at last to go to her room and try to find her own peace.

The bedroom door opened and Rowenna turned from the glass, the hairbrush still in her hand.

'Molly! What are you doing here? You ought to be in bed.'

'I couldn't go till I knew you were all right, miss.' The girl came quickly across the room and took the brush from Rowenna's hand. 'I reckoned you'd need someone to talk to. You've had just about all you can stomach these past few days.'

Rowenna sighed and nodded. She leant back her head, feeling the soothing touch of the girl's hands on her forehead and the slow strokes of the brush through her hair. She had known Molly for twelve years, ever since the maid had come as a village girl in her Sunday pinafore, asking for work. It was the year before Dorothy had died and Molly had been fourteen, Rowenna almost ten. Perhaps even then her mother had known that she was going to die and that

Rowenna would need female company, for she had instantly engaged the girl as a companion and maid. To protests that Molly was too young and untrained, she had merely answered that her youth was a virtue and training would be a pleasure. And by the time she died, a year later, Molly was Rowenna's firm friend and comforter, and had remained so ever since.

'Oh, Molly,' Rowenna said now, her voice breaking, 'why did it have to happen? If only he hadn't gone to London . . .'

'He could hev caught it here, just as like,' the maid said. 'It's been everywhere this spring. It's the damp, and the cold. And they did all they could for him, by all accounts.'

'Oh yes,' Rowenna said wearily. 'Everything. Caustic solution applied to the membrane; tincture of iron and glycerine; poppy-seed fomentations; Condy's fluid, laudanum, chlorate of potash – everything they could think of. None of it the slightest use.'

She bowed her head and let the tears fall. Poor, poor Haddie, so cheerful, so full of life, choking and shuddering his life away in London, far from all he knew and loved. Had he thought of her in his last moments? Had he called for her and wondered why she did not come?

She and Warren, summoned so hastily, had come as fast as the train would bring them. But in the last half-hour, they had been beaten by the crowded streets of London. Their four-wheel cab had been caught up in a tangle of traffic, with horses pushing against each other, neighing and stamping as their drivers struggled to find a way through. The chaos was not relieved until a policeman arrived, blowing the whistle that had recently replaced the rattle all constables used to carry and waving his truncheon to add to the turmoil. Somehow, miraculously, he found a way through for one vehicle after another, until all the coaches, carriages, cabs and traps were once more clattering on their way. But the time taken had been just too long for the Mellors, and when Warren and Rowenna arrived at last in the hospital where he had been taken, Haddon had died.

'There's some things must be meant,' Molly said, stroking the brush down Rowenna's hair. 'It's hard, but there's naught to be done about such things. We just hev to bear them.'

'I know.' But I can't bear it, I *can't*, she thought rebelliously. Haddon was all I had. And now Father wants me to be Haddon – he doesn't want *me*, he doesn't want Rowenna, or indeed any daughter at all. He just wants Haddon, and so to please him I must become my brother.

How can I become someone else, even someone I loved as much as I did Haddon? How can I become someone I am not?

'So how is your mistress taking it? Hard, I'd guess.'

Molly stretched herself out on the grass and looked up at her questioner. Leaning over her, silhouetted against the sky above, he looked broad and sturdy; when he rose to his feet his height would give him a commanding, almost lordly appearance. Yet his origins, she thought, were even humbler than her own, though he would never concede it.

'Aye, Kester, she's reet upset. Master Haddon were like a god to her. And she's got her work cut out with the old man now.'

'I saw him walking on the terrace this morning. Looked as if he had it in for the whole world.'

Molly nodded. 'He's in a reet bad temper. Drinks half the night and nothing will do but Miss Rowenna must sit beside him while he does it. It's wearing her out.'

'And when does she do her own grieving?'

'Oh, the master don't believe in that. Says Master Haddon's gone and crying won't bring him back. Well, we all

15

know that, but the tears got to be shed.' Molly shook her head sadly. 'She can't even weep when she's on her own, 'cause he don't like to see her with red eyes, and she can't talk about her brother 'cause he won't hear his name mentioned. *He* can talk about him but no one else must say a word. It's like he thinks Master Haddon belonged to him and no one else has any right to be upset.'

'He's a selfish old bastard,' Kester said. 'And always has been, by all accounts. Rowenna needs someone who'll let her pour it all out. Don't she have any aunts or uncles?'

Again, Molly shook her head. She was beginning to feel nervous about the time. She had hurried out after supper to meet Kester, but all too soon she would have to run back down the hill, and she was beginning to wonder why she had come. For the past two or three weeks she had been slipping out to meet the dark-haired gardener's lad who had almost every girl in the village in a flutter, yet he had never done more than ruffle her hair or give her a casual kiss in parting. Yet he must want something from her, or why would he ask her to come? And Molly knew, from looking in the scrap of mirror in her attic bedroom and the bigger one in Rowenna's room, that she was pretty enough, with her thick brown hair and rosy skin. John Richmond, the head gardener's son, thought so anyway – and *he* would have taken his chance to kiss her quickly enough if she'd been slipping out to him of an evening.

She stretched her body out on the grass and looked up at Kester from between her lashes. Perhaps now he might forget about Rowenna for a few minutes. But he was staring away from her, into the valley, and his dark face was unreadable. It's not her he's forgotten about, she thought sadly. It's me.

'She never comes into the garden now,' Kester said, breaking the silence. 'She used to work there a lot, but we

16

never see her now. What does she do all day?'

'Oh, she reads or sews. The old man don't like her doing rough work. In fact, he don't like her being out of the house at all, but sometimes she goes walking.'

'On her own?'

'Often with me. But quite a lot by herself.' Molly glanced at the little stone hut in which Kester had lived ever since he came to the village. It stood by the side of the old fell road and he had made a garden around it, growing his own vegetables and soft fruit. 'I'm surprised she hasn't been past here. She roams for miles sometimes.'

'Well, happen she'll come this way one fine afternoon.' Kester lay back beside Molly. 'Maybe you'll bring her yourself.'

Casual as his tone was, there was something in it which brought Molly swiftly to a sitting position. She looked down at him, at his tanned face and black curling hair, at the strong, muscled body. His life had been so different from that of the other men she knew – her father and brothers, the village boys she had grown up with, who now worked on the farms or in the mills which stood along the banks of the tumbling rivers. That was one of the things that made him so interesting. That and the fact that not one of the village girls had managed to ensnare him, not even Lizzie Hardacre who everyone had thought could get any man she wanted. But not Kester. He flirted with them, laughed at them and then went striding long-legged away up the fell, leaving them baffled.

Molly had been scarcely able to believe it when he began to single her out, first through her brother Jem who worked in the mill, then greeting her as she came to the kitchen garden or the conservatory with messages from the cook. His dark eyes challenged her and she responded with a toss of the head or a caustic retort that made him chuckle. Soon enough they were pausing for longer than a few minutes, and then he suggested that she might walk up the fell with him after supper.

'And what then?' she had asked, tilting her head. 'I hope you don't think I'm like some of those other lasses, easy for a roll in the hay. I'm a respectable girl, I am.'

'It's a walk I'm suggesting, not wedding bells,' he said, grinning. 'But if you don't want to come, I daresay Lizzie Hardacre—'

'I never said I didn't want to come. I just want it clear what I'm coming for.' She gave him a steady look, then smiled back. 'We finish our supper at seven and then I'm free till Miss Rowenna goes to bed. I'll walk up the fell road then, shall I?'

After that, she had gone regularly to meet him, sometimes for an hour, sometimes for no more than a few minutes. But although she had been ready to defend her honour, she was disappointed as the weeks passed to find that there was no need.

Now, looking down at him stretched upon the grass, she thought of all the questions he had asked about Rowenna and wondered whether he had ever been really interested in Molly herself.

'I hope you don't fancy your chance with Miss Rowenna,' she said. 'She's far above the likes of you.'

Kester grinned. 'I'd like her to prove it! There's no one, man nor woman, who's better than me just for being born in a big house. And I've got something she's never had, nor ever will if she goes on in the same path.'

'And what's that?' Molly said scornfully. 'Something you bin keeping to yourself, is it? Well, if it's Miss Rowenna you're saving it for—'

Kester laughed. 'You think there's others might appreciate it more, do you? Well, it's not what you're thinking of,

18

Miss Molly. It's freedom I'm talking about. Freedom and independence. They're the best things in the world and I'd not give them up for a crock of gold.'

'Freedom? Independence? I dunno what you mean.'

'No,' he said soberly, 'I don't suppose you do. I don't think there's many who do. But I reckon Miss Rowenna might, if only she had the chance.' He glanced up at her, his eyes bright and dark, the shimmering colour of the water that ran, stained with peat, from the fells. 'Try to get her to come out in the garden again, Moll, will you? It's what she needs, to work with the soil and the living things. It's doing her no good to be shut up in that gloomy house with an old man who's driving himself and her mad. Or bring her up here for a walk.'

Molly stared at him. His voice was suddenly serious, his expression grave, and her momentary pique disappeared. Rowenna was, after all, not only her mistress but also her best friend and she had been more worried than she'd admitted about the way old Mr Mellor had been keeping his daughter tied to the house.

'All right,' she said uncertainly. 'But you won't do nothing – well, wrong, will you, Kester? I mean, she's not like me and the other girls – she's not been about much, she don't *know* things like we do. I wouldn't like to think you'd—'

'I'll look after her,' he said, and smiled suddenly. 'I've looked after you all these weeks, haven't I? D'you have any complaints?'

Molly looked at him again, her eyes lingering on the strong brown face, the broad chest half revealed by the loose shirt he wore, the muscles of his shoulders and thighs. She thought of how she lay awake at night, imagining those arms about her, that body pressing her down into the soft turf . . . Oh yes, she thought, I've got complaints, but they're not the sort Miss Rowenna would have.

19

'I've got to go now,' she said, scrambling to her feet and brushing the loose grass from her skirt. 'I'm supposed to be back in time to help Betsy with some sewing. In fact, I'm not supposed to come out at all of an evening without permission.'

Kester got up too. 'I'll walk down the fields with you. It's getting dark and there's no moon to see your way.' They dropped down to the fell road, a rough track which led from the lane up to the wilderness of rocks and tarns above. A footpath took them down through the fields and along the river, and when they were within sight of Ashbank, Kester stopped.

'Now don't forget. Get your mistress out in the garden or up on the fells. There's things she needs and she's not getting them, nor ever will while she's shut up with that crazy old drunkard.' He looked down into Molly's face and then put his arms around her and gave her a sudden hug. 'You're a good girl, Moll,' he said. 'And I'm sorry not to be the one to change that! But there's some things not meant be – and some that must be.' And he dropped a swift kiss on her upturned lips and then turned away and vanished into the darkness.

Molly stood staring after him, her fingertips touching her mouth. *Some things not meant to be – and some that must be.* What did he mean?

Did he really believe that he might have a chance with Rowenna? It wasn't unheard of for young women to fall in love with the gardener's boy, or the gamekeeper. But such romances never came to any good, and inevitably ended with dismissal or worse for the man. Surely Kester had too much sense to involve himself with his master's daughter.

But Kester wasn't like other men. He was like no other man Molly had ever met, forever saying and doing things she didn't understand. Like tonight, when he'd talked about freedom and independence. What did he mean?

Molly turned and looked up at the big house, almost entirely dark save for a light in the drawing room and another in the kitchen. There, the rest of the servants would be gathered around the big table, or in old armchairs near the stove, each one engaged in some task – mending or sewing – while Ackroyd read to them from the daily newspaper as he listened for the bell to summon him to see his master to bed. It would be warm and friendly in the kitchen, almost like a family home.

But in the drawing room all would be quiet. Rowenna would be sitting there with her own sewing – which Molly knew she hated – watching her father slowly drink himself into his usual stupor. And grieving silently over her dead brother.

Some things not meant to be – and some that must be.

What had Kester meant? And why was he so interested in Rowenna?

Chapter Two

'Father, if you would only let me come to the mill . . .'

Rowenna wheeled round from the window and faced her father. Her hands were clenched into fists, burying themselves in the folds of her skirt. She leant forward a little from the waist, her body quivering. Her blue eyes were very dark, the delicate skin drawn tightly around them, and her hair was ruffled by the fingers she had run through the thick honey-gold curls.

'I could help you there,' she persisted. 'I could help with the accounts, with the ledgers. Ever since Haddon died—'

'That's enough!' Warren Mellor half rose from the breakfast table. His face was sagging, his jowls heavy under the thick grey whiskers. But his eyes still burned and his physique was as intimidating as ever. He glared at his daughter and brought his hand down on the table, flat and hard, so that the crockery jumped and rattled. 'I've told you, he's not to be brought into every argument. He's dead and gone and there's an end to it.' His face twisted, but even as Rowenna started forward, the spasm passed. 'Dead and gone,' he repeated with grim emphasis. 'And I'll not have his name taken in vain. I'll not have it dragged in every time you think to use it to get your own way, miss, so think on!'

Rowenna stared at him, then turned away again with a sigh of exasperation. She stared out of the morning-room window at the lawn that swept away from the house, bordered now by the shrubs and flowers she and Richmond, the gardener, had planted. Along the walls the rich blooms of rhododendrons and azaleas made a splash of brilliant red and gold, punctuated by the dark blue spikes of delphinium. Yellow iris, ranunculus, spikenard and trillium mingled with the perennials of summer, some already beginning to flower – the geraniums, the pinks and the freckle-throated mimulus, the zinnias and schizanthus.

Since leaving school there had been little for Rowenna to do at home, and when not in Haddon's company she had spent a good deal of time in the garden. There, she felt she could be herself – unconcerned with her appearance, dressed in an old holland overall with her hair roughly pinned up out of the way, grubbing in rich, warm earth and gentling the little plants into their new homes.

The sight of the leaves pushing through the soil in spring and the buds opening out in glowing colour had brought her more pleasure than she had expected, and she had extended her activities to the kitchen garden, taking delight in seeing her own vegetables – peas, broccoli, sweetcorn – brought to the table. She had even begun to take gardening magazines – the *Gardening Illustrated* and the new magazine, *Amateur Gardening*, and Haddon had given her several gardening books as birthday and Christmas presents.

But this afternoon there was little pleasure in looking out at the beauty she had created. Despite the clear May sunshine, the colours were dim, and although a year ago she would have been impatient to be out there with her fork and trowel, today she felt no urge to be weeding and planting. And she knew that her father would have forbidden it anyway, for since Haddon's death he seemed to find it obnoxious to see her engaged in any pursuit which gave her pleasure.

'I'm not taking Haddon's name in vain,' she said, her voice trembling. 'I'm not even allowed to mention it.'

'And you know why that is.'

Rowenna wheeled again. 'Of course I know! Because you're still mourning him—'

'I shall always mourn him.'

'And so shall I!' she cried. 'I'll mourn him as long as I live. He was my brother—'

'He was my *son*.'

'And I am your daughter.' She took a step towards him. 'Father, when Haddon died you told me I was to be your companion. I was to take his place—'

'You can never take his place.'

'I was to be all that he had been.' She stared at him. 'Father, I've tried my best but it seems I'm failing. What is it you want of me? Tell me, and I'll try again.'

Warren Mellor looked at her. He had aged in the past two months; his hair and beard were greyer, his skin had lost its colour and had a pallor that even regular drinking could not change. His hands trembled and his heavy shoulders had begun to stoop.

Rowenna felt again the pity that she had first known on the day of Haddon's funeral. He had so little in his life. A widower for the past ten years, there had been nothing but the papermill and his son – for Rowenna had always known that she came a very poor third. He had few friends, for not many men would tolerate his unpredictable temper and no woman his slovenliness. Any social life he had was solely with business associates and the few local functions to which everyone must be invited. And his drinking, always heavy, had increased so that he now spent almost every evening with the whisky decanter, staring into the fire he insisted must burn in even the warmest weather, and snarling at anyone who came within his reach.

Few did. But Rowenna, his daughter, must always be by his side, watching him drink the hours away, ready to ring for Ackroyd when at last the stupor overtook him and he could be taken to bed; feeling the pity and sadness of it, at war with revulsion at the wreck her father was fast becoming.

And increasingly in need herself of sympathy and comfort, a need that became more desperate as the weeks dragged by and seemed likely never to be assuaged.

'Tell me what I can do for you, Father,' she begged him. 'It will help us both. You told me I was to be your companion – to be all that Haddie had been—'

'I'm warning you, miss! I'll not have you presume on his name. *Take his place*!' He spat out the words like a foul-tasting medicine. 'No one can take his place, least of all a chit like you.'

'They were your words, Father.' She faced him bravely, knowing that everything she said was likely to inflame him further. 'And I've tried – heaven knows, I've tried. But what more can I do? I'm not Haddon – I never can be. I can only be myself, Rowenna, your daughter.' She took a step towards him, her hands held out before her. 'Can't you find comfort in that, Father? Can't you find solace in who I really am?'

Warren stared at her. His eyes were small, almost hidden by his shaggy brows. They were light brown, their colour muddied and faded by the years of drinking. Lines were etched deeply into his skin; he looked seventy rather than the fifty he actually was, and again Rowenna felt that uncomfortable mixture of pity and disgust. But the pity must win, she thought. He was her father and he had nobody else.

And I have no one else now, either, she thought, gazing at the ravaged face. Whatever his faults, whatever his temper,

I depend on him, because he is my father. Who else will care for me?

'Comfort?' Warren repeated. 'Comfort in *you*? What can you do for me, Rowenna, besides sit by me of an evening, read me the paper when my head aches and listen to me when I want to talk? Those are the duties of a daughter. You're not fitted to do more.'

'But that's just it!' she exclaimed. 'There *are* other things I could do. If you'd only let me come to the mill – I could help you there. The accounts – they must be in a sad state since Haddie died. He used to look after them for you—'

'And you think *you* could do that?' Warren snorted. 'Why, I doubt if you can add more than two and two together. You'd have no more idea of accounting than you'd have of driving a steam engine!'

'And I might know more about that than you think!' Rowenna retorted, for she and Haddon had spent many hours of their childhood at the local railway station, watching the trains and talking to the drivers. She hesitated, then said, 'Father, I think you should know that Haddon often took me to the mill with him. He told me all about it – how the paper is made from woodpulp, how the pulp is mashed and mixed together and then passed through the fourdriniers to become paper. I've stood and watched for hours. I even helped once, when the paper split and the machines had to be reset. And he took me to the office too, and showed me how the ledgers work.' She stepped forward again, forgetting her fears in her enthusiasm. 'I know more about the mill than you think – almost as much as Haddie himself knew. And if you would only let me help you—'

'You went to the *mill*?' Warren broke in. 'You went to the mill with Haddon? You went into *my* office and tampered with *my* accounts? When did all this take place, might I ask?'

27

'On days when you were away on business,' she said reluctantly, feeling that she was betraying her brother even though he was out of reach of all censure. 'And I never tampered with anything. I was interested – and Haddie knew I was capable of doing the work. I *enjoyed* it, Father.'

'Never mind that! I don't run a mill for your pleasure. And I'm surprised that Haddon should have done such a thing. No doubt you pestered him until he gave in – the boy always was too soft with you. He should have come to me and complained that you were being a nuisance.'

'I was never a nuisance,' she said indignantly. 'Haddon saw that I was interested and he also saw that I had nothing else to do with my time. What else was there for me? Only the garden, and you disliked my working there.'

'I'd no objection to you doing a little gardening, in a manner suited to a young lady. What I didn't like was seeing you running around like a gypsy. Nor do I like the idea of your going into the mill like a common working woman—'

'I didn't! I worked a little in the office, but only—'

'You stood in the drying shed, with the workmen,' he stated. 'Didn't you realise you were cheapening yourself? Didn't *Haddon* realise? What must they have thought of you? And to sit in the office, doing the work of a clerk—'

'It was good enough for Haddie.'

'It was good enough for Haddon because he would have become manager – and owner, after I'd given up.' His face twisted with the knowledge that such a thing would never happen now. 'It's not what I want of you.'

'So what *do* you want?' Rowenna returned despairingly to her first question. 'What can I do, Father, to make things easier for you to bear? Am I to be of no use at all?'

'And who says you're not of use? I've told you your duties – to sit beside me of an evening so that I'm not alone in this great mausoleum of a house.' The sudden desolation in his voice struck again at Rowenna's heart. He does need me, she thought. But what of my needs? How are we to meet those?

'You know I do that willingly, Father,' she said in a low voice. 'But the evenings are only a short part of the day. What am I to do with all the rest of my time?'

'Why, what any other young woman does,' he said. 'There must be plenty to do about the house – supervise the maids, discuss meals with the cook, some sewing or mending. And you have friends to call on and invite here for tea. Isn't that enough to pass your time?'

'No!' Rowenna cried, before she could stop herself. 'No, it's not enough. Don't you see, Father, those are the things an older woman does – a woman with a family to look after. But I'm young – I need more. And I've had an education.' She paused, searching for the words that would make him understand. 'Why did you send me to school if you didn't want me to use my mind?'

'Use your *mind*?' he repeated, as if it were news to him that she had such a thing. 'Rowenna, there was no question of your using your mind – you were educated because it's the right thing for a girl in your station in life. How could I have a daughter who was ignorant? Of course you had to be educated, and school is the best place.' He frowned. 'At least, that's what I was advised. Perhaps I was wrong. It seems to have given you some strange ideas about a woman's place.'

'Oh, I know all about a woman's place. In the home,' Rowenna said bitterly. 'But I could do so much more. I could work, as Haddie worked. I could be of real use to you.'

Warren rose to his feet.

'I've heard enough. Young women of your class do not work like common mill hands, and their education is

29

intended simply to fit them for society. To enable them to converse with a modicum of intelligence – not too much, so that they might be thought forward or precocious – and to listen with proper attention to their husbands. Or, in your case, your father.'

'But—'

'I've told you,' Warren said with a dangerous note in his voice, 'I have heard enough. I want to hear no more talk of your coming into the mill, d'you hear me? And I don't want to hear of your visits with your brother. I've no doubt you made life as difficult for him as you're trying to do for me, and if—'

'Difficult? I never made Haddie's life difficult!' The injustice brought hot tears of indignation to her eyes. 'He was my best friend – the best friend I've ever had or am ever likely to have. And I miss him every minute of the day, every bit as much as you do. I miss him because he used to talk to me, he used to let *me* talk to *him* – he didn't treat me like a baa baa black sheep – yes sir, no sir, three bags full sir. He treated me as an intelligent person, who had useful and interesting things to say. And now – now—' Her tears overcame her and she pressed the heels of her hands against her eyes. 'Now I've got nobody,' she went on after a few moments. 'Nobody who thinks my opinion is worth one jot. Nobody who is interested in *me* for *myself.*'

There was a moment's silence. Rowenna lowered her hands and looked at her father. Was there a chance that her desperate words might have reached some long-hidden depth of humanity in that cold, rigid personality? Was it possible that he might recognise her own right to grieve for her brother?

'Haddie wasn't just yours,' she said in a low, quivering voice. 'He was mine as well. He belonged to us all.'

'He belonged to *me*,' Warren said. 'He was my son. I

fathered him. You just happened to be born a few years later. If you'd been a boy—'

'But I'm *not* a boy! I can never be other than I am – but does that make me any less valuable? Am I to be second-best all my life?'

Warren stared at her. His eyes were cold and hard, like stones in a face of marble. But there was a tremor in his cheek and a tautness in his jaw that warned Rowenna of the terrifying temper that might all too easily erupt.

'Go to your room, Rowenna,' he said icily. 'You're over-wrought and hysterical. I will not have you shouting at me in this ill-bred manner, and I will not listen to any more talk of the mill or of your brother.'

'But Father—'

'*Enough*!' he roared, and she flinched away from the anger in his voice. 'Do as I say, miss, and go to your room at once. And stay there until I say you may come out.' His eyes were narrowed and glittering. 'I shall have to give serious consideration to your future,' he continued. 'You've been allowed to run wild for too long, and to have your own way in matters you should not even have known about, much less concerned yourself with. It's turned your head, just as I was told it would. Well, I have only myself to blame. Enough people warned me of the consequences of too much education for a girl, but I saw no harm in it, and Haddon—' He stopped abruptly and turned away. 'Well, we'll not go into that. It's done now. But you may as well get it into your head here and now, Rowenna, that whatever flighty ideas they gave you at that school, your place here is to keep me company of an evening, at mealtimes and at any other time I may wish it. As for the rest, you'll occupy yourself with womanly tasks about the house, and be thankful for your lot.'

'Thankful!' Rowenna exclaimed. 'Thankful! Why, I'd as

31

soon be born in a cottage! At least then I'd have the freedom of fresh air in my lungs, and a walk on the fells of a
Sunday afternoon.'

'And a cold, damp bed of straw and rags to lie on,' Warren
retorted. 'You don't know what you're talking about. You
should be thanking God on your knees daily for your lot in
life – and you can make a start now. Get upstairs to your
room, as I told you, and let's have no more argument.'

Rowenna stared at him, then turned on her heel and
stalked out of the room. She was trembling with anger
and distress, and the tears ached in her throat, but she held
her head high, determined not to let them fall while still
in her father's sight. She heard him follow her to the door
and knew that he stood at the bottom of the stairs watching
as she mounted them. But she did not look down. Her back
straight, her chin up, she climbed steadily to the top, turned
the corner and went into her room. And, before he could
think of locking her in, she did so herself, turning the key
with a loud, defiant click.

Even when she was safely inside, she refused to weep.
Her anger was a hard knot inside her, her tears turned to
ice. Instead of throwing herself on her bed, she sat by the
window, gazing out at the fells that swooped up to the distant skyline, and she clenched her hands once again into
fists and beat them softly upon the windowsill.

Why should fathers be permitted to keep their daughters
prisoner? Why should any man consider it his right to order
a woman's life to suit his own convenience – literally, to take
it away from her so that she had no control over her own
destiny, no opportunity to realise her own wishes? What
was the point of being born a woman at all, if one was never
to be allowed to enjoy life in any way? What was the point
in having a brain if one was never to be permitted to use it?

Rowenna knew very well what her father would have

answered to these questions. Women were born so that they could grow up to give birth to sons. And they were given brains so that they could bring up these sons to be fine, intelligent men. And, of course, so that they could listen dutifully to their husbands and fathers, and be satisfactory companions.

It's not enough, she thought, letting her glance wander down to the valley, where her father's mill stood beside the river. The building was old, for it had once been a cornmill and had been derelict for some time before her grandfather had taken it over to start his papermaking business. Now, more and more people were being educated and wanted books and newspapers to tell them what was happening in the world. Weekly magazines were appearing, such as *Tit-Bits*, *Bicycling News*, and the gardening magazines Rowenna favoured. The papermaking business was beginning to flourish and new methods of making paper being developed and perfected.

To Haddon Mellor, it had been an interesting and exciting time, and he had passed his enthusiasm on to his sister. Together, they had pored over maps and illustrations showing the forests of Scandinavia and Canada, where the woodpulp that almost all papermakers now used came from. Together they planned to visit such places – especially Canada, where their mother had been born – although Rowenna had never been quite sure that Haddon had seriously intended to take her with him. He expected me to be married by then, and no longer interested, she thought. But I wouldn't have been. I would always have been ready to go with him.

But now Haddon was dead, and would never go to Canada. And how could Rowenna go without him?

Rowenna spent the rest of that afternoon and evening in

her room. At supper-time, Molly appeared with a command from Warren that she go downstairs. But Rowenna shook her head.

'Tell him I have a headache, and bring me a tray. I think my father and I are better apart this evening.'

Molly went downstairs but returned without a tray, to say that the master insisted Miss Rowenna joined him at once. 'If you want to eat, you're to go down and eat with him,' the maid reported. 'If you're too poorly to walk down the stairs, you're too poorly for supper. I'm sorry, miss, but that's what he told me to say.'

'So I'm to be starved out, am I!' Rowenna said ruefully. 'Well, I daresay I can get through a night without food. Tell him I wish him a very good night and am sure my headache will be better by breakfast time. And then go to your own bed early, Molly. Or go for a walk – it's a beautiful evening.' She looked out of the window and sighed. 'I only wish I could come with you.'

She locked the door again after the maid and then returned to the window, looking out again at the long shadows of the May evening, at the reds and golds and purples of the azaleas and rhododendrons in the garden, at the green hills above. An evening walk ... It was such a waste to be indoors.

Even Molly had more freedom than she had. An hour or two each afternoon to herself – the evenings, if Mrs Partridge didn't need her help in the kitchen. The company of the other servants as they sat together, mending or reading by the stove, or perhaps out in the yard on these fine warm evenings. And no one to frown if she went walking, along by the river or up on the fell.

But I could go this evening, she thought suddenly. I could slip down the back stairs while Father's having his supper. If I lock my door he'll never know – even if he comes to talk to

34

me, he'll think I'm asleep, or sulking. And Ackroyd will take care of him later on.

Already half on her feet, she hesitated. Suppose he did come up to her room, suppose he wasn't satisfied that she might be asleep or sulking and called Ackroyd to bring another key ... But wasn't it more likely that he'd shrug and simply start drinking a little sooner, the sooner to fall into heavy slumber and have to be undressed by the men-servants and laid on his own bed?

The idea caught at her imagination. An evening walk ... and no need to hurry back, for darkness would not fall until ten o'clock and tonight there would be a full moon and enough light to see one's way.

When would she have another chance like this?

Ten minutes later, dressed in an old skirt and blouse, with a shawl in case it grew cold later, she was tiptoeing down the back stairs. The house was quiet. Warren would be having his supper in the big, dark-panelled dining-room while the servants ate theirs together in the kitchen. She could hear their voices as she came down into the basement. And then she was in the back hall, where Cook received tradesmen and where she was most likely to be seen by some small maid, sent out to the scullery with dirty dishes.

To her relief, the kitchen door was closed. Rowenna slid past and snicked open the back door. She stood for a moment in the yard, breathing in the fresh warm air and listening to a blackbird singing in an apple tree, as if in welcome. And then, aware that at any moment she might be seen, she slipped like a shadow along the walls of the house and down the narrow, twisting path that led through the beginning of the front shrubbery and out into the lane.

She had done it! She had got out of the house without being seen and was free to stay out, for as long as she liked. Everyone thought her locked in her room, and instead she was out in the long twilight, free to roam wherever she pleased and no one to call her back.

Rowenna stepped briskly along the narrow lane. It was fringed with bluebells and the white starry flowers of ramson. Above her, the trees hung heavy with leaves and blossom: lime and horse chestnut and some late wild cherry. Thrushes and blackbirds filled the air with loud music, and smaller birds flew hurriedly back and forth, their beaks crammed with gnats as they gave their nestlings the last feed of the day.

A short way along the lane, she opened a gate into a field and crossed the river. From here, she could follow footpaths through the meadows and up to the fell road that led to Potter Tarn. If she met a few people – courting couples, old men out for a stroll – it was no matter, for who knew that Miss Rowenna was virtually a prisoner these days? No one would think it odd to see her walking the paths she had so often walked with her brother.

Rowenna paused for a moment, looking down at the swift-running water. As children, she and Haddon had spent hours here, wading in the little pools between the rocks, catching lurking trout with their fingers and watching the brilliant blue flash of kingfishers and the brown sinuous otters that slid from the banks to swim and dive. With a piece of bread and a lump of cheese in their pockets, they had walked up to the fell and spent whole days there, wandering amongst the tarns and lying on their backs in the heather, staring up at the wheeling sky and listening to the high fluting song of the lark.

That was before their mother had died, for Dorothy had always encouraged her children to enjoy the surroundings in which they lived and to wander freely, making their own pleasures. And in those days Warren had taken little interest in either of them. But even later, when Dorothy was dead and Haddon old enough to warrant his father's attention, they had escaped as often as possible, going for long walks when Warren was occupied with other things.

This was the first opportunity Rowenna had had since Haddon had gone on his ill-fated journey to London. She stood on the riverbank, her hand on the gnarled trunk of a leaning willow tree, gazing down at the water and remembering the last time she had stood here, with Haddon beside her, and laughed and talked of Canada.

And now it would never be. For without Haddon, she was trapped. Without money or means, she could scarcely get as far as Kendal without her father's permission, let alone Canada. And as she stood watching the river flow swiftly on its way to the sea, she seemed to see her own life flowing away before her, swift and unalterable. An unvarying round of dutiful evenings, watching her father drink himself into oblivion, and days spent indoors, like an animal in a cage.

What would happen if she walked away tonight and never turned back? If she strode over the fells towards some distant town and found work there – as a governess perhaps, as a seamstress, as a lady's maid? Would her father search for her and bring her home, to be kept under even stricter lock and key?

Or would her new life be even more of a trap – living in some bleak room, at the beck and call of other people? She thought of her father's words – *a cold, damp bed of straw and rags to lie on.* Was that really what it could be like? Was there, in fact, no escape at all?

With a shrug, Rowenna turned away and set her face towards the hills. Whatever the future held, she would not waste this evening by worrying about it. The sun was still in the sky and although the shadows grew longer by the minute, the fading light would be followed by the brilliant glow of the moon, lighting the path before her. And that's what my life will be like, she thought with sudden determination. It may look dark and gloomy now, but it *will* become brighter. I'll make it so. And I'll find a new way to live it.

Haddon's light had been taken from her for ever, but she would not walk the rest of her days in shadow.

The old track leading up to the fell was thick with the grasses and flowers of early summer. Ragged robin, ox-eye daisy and clover carpeted the banks and honeysuckle, pink and gold, creamed the hedges. Butterflies flitted between the flowers – the elegant orange-tip, the finely marked tortoiseshell and the flamboyant red admiral; while in damp corners, sunny with yellow iris, the demoiselle dragonflies danced on gauzy wings.

Rowenna strolled between the hedges, her face lifted to the warm air. Away on her left she could see the craggy outlines of the Langdale Pikes and Wetherlam; to her right were the pleated slopes of the Howgills. In winter, there was often snow to be seen gleaming on those hills and the trains brought visitors to climb the rocks and skate on the lakes. But most people came in the summer to enjoy the long hours of daylight and the walks across the fells. The days of the poets were gone now, but Wordsworth, Southey, Coleridge and the others, who had lived here and known each path across the mountains, had written enough to bring generations of people to see the beauty that had inspired them.

The path wound on, up the hill and on to the open moorland. Here, in places, the green fists of the bracken were uncurling into delicate fronds that would soon be as high as a man, but most of the fell was covered with heather, still dark-stemmed and apparently lifeless although in a month or two it would spread a carpet of amethyst across the hills. The tarns were aflame with sunset, like beaten copper under the flushing dome of the sky, and Rowenna sat down on a rock, and held her hands out to the burnished glow almost as if to warm them.

'You're a long way from home.'

The voice startled her. She turned quickly and looked up into a pair of sparkling dark brown eyes in a suntanned face. Black hair curled over a broad, high forehead and white teeth flashed in a grin of mischief and delight.

Rowenna stared at him. For a moment, she was transported back to the churchyard on the day of her brother's funeral, eight weeks before. She saw again the crowd of mourners, the mill workers, the servants and, amongst them, this same dark face, these same eyes that had looked at her then as if there were something he needed to ask, something he should say. And then she had walked past him, and never seen him since.

'You're Kester Matthews – the gardener's boy.'

The smile vanished. He lifted his head proudly. 'I'm nobody's boy. Nor man, neither. I belong to myself.' He grinned again and thrust out his hand. 'Aye, Kester Matthews – and I may be at your service, but only if it suits me!'

Rowenna looked at the hand. It was brown and strong, with long fingers. The nails were short and cleaner than she would have expected from one who spent his days in gardens and woods. A little doubtfully, she took it, wondering if she had ever shaken a servant's hand before. But this man didn't seem to think he was a servant.

'But you do work in our gardens,' she said, still tilting her head to look up at him. He stood, tall and rock-solid, one foot up on a tussock, almost as if he owned the fells and everything on them. 'We've talked about the trees. And my brother talked about you quite a lot.'

'Oh aye,' he said, and dropped down to sit beside her.

'Hal and me were friends. He had no side about him, did Hal, he'd talk to anyone. We often sat up here and talked, him and me.' He sat quietly for a moment and then said, 'I miss him. But not as much as you do, I reckon.'

Rowenna felt the accustomed ache in her throat. She had grown used to holding back her tears, knowing how her father disliked them, but there were still times when a sudden sharp memory could overwhelm her. And such a reminder, coming in a place where she too had walked and talked with Haddon, touched her deeply. Unable to speak, she nodded, and felt the tears begin to flow.

Kester sat beside her without speaking. But after a few minutes she felt his hands on her shoulders, and at last her trembling ceased.

'There,' he said softly. 'That's what you've been needing. That's what you've been needing all this long, long time.'

Rowenna lifted her head and looked at him. She searched his dark face, tried to see the expression in his eyes, but the light was fading from the sky now and the moon not yet showing above the rolling horizon.

'Who are you?' she whispered shakily. 'How did you know what I needed? How do you know so much about me?'

His teeth flashed white in a smile. 'Do I know much about you? Or maybe it's just commonsense, knowing what we all need in times of trouble. An arm around the shoulder, someone to sit nearby and share whatever needs to be shared . . . It isn't much to do, even for a stranger.'

'But we're not strangers. It's as if – as if we've known each other a long time.'

'You've seen me about the garden. I've worked there a year or two now, on and off.'

'As long as that? I thought it was just a few months.'

'I come and go,' he said, and the smile was in his voice. 'I work when and where I like. Those I work for know me and know I'll do a good job for them, but I never stay long.'

'But why not? You could do well – you could become a head gardener—'

'And bow and scrape and touch my forelock whenever the master comes to inspect my borders and my vegetables? Not for me! I call no man master,' he said proudly. 'I sell them my labour and I sell them my skill but I will never sell anyone my life, nor my soul. That's what happens when a man takes on a "position". He's no longer his own man. Nobody owns Kester Matthews.'

Rowenna shivered suddenly and he put his arm around her waist and lifted her to her feet. 'You're shrammed with cold. Let's get you down to my hut and put something hot into you. You've a long walk home and you can't do it in this state.'

She looked at the darkening sky. The sun had gone and there was a pale glow in the eastern sky, where the moon was beginning to rise. 'It's late. It must be past ten—'

'Does anyone know you're out? Will anyone miss you?'

She shook her head. She had told Molly not to come to her again that evening. Even if the maid disobeyed her, she would think Rowenna asleep.

'Then no one'll worry. And we've got all the time in the world, till daybreak.' He led her along the narrow path through heather that brushed knee-high against their legs. 'I'll see you home safe, don't fret.'

Rowenna followed him silently, still bemused. It was like a dream, she thought, one of those long dreams that seem so logical until you wake, when they are revealed as confusion and nonsense. The quarrel with her father, the secret escape down the back stairs, the walk up through the flower lanes to the fell. The beauty of the tarn, drenched in auburn sunlight, and the sudden appearance of this enigmatic man, whose eyes had sought to give her a message in the church-yard, and who seemed to know just how to hold her, just how to give her the comfort she craved.

Who was he? What was he? He worked in the garden, yet refused to call any man master. He talked with an accent that was partly familiar, partly strange, as if he had learned his speech from a number of different sources. Yet he sounded educated, as if his intelligence had been fed and developed beyond that of any gardener Rowenna had ever known.

He had been her brother's friend. More than once, Haddon had mentioned walking on the fells with Kester Matthews, who worked in the woods. But there had been no more than that. Rowenna had never questioned Haddie about his friends, for when they were together there was too much else to talk about. And there had been long periods when Kester's name was not mentioned – times when he'd been away, working somewhere else, she guessed now – and she had almost forgotten that he existed.

She would not be able to forget again. Not after tonight.

They reached the fell road. The moon was high enough now to shed its cold, bright light over all the fields and woods that lay spread below. Far to their right were the hills of Low Furness and the sweep of Morecambe Bay, with Kendal in the valley. Ahead were the folds of the Howgills. And at the bottom of the road, just before it joined the lane leading to Garnett Bridge, was Kester's hut.

Rowenna stared at it.

'It's old William's shepherd's hut. I thought it had fallen down.'

Kester grinned. 'It had, very nearly. I put back a few of the stones that had fallen out, stuffed up a couple of holes in the roof and it was as snug as you like. I've made a bit of a garden round it too, and with these trees and the old wall shielding me from the road hardly anyone knows I'm here.'

He ducked through the low doorway and Rowenna followed him to find him lighting an old lantern that hung from a nail in the roof. The light flickered for a moment, then steadied, and she looked around.

'It's really cosy. Like a proper home.'

'And so it is a proper home,' he retorted. 'It's my home. One of my homes,' he added swiftly. 'But I think perhaps the one I like best.'

Rowenna turned and looked at him again. He stood in the soft light, the shadows playing on his dark face. His eyes gleamed and she felt a sudden qualm. What was she doing here with this stranger, late at night? No one knew she was here. No one would ever guess . . .

She drew her shawl around her. 'I think I should go home—'

'No.' His voice was quiet but definite, and her qualm deepened to fear. 'Not yet,' he said, and pushed her gently down on to a seat made from a bundle of hay with an old blanket thrown over it. 'You'll have something hot to drink first, and a bite to eat. And then I'll take you home.'

'But—'

'No one is going to worry about you. And you've nothing to fear from me.' She heard the tenderness in his voice and knew that she could only believe him, only trust him. 'I was your brother's friend, remember? Am I going to harm my friend's sister?'

The light was clear enough now for her to look into his face and see at last the expression in his eyes. And although she did not fully understand what she saw there, she understood enough to know that she could, for tonight at least, trust this man, and that she could rest easy in his company.

Who he was, what he was – those were questions that must wait for another day.

Chapter Three

By five o'clock next morning, Rowenna was back in her bed, but the curtains were drawn open and she lay gazing wide-eyed at the summer dawn. She felt curiously light-headed, exhausted from lack of sleep yet quite unable to close her eyes. Her mind was filled with images, of words and ideas – and, most of all, the sense of having found at last someone who could take Haddon's place.

No, she thought sharply, not Haddon's place. I shan't fall into the trap my father has done, nor set such a trap for Kester. No one can take Haddon's place, and Kester is the last man who would want to. Only his own place is good enough for him. He's too proud to want someone else's.

In fact, she thought, he is the only man I have ever met who is really proud. Not conceited or vain or self-important – just naturally proud to be himself. *Happy* to be himself, without any pretence, without any need to act a part. Just to be Kester, and glad of it.

And yet . . . how much did she know about him, even now? After a night spent in his company, he was still a stranger to her. A stranger to whom she had poured out her heart.

Outside in the garden, the birds were singing. The black-bird, always the first to break the silence of the night, had woken the rest with his liquid melody and now they were all busy – the chaffinches, the tits, the robin and, above them all, the songthrush, the blackbird's closest rival. In a little while they would be quiet again, occupied with their nests, but for this hour the air was loud with their music.

Rowenna sat up in bed. If she had been found with Kester... She shuddered. That was why she had not allowed him to come all the way to the house with her; why, half a mile away through the fields, she had said goodbye and sent him back to the shepherd's hut upon the fell road.

'There's nothing to hurt me here,' she had said as he stood by the stile, still half inclined to cross it. 'There's no one about at this hour, and if there were they would probably be just as anxious to keep out of my sight. I'll be home in ten minutes.'

He looked at her. Under the shadow of a tall ash tree, in the last shreds of night, his expression was once more hidden, but she could feel the warmth of his hand over hers on top of the stile. Warmth radiated from his body too, though Rowenna was shivering a little in the cool air, and she remembered how she had rested against him only a few hours before, comforted by his strength. But those moments were past, and in spite of all that had passed between them they were apart once more, two separate beings.

She felt a sudden bleak loneliness. Standing there at the stile, it seemed to her that they were at a crossroads, where ways might part never to meet again, that if she left him now he might remain for ever nothing more than the memory of a dream.

But what else could she do? With a sigh, she drew her hand from under his and began to turn away. And Kester reached out and touched her cheek.

'Come again,' he said quietly. 'Walk up to my hut again, one of these fine evenings.'

She shook her head. 'I don't know. I've told you how it is with my father.'

'Aye,' he said, and then, 'Well, I'll see you in the garden. I'm usually about, in the woods mostly. You can always find me there.'

He dropped his hand from her face and Rowenna climbed the stile and walked across the field to the lane. At the gate, she paused and looked back.

The pearly light of early dawn was creeping across the meadow, flushing the sky with primrose and lending the first hint of colour to the grey of grass and hedgerow. Under the trees, the shadows were still deep. It was impossible to see if Kester was still there.

Rowenna closed the gate and hurried up the lane, wondering if she had been missed and whether she could slip into the house unnoticed. But there was no hue and cry, no panic and no angry father, and Rowenna was able to run silently up the back stairs and into her room where she lay wakeful, thinking over the events of the night.

The 'something hot' Kester had promised her turned out to be strong tea, made with water boiled on the small spirit stove he kept in one corner. But just before handing her the large, thick cup he added something from a bottle. Rowenna, realising how cold and thirsty she was, took it eagerly, sipped and immediately began to cough.

'Whatever is it?' she exclaimed, wiping her eyes. 'Are you trying to poison me?'

Kester laughed. 'Not at all! That's just a drop of brandy to warm you. And you'd better have a bit of bread and cheese too, to keep you going on the road home.'

Rowenna took it, aware now of hunger as well as thirst. The food was plain but tasted like ambrosia and she devoured it gratefully.

'Thank you. Actually, I haven't had anything to eat since lunch-time.'

Kester stared at her. 'Why not? Have you been ill?'

Rowenna hesitated. It seemed disloyal to talk about the

47

quarrels between herself and her father, but already, after only a few hours, this strange man knew more about her then any other living being. Why hold back from him? Why not share it all?

'No, not ill. It's just that my father and I had a — a disagreement. He told me to go to my room so I — well, I locked myself in.' How petty and childish it seemed now, yet how important it had seemed at the time.

Kester stared again, then burst into a shout of laughter.

'You locked yourself in! But there's no need to look so down in the mouth about it. That's exactly what you should have done.'

'Is it?' she asked doubtfully.

'Of course it is. Why, he's trying to control you – trying to make you do what he wants you to do, every minute of the day. Locking yourself in shows him that he can't. It shows him you *can* get away from him. It shows him you're still a real person, with a mind of your own.'

'And much use that is to me,' she said. 'He'll never give me a chance to use it.'

'Then you must make your own chances,' he returned. 'Do you know what my father told me once? We make our own chances in this life, but if we don't make the best of them we may lose them for ever. They don't come again.'

'That's all very well for a man. What chance does a woman have? Her days are ordered from the moment she's born, and mostly by men – first her father and then her husband. The only person who never tried to make me into something different from what I am was Haddie.'

Kester looked at her thoughtfully. 'Tell me about yourself. What's your life been like? What have you done?'

'Done?' Rowenna said bitterly. 'Why, nothing, of course. What *can* a girl do?'

'The best with what she has, just like anyone else,' he said shortly, and to her surprise she heard annoyance in his tone. 'So, what did you have? A mother, I suppose. A nurse? A governess?'

Rowenna hesitated again. Why should she answer his questions? He was nothing but a gardener's boy, whatever he claimed to the contrary. What gave him the right to probe into her life?

But his dark brown eyes were on her, and she felt again the warm, comforting strength of his arms. She remembered the storm of weeping that he had called out of her and knew that she could not refuse him.

'Of course I had a mother,' she said in a low voice. 'She died ten years ago. She came from Canada.'

'Oh aye, Haddon told me. She was born there, wasn't she?'

'Yes, in Ontario. It's one of the eastern provinces. Her family emigrated there years ago. Her father – my grandfather – grew up on a farm near Penrith but there were several sons and not enough work for him, so he applied for a settlement there.'

'And they've been there ever since?'

'Yes. His farm was a success and he acquired more land and built a sawmill – the sawmill was the first essential in a new settlement. Other people moved in and he started a store and then other businesses, and eventually he went into timber. He's an important man in that part of Ontario now, even though he's over ninety years old.'

'And did your father go to Canada?'

'Oh no. My mother's family came here, to visit their relatives, and she met my father then. They got married and she never went back.'

'So you've never been to Canada either?'

'No,' Rowenna said, and there was a forlorn note in her voice as she remembered Haddon's plans for going to

Canada and his promise to take her with him. 'No, and now I suppose I never shall.'

'Why not? You've still got family there. Why shouldn't you go and see them some day?'

'Because – because—' But she couldn't go on. The trap seemed to be closing about her again, and to put it into words – *because my father will never allow it* – seemed to close its jaws all the tighter. Instead, she put down her empty cup and said, 'I think I should go home now.'

'Will they miss you? You told me no one knew you'd come out.'

'I know, but—'

'What time do they call you? You've a maid – what time does she bring your tea or whatever you have?'

'Just before eight. But they'll be about long before that. The housemaids are up soon after five, cleaning out the fireplace and dusting and sweeping the rooms.'

'At five in the morning? Can't they do such things during the day?'

'It's supposed to be done before the family come downstairs. Then they can do the upstairs rooms. Anyway, if they started any later they'd never be finished.'

'And what time *do* they finish?'

Rowenna looked at him in surprise. 'I don't really know. At bedtime, I suppose. Though they don't have much to do in the evening, once they've finished washing up.'

'And you think *you're* in a trap!' Kester said. There was a moment's silence, then he said, more gently, 'Perhaps it seems worse to me than it really is. Perhaps they're happy enough. There's nothing wrong with hard work, after all . . . But the main thing is that no one's going to miss you for a bit longer.'

'No. But I ought to go back, all the same,' Rowenna said, a little uncertainly.

'And I think you should rest a bit first. You've had a long walk and a lot of crying, and not much to eat from all accounts. Stay here with me a couple of hours and get some sleep. Then I'll take you back.'

'Sleep? Here?' Rowenna looked around the little hut. It had stone walls and an earthen floor, covered in straw. In one corner stood a narrow bed, little more than a wooden frame, with legs to raise it from the ground, and a palliasse with an old blanket or two. Apart from a couple of wooden boxes in which Kester evidently kept his belongings, there was no other furniture.

'Why not? It's better than fainting in a ditch.' He slid his arms around her and, before she could protest, lifted her across to the bed. 'There,' he said as he laid her down on it, 'you'll do better for a bit of sleep. And you needn't fear – I'll take care of you.'

Rowenna lay still, too startled and all at once too weary to move. She looked up at the brown face and glimpsed a sudden change in expression, a shift in the features that caught at something deep inside her. For a moment, she and Kester Matthews stared at each other, breathless. And then, abruptly, he moved away.

'Sleep now,' he said in a low tone, and his voice was oddly roughened, as if he had been suffering from a cold. 'Sleep, and I'll wake you up when it's time to go home.'

Afterwards, Rowenna was astonished that she had been able to sleep in such surroundings. But when she woke, it was with Kester's hand touching her brow, and the stone hut filled with the creeping grey light of dawn, and a cup of tea steaming beside her. And a feeling of rest in body and mind, such as she had not known for many, many weeks.

As Rowenna had said she would, Molly came to her room just before eight, carrying a tray of tea and thinly cut bread and butter. She set them down beside the bed and stood for a moment looking down at her mistress.

'You look reet done up,' she said. 'Have you slept at all?'

'Enough,' Rowenna said, thinking of the dreamless sleep she had had in the shepherd's hut. She stretched her arms, realising that she must have slept again for an hour or two. 'Is my father about yet?'

'I took in hot water for his shave. He near threw the razor at me.'

'Oh Molly, no!'

'It's all right,' the maid said with a grin. 'I stood in front of that vase he's so particular about. If I'd ducked he'd have knocked it off the mantelpiece.'

'And if you hadn't ducked, he'd have killed you!'

'Ah, but he knew I'd duck, you see. And now,' Molly said coolly, 'why don't you tell me what you got up to last night?'

Rowenna stared at her.

'What do you mean?'

'You know well enough what I mean,' the maid retorted. 'You were out most of the night. I come up afore I went to bed, to see as you were all right, and you weren't here. Nor were you in your bed at midnight, nor at two in the morning, nor at four. I was in two minds whether to raise the alarm but I reckoned you knew what you were doing and when I peeped in about six and saw you sleeping like a baby, I was glad I hadn't. But I'd still like to know where you were.'

For a moment, Rowenna struggled with the desire to tell her it was no business of hers. But Molly had been her friend too long. After a few minutes, she said, 'I went for a walk, that's all.'

'All night? By yourself?'

'Why not?' Rowenna said, but she could feel the colour rising in her cheeks and knew that Molly must notice it.

'Well, I began by myself,' she admitted. 'It seemed too good a chance to miss. It's so seldom I get an evening to myself nowadays, and it was so lovely. I *couldn't* stay in my room all that time. I walked up through the meadows to Potter's Tarn, and sat looking at the sunset on the water.'

'And then what happened?'

'Who says anything happened?' Rowenna prevaricated, then caught her maid's sceptical eye and gave in. 'Oh, very well. Someone came along and found me there. We talked.' Once again, she tried to make light of it with a shrug and a dismissive note in her voice. 'That's all.'

'You talked all night? Up by Potter's Tarn?' Molly's tone was now openly disbelieving. 'Come on, miss. Who'd be wandering around Potter's Tarn at that hour that you'd want to spend all night talking to?' She caught her breath and said sharply, 'Unless . . . It weren't that chap as works in the garden? Him as lives in the hut up by Garnett Bridge Road?'

'If you mean Kester Matthews,' Rowenna said resignedly, 'yes, it was. I suppose you've met him about the place.'

'Aye, I have.' Molly was silent for a moment or two. 'More than once, as it happens. And I've been up to that hut of his too. Did he take you there?'

'Yes, he did.' Rowenna looked at her. 'There was nothing . . . untoward, Molly. He behaved like a gentleman.'

'Oh, he would. But you'll not get many to believe it.' Molly sat down suddenly on the bed. She looked tired, Rowenna thought guiltily, realising that the maid had stayed awake most of the night, worrying about her. And she looked upset, too. How well did she know Kester? Why hadn't he mentioned her last night? Had he and Molly discussed Rowenna between them?

'Look, miss,' the maid said, 'you shouldn't go out walking on your own late at night – you know the master'd have a fit

53

if he knew. And you didn't ought to go into places like Kester Matthews's hut. As for staying there – why, you must have been hours together!'

'I was asleep most of the time.' Again, Rowenna caught the expression in the other girl's eyes. 'Molly, I told you, nothing happened that shouldn't.' Indeed, she scarcely knew what might have 'happened that shouldn't'. 'Kester found me on the fell and took me back to have a hot drink and something to eat before coming home. And I was tired, so I rested for a while as well. There was nothing more than that.'

'And like I say,' Molly said, 'I'd believe you but many wouldn't.' She looked at her mistress as if debating something in her mind.

'And what about you?' Rowenna asked. 'You say you've been up to his hut. What happens when you're alone with him, Molly?'

Molly flushed to her forehead. 'Nowt that you need bother your head with, Miss Rowenna,' she said sharply. 'And I'm sorry if that sounds impertinent, but there's some things a girl has a right to keep private.'

Rowenna stared at her. Although Molly was her maid, the two had known each other long enough to consider themselves friends. They very rarely exchanged sharp words and there had never, as far as Rowenna knew, been any secrets between them. Now it seemed that there was a secret, and had been for some time.

'Very well, Molly,' she said a little stiffly. 'I'm sure I don't want to pry into your personal affairs. But I hope you'll let me know in good time when I need to start looking for another maid.'

Molly's face coloured again and she looked ready to burst into tears. She looked down into her lap, twisting her fingers together, and then blurted out, 'I don't suppose you'll ever need to do that, miss. Kester Matthews ain't interested in me. Nor any of the village lasses. He—' She stopped suddenly and bit her lip. 'He never stops in one place long enough to walk out steady with anyone.'

'What do you mean? He looks very settled in that old hut. And he works in our garden.'

'Aye, when it suits him.' Molly pleated her apron between her fingers. 'You might as well know, miss, he stays only as long as he wants to, in any place. He's a wanderer. Here today and gone tomorrow. He might be sitting in his doorway one evening looking at the sunset, and next morning he'll be gone and no sign he'd ever been there. He's like the rest of his folk, can't never stay put for five minutes together.'

'The rest of his folk? You mean you know his family?'

Molly gave her mistress a brief, incredulous glance. 'He's a gypsy, miss. Don't say you didn't cotton on.'

'A *gypsy*!' But of course he must be, Rowenna thought, with that dark skin, that black hair and those deep brown eyes. And that steadfast objection to calling any man master. 'But why doesn't he live with his people?'

'As to that, you'll need to ask him,' Molly shrugged. 'Maybe he does, from time to time. Who knows where he goes when he's not here? Maybe he's got a wife and children – he's never said so, but then he's never said not. If he has, good luck to her and them. They'll need it.'

'You mean he's untrustworthy?' Rowenna thought of her certainty last night that there was a man she could trust, a man who could – no, not take Haddon's place, but stand in place alongside her brother. She thought of the pride she had sensed in him, the sure confidence. Could she have felt those things about a man who couldn't be trusted?

Molly shook her head. 'I don't know, miss. I don't know what I mean. I'm like everyone else – can't make him out.

All I know is, every girl in the village is wild about him, and I'd not like to see you go the same way.' She stood up and held Rowenna's teacup out to her. 'It's getting near breakfast time, miss. Drink this, and forget about him. He's not for the likes of you.'

And how did we come to be discussing him as if he might be, Rowenna wondered, sipping the lukewarm brew. But Molly was right. There were other things to be thought of now. In a few minutes she must be at the breakfast table, ready to pour her father's coffee and see that his toast was to his liking. And it seemed, from Molly's account, that his temper was no better than it had been yesterday.

She sighed. Somehow, much as it went against the grain, she would have to try to smooth him down. Life would be more comfortable for everyone if he were to leave the breakfast table in a less belligerent frame of mind. If she could do nothing useful in the world, she could at least in that way make life easier for the servants, the millhands and anyone else unfortunate enough to cross Warren Mellor's path today.

Today and every day, she thought as she washed in the hot water the housemaid had brought up, and stood still for Molly to fasten the row of tiny buttons down the back of her dress. My life's work. And will anyone remember me for it?

Kester Matthews worked steadily in the woods, clearing dead branches and repairing the rock path that led down to the banks of the river. It was his favourite part of the garden of Ashbank and he took pride in looking after the trees, seeing that each one had the light and space it needed and tending any that might be damaged or diseased. He sometimes felt like a doctor, caring for his patients, or a father watching over a growing family.

Kester loved trees. It was one of the reasons why he had

left his family and the travelling life, for a gypsy never had time to watch a tree grow, never had land in which to plant an acorn and know that it would mature into a great oak. For Kester, a wood or forest had always been the place where he felt most at home. He had always been reluctant to depart from camps made amongst the trees and disliked those on windswept moorlands. More than that, he disliked the way the travelling life was changing.

'I don't like fairgrounds and roundabouts,' he told his father. 'I don't like steam engines. They're noisy and dirty. The old dobbies, with a pony to turn them, are better.'

Kieran Matthews looked at his son and scratched his head. 'I thought it was you young ones who were all for new ways and new inventions. The other lads are keen enough.'

Kester shook his head. 'I'd rather live the old life. I'd rather be in the woods, snaring rabbits for the pot and guddling trout. And I'd like to grow my own food – vegetables and fruit.'

Kieran looked at him in surprise. 'But you'd need to live in a house for that! You'd be a *gauje*. You'd never stand up to it.'

'I needn't live in a house. A tent or a wagon would do. But I'm tired of wandering about from one place to another, never stopping more than a week or two.'

'You'll have to work for your living. It's not easy to live off the land by yourself. And what will you do for company?'

'I'll manage.' Kester looked at his father. 'I know you always tell us to call no man master, and I reckon I believe in that too. I don't mind working, but I'll never take a *job*. And I'll never give up the travelling – I don't see myself ever staying in one place for good. I reckon I'll try it on my own for a while anyway.'

Kieran nodded. He was nearing seventy then and Kester

was the last of his sons, for his wife had died only a year after the boy had been born and Kieran had never taken another woman. A man needed a good quiverful of boys, but there was barely work for them all, despite the number of horses they had to look after and the different rides and sideshows they managed. And with the new steam roundabouts there would be even less work.

He sighed a little. Travelling had changed since his young days; it had been a much more easy-going affair then, with time to camp in sheltered valleys and weave baskets, or make crooks from the sheeps' horns picked up on the moors. He remembered long, lazy days in the heather, lying beside a sparkling stream with one hand in the water, fingers moving so idly that a trout would swim between them and almost beg to be caught. And if it wasn't trout for supper it would be a rabbit, snared in the early dawn, or a pheasant picked up in the woods . . .

Perhaps Kester had the right of it.

'Aye,' he said, 'you try it. It's a chance for you now, before you jump over the broomstick and get yourself a barrowload of *chavvies*.'

Kester laughed. 'It'll be a long day before I do that, Pa. A wife and a barrel of kids won't suit me. I'd rather be on my own.'

'Well, there's plenty who've said that in their time and woken up one fine day to find themselves with a family to rear,' his father said. 'But mind what I say, Kester. You must always take your chances when they come your way. They don't come twice.'

It was his favourite saying, and there was always a strange, faraway look in his eye as he said it. But he didn't take kindly to questions, so it was with a sense of danger that Kester took his courage in both hands and asked, 'Have you ever missed a chance, Pa?'

Kieran laughed shortly. 'Aye, and more than one if I could but remember. But I wasn't much older than you when I first learned about chances. I missed one then. I went away, thinking it would come again, but it never did. I've never forgotten it.'

'What was it?' Kester asked, but his father had had enough.

'Never you mind. Just don't make the same mistake. Know what's right for you and make sure you get it, or you may go on looking for it till the end of your life.' He gave his youngest son a sharp glance from dark brown eyes. 'They say you're the most like me of all my boys. Well, if so you'll make your own way and you'll do well at whatever you turn your hand to. If it's trees you want, and growing plants, then go with my blessing. And there'll always be a place for you back here, whenever you want to come.'

Kester left him and the rest of the family with an ache in his heart, but before he had reached the end of the road the ache was easing and he knew he had made the right decision. From then on, he wandered alone wherever fancy took him.

But gradually his wanderings evolved into a pattern. A forest here, a big garden there, an estate in another county. And at each one, a welcome for the enigmatic young gypsy who was willing to sell his labour but not himself, who would work hard and well yet vanish overnight when the task was done; who tended the trees and plants as if they were his children, and who asked nothing but a hut to live in or a place to pitch his tent, vegetables from a garden and enough money to buy meat and clothing.

So it was that he came to Ashbank, close to the river Kent. And here with the wild fells near at hand and the old shepherd's hut to make his home, he liked it best. He made the woodland his own, working there under the bright clamour of birdsong, content and at ease; until he looked up one morning and saw Rowenna Mellor, dressed in an old brown holland overall, grubbing in the garden, and was lost.

Since Haddon had died, Rowenna had spent little time in the garden. Although her days were free of her father's presence, she was nevertheless kept busy with the various tasks he had set her to do while he was at the mill. He always expected her to be at hand if he came home unexpectedly and at supper he demanded a detailed account of her day, though Rowenna noticed as she began her tedious catalogue that his eyes immediately began to roam about the room, as if he were as bored as she. Clearly, he had no real interest in her doings, and she was reminded of Kester's remark that he simply wanted to control her.

That's exactly it, she thought at breakfast after that strange night up on the fell. He wants to tie me with a string. He wants to know that every minute of the day I'm doing what *he* wants me to do – as if otherwise I'll escape. Like a dog, chained to its kennel whenever its master is away.

She sat opposite her father, looking at him across the table. He was deep in the morning copy of *The Times*, which was brought from the railway station early every morning, eating toast as if he barely saw it. I could give him cardboard spread with butter and marmalade, she thought, and he'd never know the difference. And why does he want me here at all? What use or pleasure am I to him? Is this to be the pattern for the rest of my life? Chained like a dog, never able to do a thing I want to do, never allowed to be myself?

And then, with a sudden flow of anger and determination – am *I* going to allow this to happen?

What had Kester said? *You must make your own chances.* And in answer to her bitter question as to what a girl could do with her life, he had retorted with some asperity – *the best with what she had, like everyone else.* Clearly, he had thought her capable of taking her life into her own hands and she sensed a certain disappointment that she hadn't done so.

But how can I, she demanded silently, as if she and Kester were continuing their conversation. How can I defy my father when without him I have nothing? No home, no money, no means of making a livelihood, nothing.

No, that wasn't true. She had been educated as well as any girl. She could apply for a post as a governess. One of her teachers might give her a reference. It was by all accounts a hateful job, but there must be some families for whom it would be a pleasure to work. And she would at least be her own woman.

Or she could be a teacher herself, in a school such as the one where she had spent the last five years. Again, it was not a life she had ever thought attractive, but her life would be her own – or would it? She thought of the women who had taught her, the rules they had been forced to live by just as much as the girls they taught, the sheer tedium of trying to force knowledge into the heads of children who didn't want it.

Perhaps everyone lived in a trap, she thought, looking once again at her father, and she knew then the real reason why she did not leave him and seek her own life.

That moment of pity in the churchyard and, later, at home. The stark loneliness she had seen in his eyes. The bond of grief that held them together, even though he refused to acknowledge it.

I can't leave him, she thought. I have to stay. But I can't go on living like this either.

He shall have my company while he is in the house. But when he is out of it, I shall please myself.

I'll make my own chances.

* * *

61

By nine o'clock the sun was already hot. Warren Mellor left as usual for the mill and, as usual, gave Rowenna a list of instructions as to how she was to spend the day. She listened, saying nothing. And as soon as he was gone, she hurried upstairs and changed out of her morning gown and into her old holland overall.

'Whatever are you doing, miss?' Molly exclaimed, coming in to tidy the room and finding her scooping her hair up in a careless knot. 'Didn't your pa say you were to mend the winter curtains today?'

'Yes, and they can wait,' Rowenna retorted gaily. 'Can you imagine a worse job, Molly, than to sit hemming and darning great heavy velvet curtains on a day like this? I'm going out in the garden!'

'But he'll ask you—'

'And I shall tell him.' Rowenna snatched up a wide-brimmed sunhat. 'I don't intend to deceive him, Molly. I'll tell him – when he asks – what I've been doing. And I'll do it again. And again.' She faced her maid with glittering eyes. 'He may shout at me all he likes, he may lock me in my room if he wishes, but he can't shout for the rest of his life and he can't lock me up for the rest of mine. So long as I'm a dutiful daughter to him when he needs me, he can have no complaints, and the only way he can control me when he's at the mill is to take me there with him. Which he'll never do – I've already shown him how much I'd like it, and that's enough for him!'

Molly gazed at her. Her eyes were frightened but there was a spark of admiration in them too. 'He'll half kill you,' she said.

'No,' Rowenna answered, 'that's what he's *been* doing, Molly. He's been slowly crushing me to death. But now I'm alive again and I intend to stay alive. I'll do my duty by him – I'll be all a daughter should be – but I'll never allow myself to be crushed again.'

'It's that Kester that's done this,' Molly said slowly. 'You only met him last night and he's changed you already. Oh, miss—'

'Is it? Or is it just that he's opened my eyes and helped me to change myself? In any case, it hardly matters. The important thing is that I now know I *can* help myself. And that takes away all my father's power.' She smiled. 'I wonder what he'll do when he realises that!'

Molly shivered. 'I don't even like to think about it. Miss Rowenna, are you really sure you're doing the right thing? He is your pa, and you're not even twenty-one. He could do so much—'

'What?' Rowenna challenged her. 'Beat me? Chain me to the wall? Just let him try.' She lifted her head proudly. 'I can walk out of this house tomorrow if I wish.' She marched towards the door.

'And where would you go? To Kester Matthews?'

Rowenna stopped. Slowly, she turned about. She stared at her maid.

'To *Kester Matthews*? Why do you say that?'

'Well, it's him that's done this, that's plain for anyone to see. Maybe it's true that nothing happened last night – but you bin in a fever ever since you come home. And if you're thinking of running off—'

'I'm not! I'm not thinking of that at all. I simply want to live in my own way.'

'Or his,' Molly said. 'Maybe you like the idea of the gypsy life wandering here and there, wherever the fancy takes you, living off the land. Well, let me tell you, it'd soon wear thin once the snow started and you found your tent buried and the ground frozen beneath you of a night and nowt but a rotten turnip to gnaw on.'

Rowenna snapped her fingers impatiently. 'Really, Molly, your imagination's getting the better of you. I've never said a word about wanting to be a gypsy and I've no intention of living in a tent – with, or without, Kester Matthews. And I can't think why you're so upset about this – unless it's *you* who wants to live in the tent with the gardener's boy!'

Their eyes met. Molly flushed scarlet and turned away. She picked up Rowenna's nightgown and shook out the folds.

'I just don't want to see you getting hurt,' she said in a muffled voice. 'You don't know nothing about Kester. And your pa could cut up really rough if he thought you were slipping out to meet a gyppo—'

'Molly, I did not "slip out" to meet him,' Rowenna interrupted. 'It was quite by chance and I don't expect it to happen again. All I want to do is to live a little of my life in the way I enjoy – and I intend to start this morning, by doing some gardening.'

She jammed the wide-brimmed hat on her head and turned back to the door. But with her hand on the knob, she paused. She could not leave Molly like this.

'Don't worry about me, Molly,' she said gently. 'We all have to do what we think is right. And how can it possibly be wrong for me to want to do a little grubbing in my own garden, and grow a few flowers to make the world a little bit brighter?'

Molly turned swiftly and came across the room. She stood in front of Rowenna and laid one hand on her arm.

'There's nowt wrong in it, miss. It's wrong that the master should try and stop you. But I've bin with you such a long time now, ever since I were a little lass. I can't help but worry, can I? Specially when there's nowt I can do to help.'

Rowenna's face softened. She took a step closer and put her hand on the maid's shoulder.

'You do help,' she said quietly. 'And I know how you feel. Sometimes I think we're more like sisters than mistress and maid. Ah, don't cry, Molly – there's nothing to weep for.'

She folded her arms about the girl and held her for a moment. 'Let me go my own way, Molly,' she said. 'It's little enough I'm asking, after all – a few hours in the garden, a walk now and then. My father will get used to it in time. He's not really an unreasonable man, just very unhappy at present.'

Was it true? She let Molly go and kissed her, and then went out of the room and down the stairs. Outside, the sun was beating down, already hot. The garden was bright with colour, much of it colour she had caused to come about with her planning and planting. She drew in a deep breath and gloried in the freedom she had granted herself.

Yes, it was true that her father was an unhappy man. Perhaps he had always been unhappy, perhaps this was why he had always behaved as if Life itself were set against him in spite of the good fortune he had been given. And perhaps that was what happened to all such unhappy people – that they should be constantly striving to control the people about them, constantly endeavouring to mould life to their own pattern.

It might even happen to her, if she didn't take this step now. If she didn't do what Kester had called 'making her own chances'.

With firm steps, Rowenna marched round to the gardener's shed. It was open, for Richmond and his assistants had been at work for the past two hours. She took out a small fork, a hoe and a wheelbarrow and set off towards the kitchen garden.

At the far end of the garden was the little woodland where Kester spent most of his time. But Rowenna had no intention of letting her footsteps take her there.

She had met Kester Matthews by chance on Potter's Fell. If she met him again, even in her own garden, it must again be by chance. She would have no one say that she had deliberately sought him out.

Yet all through that morning, as she worked under Richmond's directions amongst the vegetables and fruit bushes, her eyes kept glancing towards the green door that led out of the kitchen garden and through which anyone might, at any moment, come.

And each time it opened she caught her breath, hoping that this time it might be the dark-eyed gypsy who had held her in his arms last night and spoken words of comfort in her ears.

Chapter Four

Kester knew when Rowenna was in the garden. There was a different feel to the air, as if she had disturbed it slightly by her presence, as if the movement of the breeze about her body brought him a sense of her shape. He knew that she was nearby, working with her trowel and her fork; he knew that if he left the woods and went into the garden he would find her.

He did not go to look. He was as aware as she was of the impossibility of their position. He had asked her to go to his hut again but, even as he had said it, he'd known she never would. If I had any sense, he thought, I'd go away now, before it gets any worse. But he could not bring himself to leave.

A wife and a barrowload of chavvies . . . He'd laughed when his father had said that, convinced that no woman would make him want to change his wandering ways. Yet, for Rowenna he might settle down; and for Rowenna's *chavvies* he would make a home.

Ach! This was crazy talk. Rowenna Mellor was as far out of his ken as the Queen herself. And if he was going to lose his senses over her this way, he'd be better to take to his wandering again and put the length and breadth of the country between them. For it was certain that no good would come of his being here and likely to see her face and hear her voice at any minute.

He remembered the first time he had seen her. She was in the kitchen garden, dressed in an old brown frock, wielding a hoe. It was a summer ago, and although he had been working at Ashbank for almost a month he had never set eyes on her before. He stood watching for a moment, thinking she was a maid or perhaps the sister or daughter of one of the gardeners.

But there was something about her that set her apart. The silky hair, the colour of honey blended with cream; the soft glow of skin barely touched by the sun; the hands that, even at this distance, he could see must be white and soft, unaccustomed to toil.

Who was she? And even as he asked the question, he knew what the answer must be. Rowenna. Haddon's sister, who had been away at school.

Haddon had talked about her occasionally as the two young men walked on the fells, for by then they were friends. They had first encountered each other in the woods, where Kester was clearing brush. Haddon had been walking on the fell and came back through the woodland gate, stopping when he saw Kester at work. They talked for a few minutes about the trees, then Haddon went on his way. But he came again a few days later and they talked again, each discovering in the other a love for trees. The next morning, Haddon arrived with a parcel of books for Kester to read. They turned out to be eight heavy volumes under the title *Arboretum et Fruticetum Britannicum* and Kester stared at it uncertainly.

'I can't read that. It's not English, is it?'

Haddon laughed. 'No, it's Latin. But the book's written in English. See' – he seized and opened one of the volumes – 'here's its title in English: *The Trees and Shrubs of Britain*. It's by a man called John Loudon. He was a famous gardener and wrote lots of books but I think this is his best.

Look at the plates – four whole volumes of them, pictures of every tree he mentions. What a work!' He stopped and looked at Kester. 'Er – I suppose you *can* read?'

'Oh yes,' Kester said. 'My father taught me. Not many of our people can, even now – we never stay in one place long enough to go to school – but someone taught him years ago and he passed it on to us all. My brothers say that's what's wrong with me – if I didn't read so much, I wouldn't be such a wanderer!'

'But all gypsies are wanderers,' Haddon said.

Kester shook his head. 'No. They stay with their tribe. They live in a village just as *gaujes* do, really. They may go from place to place, but they take their village with them.'

'Well, anyway,' Haddon said, 'you can borrow these books if you like. They're not from my father's library, they're my own. They'll tell you all you want to know about trees.'

The books were still in Kester's hut, locked away in a box. Since Haddon had died, he hadn't known quite what to do about them. They should be returned, but how, and to whom?

It was soon after that when he had first seen Rowenna, hoeing the lettuces. Her hat was off and lying on the ground beside her, and her hair tumbled over her face like a fall of peaty water from the moor, glinting dark and golden in the sunlight. With an impatient gesture she brushed it back, then straightened up and lifted it with both hands away from her neck. Her body curved gracefully from her narrow waist, her breasts outlined against the skimpiness of the brown overall. The loose sleeves fell back to reveal the soft, white plumpness of her arms.

Kester stared at her and felt his heart move.

Ever since then, he had watched for Rowenna every day. He had stayed at Ashbank, working at whatever tasks

69

Richmond cared to set him, in the hope of seeing her. He had struck up acquaintance with her maid, in order to find out more about her. And he had even spoken to her occasionally, when she came down to the little woodland to walk under the trees.

He had gone to the church for Haddon's funeral, partly to mourn his friend and partly to see Rowenna, to try to convey to her some small grain of comfort. He had looked into her eyes in the churchyard and felt sure that she understood.

When he had come upon her sitting in the heather by the tarn, he had for a moment thought her conjured there by his own yearning. But he had quickly seen that she was unhappy and after that he had forgotten to think about himself and had concentrated his attention on her, on her unhappiness and need. He had taken her back to his hut, wishing it could be for ever, but he had known that he could not keep her there, nor give any hint of what was in his heart. And afterwards, when he had walked back down the meadow paths with her and bade her goodbye at the stile, he had felt as if that goodbye were for ever.

Take your chances when they come your way. They don't come twice.

His father's voice sounded in his head, so clearly that Kester turned sharply, half expecting to see him there. But he was alone. Only the birds, flitting amongst the trees, were present to witness his turmoil. He sat down on a log, leaning his chin on his hands, and stared at the bare earth.

It was easy to say *take your chances when they come*. How did you know what was a chance? Had last night been a chance?

No. He could not have said to Rowenna – *come away with me*. He could not have told her his feelings for her – that she was his woman. That was the last thing she wanted to hear at present. She wanted to be her own woman, she wasn't ready to be possessed by any man. She was still trying to escape from her father.

He remembered his father teaching him to guddle trout. Lie quietly and wait, he had said. Just let your fingers dangle in the water, moving gently with the current, and wait for the fish to swim between them. And then slowly, slowly, tickle it until it's almost asleep in your hand – until it's yours.

Patience. That was the answer. Patience. Stay quietly and wait. It was all he could do.

Warren Mellor sat at his desk in the office at the papermill. His ledgers lay open before him, half a dozen quills awaited sharpening by the inkstand and paper samples littered the benches that ran around the walls. Through the window opening to the outer office he could see the row of clerks, scratching away busily, and beyond that the mill and the great fourdrinier, the papermaking machine itself, with the endless sheet of paper winding between the rollers which would turn it from wet pulp to a paper fine enough to print newspapers on. A hundred and fifty feet of paper a minute, and a hundred inches wide. A growing industry to supply the rapidly increasing demand for books and newspapers.

And yet the ledgers were not showing the healthy profits that would have made Warren happy. He stared at them with bleary eyes. Last night had been a bad one; that minx of a daughter had defied him and locked herself in her room, refusing to come down either to dinner or to sit with him afterwards. As a consequence, he had taken more drink than was good for him and Ackroyd had found him on the stairs, scrambling up on his hands and knees, and put him to bed like a baby.

Had ever a man been cursed with such a daughter? Awkward to a degree, she seemed determined to make life miserable for him. In spite of years of schooling, she had none of the feminine graces, never sat at her embroidery of an afternoon, never played the piano or sang, though she had a passably pretty voice when she cared to use it and he had heard her singing like a lark out in the garden.

The garden! It was almost all she seemed to think about. He had caught her many times, dressed like a vagabond and with her hair all awry, digging as if she were being paid for it. And laughing and joking with the gardeners like a common labourer.

He supposed that it came from losing her mother so young. And also from Dorothy's habit of letting both children run wild and spend all their holidays climbing trees or making camps up on the fells. All very well for Haddon, but not in any way the right upbringing for a young lady.

If only Haddon were still here!

Warren stared again at his ledgers. The past few years had been disastrous for the paper trade. First there had been the shortage of rags, which had been talked about for years. People were simply not throwing away their clothes as they had done in the past, perhaps because they couldn't afford new ones so often. There had been a sudden frantic search for new fibres and several manufacturers had believed that esparto grass was the answer. A group which included Warren Mellor had banded together to lease a hundred thousand acres of land in southern Spain, on which to grow the esparto, believing that this would end their difficulties.

It had taken only two or three bad harvests to persuade them otherwise. After that most manufacturers had agreed that woodpulp was the best source of fibre and one firm had broken away to build its own pulpmill in Norway. A few, including Warren, hung on to esparto but the difficulties became too great and paper produced from woodpulp began to take the market. In the end, they decided to abandon the Spanish land and search for new sources of wood.

There were only two worth consideration – the Scandinavian countries, where white pine grew in profusion, and Canada. And it was the thought of Canada that caused Warren Mellor most aggravation.

If only his wife hadn't died! With her family now so prosperous, she could have been of real value to him. But since her death, he had communicated little with the Tysons in Ontario and there was not much chance that they would help him now. And meanwhile he had lost money over the Spanish fiasco, money he sorely needed to buy into the woodpulp market. If something wasn't done soon, he would be in deep trouble.

Haddon would have had the ideas and the energy to get them out of it. But Haddon had gone, and all he had left was that useless daughter, who was no good to anyone.

Warren's mind felt as bleary as his eyes. He could not focus his attention on anything for long. He stared again at the ledgers, trying to make sense of them, but his vision swam and his head ached. He longed for a brandy, but the bottle he had taken to keeping in the office was empty, and he had forgotten to bring a replacement.

He cursed and began to rise to his feet, but before he was properly upright the door swung open and his chief clerk, Grandison, came in.

'Mr Boothroyd's here to see you, sir.'

'Boothroyd?' Warren's eyes peered past the clerk. 'Boothroyd? Why, what brings you here?' He slumped back into his chair and gestured towards the clerk. 'A seat for Mr Boothroyd, and bring us something fit to drink. Brandy – there's some at the house if you've none here.'

Grandison pushed forward a chair. He gave Warren a

doubtful glance, but a thunderous scowl sent him scuttling away and Alfred Boothroyd closed the door and sat down.

'Well, Mellor. I hope I find you well.'

'Well enough.' Warren watched him suspiciously. Why was he here? Although their two mills were on opposite banks and shared the water, the two men rarely visited each other and there was not even a footbridge between the two properties. 'You look blooming.'

'Aye, I keep myself pretty fit. Abstemiousness, that's the secret. I never take drink during the day and I never smoke, apart from a cigar or two after supper.' He let his glance rest for a moment or two on the empty glass on Warren's desk. 'And how are times with you?'

Warren shrugged. 'Much as for anyone else, I imagine. The demand for paper seems to increase every day. Newsprint more than anything. I daresay you're finding the same. It's good news for us all, provided we've the capital to work with.'

'And d'you have that?'

Warren raised his eyebrows. 'You're pretty inquisitive, aren't you?'

Alfred Boothroyd folded his arms and stretched out his legs. 'I believe in coming to the point. And I've a reason for asking.'

'Maybe you'd better tell me what it is. I'll know then whether I want to answer.'

The door opened and the chief clerk entered with a bottle of brandy and a fresh glass on a tray. He set it down at Warren's elbow and withdrew.

'You'll take a glass?'

Boothroyd shook his head. 'I told you, I never take alcohol during the day. It dulls the senses.' He watched as Warren poured some into his own glass. 'I've a proposition to put to you, Mellor.'

'You have, have you? And what might that be?' Warren raised the glass to his nose, sniffed and then took a swallow. 'Ah, that's better. Well, out with it, man, what is this proposition?'

Alfred Boothroyd unfolded his arms and leaned forward, resting one on Warren's desk. With the other, he made little jabbing motions in the air.

'You're not doing so well, Mellor. Don't bother to deny it – there aren't many secrets in this business. You caught a bad cold over that Spanish business and you're having a hard time pulling out of it. You need new machinery if you're to keep up – hundred-inch fourdriniers are nowhere near big enough these days – and you need a cheaper supply of woodpulp. No' – he held his hand up, palm outwards – 'I know what you're being charged, and you ought to be paying less. If you go on like this, you'll be in Carey Street, facing the bankruptcy judge. Now isn't that so?'

'I don't know where you get your information—' Warren began angrily, then subsided. 'Oh, very well. Yes, you're not far off the mark. It's been a poor time for me, what with Mawkins and Trent both pulling out of the Spanish group and leaving me in the lurch, and then my son being taken from me. He was my right hand, you know. I'm hard pressed without him.'

'I know that. And that's why I'm here.' Boothroyd's small round eyes watched Warren carefully. 'You need someone to take his place—'

'No one can do that! How can anyone replace a son?'

'As a son, no one can. But as a working colleague – as a partner—'

'I'm not looking for a partner. And if I were, I doubt if you'd apply. You've got your own business.'

'I have. And I'd like to expand it. And I was about to say, that as a working partner, if you can't have your son, what

75

better substitute could you find than a son-*in-law*?'

He sat back, arms folded again, and watched as Warren frowned, trying to make sense of the idea.

'A *son-in-law*? Are you trying to tell me—'

'I'm making an offer for your daughter,' Boothroyd said bluntly. 'Miss Mellor.'

'*Rowenna?*'

'Have you more daughters?' Boothroyd smiled. He had pointed teeth, like a wolf. 'She's of marriageable age, is she not? Left school a year or so ago, I'm told. She should be accomplished enough, and have all the housewifely skills if she's been looking after your house since then. And it would be a good thing for both our businesses.'

'You mean you'd want to take over my mill?'

'I mean we could work together. Share our assets. You've got a good position here, Mellor, and it touches mine on the riverbank. We could expand, build a fine new pulpmill on the land we've got between us. We could import our own wood, do the job ourselves and cut out half the expense. And we'd have a family to pass it all on to – my children, your grandchildren. Now what d'you say to that?'

Warren stared at him and took another gulp of brandy. The liquid burned the back of this throat and lit a streak of fiery light in his brain. His thoughts raced.

It might be the answer to all his troubles. It could solve his financial problems and rid him of a daughter who was becoming a trial to him. At the same time, he'd still have some control over both her and the business. The idea of losing either entirely was one he didn't want to accept, but to retain his rights as a father and as a mill owner . . .

'Well?' Boothroyd said after a few moments.

Warren frowned. 'Have some patience, man. I can't answer at once. I'll have to think it over – take advice. I need to see your figures – what you're prepared to put into the business, what you're proposing to do. I'm not bankrupt yet, Boothroyd – I've still got a good business here and I've been considering other ways of making the place pay better. You'd better set it all out on paper and then I'll see what I think.'

'And Rowenna – Miss Mellor?'

Warren's eyes took on a calculating look.

'I'll have to think about that too. Since my boy died she's all I have left. She's been a good companion to me these past months. I've been counting on keeping her company for a good few years yet – maybe for the rest of my life if she shows no desire to wed.'

'And if she does show such a desire? A husband could take her away, Mellor. And you might find yourself with a son-in-law you can't get on with.' The dark marble eyes watched him. 'Let me have her and she'll be within reach for as many years as you care to have her, aye, and your grandchildren too, in and out of your house as much as you please. Why, we'll be bringing them up together, man – now what could be better than that?' He waited a moment, then added, 'Grandsons, no doubt, and I'd have no objection at all to the first of them bearing whatever name *you'd* like to choose.'

Warren stroked his beard thoughtfully. There was no denying it was a temptation. His financial situation was every bit as bad as Boothroyd hinted, and something would have to be done soon if he were not to slip into a worse mess. As for Rowenna, his feelings were mixed. The girl irritated him but she was the only member of his family remaining to him and he had made up his mind that, however wilful she might be now, she could be trained to become in time a useful companion to him, as meek and submissive as any father could wish. He had toyed with the idea of marriage for her, and discarded it, fearing the loneliness of an empty house.

But Boothroyd's proposition shed a different light on the

matter. If he let the man have Rowenna, she would still be within reach, able to give him her time and attention whenever he required it. Their house would be open to him whenever he felt like taking a walk along the riverbank. And if he and Boothroyd were partners ... He glanced again at the man opposite. Yes, he could very well make a suitable partner and son-in-law. Old enough to have a sensible head on his shoulders where his wife was concerned, cool enough not to run away with any fancy romantic ideas about marriage, and by his own showing, a good businessman.

And the children – Warren had had little time for his own babies, but babies grew into useful adults. Rowenna was young and strong enough to produce a quiverful of them, not like her mother who had only managed two to survive childhood. And as Boothroyd said, some of them were sure to be grandsons.

A grandson to leave the mill to. A grandson whose name he could choose himself.

Another Haddon.

'Well?' Boothroyd said, and Warren removed his hand from his beard and laid it palm down on the desk.

'I told you, I'll think on't. It's not a matter that can be decided all in a minute. I need to look at the question from all sides.'

'You'll not need to take too long,' Boothroyd told him. 'The word is that you're about to lose the contract for Titus Wilson.'

Warren scowled. Titus Wilson was one of the foremost printers in Kendal, established almost twenty-five years ago, and a good customer. Warren had had some uncomfortable brushes with his agent in the past few weeks and was aware that if he lost the contract he would be in a very awkward spot indeed.

'I don't know how you've come to hear that,' he blustered. 'Maybe you ought to change your spies.'

'Oh, come on, man, what's the use of denying it? We'll have to be open with each other if we're to be partners—'

'Aye,' Warren said emphatically, '*if* we're to be partners. I told you, I'll think about it before I make up my mind. You'd not want me working with you if I were one to make snap decisions, would you, now?'

Alfred Boothroyd laughed. 'No, indeed! You've made a good point there, Mellor. Well, we'll leave it at that for today, shall we? I'll leave you to turn it over in your mind. And of course I'll not mention anything to Miss Mellor, though I take it you won't object if I exchange a civil word or two with her now and then. In fact' – he was rising to his feet as he spoke and slapped his thigh suddenly, as if the idea had just occurred to him' – why not bring her over to supper one of these evenings? Just the three of us, eh? Or maybe I'll ask my sister Matilda along to keep her company. It'll give her a chance to have a look at the house, too.' He smiled at Warren, showing the wolfish teeth. 'Shall we say next Tuesday?'

'Aye,' Warren said after a moment's consideration, 'I don't see any harm in that. It doesn't mean I'm accepting your offer, mind,' he warned.

Boothroyd laughed again. 'Of course not, my dear fellow! But you'll have had time by then to give it some thought, won't you? Perhaps we'll have a word or two over the port, after the ladies have retired. In any case, there's no need to rush into things, is there?' He glanced again at the brandy bottle. 'I daresay you'd be glad to have less to worry about. Daughters are expensive, so I've heard.'

'So how is she now, your mistress?'

Kester sat in the heather at the door to his hut, gazing out

79

over the valley. Below him, the fields sprawled between grey stone walls to the valley where Rowenna lived with her father on the banks of the river Kent. The long ridge of Whitbarrow Scar was blue and hazy on the horizon, and beyond it Kirkby Moor and the hills of Furness were little more than shadows. There was a glitter on the estuaries and the sweep of Morecambe Bay, but no sails could be seen and even the rolling Howgills and the Helm, so close at hand, were blurred with heat.

Molly sighed and wondered why she had come, why she kept on coming. Kester wasn't interested in her, it was plain to see. He never seemed to notice her dark brown hair, waved especially for his benefit, or the coloured ribbons she twined through it. He didn't spare a glance for her waist, drawn in tightly by the wide sash she had bought in Kendal Market last week. He didn't even seem to notice the buttons left undone on her bodice, revealing skin still white, unkissed by the sun. She would have liked it to be kissed . . . And John would have kissed her readily enough if she'd only given him the eye. But Kester didn't seem to have heard of kissing.

Even if he did hanker after Miss Rowenna, she thought irritably, he must know she would never so much as look at him. Even though they'd spent a night together here in this very hut. A *night*! And nothing had happened. Why, if *I* had the chance of a moonlit night here alone with Kester Matthews, I'd make sure something happened all right, she thought.

'Miss Rowenna's well enough,' she answered. 'Considering she has to live with that miserable old cur. Drunk half the night and surly all next day. It makes me glad to be what I am. At least no man's got the mastery of me.' She glanced at him sideways. I wouldn't mind you being my master, she thought.

80

'Ach, you're as trapped as Rowenna,' Kester said. 'How can you call your life your own, when you've only got an hour of an afternoon to get out of the house and even then you're not supposed to do what you want with it? Isn't there some rule about "followers"? What would your house-keeper say if she knew you were up here with me?'

'She wouldn't say nothing,' Molly said with a grin. 'She'd just give me the key of the street . . . No, I reckon she turns a blind eye. There's not many girls who won't have a boy or two at their heels. It's human nature.'

'Aye, and it's human nature to want to be free. Catch *me* selling myself to a man like Warren Mellor. Any man who wants to be my master has to be a man I can look up to, a man who's *worth* calling master, not some old drunkard who happens to have inherited a business and a fine house and looks set to destroy both.'

'My!' Molly said, opening her eyes wide at him. 'We *do* think a lot of ourselves, don't we! And who are you to talk so fine, Kester Matthews? You're nowt but a gyppo!'

Kester's face darkened and his hand shot out to grip her wrist. 'Don't call me that! Gypsy, I don't mind – or Romany, since I can speak the language. But my folk call themselves travellers, plain and simple, and don't give themselves any airs about it. And if there's one thing we know, it's that we're as good as any man living and we don't bare the head to anyone unless we reckon he's earned it. And that's not by taking what his father left and making a mess of it.'

'You're just like them Quakers,' Molly said. Kester's strong fingers were hurting her wrist but she wasn't going to say so. At least he was touching her – taking notice of her. 'They talk like that. About everything being equal in the sight of God. Mind, that's in the Bible, but it's not really true, is it?'

'Isn't it? Why not?'

81

'Well, it stands to reason,' Molly said impatiently. 'You got to have masters to run things. I mean, there's *always* been people like that. Kings and queens and such. And mill owners and folk with grand houses. And there's got to be people to work for 'em and keep it all going.'

'That's right enough,' Kester agreed. 'But they don't have to be treated like slaves, or as if they don't matter. There's no reason on earth why old Mellor should think he's got the right to treat Rowenna like she's just been born for his convenience. Or for your housekeeper to think she can make you go against human nature and not have a young man to kiss you and mate with you.'

Molly's face grew warm. She looked down at Kester's hand, still fastened around her wrist though his grip had relaxed now and he held her loosely.

'Well, I don't, all the same, do I?' she said. 'I don't have a young man to kiss me and – and—'

Kester too had been looking down at their hands, lying together on the sheep-nibbled turf. He raised his eyes to her face.

'And you don't have a girl,' she went on. 'Both of us, hankering for summat we can't ever have. Daft, isn't it?'

'Yes,' Kester said slowly, 'it's daft.' And he reached out both hands and pulled Molly towards him.

Rowenna came in from the garden that afternoon with a sunburnt face and a sense of healthy tiredness. Lack of sleep was making her feel lightheaded, as though the world were somehow unreal, but out in the garden, tugging at weeds and clipping the over-exuberant growth of roses and shrubs she had planted, she had felt more herself than she had for months, and the exercise had refreshed a body that had stayed still or moved only slowly for too long.

She came into the hall, dropped her hat on a chair and sat

down to take off her boots. The house was quiet. It was not quite tea-time and the servants were probably in the kitchen, or perhaps taking the sun in the yard. Lunch was in the past and the bustle of supper preparations not yet begun. Soon the housemaid would prepare a tray for the drawing room, and then they would all gather round the big kitchen table for their own hearty meal of bread and jam, followed by one of Mrs Partridge's fruit cakes. As small children, Haddon and Rowenna had been in and out of the kitchen all the time, and had frequently shared in these teas. Rowenna cast an eye towards the door which led to the kitchen quarters and wished she could share in one now. It would be so much friendlier, so much more comforting, than sitting alone in the over-furnished drawing room.

Her boots off, she pushed them under the chair and looked around for the slippers she had left ready to put on. But as she reached out for them, the drawing-room door opened and she looked up in surprise to see her father looming over her.

'So there you are. I was beginning to think you had deserted us.'

Rowenna could think of nothing to say in answer to this, so she continued to fasten her slippers in silence. Her heart was beating quickly. She had gone straight out into the garden this morning after breakfast, and had slipped into the kitchen and begged some bread and cheese for a midday snack. Never before had she been absent from a meal without illness as an excuse, and she knew that he was likely to be even angrier with her now.

But she had decided to take her life into her own hands, to refuse to let him bully and browbeat her any longer. Was she going to fail at the first fence?

She pulled the knot tightly and stood up to face him. For the first time, she realised that they were almost the same height, and she could look him straight in the eye.

'I haven't deserted you, Father. I've only been in the garden.'

'*All day?*' He spoke as if she had said she had been on the moon.

'Yes. It was so beautiful. And I've been so busy, I barely noticed the time.'

'And never felt hungry, I suppose?'

'I had some bread and cheese at lunch-time.'

'Bread and cheese. So you knew it was lunch-time but you didn't think it proper to come indoors and share the meal with your father, like a civilised being.'

'I thought we were better to have a little time apart,' Rowenna said quietly. 'It was too pleasant a day to quarrel—'

'Quarrel? *Quarrel?* And is that what we've come to, that you're afraid to be with me for fear of a quarrel? May I remind you, miss, that a daughter's duty is *not* to quarrel with her father but to be a comfort and companion to him in his bereavement? May I suggest that any daughter worthy of the name would be glad to serve in such a way, that she'd be pleased to sit quietly and ease his loneliness a little?' He glowered at her. 'Is it too much to expect you to come in and take a cup of tea with me?'

'Of course I will, Father. But I'm rather dirty from the gardening. I should go and wash my hands at least.' She got up and went to the little cloakroom by the side of the front door, where there was a tap and a fixed basin. She closed the door and leaned against it, trembling a little.

It had cost her some effort to remain calm and not to rise to her father's taunts. But how otherwise were they to continue living in the same house? And for all her fine words and decisions, what else could she do? Despise her father as she might, there was always, at the bottom of it all, that terrible pity. She could not abandon him to the grip of the loneliness he feared, to the memories he could not endure.

Tea had been brought to the drawing room when she went in, and her father was sitting by the small table, his cup before him, evidently waiting for her to come and pour. She did so, determined to remain calm but knowing that her temper could be as hot as her father's.

'A fine state in which to come to the drawing room,' he remarked caustically as soon as he saw her. 'Look at you! All over earth, like a common gardener's boy. It's as well we've no visitors to see you like this.'

'I've washed my face and hands, and taken off my overall,' Rowenna said. 'I'm sure my dress is clean.' She picked up the teapot.

'Dress! Is that what you call it? It looks like something the housemaid might wear.'

Rowenna glanced down at the light cotton print, simply cut and unembellished with lace or frills. She handed her father his tea.

'It's one I used to wear when I was home from school, to go for walks in.'

'Quite. Appropriate enough for a schoolgirl to go tramping about the fields in, but not at all suitable for a young lady taking tea with visitors in the drawing room. I'd order you to go up and change it this minute if I weren't so damnably tired.'

Rowenna passed him a plate of bread and butter which he declined with an irritable shake of his head. She cut him a slice of fruit cake and laid it on his plate. He picked it up and took a large bite.

'Ugh! This cake's quite dry. Has that woman forgotten how to bake?'

'It seems excellent cake to me, Father.'

'Your mother used to bake good cakes,' he went on, as if she had not spoken. 'Pastry, too. Partridge has never had the knack she had. Look at these scones, as dry as dust.' He crumbled one between his fingers. 'I suppose they taught you to cook at that school?'

'They taught us all the housewifely skills,' Rowenna said, guessing what was coming.

'H'm. Well, it's time you started to be of some use about the place. You can start tomorrow. Take over the ordering of the household. Some of the cooking. I'll look for the results at supper.'

'I'll bake you a cake willingly, Father,' Rowenna said. 'But I'm afraid I can't take Mrs Partridge's place as house-keeper and she'd be most offended if I tried to usurp her position as cook. Why, she'd probably give notice on the spot.'

He glared at her. 'Are you refusing?'

'I'm simply trying to point out—'

'Richmond doesn't seem to object to your spending all day in the garden.'

'But I'm not taking over from him. In fact, I take my orders from him. He knows far more about gardening than I do, and—'

'You *take orders* from him? The man's an employee—'

'He's in charge of the gardens – just as Mrs Partridge is in charge of the house. And I enjoy working in the garden—'

'And you wouldn't enjoy working in the kitchen! Oh, you don't have to tell me that, miss. You've always been the same – rather grub about in the dirt than put yourself out to please your father. Have you mended those winter curtains as I told you to do?'

'No, Father.'

'And why not? I specifically said they were to be done today.'

Rowenna cast a glance at the window. The sun still shone down from a cloudless sky. Surely even her father could see the impossibility of sitting with a hundred yards of thick velvet draped across one's knees on a day like this.

'There's plenty of time to do that, Father, when it's raining. Today I—'

There was a crash as her father came suddenly to his feet, tipping his chair back behind him. Rowenna put out a hand to prevent the small table from tipping as well, and caught the sugar bowl as it slid dangerously close to the edge. Her father towered over her.

'Let's get this quite clear, miss! *I'm* the one who says when there's time to do the jobs that need to be done, aye, and who's to do them too. If I say you'll mend curtains, you'll mend curtains, whatever the weather outside, and if I say you'll bake cakes, you'll bake cakes. And no more mealy-mouthed objections about offending the cook or the gardener. They're my employees, d'you understand, my servants, and they'll do as they're told just as you will, or be shown the door. There are plenty more outside as good as them, and they've got the sense to know it.'

'But not so many who'll he willing to work for a tyrant!' Rowenna flashed. She stood up too, facing her father, forgetting all her good resolutions and glorying in her ability to defy him. 'Mrs Partridge and Ackroyd and Richmond and the others have been with us for years, they were here when my mother was alive. They loved her and they loved Haddon – I think they even love me. And that's why they stayed. But they'll not stay if you start to bully them – and neither will I.' She lifted her chin, meeting his furious eyes, seeing them small and red with rage. 'I'll leave you, Father. I'll find work as a governess – a seamstress – anything, rather than stay here and put up with your domineering.'

'You'll leave me when I say so,' he rasped. 'And it'll be in a decent manner, as the wife of someone who can control you as you need to be controlled. And meanwhile you'll learn some better manners. Go to your room!'

Rowenna did not move. She stayed quite still, facing him. She saw his fists clench and the muscles of his face tighten, and braced herself for a blow. What she would do if he struck her, she had no idea, but she almost welcomed it, knowing dimly that it would set her free as nothing else could do. And perhaps Warren read the message in her eyes and knew it too, for after a moment he turned away.

'Are you defying me, miss?' he asked, but there was now no challenge in his voice and immediately Rowenna felt her resolve ebb. He was, after all, nothing more than a lonely and pitiful man.

'I'm not defying you, Father,' she said gently. 'I simply want to live a part of my life in the way that makes me happy. And only when you're away at the mill. I'm quite willing to devote the rest of my time to you.' She sat down and poured another cup of tea. 'Here. Drink this and you'll feel better. I'll mend the curtains this evening while we're sitting together. And tomorrow I'll bake you a cake.'

Warren turned and looked down at her. His rage had gone, leaving him appearing oddly smaller. His eyes looked flat and expressionless.

He sat down slowly and drank the tea Rowenna had poured, and she looked at him with compassion.

Had either of them won? Or had they simply locked themselves tighter in a bond that neither could escape?

Chapter Five

Rowenna half expected her father to return to the subject of the garden at breakfast next morning, and forbid her to go out there. But it seemed that he had decided that, for the time being at any rate, the conversation had not taken place. He did not ask how she intended to spend the morning and she took it that, so long as she appeared decently garbed at lunch, he would not mention the matter again.

The sun was already warm as she went to the head gardener's shed and collected her hoe and a trug in which to put the weeds she dug up. For a while she worked in the flowerbeds, mostly on her hands and knees for the plants were too closely packed to use the hoe, and it was eleven o'clock before she realised that she had forgotten to wear her hat.

She sat back on her heels. The heat was almost visible, a shimmering haze over the garden. Perspiration was running down her face and neck, and soaking the thin cotton shift she wore beneath her overall. If I stay out here, she thought, I shall have heatstroke. I ought to go indoors.

Instead, she glanced about the garden for shade. There were several trees – a large weeping willow, hanging its green curtain over the lawn, a spreading cherry under which she and Haddie had often lain telling each other stories – but none seemed to promise the deep, cool shade she needed at this moment. Her glance fell on the little wood at the far side of the wide lawn.

Leaving the trug where it was, she rose to her feet and walked across the grass. It was short, for John Richmond had been marching the old pony up and down it yesterday, dragging the grass-cutter. At the far edge, a few shrubs spread their feet across it, and beyond them were the trees and the deep shade she needed.

Rowenna walked quietly along the narrow path. Sometimes one could surprise a red squirrel or two here, or even a deer. In the middle of a thicket there was a hummock, pocked with the burrows dug over the years by a colony of badgers. But you had to be quiet indeed to spot them, and then it must be dusk or even later. Haddon had brought her here one night, when they were both supposed to be in bed, and they had watched entranced as three cubs came out and tumbled together in the moonlight.

At the centre of the wood was a little dell, where the sun could reach in and dapple the grass with coins of light. It was filled with bluebells now and looked like a piece of fallen sky. Rowenna sat on a log at the edge and gazed at them. Almost without thinking, she unbuttoned her overall and pulled it off. The air whispered against her bare arms and the low neck of her shift, which was still clinging damply to her body.

A *proper* young lady would be wearing a chemise and perhaps even a bust-improver, she thought with amusement. But I'm not a *proper* young lady – nor ever wish to be. Poor Father!

She slipped down from the log to the grass and lay stretched out, revelling in the shade, as cool as running water yet with the sun near enough to roll into should she need its warmth. A few yards away she could hear the sound of the river, making its way swiftly past the mills and down to the estuary at Grange-over-Sands. The water was low, for the level soon dropped in dry weather, but there were several pools and always enough for the mill. She thought how pleasant it would be to bathe in it.

Well, my clothes are wet enough already, she thought, looking down at the damp shift. And there's no one about – the gardeners will be having their lunch. Why shouldn't I?

She got up and ran across the little grove to the bank, looking down towards the water. It glittered beneath her, flashing over rocks lit by sunlight glancing down through the trees. The pools were dark and mysterious, brown as peat, with the water sliding as silky and sinuous as an otter until it curved up over the next rock and broke into smithereens of diamond brilliance.

Rowenna climbed down the bank and stood for a moment on the brink of a pool. She hesitated. It wasn't deep enough to swim in, merely to wallow. But the morning was so hot and she felt so sticky, that even a wallow would be refreshing. She stepped into the pool and lowered herself into it until it ran cold and breathtaking over her whole body.

Gasping, she splashed a little. But the shift, which had seemed so skimpy on land, was getting in her way, and with a sudden flash of impatience she tore it off and flung it to the bank, where it draped itself like a pale ghost on a branch. The water flowed around her, sliding about her skin, teasing into every minute crevice. It lapped over her breasts, curled itself over her thighs, pulled gently at her toes and fingers. Like cool liquid silk, it wrapped itself around her body and she lay in its pampering embrace, resting gently against the smooth rocks as it wafted her to and fro, feeling the warmth of the dappling sun which filtered down through the shivering leaves.

A sudden change in the quality of the light, an almost

imperceptible movement on the bank, caught her attention and she glanced up. There was nothing to be seen – and yet she felt sure that there was something different, perhaps in the arrangement of the trees, as if two or three of them had gathered close together. Suddenly fearful, she sat up, drawing her legs up beneath her. Still there was no movement. And then, her eyes growing accustomed to the darkness between trees, she realised that what she had taken to be branches and wood was in fact a human figure.

A man, watching her.

Rowenna uttered a small scream. Instinctively, she crossed her arms over her breasts. She stared up at him, her eyes dilated, and he detached himself from the trees and came down the bank towards her.

Kester. Kester Matthews.

Rowenna let out her breath on a long sigh. Whatever Kester Matthews was, he was no threat to her. Hadn't she spent a whole night with him in his hut, unharmed? Hadn't he brought her home in the pearly dawn light and done no more than lay his fingertip on her cheek? She could feel the touch of it yet . . . Her heart thumping again, she gazed up at him and watched him come down the bank, his dark eyes fixed upon her.

'You seem set on surprising me,' he said. 'You turn up just when I don't expect you. And looking . . . His eyes moved over her and she remembered that she was naked. Her shift was hanging on the branch near his head, beyond her reach.

For a few seconds she stood in the pool, the water running in a shimmering cascade down her naked body. The sun cast its trembling, dappled light through the canopy of the trees, clothing her in flickering shadow as if in shot silk. Her hair lay in heavy, damp waves on her shoulders, a few tresses curving down over one breast, and her thighs gleamed white against the green and brown of the river.

What should she do? Now that she had recovered from her first fright at seeing him, her relief was making her angry. What right had he to stand watching her, when she clearly wanted to be private? Why hadn't he made some sound, to warn her that she wasn't alone?

'Give me my clothes,' she commanded imperiously, and he laughed.

'Well! Aren't we the royal princess! Have you never heard the word *please*?'

Rowenna flushed.

'I don't have to plead for my own clothes. If you were a gentleman, you'd give me them at once and turn your back while I put them on.'

Her eyes reflected the changing colours of the water as they challenged him and Kester reached up one hand and lifted down the garment that hung across the branch.

'You're like a water-nymph,' he said softly. 'A naiad, coming up out of the river.'

'That's not a word I'd have expected you to know.' She took the shift from him and lifted it over her head.

'No, because you think I'm an ignorant gypsy. I told you, my father taught me to read and I read every book I could lay hands on. I borrowed them, bought them, even stole some from folk who had no use for them and just kept 'em for show. It didn't matter to them – they never missed 'em. But I read them over and over again. I take them wherever I go.'

Rowenna remembered the boxes in his hut. She had supposed them to contain personal belongings like clothes. Were the boxes filled with books?

Her shift was on now, concealing her wet body from his gaze, though eyes like his seemed capable of seeing through anything. With another imperious gesture, she lifted her hand.

'Help me up the bank, please.'

He grinned and reached down. She felt his warm brown fingers close around hers and draw her up out of the water. As she came towards him he did not back away but stood firm, pulling her close against him. She felt his body, hard against hers, and caught her breath.

'I ought to demand payment for this,' he said, looking down into her face. His eyes were very dark and she could feel the pounding of his heart under his shirt. 'A toll, as you might say. What do folk like you do for forfeits at Christmas parties?'

'All kinds of things,' she answered, dismayed by the quaver in her voice. 'A recital, perhaps – a silly trick, like standing on one leg for two minutes. A – a—'

'A kiss?' he suggested. His lips were very close. She could feel his breath, cool and sweet.

'Sometimes.'

Her voice was no more than a whisper. She raised her face and his lips brushed against her skin. She closed her eyes and felt his mouth upon hers, gentle, tender, yet trembling with promise. His arms were about her, holding her closely, yet she knew that if she wanted to break away he would not try to keep her.

If she wanted to break away . . . But she did not want to move.

Kester lifted his head. He looked down at her and his expression was grave. For a moment, they gazed into each other's eyes and then his dark face broke into a laugh.

'That's your forfeit paid!' he exclaimed. 'And now you may pass, my lady.'

His arms dropped away and Rowenna felt suddenly cold.

She gave him an uncertain glance, then climbed up the bank past him, back to the little blue hollow. She found her overall and slipped it back on, then sat down on the grass and waited.

Kester appeared a moment or two later. He looked at her, grinned again and came across the dell to throw himself at her feet.

'I thought you might have gone.'

'Why should I do that?'

He shrugged. 'I might have offended you.'

'Yes, you might,' Rowenna said. 'But you didn't. Why should that be, d'you suppose?'

He slanted a look up towards her, as if weighing up whether she intended the question seriously. 'Maybe you wanted to be kissed.'

'Indeed not!' Rowenna exclaimed. 'The idea never entered my head.'

'Why not? Haven't you ever been kissed before?'

'Of course,' she answered with dignity. 'My brother kissed me often—'

'I don't mean a brother's kiss!'

'—and I was kissed during a game of charades when I spent a holiday with one of my schoolfriends,' she concluded, aware that none of these kisses had felt in the least like the one Kester had just given her. She looked at his teasing eyes and then quickly away again, aware of the sudden warmth of a blush in her face.

'So you've never been kissed,' he said quietly. 'Well, it's a sad thing when a girl like you can bathe naked in the river on a summer's morning and no man to see and make love to you—'

'You saw me,' she said involuntarily and stopped, blushing even more fiercely. 'Not that you were supposed to. I'd never have dreamed of doing it if I'd known you were about.'

'You knew I was about. I told you yesterday morning. I'm always about in these woods.'

'I did not! I thought myself alone. There was no sign of anyone when I came here – no sound of any work going on, or anything.'

'I was resting,' he said matter-of-factly. 'I've been working since dawn, putting in a new fence. I saw you in the garden an hour ago.'

'Well, I didn't see you.' Rowenna paused. Why was she arguing with him? Hadn't she just said that his kiss had not offended her? 'I really didn't,' she added more quietly, and he smiled and took her hand.

'I believe you. But you should be careful if you're going to do such things. There are some men I'd not like to see you as I saw you, and who might not be so careful with you either.'

Careful? What did he mean? Rowenna looked at his fingers, playing with hers. She wondered what they would feel like, stroking her skin. Soft and gentle like his lips, or hard and firm? Which would she prefer?

'So how did you fare when you got home yesterday?' he asked. 'Did anyone see you?'

'No. Only my maid knew I'd been out, and she won't tell. I slept for a while and then I came down into the garden and worked all day.' She glanced at him. 'I wondered if I might see you.'

'I thought it was better to keep out of your way. I saw you, though.'

'You mean you watched me and never let me know?'

'Listen,' Kester said. 'Things can't be easy between you and me. You know how it is. I'm just a gypsy. I don't have any proper job, I wander from place to place – I don't even stay with my own folk. If anyone thinks I'm taking more interest in you than I should, there'll be trouble and I'll likely be dismissed with no chance to come back ever again. Same for you – only you'll be locked up, or maybe wed to someone who'll take you away and keep you busy producing *chavvies* – children.'

'I don't see why we can't be friends, though,' Rowenna argued. 'My maid Molly is my friend, and no one sees any reason to object to that.'

'And you think no one would object to us being friends! It's not the same at all.'

'Well, I know it isn't the same. You can't come into the house or anything like that. But out in the garden – we can see each other every day.' She gazed at him appealingly. 'We can work together – talk. You don't have to be in the woods all the time. You can work in the kitchen garden, or with the roses. I often work with John Richmond there, or in the greenhouse. Nobody would take any notice of that.'

His face darkened. 'And I'm to dance attendance on you in the garden just like Molly dances attendance on you indoors, is that it? I'm to take orders amongst the cabbages, just to suit your whim. And what about the days when you've got summat better to do? What about when I want to go off and work somewhere else?'

'Oh, you wouldn't do that. You'd stay here, surely.'

'Would I? Stay here and give up my freedom just for a chance of a word now and then – a kiss when nobody's looking?' He regarded her sombrely. 'Or are you offering more for my time?'

'I don't know what you mean,' Rowenna said angrily, snatching away her hand. 'And I don't really know why we're even discussing this. I simply thought that after the other night, you were – well, you were my friend. You seemed to understand so much – about Haddie and about my father.' She paused, then added in a small voice, 'I don't have any other friends – not real friends. Only Molly. And even she doesn't always understand.'

Kester's face softened. He picked up her fingers again and folded them in his. He carried them to his lips and kissed them gently, one by one.

'I know,' he said. 'We all need a friend or two. And I'm yours, Rowenna. There's no two ways about that. But like it or not, it can't be easy. And we can't ever be more than that.' He stopped and looked across the little dell, filled with blue light, towards the bank of the river. 'It's a pity I came here today and found you bathing with nothing to hide your loveliness,' he said. 'And a pity I kissed you. Because that's something we'll never be able to forget.'

'I don't want to forget it,' Rowenna said in a low voice. 'I want to remember it for ever.'

'Aye,' he said, 'and so you will. And so will I. But it's a memory we may come to curse, for it's a memory that will never let us rest again.' His eyes met hers and it seemed that their darkness caressed her heart. 'We'll want it again and again, and more,' he said. 'And that's what can never be, my Rowenna.'

An invitation to supper was not something that occurred often to Rowenna and at first she demurred, convinced that Mr Boothroyd had invited her simply out of courtesy and did not expect her to accept. To her surprise, her father told her sharply that she must indeed accept, and take the trouble to look her best.

'You're not a schoolgirl any longer,' he said. 'I expect you to be a credit to me. You'll be attending other functions as my companion, and acting as hostess as well, so you may as well accustom yourself to the idea.'

'Hostess? But we never have any dinner parties here.'

'Not since your mother died,' he corrected her. 'But now that you're a young woman I can resume my local duties.

I've always had a fancy for standing for the town council – perhaps eventually as mayor – but without the right helpmeet . . .'

Rowenna gazed at him. 'Father, I don't think I'd enjoy that kind of thing at all—'

'Who's talking about your enjoyment?' he said sharply. 'You've had years enough of running wild and doing as you please. You're of an age to be useful to me now, so you can start repaying your debts.' He stared critically at her. 'You'd better get the dressmaker to run you up a few new gowns. I doubt if you've anything fit to wear in public, other than those two mourning dresses, and they're as plain as charity. You need something showier for such events.'

'My black silk looks well—'

'I've seen it a hundred times. You ought to have at least two others, to ring the changes. See to it, and don't run mad with expense. I'm not made of money.'

Rowenna went upstairs and looked inside her wardrobe. Of the few clothes which hung there, most were old school clothes which she was 'wearing out', with the dark blue silk her father had given her for her eighteenth birthday, and her mourning dresses. None were really fashionable, for she hated the new 'bustle' – clothes were restricting enough without wearing a great pad of horsehair attached to the back of the waist – and the blue silk had been made in the old tie-back fashion, and as simply as the dressmaker could be persuaded. As evening clothes went, it was relatively comfortable, and she made up her mind to have any new gowns made in the same style. Perhaps in deep violet, which counted well enough for mourning now, and suited her colouring.

Why was her father suddenly interested in social functions, she wondered. Did he really intend standing for the town council? Was this why Mr Boothroyd had invited them to supper? And did he really mean to hold dinner parties at Ashbank, parties at which she would have to preside as hostess?

'I can't think why he doesn't marry again if he needs someone to accompany him,' she said to Molly as the maid dressed her hair the following Tuesday evening. 'A wife of his own generation would be far more suitable. I'm just not the right sort of person to go to all these affairs, Molly. I'll let him down all the time.'

'Nonsense,' the maid said robustly. 'You're as good-looking as any you're likely to find round here. You'll have all the men at your feet, see if you don't.'

'And I can't think that *that* will please Father,' Rowenna returned. 'He's not entering me for the marriage mart – he wants me to himself, to act as wife, daughter, companion – whatever's needed at the moment. He won't want someone carrying me off to the other side of the country, where I'm of no further use.' She sighed, and added, 'Though why he wants to keep me at his side I don't really know, since I seem to irritate him with every breath I draw.'

Molly piled the honey-cream hair on top of Rowenna's head, allowed a cascade of loose waves to tumble down the back, and fastened it skilfully with a few pins and a trailing ribbon.

'There. You look lovely.'

Rowenna stood up and looked critically at her reflection. The violet silk of the gown which the dressmaker had laboured all week to have ready darkened her eyes so that they were almost the same shade, and its sheath-like cut fitted her slender figure perfectly, the low neck showing off her skin that was faintly and unfashionably golden from the sun. Her cheeks glowed with the same burnished shimmer and her only jewellery was a gold locket and chain that Haddon had given her.

'I suppose I look well enough,' she conceded. 'Though why it should matter, heaven only knows. We're only going to supper with Mr Boothroyd.' She grimaced. 'It doesn't matter how hard I try, I can't like Mr Boothroyd. He makes my flesh creep. I'd rather be at home, dressed in an old wrapper and eating plain cold mutton, to tell you the truth.'

Molly laughed. 'And that tells me just how much you don't want to go! You hate cold mutton. Well, I daresay you'll get better food than that, and you won't see much of him. He and your pa will sit all evening over their port and you'll be left in peace with the other ladies. D'you know who else is going?'

'Mrs Oaksey, I believe, Mr Boothroyd's sister. She's pleasant enough, I suppose, though she hasn't anything to talk about except local gossip.'

'Nobody else?' Molly asked. 'Oh well, it'll be quiet enough then. I suppose your pa wouldn't be going, else. It's still not so long since Mr Haddon passed away.'

'People don't observe such long mourning now,' Rowenna said. 'And I think that's a good thing. What help is it to sit at home bewailing? Haddie wouldn't have wanted that. He was too full of life – he'd have wanted us to enjoy what we had.'

'Aye, he was a bonny lad.' The two girls stood silent for a moment, then Molly shook herself and said briskly, 'Well, you'd best be getting yourself downstairs, Miss Rowenna. Your pa'll be shouting for you any minute. Now, you have a pleasant evening and try not to let your flesh creep too far. He can't hurt you, after all.'

No, Rowenna thought, he can't hurt me. But he looks at me as if he would like to, in some queer, horrible fashion. And she remembered how he had oozed up to her in the churchyard, at Hadden's funeral, and pressed his fishlike hands into hers, and shuddered.

101

But there was no time for further thought. As Molly had predicted, her father was already calling her name impatiently from the foot of the stairs, and she picked up the little satin purse her mother had embroidered for her when she was a child and went quickly out of the room.

It was an evening for roaming the fields and fells rather than for sitting indoors in a stuffy room, eating supper with stuffy people, she thought as she and her father entered Alfred Boothroyd's house a quarter of an hour later. After the brightness of the early evening, it seemed almost ominously dark in the hall with its deep red embossed wallpaper and its heavy furniture. Large portraits of old men with heavy frowns and stern mouths loomed down from the walls, and an array of stuffed birds perched stiffly on twisted branches in glass-domed cases.

Although it was only on the other side of the river from Ashbank, the nearest bridge was in Burneside itself, necessitating a drive down to the village and then back along the other bank. As Boothroyd welcomed them, his cold hands lingering on Rowenna's shoulders as he helped her to remove her light evening cloak, he apologised for the journey.

'It would be so much more convenient to have a little footbridge across the river between our two properties, don't you agree? Then you could slip over whenever you had a mind, Miss Mellor.'

Rowenna smiled faintly, wondering when he thought she would have 'a mind' to slip over to Meadowbank. She turned to greet Mrs Oaksey.

Matilda Oaksey had been widowed several years earlier, and although she did not live with her brother she often acted as his hostess. She had a house in Staveley, where her husband had managed another of Alfred Boothroyd's mills, and lived comfortably enough on what he had left her. Perhaps being a widow was best of all, Rowenna thought, for you could then be totally independent and manage your own affairs without anyone else having rights over you. A difficult state to arrange, however – and the idea brought a smile to her lips which was still there as she turned back to her host.

He stared at her for a moment with a queer, hungry look in his marble eyes, and Rowenna felt the smile fade abruptly. Her skin coloured and she let her glance fall. At that moment, Mrs Oaksey moved forward and slipped her hand under Rowenna's elbow.

'Come into the drawing room, my dear. Alfred, I can't think what you're about, letting your guests stand around in the hall. They must need some refreshment. The maid has already brought in a very pleasant fruit cup, so let's go in and sample it.'

A journey of fifteen minutes scarcely warranted refreshment, but Rowenna accepted the fruit cup and sat down in the window seat, looking out at the garden and wondering if she had ever seen a home which so echoed its owner's character. Just as the house was dark and gloomy, stuffed with furniture that seemed to loom and threaten, so the garden too was sombre, its trees all dark-leaved or evergreen with scarcely a flower to be seen. They seemed to be advancing towards the house – indeed, one or two had already reached it and were pressing their branches against the windows – and at the same time they reached up to blot out the sky, their solid mass like a deep thundercloud obliterating the sunset.

'And how are you faring these days, my dear?' Mrs Oaksey was beside her, fanning herself gently. 'You must be such a comfort to your father. He would be very lonely without you.'

'I think he would. But I'm really no replacement for my brother.'

'Oh, I'm sure he relies on you a great deal. After all, he has no wife either. That must be true loneliness for a man.'

'I suppose so. But he's talking of my going with him on social functions, and of holding our own dinner parties.'

'Well, naturally you're the only one who can help him unless he finds a wife. But what of when you marry?'

'Oh, I don't suppose I'll marry,' Rowenna said. 'Father won't let me go away, and I can't leave him. I'm all he has.'

The thought of Kester's laughing face came into her mind, and his gravity when he had kissed her by the river. She had been as much gypsy as he for that moment, standing almost naked in his arms beneath the trees. She had known for a few moments what it must be like to be free – free to love beneath the wild sky, free to choose her own way. But it had faded all too soon; the reality of her life had broken in again and Kester himself had destroyed the moment. *We can't ever be more than friends . . . we'll want it again and again . . . and that's what can never be . . .*

Mrs Oaksey was watching her. She said, 'It's not easy for you, my dear, I can see that. But I daresay some solution will present itself. A pretty young thing like you ought to be married. I'm sure something will happen to make your father change his mind.'

There was an odd note to her voice, as if she knew more than she was saying, and Rowenna turned her head to look at her. But there was no hint of hidden knowledge in the pale, rather fat face, and the small eyes, brown like her brother's but not so much like marbles, stared back innocently.

All the same, Rowenna thought uncomfortably, she does know something she's not telling me. What can it be?

And the idea came to her that Mrs Oaksey might be looking for another husband. And that her glance had settled on Warren Mellor.

The evening wore on. After the fruit cup, dinner was served, and it was almost as uninteresting as the cold mutton Rowenna had said she would prefer. Alfred Boothroyd's cook was evidently unaccustomed to cooking the kind of dinner he had ordered tonight and almost every dish was either undercooked, overdone or spoiled in some other way. The spring soup was lumpy rather than thick, the boiled fish like cotton-wool but rather less tasty, and the sirloin tough. The sorbet was nearly liquid and the roast quail dry and stringy. The vegetables were boiled to a mash and the fruit jelly so tough it needed almost a hammer and chisel to serve the portions. By the time the savouries were reached, Rowenna was forced to repress an increasing desire to giggle, and the ice, which was even more melted than the sorbet, almost lost her her composure entirely.

Thankfully, she retired with Mrs Oaksey to the drawing room. There, a tray of tea had been brought in by the house-maid and Mrs Oaksey poured a cup and handed it to Rowenna.

'My poor brother suffers from having no one to order his house,' she remarked. 'I do my best, of course, but he sadly needs a wife. Men are so lonely without women, don't you agree? Well, of course you do – you were telling me before dinner about your father. I can understand why you feel it impossible to leave him.' She smiled at Rowenna and carried her own cup across to the sofa where Rowenna sat. 'But as I said, I'm sure something will happen to make it possible. And I daresay you'd welcome that. It's no life for a young woman, to be dancing attendance on an old man. Not that your father's old, by any means,' she added hastily. 'Why, I don't suppose he's a day over fifty, is he? And a fine man too. I'm surprised he's never found himself another wife.'

She *is* setting her cap at him, Rowenna thought. And suppose she succeeded? What would happen next? What would happen to me?

Perhaps it would indeed be the answer to her problems. With a wife to attend to his comfort, her father would forget about Rowenna, just as he had when Haddon had been there to talk about the mill and play cards with him of an evening. She would be free once more to spend her days in the garden and her evenings with a book. She would be able to go walking on the fell. Perhaps even to marry, if she chose.

Once again, Kester's face came to her mind and she heard his voice. *Take your chances when they come . . .* Was this to be her chance?

The door opened and she looked up, surprised to see her father and Mr Boothroyd so soon. She had expected them to spend longer over their port. But they came in, evidently pleased enough with one another, and Mr Boothroyd poured brandy for them both. He came over to sit beside Rowenna, and Mrs Oaksey, smiling, got up and moved across the room to speak to Warren.

'It's pleasant to have your company here this evening, Miss Mellor,' Alfred Boothroyd said in his smooth tones. 'We haven't seen enough of you since you left school. You're quite grown up.'

'Thank you,' Rowenna said politely, wondering why this was supposed to be a compliment. Nobody could help growing up, after all. She wondered what he would say if she told him that he was quite grown up too . . . 'I've been looking at your garden,' she added, for want of anything else to say.

'Ah, the garden, yes. I understand you're quite a gardener yourself. I'm afraid it isn't in my line – I leave it all to my man. So long as I have my privacy I don't concern myself much with what he grows.' He glanced out at the encroaching thickets. It's rather like the castle in the story of Sleeping Beauty, Rowenna thought. Is there a princess somewhere asleep in this big dark house, and does her prince have any hope of fighting his way through to find her? The thought made her shudder.

So too did Alfred Boothroyd's presence, so close beside her. She looked at him, seeing the pallor of his thin, cadaverous face, the marble coldness of his eyes. His hands were white too, his fingers as pallid as slugs. She remembered the feeling of them on her shoulders as he removed her cloak, and felt the goose-pimples rise on her skin.

He had a way of tilting his head slightly and moving his neck as he spoke to her, like a snake. He stretched his long, spidery legs out in front of him and showed his teeth in a smile.

'Perhaps you'd like to come and look at the garden with me one afternoon. You could tell me what I should be doing. I have a fancy for a grotto. We could plan it together.'

'That would be pleasant, but I doubt if I'd be able to come. My father likes me to attend to the house during the day.'

'Of course, but I'm sure he can spare you for the odd afternoon. Better still, why doesn't he come with you? I can ask my sister too and make it a tea party.' He smiled again and Rowenna glanced at her father and Mrs Oaksey, engaged in conversation across the room, and her suspicions increased. Mrs Oaksey had definitely decided to pursue Warren Mellor, and Alfred Boothroyd was aiding and abetting her. 'I'd like to show you the house too,' he went on. 'I'm sure you'll be interested. And you might be able to help me with a little interior decoration and refurbishing, too. It sadly needs it, in places.'

107

'I really know nothing at all about decoration,' Rowenna protested, but he was already on his feet.

'In fact, there's one matter I'd like your advice on at once. Come and look at the guest bedrooms. I'm thinking of ordering new carpets for them and have only a hazy idea as to what's required. I'm sure your father and my sister won't miss us for a while.'

He closed his cold white fingers around Rowenna's wrist and drew her up beside him. She cast a glance of appeal towards her father, but he only glanced up and nodded, as if to give approval for the expedition, and Mrs Oaksey's plump face beamed. Then they both turned back towards each other and resumed their conversation. Clearly, they were interested only in each other.

Alfred Boothroyd pulled Rowenna towards the door. He closed it behind them and they stood a moment in the darkened hall, looking at each other. Then he started up the stairs, his fingers still closed around Rowenna's wrist, and she was forced to follow him.

'This is the main guest bedroom,' he said, throwing open a door. 'It's a fine room, don't you think?' He was speaking quickly, as if nervous. 'I thought of decorating it in shades of brown. A good, serviceable colour. It already has oak panelling, as you can see, on the lower half of the walls, and good rich wallpaper above that will set if off nicely. And a patterned carpet, of leaves perhaps. Velvet curtains, of course, on both the windows and the bed. A rather fine small four-poster, isn't it? I have another like it in my own room.' He turned her to face him and Rowenna saw with a shock that his eyes were no longer cold marbles, but like coals that had begun to smoulder. 'My own room is quite close to this one. I've sometimes thought that if I ever marry, this would be my wife's. It would be suitable, don't you agree?'

'Yes,' Rowenna said bemusedly. 'Oh yes, very suitable.' She glanced around and added politely, 'It's a beautiful room.'

'Oh, I'm glad you think so. Very glad. And brown would be a good colour?'

Rowenna looked at the dark, panelled walls, at the window from which she could see only the mass of trees pressing around the house. She thought of the guests who might find themselves having to sleep here, of the wife who might one day look on it as a haven – wouldn't any woman, married to Alfred Boothroyd, need a haven? And a small devil entered her soul. He had asked for her opinion. Very well, he should have it.

'Brown?' she said consideringly. 'Oh no, I don't think so. Brown's quite out of fashion these days.' She had no idea what was in or out of fashion. 'I think you should paper it in white. That will lighten it up. Or – no – a very pale, delicate pink. With rose-pink curtains and a grey carpet to set it off. There could be some pink flowers in the carpet too. And the bedroom china should be white, with pink flowers on it just the same. And there should always be flowers on the mantelpiece and side table, and in winter a fire laid in the grate.' She stopped, surprised by the picture she had conjured up. It really would look quite nice, she thought. Light and pretty and so much more welcoming than the dark browns Mr Boothroyd had proposed.

'Pink?' he echoed, as if he had never heard of the colour before. 'You really think that would be best?'

'Oh yes,' she assured him. 'Much the best.'

'And it would appeal to a young lady? A – a bride?'

'I'm sure it would,' she said, wondering if he already had someone in mind.

He stared at her for a moment. 'Then it shall be done,' he declared.

Rowenna began to feel alarmed.

'Oh, you mustn't take any notice of me! I told you, I know nothing about decorating rooms. I'd be much happier giving you advice about the garden.' She cast a nervous glance at the door. 'I think we ought to be going back to the drawing room now, Mr Boothroyd. My father will be wondering what's become of me.'

His eyes burned into hers. He had not released her wrist and she could feel his thin, bony fingers, still cold against her skin. He was standing close, so close that she could feel his breath on her cheek. It smelt of cabbage. She took a step back.

'Mr Boothroyd?'

He frowned a little and his vision seemed to clear. His fingers fell away from her arm and she stepped further away, thankful to be out of his reach. She opened the door.

'I think you must decorate your room exactly as you want, Mr Boothroyd. And now I really must go back to my father. It's getting late – he must be ready to go home.'

She turned back and looked at him. In the dim light of the room, Alfred Boothroyd was standing still. His face was shadowed and she could not see his expression, but from the way he stood she had the impression that he was pleased. Pleased and satisfied.

Because she had told him he ought to decorate the room in pink? Or for some other reason?

Perhaps he thought that when they returned to the drawing room, her father and Mrs Oaksey would be announcing their engagement!

Chapter Six

Warren Mellor continued to disapprove of his daughter's activities in the garden, but short of tying her up in her room there was little he could do to prevent her from doing as she wished when he was not at home. If he complained, she simply asked him again to take her to the mill with him, and this he refused point-blank to do. At which, Rowenna shrugged and went up to her bedroom to put on her gardening overall.

She saw Kester almost every day now. They generally met in the little dell by the river, at a time when the other gardeners were having their bait in a corner of the kitchen garden. Nobody missed Kester, for he frequently preferred to take his break alone, amongst the trees, and nobody came wandering along the little paths to disturb them.

Rowenna did not bathe naked in the river again, for she was afraid of being seen from the opposite bank, perhaps by Alfred Boothroyd himself. But in the sheltered grove, with the air fragrant from the scent of bluebells, she and Kester would lie in each other's arms and he would move his lips softly over her skin, whispering softly in a tone that was tenderness itself.

Sometimes, as she lay against his warm body, looking up at the sky that showed blue through the screen of leaves that moved gently above them, she felt a warm spreading heat that made her press herself more closely against him and turn her head, seeking his mouth with a desire to feel it harder against hers. As she did so, she could feel Kester's arms tighten about her. But immediately, though her joy soared, he would loosen his grip and move away.

'Kester – please—'

'No,' he said, his voice hoarse. 'No. You don't know what you're doing.'

'I just want to hold you closer—'

'*No*,' he repeated, and pushed her away from him. 'Lordy me, Rowenna, d'you think I don't want to love you as God meant us to love? D'you think I don't want to hold you tight against me and do all the things a man and a woman *should* do together? I know just how it'd be and I lie awake at night, just wanting you that way. But we can't – not here. It's too dangerous. And maybe we never can.'

Rowenna stared at him, barely understanding his words. Of course she was aware that if anyone came upon her and Kester lying so intimately together, there would be trouble. But his kisses stirred her blood, making her desire more, even though she hardly knew what she desired.

'I only want you to kiss me a little more—' she began, but he turned on her, his face dark with a passion that made her catch her breath.

'*Only kiss you*? If I kiss you any more than I have done, I'll go mad if I can't have you. It's driving me crazy as it is. Holding you in my arms – feeling your body – wanting you – why, there's times I don't know how to stand it.' He beat his fist upon the grass. 'Don't drive me too far, Rowenna. Don't. I'll kiss you and hold you, but if you ask for more I won't answer for the consequences!'

Rowenna shook her head, bewildered, and felt the tears hot in her eyes.

'What have I done?' she whispered. 'What have I said?

112

You look so angry . . . All I want is to love you . . .'

For a full minute, Kester's dark eyes looked into hers. And then he reached out and gathered her against him, holding her close to his heart.

'All you want is to love me,' he whispered in a ragged voice. 'Oh my sweetling, if only you knew – if you only knew how much *I* love *you*. Oh, I'd like to take you now, right here on the riverbank amongst the bluebells, and then I'd like to take you up to my hut and love you again, and take you over the hills and away, somewhere where we could be on our own for the rest of our days . . . But I can't do it. I can't do any of it.'

'Why not? Why can't you love me, Kester?'

'You know why not!' he returned roughly. 'Because of what I am and what you are. A gypsy and a fine young lady – it's impossible. And because things are bad enough for you already and I don't want to make them worse.' He kissed her then, hard. 'There. That's what you wanted, isn't it? And it's all you can have – all either of us can have.' He sat up away from her, and ran his fingers through his black, curly hair. 'I shouldn't ever have let this start.'

Rowenna sat up too. She reached across and laid a timid hand upon his shoulder.

'I'm glad you did,' she said quietly. 'Coming here in the mornings, meeting you – it's all I live for now. And I won't ask you to kiss me like that again, not if it upsets you. We'll just be quiet together, as we've been these past few days. Will – will that be all right?'

Kester sat for a moment looking down at the grass. He pulled at a bluebell head and scattered its seeds at his feet. Then he turned and smiled at her.

'I don't think you understand even yet what's happening atween us,' he said. 'But no matter. Time'll have its way, as my dad would say. And if I can't have what I want, it's certain I can't give up what I've got. And now it's time one of us was seen doing a bit o' work – so give us a last kiss and then tidy yourself up a bit. You're all over grass.'

And after that there was no more talk of kissing or making love. They met each morning still, and lay together, but now Rowenna knew that the gentle kisses were all that could be allowed, and the caresses that made her long for more must be restrained. And she lay in the grass, with the bluebells echoing the sky above, and gave herself up to the tenderness in Kester's hands and lips, and remembered them at night when she was alone. And she thought of the day when her father's demands would cease and she could be free to go where she would and love whom she liked.

Since the dinner party at Alfred Boothroyd's house, she had become more than ever convinced that her father intended to marry Mrs Oaksey. Twice during the following week he drove round to Meadowbank, and once Mrs Oaksey had accompanied her brother to tea with the Mellors. Rowenna had been dragged in from the garden for the occasion and had been forced to wash and change hurriedly without Molly's help, which meant that she could not wear her day-dresses, each of which had fifteen or twenty buttons down the back, but had to put on an old school dress which buttoned in front but was too tight. Her breasts, small as they were, strained against the cotton and she was in constant terror that the buttons might burst and fly off during tea.

'What in God's name possessed you to wear that appalling garment?' her father demanded as soon as they were alone again. 'I was ashamed to look at you. It's positively indecent! Heaven knows what Mrs Oaksey thought, and as for Boothroyd – he must have thought you nothing but a trollop.'

'It was all I could put on,' Rowenna said. 'Molly always

has an hour off in the afternoon and the other servants were picking strawberries in the kitchen garden, so there was no one to help me. Would you have had me appear at tea in my overall, Father?'

'You know perfectly well I would not,' he growled. 'But if you behaved as a young lady should and dressed properly all the time, there'd be no need for these panics. You should have been in a – what do they call it? – tea-gown before our visitors even arrived, and somewhere in the house ready to receive them.'

'But we didn't know they were coming!'

'You should *always* be ready to receive visitors,' Warren stated. 'Or you should have two or three At Homes each week. Then people would know where they were.'

'At Homes? Me?' Rowenna began to laugh. 'Really, father, the idea's absurd. Nobody comes to see *me*. I hardly know anyone, I've been kept in the house so much.'

'That will do!' he thundered. 'How dare you laugh at me, you hussy! I can see I've allowed you too much of your own way yet again. You've been doing just as you pleased this past week and now you think you can behave like a hoyden to your own father and shame me before my visitors. Well, let's see how you like this. I'll be in for my tea every afternoon at three-thirty and I expect you to be here and ready, *suitably* dressed, to attend me. D'you understand?'

Rowenna's cheeks grew cold as the colour left them. Through stiff white lips, she answered, 'Yes, Father. I understand you. But that means I won't be able to go into the garden at all after lunch. I shall have to get Molly to help me dress before she has her hour off, and just *sit* here until half past three doing *nothing*. I'll be driven mad with boredom.'

'No, you won't. I'll find plenty for you to do. I daresay you've not finished those winter curtains yet, have you? And there's plenty of other mending to be done. And when

115

you're tired of that, you can start some work of your own. A patchwork quilt – my mother made one for her wedding day and it's on my bed yet. That'll keep your fingers busy. And some fine embroidery. You've done little enough of that kind of thing since you left that expensive school. Oh, you'll not have time to be bored.'

'But I shall.' She gazed at him imploringly. 'Father, you know how I hate sewing, and sitting indoors on fine days. It will kill me to have to spend my afternoons in that way.'

Warren snorted. 'Kill you! Don't dramatise things so – why, you're worse than your mother used to be. Of course it won't kill you. It's the proper way for a young lady to spend her time. And don't think you'll go grubbing about in the garden during the mornings, either. I told you before, they're for seeing to the house and making sure the servants are up to the mark. It'll be good training for when you have a home of your own. A fine wife you'd make in your present condition!'

'I doubt if I'll ever make any kind of wife at all,' she retorted. 'Who is going to want to marry me? Who would you *allow* to marry me? You'll keep me here a prisoner for the rest of my life, chained to a sewing-needle, just for the pleasure of making me miserable. I shall die an old maid, or else become a lunatic, driven mad by a patchwork quilt that I'll never, never be able to finish.'

Warren stared at her. His whiskers bristled dangerously and his eyes narrowed.

'How dare you speak to me like that? Apologise at once!'

'I won't. I've nothing to apologise for. Everything I say is true – you *do* just want to make me miserable. You get some horrible kind of pleasure out of it. You like to think you've got control over me, that you can make me suffer. You've been doing it ever since – since Haddie died, and it's getting worse.' The tears were thick in her throat now, but she struggled on, knowing the words must be said. 'It's as if – as if you're punishing me. As if you blame me for Haddie's death. As if you thought it was all my fault and it was I who should have died, instead of him.' Her sobs overcame her and she covered her face with her hands, then took them away to stare with wild eyes at her father and cry, 'I believe you wish I *had* died . . .'

There was a silence. Outside, one of the gardeners could be heard wheeling a barrow along the path. A bird called out a 'chink-chink' of warning as it was disturbed from a bush.

Slowly, Rowenna removed her hands from her face. She felt in her pocket for a handkerchief and shakily blew her nose. She looked up at her father and flinched at the fury in his eyes, at the curl of his nostrils and the snarl that drew back his lips and exposed his yellowing teeth.

For a moment, she feared he would strike her. At his sudden movement, she recoiled. But he paused, to stand like a pugilist about to begin his fight, his fists bunched at his sides.

'And now, if you've finished, you'll go to your room,' he ordered harshly. '*At once*, d'you hear? And you'll stay there until I tell you to come out. The maid will bring you your meals. I don't wish to see you again, until I can be certain that I can trust myself not to wring your impertinent little neck.'

Rowenna took a deep breath and faced him, swallowing the tears that had welled up as she thought of her brother. She tilted her chin and looked at him with defiant eyes. The tight school dress had a simple naivety that contrasted incongruously with her slender height and curving figure, and even more with the tone in which she spoke as she said, 'No, Father. I won't go to my room. You'll never lock me up again. You can't, unless you carry me there by force, and it

117

will take more than you to do that for I'll fight and I'll scream every inch of the way. And I don't think Ackroyd will help you, for he has enough to do getting you to *your* room of an evening.'

She stood still, forcing herself not to move as Warren started forward, his face suffused with rage. 'Don't hit me, Father,' she said quietly. 'I know you have a right to, as my father, but the servants will gossip all the same and it won't help you, in your stand for the council, to have people know you're violent towards your own daughter.'

'Violent!' he spluttered. 'Violent! It would be no more than the discipline you need, my girl, and nobody would blame me for it. Now, miss, do you dare to defy me?'

'I've told you,' she said, 'I'll be a dutiful enough daughter to you while you're here in the evenings. The rest of the day I consider my own. If I wish to spend my time in the garden, I will. If you are expecting visitors for tea, naturally I'll be present and wearing the proper clothes, but I will not sit here day after day waiting, just in case Mr Boothroyd or his sister chance to call. In any case, they don't come to see me, and well you know it.'

'Don't come to see *you*?' Warren demanded. 'And what do you mean by that?'

'Oh come, Father,' Rowenna said. 'It must be clear to everyone why you and Mr Boothroyd have started to visit each other so suddenly. And especially why Mrs Oaksey is always present. You're thinking of marrying again, aren't you? Soon, you'll have a wife to dance attendance on you – and I can tell you this, as far as I'm concerned it can't happen a moment too soon!'

'And did he deny it?' Kester asked when Rowenna described the scene to him the next morning. They were lying in the dell, though the bluebells were fading now and the canopy of leaves overhead was thicker, shading them more completely from the sun. Kester was on his back, his arm flung out to the side, cradling Rowenna's head.

'I didn't give him the chance. I walked out of the room before he could answer. I was really afraid that if I stayed longer he would either kill me or have an apoplexy.' Rowenna turned her head and looked at Kester. 'It sounds funny, I know, but it was truly frightening. He has such terrible rages, and they've been worse since Haddie died.'

'Aye, I can tell that.' Kester spoke soberly. 'And you know what I reckon? I reckon you ought to get out of there. Get away. Go somewhere where he can't find you and harm you. Otherwise one of these fine days he'll do just what he said, he'll lose control of himself and kill you.'

'Oh no,' Rowenna said. 'Of course he won't. After all's said and done, he is my father.'

'And fathers can lose their tempers, same as anyone else. Look, I've seen it happen – there was a man in our camp took leave of his senses one night and flung his own son across the fire and kicked him till he was dead. Before anyone could lift a finger to stop him. And he loved his son – thought the world of him. It was nowt but a quarrel, but old Jake hanged for it.'

Rowenna stared at him, horrified.

'Kester, how dreadful! But – that man was a gypsy, wasn't he? And – '

'Gypsies aren't savages,' Kester said. 'They're ordinary human beings. Anyone can let his temper get the better of him, and you aren't helping, goading him the way you do.'

'*Goad* him! I do no such thing. I've just got tired of letting him browbeat me, that's all. I stand up to him. And why should I not? Am I to spend the rest of my life with my needle, doing things I hate and never doing anything more in the garden than walk in it, twirling my parasol?' She paused for a moment, then added in a low voice, 'Am I never to be able to see you like this, and talk to you? You're my only real friend, Kester.'

'I thought Molly was your friend.'

'Oh yes, she is – but I can't talk to her, not as I can to you. And besides—'

'Besides, you can't do this with her,' he said with a grin, and pulled her close to kiss her. 'Or this.' And with his free hand, he stroked her breast.

'No. I can't.' She lay still, trembling slightly, in the circle of his arms. 'Oh, Kester, what am I going to do?'

'I already told you. Get away from him.'

'But how? Where could I go? I've no friends, no other family, no money. I've thought about it – trying to find work as a governess or a teacher. But it's impossible without a character reference and I can't go begging on the streets.' She lay staring up at the leaves, then turned to him. 'But I could come with you!'

'With me?'

'Yes. I could come and live in the hut up on the fells. Father would never know I was there. I could cook your food and mend your clothes and we could live together. Oh, Kester—'

Kester's fingers stroked her absently. He looked up at the leaves above, then back into her eyes.

'But I'm not staying there. I'll be moving on soon—'

'Moving on?'

'Aye. There's not much work here for me through the summer. Not the sort of work I like doing. I'll go south for a bit, see what I can pick up, maybe join my folk for a while and work a fair or two. There's the Horse Fair at Appleby, I'll find them there and see what's doing.'

'But I could come too. My father would never find me – he'll never think of looking in gypsy camps.'

Kester shook his head. 'It's not so easy as that, Rowenna.

Look, if the world spun the way we want it to, you'd be my woman. But it can't happen, not the way things are. And I've made up my mind it's best for me to go. I'm no good to you, my love. If I stay, it'll mean trouble – trouble for you. And—'

Rowenna sat up. She looked down into his face, trying to read the expression in his eyes, but they were veiled and enigmatic. Suddenly, she felt that she did not know him at all, that she had never known him.

'You're going to leave me? You're going away, with never a word?'

'No! I'd not have done that. But – oh, my sweetling, can't you see? This is no good for us, this kissing and canoodling in corners. We need to love each other properly, we need to be together. And since we can't be that, it's best to stop now. You'll have a chance then to find someone who can marry you and give you all the things you ought to have—'

'*Marry* me? But I don't want to marry anyone. I love you.'

'And I love you. But we both know that nothing can come of it,' he said soberly. 'My life isn't for you, Rowenna. You've only seen it in the summer – and you've only seen the hut where I live now. It's a good place, that hut, but it's not always like that. There's times when I live in a tent, with the rain lashing on the canvas and maybe the snow piling up outside. There's times when it's impossible to keep a fire going and I just have to sit it out till the rain and the snow stop. And times when I'm hungry and have to live on what I can get. It's a hard life, Rowenna, and not one I'd ever want you to live, if there was any way round it.'

'But there is a way,' she said. 'You could get a job. You could work in a garden somewhere – Richmond would give you a character. We could live simply enough in a gardener's cottage—'

'No,' he said flatly. 'No, I'll not work for any man. I've

told you before – I call no man master, nor ever will. I don't need to live like that.'

'But if you loved me—'

'I still have to be myself,' he said doggedly. 'I'll not ask you to give up being yourself for me, and I'll not give up the mainspring of my own life. If I did, I'd not be the man I am, and we'd come to hate each other for it.'

'I don't understand. We could never hate each other.'

'We could,' he said, 'if we tried to put each other into boxes. I couldn't live in a box, Rowenna, not even with you.'

'So what am I to do?' she asked miserably. 'You say I've got to get away – but where am I go go? There's nobody else, Kester.'

'Don't you have any other family?' She shook her head. 'What about Canada? You've got folk there.'

'And how do I get to Canada, without money?' she demanded. 'Stow away on a ship? Work my passage? Canada could be on the moon, for all the chance I have of going there. And I can't write and ask them to send me my fare. My father's hardly written to them in years. In any case, if I did and they wrote back, he'd see the letter and open it.'

There was a long silence. Then Kester said, 'It looks like you'll have to come away with me, then.'

Rowenna sat up slowly. She looked down into the dark face. She searched the brown eyes, looking for a hint of laughter, of mockery. But there was none. Only grave truth.

'You mean it,' she said wonderingly. 'You really mean it.'

'I wouldn't say it if I didn't.'

She lay down again, feeling his body warm and strong beside her. If she went with him, she knew that he would protect her, that he would look after her. He would teach her to cook on an open fire, to find the food to cook – the rabbits and fish, the berries and herbs gathered from the hedgerows. They would wander under the broad sky, free as she had never been free, as she had never thought she could be free. They would lie together at night, warm and close in the heather.

'Are you asking me to marry you?' she asked.

Kester let out a shout of laughter. 'Marry! Well, we can jump over the broomstick together if it'll make you happy. I've not done it with any other girl, so it can be as legal as you wish. But I've nowt to give you, Rowenna. No fine house or stable full of horses, no fancy gowns. You'll lose all that if you come with me.'

'Oh, I don't care about that. None of those things matter to me. I should be sorry to say goodbye to the garden, but that's all.'

He looked at her seriously. 'I've told you how it'll be. I'll not sell myself to live in a cottage.'

'I'll never ask you to,' she said. 'You'll always be your own man, Kester. So long as you're mine too!'

He held her close and then said, 'We'll do it quick. Come up to my hut tonight. We can be away with the dawn.'

Tonight! The word thrilled through Rowenna's body. She turned into his arms and he held her close, his hands moving slowly on her back, his lips in her hair. Tonight, she knew, he would love her as she longed to be loved. Tonight, she would understand.

The stable clock began to chime and they heard footsteps on the path above. The mid-morning break had long since been over and the gardeners were about their work again. Kester put her from him and knelt up. He brushed the grass from her hair.

'Go back in and make yourself ready, my sweetling. Bring as little as you can do with you, but remember the nights can be cold, even with me to keep you warm. I'll be waiting for you as soon as the sun goes down.'

'I'll be there,' Rowenna promised, and she kissed him once more, then scrambled to her feet and climbed to the rim of the hollow. 'I'll be there.'

Her heart alight, she picked up her gardening tools and ran swiftly along the path to the kitchen garden. There would be no more work outside today. She had things to attend to indoors, and for these last few hours she would be as pleasant as she knew how to the father she was soon to leave behind.

The day passed with agonising slowness. To Rowenna, it was as if the sun stood still in the sky, hanging endlessly over the quiet house. The shadows were changeless, growing neither longer nor shorter. Inside, everyone seemed to move more slowly and luncheon seemed to take the whole afternoon, though it was barely two o'clock when her father rose from the table.

'Well, I must be getting back to the mill. I'm glad to see you've decided to see sense, Rowenna, and dressed yourself properly for once. Make sure you're here at tea-time, for I might bring Mr Boothroyd with me.'

'Mr Boothroyd? But he was here yesterday.'

'And does that mean he mayn't come again?' Warren's momentary approval evaporated and he glowered at her. 'I suppose I am permitted to invite what guests I like to my own house?'

'Of course, Father, I was just surprised, that's all.'

'Well, have the courtesy to conceal your surprise when he comes,' Warren snapped. 'I want Mr Boothroyd to feel welcome in this house, not like some unexpected interloper.'

'Will Mrs Oaksey be with him?' Rowenna enquired and was surprised when her father raised his eyebrows.

'Mrs Oaksey? No, of course not. We'll be coming from

the mill. Unless she happens to look in at the same time, but I can't imagine why she should.'

He went out, leaving Rowenna baffled. Why should Mr Boothroyd be coming without his sister, and why should her father be so obviously surprised by the notion that she might come too? Wasn't the entire friendship between the two families simply a prelude to an engagement between Mrs Oaksey and her father?

Well, after today it would be no more concern of hers. They could marry or not, as they wished, and she would be far away and need never give them another thought.

She went upstairs to make her preparations. She was already in the flowery muslin tea-gown her father had decreed she should wear for such occasions, so need not bother any more about that. Of far more interest to her were the clothes she should wear tonight, for her flight with Kester. As little as you can manage with, he had said, but the nights can be cold. And it would be autumn before long, and then winter. She would need warm clothes then.

She opened the big chest that stood in a corner of her bedroom holding her winter clothes. On top was the fur mantle she had bought for Haddie's funeral and not worn since. She took it out and laid it on the bed. Beneath it lay a warm woollen skirt, plainly cut, and a blouse with no elaborate decoration other than a few tucks. Well, they would have to do. She certainly could not carry more. She hastily rolled the three garments into a bundle and secured them with a ribbon.

In another bundle, she wrapped a few undergarments – no corsets, she thought with glee – and a shawl. Then she pushed the whole lot under the bed and looked around the room she had slept in ever since she was a small child.

Could she carry any more? For the first time, she realised how much a haven this room had been to her, how much things in it meant. There were the shells Haddie had brought back once from the seaside, and the big smooth pebble of agate they had found on the beach near Bardsea. There was the rag doll her mother had made her, with the face rubbed off by loving, and painted on again with a bigger smile than it had had in the first place. There were the toy dog and the farm animals and the Noah's Ark with its collection of exotic creatures – Noah having apparently done all his collecting in the jungle, and left the pigs and the cattle to drown. There were the books she and Haddie had read over and over again, and the games they had played together on wet afternoons.

All these must be left, and Rowenna felt a tearing sensation in her heart, as if they were a physical part of her body and were being wrenched away. It is as if I am leaving a part of myself, she thought.

And perhaps that was just what she was doing. For tonight, she would leave for ever the Rowenna who had been a child here, who had grown up in this room. From tonight, she would be a woman, facing a world of which she knew nothing, her only companion a gypsy, whose life had been as different from hers as if they had lived on different planets. A man she barely knew, except to know that she loved him.

As he had promised, Warren Mellor brought Alfred Boothroyd home for tea, and the two men sat eating scones and fruit cake, drinking tea and discussing business as though Rowenna were in a different room. Sitting in the window with some of her hated embroidery on her lap and gazing at the garden, bored and only half listening to their talk, she thought sadly of how Haddon would have joined in with his own ideas, and wished she could do the same. Esparto grass, woodpulp, white pine and hemlock – they were subjects she had discussed more than once with her brother, and she knew his opinion of each one and his thoughts on how the mill should be managed in the future.

She was a little surprised to find that Alfred Boothroyd seemed to share those opinions. He was offering her father advice and Warren Mellor, far from taking offence, was actually listening and accepting it. Rowenna too began to listen more carefully, and the direction the discussion was taking began to puzzle her even more.

'Manufacturers who want to expand are going to have build their own pulpmills,' Boothroyd said. 'It's the only way forward. Bring in the logs themselves and process them on the spot. As things stand now, the woodpulpers have got us all over a barrel. We have to pay their prices. And the Scandinavians are going to get more and more expensive, mark my words. It's to the New World we ought to be looking.'

'Aye, but how do we get a foot in that particular door?' Warren demanded. 'And I know what you're thinking, Boothroyd, but my contact there is no more than any other man's. I can assure you that my wife's relatives would be less than welcoming if I were to come knocking on their door, cap in hand. If I'd known ten years ago what I know now—'

'Most of us could say that,' the other man interrupted smoothly. His marble eyes were as expressionless as his tone. 'But I'm sure matters could be mended, with the right incentive. And there's that other proposition I put to you, too.' His glance flickered towards Rowenna and she bent her head quickly over her sewing.

'We'll discuss that another time,' Warren said abruptly. 'And now I should be getting back to the mill. You'll excuse me, Boothroyd, I'm sure. My daughter will be happy to entertain you should you like another cup of tea.'

Rowenna lifted her head sharply. Surely he was not going to leave her alone with Alfred Boothroyd! In any case, the other man must have affairs of his own to attend to. But before she could speak, Boothroyd said smoothly, 'Indeed, I should very much like another cup. It's a hot afternoon. And perhaps Miss Mellor would be kind enough to show me the garden? She's promised to come and look at mine one day and I'd like to see just what she's made of this one.'

Rowenna cast an agonised glance at her father, but he refused to meet her eye and left the room. Without looking at Mr Boothroyd, she refilled his cup and handed him another slice of cake. He munched for a few minutes in silence, then said pleasantly, 'You're looking very well today, Miss Mellor. Quite beautiful in fact, if you don't mind my being so personal. That's a very pretty dress.'

'Thank you,' Rowenna murmured. 'It's one of my favourites.' In fact the thin muslin, with its sprinkling of small, bright flowers, was as cool and comfortable as the holland overall she wore in the garden – though not, with its yards of material and flowing lines, as practical. She glanced up at her guest, wondering what to say next. Should she compliment him on his shirt or jacket? The thought brought a bubble of hysterical laughter dangerously close to her lips.

He set down his cup. Now he'll go, she thought with relief. But instead, he stood up and said with decision, 'And now the garden.'

'Do you really want to see it?' Rowenna asked in surprise.

'Didn't I say so? And you did promise.'

Rowenna could remember doing no such thing, but she knew her silence could be – and had been – taken as acquiescence. Well, if there was no help for it she might as well put on a brave face, and it surely must be better than sitting indoors with him. She got up.

128

'Let's go out, then. But you must tell me the moment you start to feel bored, or if you don't have time.'

'With you,' he said gallantly, 'I shall never be bored. And I can spare all the time in the world.'

Rowenna gave him another glance of surprise but said nothing. She led the way through the hall and outside.

'Which part of the garden would you like to see?'

'Oh, all of it,' he said, to her dismay.

'But that will take some time, Mr Boothroyd. I'm sure you're too busy.'

'Not at all,' he responded, still with that ghastly gallantry. 'I've the rest of the afternoon at my disposal. At *your* disposal,' he corrected himself. 'And there's nothing I should like better than to spend it walking in the garden with you.'

Rowenna's bewilderment increased. Alfred Boothroyd had never been known to take a holiday in his life, except for those he was forced to take, such as Christmas and the bank holidays declared by law. Even then, he was suspected to spend the greater part of them working in his study at home. An afternoon spent wandering in a garden was surely beyond his experience.

'Well,' she said doubtfully, 'let's start with the flower garden. The roses are doing beautifully this year.'

'They look extremely fine. Do you know all their names?'

'Most of them. This is one of my favourites – the *Botzaris* damask rose.' With gentle fingers, Rowenna lifted the heavy blossom, as creamy white as a magnolia, and bent to sniff its fragrance. 'And this is is Leda, the Painted Damask. They have such beautiful perfumes, I love them.' It struck her suddenly that after today she would never see these flowers again and tears misted her eyes as she straightened and walked quickly on. 'There are too many here to tell you all their names,' she said, when she could trust her voice again, 'but I daresay you have some of them in your garden.'

'Possibly. I seldom look.'

Rowenna stopped and looked at him. 'Mr Boothroyd, are you sure you really want to do this? Please don't say yes, just to be polite—'

'My dear Miss Mellor, I never say anything "just to be polite". I asked you to show me your garden because I want to see it. I want to walk with you. I want to hear you talking about the things you enjoy.'

Once again, Rowenna gave him a baffled glance. What possible interest could he have in her? And then it occurred to her that perhaps he was doing this on behalf of his sister. Perhaps Mrs Oaksey had asked him to spend some time with her, to find out what she was really like. No doubt Rowenna's father had told her of their difficulties and she was wondering what kind of stepdaughter Rowenna would make, and perhaps even whether she wanted to live in the same house.

The thought brought a shiver of dismay. Suppose Mrs Oaksey decided not to marry Warren after all! He would be alone then, just as Rowenna had dreaded, and a source of guilt for the rest of her life.

I must impress Mr Boothroyd, she thought. I must make him think me a sweet and gentle daughter, who will be nothing but a pleasure about the place. Then he'll go back to his sister with a good report of me and she'll agree to marry my father – and I shall be free.

But you're going to be free anyway, a small voice reminded her. You'll be free tonight – when you run away with Kester.

Rowenna hesitated. She looked around the garden, at its height of summer beauty. She thought of the fur mantle and the winter skirt and blouse, bundled under her bed upstairs. She thought of herself, slipping out after dark and making her way up through the meadows to Kester's hut.

Of course she would be free. But there was still a tiny doubt in her mind. Everything might not go so smoothly as it seemed. There was always something that could go wrong. Already, she had lost a mother and a brother. And if she were to lose this too, this love that had come so suddenly upon her, then her life would be even more of a trap than it was now.

Mrs Oaksey might be her last hope. Better do nothing to spoil that hope, should it ever be needed.

She spent the next hour and a half walking Mr Boothroyd round the garden. Setting out to be as agreeable as she knew how, she showed him the conservatory where her mother had once grown orchids, the pond where the golden carp that she and Haddon had dropped in years ago still swam, each nearly a foot long, the herb garden where the air was aromatic with lavender and camomile, sage and thyme, and the kitchen garden where rows of neat vegetables were being hoed and gathered.

'You grow a good variety,' he observed, looking at the array of beans, peas, cauliflower and kale. 'Surely that's asparagus. And sweetcorn.'

'Oh yes. We grow everything – as much as we can find the seed for. Richmond is a very good gardener.'

'And so, it would seem, are you.' He glanced at her. 'I hear you spend a good deal of your own time out in the garden.'

So I was right, Rowenna thought. He's been sent to see if I'm really the hoyden Father tells them.

'Oh, not so much,' she said casually, leading him past the seed-bed where some of Haddon's young trees were just beginning to germinate. 'I like to come out when I can talk to Richmond about plants, especially when the weather's fine as it's been recently, but Father really likes me to spend my time with my needle.'

131

'Ah yes. I noticed you were doing some embroidery at tea. A pleasant accomplishment for a young lady, I always think, and useful too. What are you making?'

'Oh, just a cloth for the table. And then father suggests I should make a patchwork quilt.'

'For your trousseau, I daresay,' he suggested, and Rowenna blushed scarlet. Mr Boothroyd was becoming arch – almost flirtatious. She looked away, unable to meet the marble gaze.

'I'm afraid any prospective bridegroom would have a long wait if he wanted to sleep beneath that on his wedding night,' she said, and blushed again. How had the conversation come to such intimacy? She stopped at the gate leading out of the kitchen garden, and laid her hand on its latch. 'I think I've shown you everything now, Mr Boothroyd.'

'Oh, but we haven't seen the little woodland. I've been hoping you would show me the trees your brother planted.'

So he knew about those! Rowenna had been deliberately avoiding the wood, knowing that she could not bear to take him to the little dell where she and Kester had lain together, or to the river where she had bathed and he had first kissed her. But now it seemed that there was no choice. She turned and led him along the little path across the lawn.

'Very pleasant,' he remarked, standing at the edge of the trees. 'And did Haddon plant all these?'

'No, some of them were here already.' Did he really not know the difference between an exotic species and the ordinary ash and birch and willow which fringed the little plantation? 'We got some of the seeds from a man who used to live in Furness and went to India – Walter Sherwin. He collected a lot of plants and sent them home to his sister and she gave a few to Haddon and me – my mother's family knew the Sherwins before they went to Canada, and she visited them for a while before old Mr Sherwin died. Miss Martha was very interested in gardening – she has a fine collection of primroses.'

'Indeed.' He sounded bored again and she stopped, aware that she had been chattering. She turned away, hoping that now he had seen the trees he would be satisfied, but instead he stepped a little further into the wood. 'And so what are these called?'

Rowenna felt her patience begin to give way. He could *not* be interested in the names of all the various trees – not when he couldn't even tell a birch from a rowan! And she desperately did not want him to set foot in the little dell. It was her place, hers and Kester's, their place of magic, and to have Alfred Boothroyd set his foot on its hallowed earth would be to besmirch it. Moreover, she was aware of the sounds of someone working on the far side, near the river, and knew that it must be Kester.

'I'm afraid I don't remember their names,' she lied. 'Haddon was more interested in the trees than I . . . And I'm afraid I must have kept you long past your time, Mr Boothroyd. There must be a hundred things you have to do.'

He turned and smiled at her, that sharp-toothed smile that reminded her of a wolf. Then, to her dismay, he walked a little further into the trees and stopped, on the very edge of the bluebell grove. He held out his hand.

'Nothing more important than this,' he said smoothly. 'Miss Mellor, won't you join me in this delightful place and admire these lovely blue flowers?'

He didn't even know a bluebell when he saw one! she thought. She hesitated, reluctant beyond words, to stand beside him in the place where she and Kester had passed so many magical hours. But he moved his hand, curling the fingers in a gesture that was half invitation, half command, and there was nothing she could do.

'That's better,' he said softly as she stood beside him. 'A pretty place, don't you agree?'

Rowenna nodded, unable to speak. Pretty! It was a word for it, she supposed, but there were so many others to use instead.

'A place for lovers' trysts, I would imagine,' he went on, and she looked up sharply. Had he seen her and Kester together? Had he stood on the opposite bank, watching as they came into this little dingle to kiss and caress? Had he – worst thought of all – seen her bathing there, almost naked, her bare skin showered with drops of sparkling water?

'What lovers would meet here?' she asked lightly, her heart beating fast. 'They must be old by now, if any ever did.'

'Oh no,' he said, 'not old at all. They would be young. Lovers are always young, Miss Mellor, don't you agree?'

Why was he doing this? Rowenna thought in agony. Why was he tormenting her? He must have seen . . . Was he about to demand some favour of her, in return for his silence? But what favour could she possibly do for him? Unless it were something concerning his sister and Rowenna's father.

It must be that. It must. And yet . . .

She could still hear the sound of someone working, out of sight in the bushes. If only Mr Boothroyd would come out of the wood before Kester saw them together, in the little hollow that had become their own.

'In their own eyes, if in nobody else's,' he continued. 'But why am I talking to you like this, Miss Mellor? You can have no knowledge of lovers and their ways. You're so young, so innocent, so pure . . .' He was standing very close to her. The stale-cabbage smell of his breath invaded her nostrils. There was a faint sheen on his brow, as if of perspiration, yet here under the trees it was cool and shady.

134

'Shall we go back now?' she suggested desperately. 'Please, Mr Boothroyd, my father will be home and wondering where I am . . .'

'He won't worry, I'm sure. After all, it was his suggestion that we should walk in the garden. But we were talking of lovers – '

No, she thought. *No.*

'And what an ideal place this is for a tryst,' he went on, his voice so smooth that it might have been oiled. And then, so unexpectedly that she did not at first understand what he was saying, 'Miss Mellor, I wonder if you have any idea of the regard I have for you?'

'R-regard?' she stammered. The wood was silent now, save the rustle of the leaves.

'Yes, regard. It's very high indeed, Miss Mellor. So high, that—' He paused. His cool suavity seemed to have left him. He flushed and wiped his brow. He looked at her almost in appeal, then reached out and closed the fingers of both hands around her arms. They dug into her soft flesh like the fingers of a skeleton, all bone, but they were as clammy as if they were fish.

Rowenna gave a little scream and backed away. But Mr Boothroyd caught her tightly against him. He pressed his mouth upon her face and she felt the moistness of his open lips against hers. Too shocked to move, she stood in his arms, trapped against his body. And then she saw Kester come crashing through the trees; and, at the same moment, heard a voice calling in panic from across the lawn.

'Miss Rowenna! Miss Rowenna! Oh, come quick – come quick. Oh, where is she, where can she be?'

Alfred Boothroyd let go of Rowenna as if he had been stung. His eyes wild, he dragged her up out of the dell. Across the lawn, Rowenna could see Molly, running with her apron up, her face white with terror; and as she glanced back into the dell she saw Kester standing baffled where a moment ago Mr Boothroyd had clasped her to his body.

Chapter Seven

It was past nine o'clock, the doctor had come and gone and a nurse been hastily summoned to watch over Warren Mellor at night, before Rowenna had a chance to think about Kester.

As yet, he would not have started to worry about her. He wasn't expecting her until after dark and the long northern twilight was still in the sky. He knew, too, that her father often sat up late drinking, and demanded her presence at his side until Ackroyd saw him to bed. But soon, as night fell, he would begin to look for her and to wonder why she did not come.

And she would not be coming. Rowenna knew as soon as she ran into the house, with Alfred Boothroyd beside her, that she would not be able to keep her tryst with Kester that night, nor perhaps any night, for her father was sprawled on the hall floor, his face ashen. He was breathing rapidly, his right arm flung across his chest while the fingers clawed the air. His lips were drawn back in a grimace of pain and his eyes rolled as he stared desperately at the servants who were gathered about him.

'Oh, my dear lord, whatever can we do?' the cook was crying as Rowenna hurried through the door. 'The master's dying! Oh, Miss Rowenna, there you are. Look at your poor father. Oh, it's the end for him, poor man, the end!'

'Don't be ridiculous, Mrs Partridge,' Rowenna snapped. 'Of course he's not dying. You'll frighten him with that sort of talk.' She knelt beside the groaning man. 'It's all right, Father, I'm here. Tell me what happened.'

'Pain,' he gasped. 'Pain – all down my arm. And my chest. My heart—' He groaned again and rolled his head. 'Partridge is right,' he whispered. 'Dying . . .'

Rowenna lifted his head into her lap and stroked the grey hair. 'Of course you're not dying, Father.' She glanced up. 'Has anyone gone to fetch the doctor?'

'I've just sent Bill, miss.' Ackroyd appeared with a small bottle in his hand. 'Here. Give him this – it's *sal volatile*. It'll help bring him round.'

Rowenna held the bottle under her father's nose. He coughed and choked, his body convulsing, and she snatched the bottle away again in alarm. 'It's making him worse.'

Alfred Boothroyd knelt beside her. 'Perhaps we should get him somewhere more comfortable. You' – he spoke abruptly to Ackroyd – 'you and the menservants, lift him up gently and carry him into the drawing room. There's a sofa there, if I recall correctly. And one of you women, fetch blankets and a pillow or two. He needs to be kept warm.'

He pulled Rowenna away and they watched as the men did they were bade. Warren groaned protestingly but seemed easier when laid on the sofa with a couple of blankets over him, and Rowenna knelt beside him, stroking the damp hair back from his cold, sweating forehead. The servants followed and stood around, staring anxiously, and Rowenna looked up at them.

'Please go back to your duties, all of you,' she said crisply. 'You can do no good here and you're simply using up the air my father needs. Ackroyd, open some windows, it's far too hot and stuffy in here. And bring some cold water for my father to sip. Molly, you stay with me please. The rest of you

138

have done very well, but there's no more to be done until the doctor arrives.'

'Except to bring some tea for your mistress,' Alfred Boothroyd interrupted smoothly as they turned away. 'Or we'll have another patient on our hands. You look as white as a sheet, my dear,' he added to Rowenna. 'I hope you have no objection to my giving orders to your servants.'

'Oh – no, none at all,' she said, confused. It seemed an odd moment to be paying attention to the social niceties. As for tea, she wondered that he could even think of it at such a time, and knew she would not be able to touch it.

When it came, however, she took a sip for politeness' sake and found that she was glad of it after all. The hot, sweet drink soothed her anxious nerves and warmed her shivering body, making her feel both relaxed and more alert. She set down the cup and smiled at Molly, who had put it down beside her.

'Thank you, Molly. That was just what I needed.' Her eyes went past the maid to Mr Boothroyd, who had left the room for a few minutes and now returned to stand behind her. 'Oh, Mr Boothroyd, you're still here! Really, there's no need for you to stay. I'm sure we'll be able to manage once the doctor comes—'

'Nonsense, my dear. How could I leave you in this trouble? In fact, I've taken the liberty of sending one of your men to ask my sister to come round. We'll stay with you for as long as you need and do whatever is necessary. You need not worry about anything other than looking after your father.'

'It's very kind to you,' Rowenna stammered, not at all sure that she wanted Mr Boothroyd and his sister staying in the house. But what else was she to do? She had no one else to turn to.

She looked down again at her father's face. He seemed

to be half asleep now, his face still grey, and his breathing was difficult. Spasms of pain crossed his face and she felt a surge of her old pity for him. No wonder he feared being alone.

How much longer would the doctor be? She tried to reckon in her head. Billy, the boot-boy, had gone down to the village at least twenty minutes ago, perhaps more. He would surely have taken the old pony, who might be past his galloping days but could still raise a creditable trot. Ten minutes, perhaps, to the doctor's house and then, if Dr Cooper were at home and came immediately, another ten to get back – perhaps longer for the doctor, who might have to wait for his own pony to be harnessed into its trap. But help must surely arrive soon. She hoped that it would not be too late.

Warren opened his eyes and looked up at her. His breathing was surely a little steadier now, though his face was still the colour of ashes. His lips moved and a faint whisper issued from them. Rowenna bent closer to try to understand.

'. . . leave me,' she heard on a faint thread of sound. 'Not while I'm sick. You won't . . . will you . . .'

'No, Father,' she assured him, while her heart sank within her. 'I'll not leave you. And you'll soon be better. It's only the heat that has been too much for you.'

He closed his eyes again and she knelt there, silent, holding his hand. And almost as if it stirred the air, a bird's wings fluttering as it flew away through the window and out of sight across the hills, she felt her chance of freedom escaping her.

Take your chances while you have them. They may not come again.

The words beat at Rowenna's brain as she lay that night

in the bed she had thought never to sleep in again. Beneath it, her winter clothes still lay bundled, for there had been no time to put them back in the chest. But she knew that tomorrow she would replace them.

Would she ever take them out again, to go up the fell to meet Kester?

Rowenna gazed out of the window. The sky was prickling with stars. She could hear an owl hooting as it hunted over the garden, and the sharp bark of a dog somewhere in the village. What was Kester thinking now, up in the shepherd's hut? What had he thought when he saw her standing in Alfred Boothroyd's arms, in the bluebell grove?'

The last few hours had been filled with activity. Mrs Oaksey, who had been at Meadowbank, had arrived on the heels of the doctor, who had marched in with his coat-tails swinging and flung his hat on the table before bending to examine Warren Mellor. Rowenna watched anxiously as he placed his stethoscope on her father's chest and listened to the fluttering heart. She tried to read his absorbed expression but could make nothing of it. At last he straightened up, laid down his instrument and said briefly, 'He'll do.'

Rowenna stared at him. 'What do you mean?'

'What I say.' Dr Cooper was a tersely spoken man. 'He's had a nasty attack, but he'll pull through. Mind you, he don't deserve it – eats too much meat, drinks too much wine. But he'll live to eat a few more hot dinners yet.' He pulled a notepad from his pocket. 'I'll give you a few instructions – what he's to be given for the next few days. Keep him in bed – they'll know how to handle him. And no worry or excitement or he'll have a relapse, and that could be the death of him.'

'But what happened? What's the matter with him?'

'Inflammation of the heart,' the doctor said brusquely,

141

already packing his stethoscope away and looking round for his hat. 'That's what caused the pain down his arm. Nothing much to be done about it, just complete rest, hot fomentations, a vapour bath and sleeping pills. Nothing to eat, only milk or chicken broth with a little thin cornflour, and some wine and stronger soup after a day or so. The most important thing is not to let him get anxious about anything. Worst thing possible for inflammation of the heart.'

'Yes, I see. Thank you very much, Doctor.' Rowenna moved over to the sofa and looked down at her father. The doctor had already given him a sleeping pill and he had fallen into a doze. He looked pale and somehow smaller, and she felt another sharp stab of pity.

No worry. No excitement. No anxiety.

If she left him now, she might be responsible for his death.

Now, sleepless despite her exhaustion, Rowenna tossed and turned in her bed. Along the corridor, Matilda Oaksey was sleeping, though Mr Boothroyd had agreed that it was less trouble for him to return home. He had left with many promises to return next morning and to do all that was required in the mill. 'Your father has taken me into his confidence in most of his business affairs,' he said to Rowenna, folding one of her hands in both of his and looking into her eyes. 'I feel sure he would be happy for me to give him all the help I can ... And of course I'll do nothing without consulting him, as soon as he's well enough.'

'Thank you,' she said. 'But there's really no need to worry. I know quite a lot about the business myself and I'll be happy to take over—'

'You?' he exclaimed. 'Oh no, my dear, that wouldn't be at all appropriate. Why, you're not even of age! And whoever heard of a woman managing a papermill? In any case, you'll be needed at home, by your father's side. No, I'll see to everything. You needn't give it another thought.'

Rowenna sighed but knew there was nothing she could do. Even though Alfred Boothroyd had no rights at all in her father's mill, if it came to a tussle between him and herself, everyone would take his side. She would not even be able to order him from the premises. Women – especially young women, barely twenty years old – did not manage businesses. And she dared not do anything that would make her father's illness worse.

'It's a bad do, miss,' Molly said sympathetically when at last Warren was in his bed and the nurses established nearby. Mrs Oaksey, who had taken it upon herself to order meals and announce to the servants that she would be staying for the foreseeable future to look after 'poor Miss Mellor' and her father, had retired to the room along the corridor. And Rowenna, exhausted, was sitting at her own bedroom window, gazing up towards the shadowy fells.

'I reckon you must feel like nothing on earth. Coming in all of a rush and panic like that, to find your poor father half dead on the floor and Mrs Partridge throwing a fit. And now old paleface from over the river's got his foot in the door, you won't have a minute to call your own, not to mention dancing attendance on his sister and trying to please your pa. It's a shame, just when you were beginning to find your feet again.'

Rowenna looked at her. She barely heard the maid's words. Her thoughts were filled with Kester and her need to get a message to him, to tell him why she wasn't coming, to assure him of her love.

'Molly,' she said, 'you know Kester, don't you? You know where his hut is.'

'Aye,' the maid said, startled. 'I do. Why?'

'I want you to go up there,' Rowenna said quickly. 'Tonight. I have to get a message to him.' She paused for a moment. She hadn't even told Molly that she meant to run away, for it had been decided so quickly. She had never even confided in her maid about the trysts in the bluebell dell or the love that had been growing between herself and the gypsy. 'I was going to go to him tonight,' she confessed. 'We were – well, we were going to run away together. It was my only chance,' she said as Molly's eyes widened. 'My only chance to be happy – don't you see? Kester and I love each other.'

'*Love* each other?' Molly gasped. 'But miss – that's crazy. You and him? Why, he's nobbut a gypsy!'

'And what's wrong with that? He's a man, and a fine one – a great deal finer than most of the men I know of my class.'

'Oh, I'll grant you that,' Molly said. 'But all the same – his life's not your life, Miss Rowenna. He lives wild and rough, wandering here and there. He sleeps out in the open as often as not, and lives on whatever he can grub up out of the fields. You could never stand up to that.'

'I'm not standing up to this sort of life either,' Rowenna retorted. 'Can't you see, Molly, since Haddie died my father's been keeping me a prisoner. After only a few months, I feel as if I'm going mad – what will I feel like after a year? Two years? Twenty? I'd rather take my chance with Kester. And we needn't always sleep out in the open. There are other shepherds' huts. Or perhaps we'll buy a gypsy wagon. They're snug enough.'

'A gypsy wagon? You?' Molly shook her head. 'Well, I never thought I'd live to see the day . . . And you say you were going *tonight*?'

'Yes. We planned it only this morning. And now – with my father so ill – I can't go after all.' She gazed at Molly and her eyes filled with tears. 'You heard what the doctor said. The slightest upset might kill him. I couldn't have that on my conscience, Molly.'

'No, you couldn't,' the maid said slowly. 'So I suppose you want me to go up there and tell him?'

'Please. I'd be so grateful.' Rowenna reached out suddenly and took both Molly's hands in her own. 'Tell him I love him. Tell him I'll come – as soon as I can. Tell him – oh, tell him not to go away, to wait for me.' Her voice broke. 'Don't let him go away without me,' she whispered.

Molly stared at her. Then she gently disengaged her hands and felt in her apron pocket for a handkerchief. She wiped Rowenna's eyes and face, and leant forward to cradle her head on her breast. They sat for a moment, quite still, while Rowenna sobbed.

A knock on the bedroom door startled them both.

'Are you all right, Rowenna dear?' came Matilda Oaksey's voice. 'I thought I heard you crying. If there's anything I can do—'

Rowenna shook her head violently at Molly, and the maid went quickly to the door and opened it. 'Miss Rowenna's all right, thank you. Just a bit upset, like. I'm seeing her to bed now.'

'Oh.' Rowenna could see Mrs Oaksey in the corridor, craning to see around Molly's buxom figure. 'Well, if you're sure. Rowenna? Would you like me to come and sit with you for a while, until you drop off to sleep? Perhaps a few verses from the Bible—'

'No, thank you,' Rowenna said, and tried to make her voice sound sleepy. 'I'm quite all right, Mrs Oaksey, really I am. In fact, I was almost asleep . . .' She forced a yawn. 'Don't let me keep you from your bed.'

'Well, if you're sure . . .' There was a slightly disappointed note in Mrs Oaksey's voice, but she moved away and presently could be heard closing the door of her own room. Molly shut Rowenna's door firmly and came back to look at her mistress.

'Nosy old besom! She just wanted to gloat over you. So you want me to go up and see Kester Matthews for you, do you?' She sighed. 'I've never thought much up till now about that old saying that it's an ill wind brings nobody any good, but I reckon it's true after all. It might be an ill wind as struck your pa down this afternoon, but it's not as ill as all that if it's kept you from running off to be a gypsy. You'd live to regret that, Miss Rowenna, and don't you think otherwise!'

Kester sat at the door of the shepherd's hut and stared down into the valley. A few cottage lights were appearing here and there but most people, at this time of year, went to bed with the fading light. He tried to pierce the gathering darkness with his eyes, to see if that really was a hurrying shape below him or just a gorse bush humped into the dusk. Behind him, his few possessions were already thrust into the large pack he slung over his shoulder when travelling.

He put his hand on the pile of books at his side. They were the encyclopedias of trees that Haddon had lent him and he had never returned. Several times, he had opened his mouth to tell Rowenna about them but always something else had intervened – the sound of someone approaching, a reluctance to spoil the moment by mention of her brother, or, more likely, a kiss. Now he was not sure what to do about them. They were too heavy to carry yet he was loth to let them go and he felt instinctively that Rowenna would want to keep them.

Well, time enough to discuss that when she arrived. He stirred anxiously. It was almost full dark now and he'd have thought her here while there was still light to see the way. He ought to have gone down to meet her, and would have done save that there were two or three paths up through the fields and he didn't know which she might take. He stretched his legs out and then drew them up to rest his chin on his knees, frowning as the darkness grew deeper.

Once again, he wondered if he was making a mistake in taking Rowenna away with him. He'd always been so determined to travel alone, to go where he pleased without encumbrance. And to take a *gauje* woman, one who had never slept under the stars or cooked a meal over a fire – never cooked a meal at all, he guessed – why, it was a little short of madness. True enough, she was different from most young women of her class, happier in the open air, could ride a horse or dig a trench, didn't seem to mind getting her hands dirty or care about her clothes . . . but all the same, she'd been brought up soft, you couldn't get away from that, and she'd find a wandering life hard. Hard enough in summer, when the sun hid for days on end and the rain fell from clouds that looked as if they would never roll away – but in winter it could be deadly.

Well, time enough for that too. He couldn't feel down-hearted for long. He'd been hankering after her ever since he'd first seen her, two years ago, walking in the garden with her brother. He'd watched her, grubbing in the kitchen garden in her holland overall and hoeing the flower borders. He'd seen her dark blue eyes, brightened by the sun, sparkling as she laughed at something Haddon had said to her, and he'd smiled to see her mowing the grass with the old pony and then climbing on its back to go back to the stables.

He thought of her hair, the shade of the honey he sometimes collected from beehives, blended with streaks of cream. In the past few weeks he had held that hair in his own hands, letting the tresses lie across his fingers, and had lifted it to his face and smelt the good clean perfume of it. He had stroked the proud, curving neck and laid his lips upon the cool, silky skin. And he had kissed her lips too, so sweet and soft, and the breasts that were full and round, yet small enough to cradle in his hands.

The heat of longing spread through his body and he shifted impatiently. Did Rowenna have any idea how he had yearned to possess her in that little dell of flowers, how he had dreamed at night of making love to her, naked, as she had been when he came upon her bathing in the river? Did she understand how his body tortured him with a desire that burned more hotly with every kiss, every touch?

He wanted nothing more than to stroke her skin, his fingers tenderly seeking each sensitive crevice, until she too burned with the flame that threatened to consume him and he could at last sink himself into her willing body and share with her the transport of joy that he knew must be theirs. But until now he had kept his passions severely under leash, for he knew that while she lived beneath Warren Mellor's roof she must not be touched. He had heard too much of what came to men and women like himself and Rowenna who transgressed the rules. Little use he would be to her, if Warren threw her out, if he was behind bars in jail, serving a sentence for enticement!

But tonight she was coming to him of her own will, and by dawn they would be away together. And before they went, he would lie with her in his arms and make her his woman.

A rustle in the nearby bushes brought him to his feet, peering into the darkness. The sky was peppered with stars now but they shed only a faint light, and she was almost at his side before he saw her. With a gasp of relief, he caught her and drew her into his arms, covering her face with kisses. And then he drew back again, shocked and unbelieving.

'Rowenna?'

'It's not Rowenna. It's me – Molly. I– ' The maid's voice faltered. 'Please, Kester, can we go inside for a minute? I – I've got summat to tell you.'

He stared at her face, no more than a pale smudge in the darkness. Something to tell him ... And with a hollow feeling of shock, he knew what it must be.

'What is it? Is she not coming?' He laid his hands on her shoulders and shook her. 'Tell me, Molly, for God's sake! *Is Rowenna not coming*?'

Molly began to cry. He drew her inside the hut and sat her down on the bed of grass and heather he had prepared for Rowenna. As she sat there sobbing, he lit the lamp and then looked into her swollen face.

'What's happened? Why isn't she coming?' He remembered the scene he had witnessed earlier. 'What was all that commotion this afternoon, and what was that skinflint Boothroyd doing at Ashbank?'

Molly shook her head. 'Don't shout at me, Kester. I'm telling you. But – oh, I can't, I *can't* ...'

'You can. You will. Molly, for God's sake' – he laid his hands on her shoulders and shook her – 'can't you see what you're doing to me? What's *happened*? Is she ill?'

'No – oh no, Mis Rowenna's well enough. But she sent me up here to say she couldn't come away with you after all.' She hesitated, then said in a low, rapid voice, 'She said you were to go without her – not to wait ...'

'Not coming? Not to wait?' Kester stared at her in disbelief. 'Molly, what are you telling me? It was all planned – we were to go tonight—'

'I know. But at the last minute ...' Molly shook her head and covered her eyes with her hands. 'I reckon she just couldn't face it,' she whispered.

Kester gripped her shoulders, his fingers biting into the plump flesh. 'I'll go down there. I'll talk to her myself. I *know* she meant to come—' He twisted away, as if to set off down the hill at once.

'No!' Molly caught at his arm. 'No, you mustn't do that!

149

She's upset enough – it's cost her a lot to send me up here. She knows how much it meant to you – but it wouldn't do, Kester, not for a lady like her to come tramping with a gypsy. She'd never stand up to the life, never. And besides—'

She broke off, and Kester turned back to look at her with narrowed eyes.

'Besides what? Is there summat you're not telling me, Moll? Some other reason why she won't come?' He watched her bite her lip and grow red, and grasped her shoulders again, shaking her as if to loosen the truth from her unwilling tongue. 'Tell me! *Tell me!*'

But there was no need for Molly to tell him, for didn't he already know? Like a lightning flash, he remembered the scene he had witnessed in the garden only a few hours earlier. Rowenna in the bluebell grove – *their* grove! – being kissed by that skunk Boothroyd. And making no attempt to escape! He shook his head, seeing her again, standing in the man's arms, her own arms at her sides. He'd thought she had been caught unawares, had simply stood unresisting – but why hadn't she struggled? Why hadn't she told the man to let her go?

He saw Molly open her mouth and knew she was about to tell him the truth. And knew too that he could not bear to hear it.

'It's all right,' he said roughly, turning away, 'you don't have to say no more. She ain't coming, and that's all there is to it.'

He thought of the life they had planned, the wandering they could have done together beneath the wide blue sky, and his throat ached. Why hadn't he done this sooner? Why had he ever had any doubts? He had wanted Rowenna to come away with him as much as she wanted to come. If I'd only asked her before, he thought. Even yesterday . . . I had my chance, and I missed it, and now it will never come again.

He would never lie with Rowenna in his arms. Never stroke that silken body, never trace its curves with his fingers, never kiss the willing lips again. Never merge his body with hers, never delight in the soaring, joyful pulsing of mutual passion, never know the warmth of the loving afterwards, entwined together, the tender sweet kisses, the soft caress.

Never, never, never . . .

He sank his head in his hands, feeling the stab of bleak, bitter disappointment in his heart. A cold black cloud of despair filled his mind. The only warmth in the world came from Molly's hand on his knee and the tears that fell from her eyes on to his arm.

They sat together in silence for a long while. Outside, Kester heard the occasional hoot of an owl as it hunted, and once or twice the bleat of a sheep. Through the open doorway he could see the stars still pricking the black sky. Dawn was a long way off, yet he and Molly seemed to have been sitting here for years rather than just an hour or so. He rubbed his hand over his face, as if expecting to find a growth of beard there, and turned towards her.

'Thanks for coming, Moll,' he said, and his voice felt rusty as if unused. 'It was good of you.'

He laid his hand over Molly's. He knew quite well that she was in love with him, but he did not think that she would have followed him if he had asked her to go. She was too practical, too sensible. She knew the life he led and that it was not for her. She might love him, but she would marry the gardener's son and have a bushel of *chavvies* and be happy enough.

But Rowenna . . . Rowenna was wild in her soul, and needed the open air and the wide skies. She needed freedom and space.

She'll never have them now, he thought. And I shall never have her. I'll never again see her walking with the wind in her hair and the laughter in her eyes and the sting of the cold air in her cheeks. I'll never lie with her in my arms and look up at the stars . . .

And his body, that had yearned so much and waited so long, stirred in protest, as if demanding the satisfaction it had been promised. He felt the longing spread like fire through his body, deep into his loins. He felt it tingle through every muscle, throbbing with a fierce, intolerable heat. It caught him like an iron band, crushing him in its grip, and he knew that he could wait no longer, that it must be released or he would go mad.

He turned to the girl beside him. She was warm and tender. He looked down into her face, lit only by the stars, and saw her eyes gaze back into his. He felt her lips, soft against his mouth, felt her body soft and warm and pliant against his and with a groan he caught her against him and pressed her back on the grass and heather bed he had meant for Rowenna.

He had touched and kissed her before and found comfort in her warmth. Now she tangled her fingers in his thick curly hair and drew him down against her. Her arms held him close, and she pressed herself against him. But for Kester she was at that moment neither friend nor lover. She was nothing but woman. Not herself, not Rowenna, simply woman, offering the warmth and release his body craved and hungered for. Even in that moment, as he ran his hand down the length of her, from neck to knee, he knew that she could not give him all he desired. But as he rose above her willing body and thrust himself deep inside, he knew that this was the only loving left to him. For he would never, without Rowenna, know the total joy of loving a woman who would go with him to life's end.

Dawn was painting its first few streaks of rosy gold on the

summit of the Howgills when Kester left Molly at the stile where once he had bidden Rowenna goodbye. He watched her go across the field to the gate, turn and lift her hand once in farewell, and then disappear along the lane. When he was sure she was out of sight, he followed her and walked slowly into the garden of Ashbank.

He did not go to the door of the house. He walked instead to the bluebell grove, and sat down for a while, listening to the river and looking at the trees. The large ones, the beech and the ash and the old birch, had been here for years, self-seeded or planted by an earlier generation. The smaller ones – the Japanese cherry, the gingko, the copper-leaved acers and the creamy magnolia – had been planted by Haddon to make a wood of curious beauty and interest. It was not mature – it would not be mature even in Rowenna's lifetime, for the redwoods and giant sequoias were still in the seed-bed, not even yet germinated – but it was already lovely, and Kester had felt proud to work in it.

Who would work in it now? Nobody else, save Rowenna, had shared Haddon's interest, nor even known of it. Only Kester had fully understood and gone on working there after Haddon's death, and now he too would never come back again.

He put out a hand and touched the bark of the nearest tree. They were his friends, these trees. He had worked with them and amongst them, keeping them free of entangling brush and bramble, watching them through the seasons. In spring they opened their buds first cautiously, then gladly, to green leaves; in autumn they changed colour to a dress of gold and bronze. He had watched them grow, had nurtured and tended them, and now he was saying goodbye.

But the dell meant more than a few trees. It was here that he had seen Rowenna like a water-nymph in the stream, the bright water glittering on her silky skin. It was here that he had lain with her head on his arm and talked of freedom, of wild and flying clouds, of rain and sun and snow. It was here that he had kissed her and told her he loved her.

It was here that she had begged him to make love to her and he had refused. *Take your chances while you have them; they won't come again* . . .

Kester lay back in the grass and watched the pearly, rose-flushed sky above deepen to the blue of morning. And he saw the colour blur through the haze of his tears, and felt them run hot down the sides of his face, and his body shook with sobs.

The house was astir when he finally stood up and walked away from the dell, leaving behind the parcel of books he had brought with him. For a few moments he stood at the edge of the wood, looking up at the window that he knew to be Rowenna's. And then, without once looking back, he walked out of the garden and away up the fell.

When Molly brought Rowenna's tray at eight o'clock, she found her mistress already out of bed and sitting at the window in her wrapper. She was pale and her eyes were dark and haunted.

'I've been in to see my father,' she said. 'He's had a good night, the nurse says. He slept a good deal. And he's had some milk and cornflour, and some of the medicine the doctor prescribed.'

'He'll be right as rain in a few days, you'll see,' the maid said, setting the tray down on the little table that stood beside the bed. 'And how did you sleep, miss?' She went over to the dressing table and began to fiddle with Rowenna's hairbrushes.

'Oh, not very well. There were too many things on my mind. And the light woke me early.' She hesitated, then said, 'I was sitting here earlier and I could have sworn I saw

154

someone down in the garden. Near the trees – just standing, looking up at the house.'

'Did you, miss? I don't know who that could have been. Perhaps it was just a shadow.'

'Shadows don't appear by themselves,' Rowenna said. She turned away from the window. 'Well, perhaps it was my imagination. Molly, did you go and see Kester last night?'

'Aye, I did, miss.' Still Molly did not turn from the dressing table. She picked up the brushes and rearranged them, then altered their positions. 'And I give him your message.'

'And what did he say?' Rowenna asked tensely.

'Say? Why, miss, what was there for him to say? He were upset, of course, but you'd expect that, wouldn't you.'

'Yes, I suppose you would. But did he say nothing else? Nothing about what he would do?'

'Why, what d'you expect him to do, miss? Whatever he was planning, I suppose. Going on to the next place, wherever that might be.'

Rowenna flinched. Molly's voice had had a sharp edge to it, as if she were angry. Rowenna watched her for a moment, still playing with the brushes.

'Molly, what's the matter? Has something upset you?'

'Me? Why should *I* be upset? It ain't *my* father who's sick or *my* young man who's gone off. Everything's the same for me as it always is – why should it be any different? I'm nobody, after all.'

Rowenna stared at her. She had never known Molly give vent to such an outburst, never heard such bitterness in the maid's tone. For a moment, she forgot her own distress.

'Molly, what is it? You *are* upset – dreadfully upset. What's happened? Is it Kester? Was he angry with you?'

Molly shook her head. She stared down at the brushes in her hands as if she were seeing something else. Then she

155

lifted her head and met Rowenna's eyes in the mirror. Her lips trembled, her face distorted, and she burst into tears.

'*Molly!*'

Rowenna came to her feet and crossed the room swiftly. She took the weeping girl in her arms and held her close. She patted the shaking shoulders and stroked the smooth hair. And as she did so, her fingers found a strand of heather caught up in the neat bun Molly wore at the back of her head.

'Molly . . .'

The maid lifted her head and looked at what Rowenna held in her fingers. She blushed a deep scarlet and the tears overflowed again. She laid her head on Rowenna's shoulder.

'Oh, miss – I'm that sorry. I never meant it to happen, nor did he, but he was so unhappy and I – I've always wanted him. It didn't seem wrong then, to give him what I could – it weren't what he wanted, not by a long chalk, but I reckon it helped a bit. And I'm sorry, but I'd do it again, even though he'll never care for me, not the way he cares about you. Even while – while he was doing it, it weren't me, he was thinking about, not really. It's been you all along, I've always known that . . . And now it don't matter anyway. He's gone and neither of us'll ever see him again.'

Rowenna stared at her. The last few words passed over her head. Her mind caught at the meaning behind Molly's outburst, trying to make sense of it.

'What are you talking about, Molly? What happened? What did you and Kester do?' The first hint of the truth scraped the edges of her mind with the roughness of a shard of broken glass. 'Molly, *what did you do*?'

The maid looked at her with reddened eyes. 'Why, what do you think, miss? He's a man and I – I've always hankered for him. He were disappointed, he'd been thinking to lie

156

with you last night and you didn't come. And I was there . . .' She burst into fresh tears. 'I wouldn't hev stopped him even if I could!' she cried. 'I'd bin wanting him for myself – and could hev had him, too, and more fitting than for a lady like you. Why should I say no? Why should I, when he needed a woman so bad and I was there and ready?'

Rowenna stared at her. The pain of betrayal was in her heart, yet she could not but accept that Kester's anguish had been as great as her own. Would she have behaved so? She could not tell. And before she could think of it, the rest of Molly's words burst in her mind like an explosion.

'*Never see him again*? Molly, what do you mean?'

Molly raised her head again. She looked into Rowenna's eyes, and Rowenna read there a message of misery and hopelessness that spoke directly to the anguish in her own heart. Until this moment, she had kept it firmly suppressed, but now it rose up and threatened to overwhelm her.

'Why, he's gone now,' the maid said. 'He's gone and he'll never come back. You didn't think he'd wait, did you?'

Rowenna let her go. She walked to the window and stood looking down at the garden, bright now with morning sunshine. The only shadows at the edge of the lawn now were those of trees, and she knew that Kester would not again stand looking up at the window, nor lie with her in the little valley of bluebells.

She turned away and sank down on her bed. And all the tears she had kept pent up inside her broke loose like a dam that has been breached, and flooded her heart.

Chapter Eight

Warren Mellor recovered quickly from his attack, but demanded Rowenna's presence by his side at every hour. He would not go out into the garden, however warm and fine the weather, but stayed indoors in his study or in the drawing room, where Rowenna found it unbearably stuffy. Her only escape was in the early morning, for he continued to take breakfast in bed and did not appear downstairs until ten.

Often she would get up before Molly came to her room and go down to the little dell by the river. Kester had come there on that last night, she knew, for she had found the parcel of books and recognised them as her brother's. And she knew that she had seen him that morning, looking up at the house. Suppose she had slipped out then and gone to him . . . what would have happened?

But the moment had passed and Kester had slipped away, as a shadow melts beneath a cloud, and vanished over the fells.

Another chance left untaken.

The bluebells were all gone now and the trees beginning to show the wear and tear of summer, their leaves a darker, dustier green than the fresh canopy which had hung over her and Kester. It was a cool retreat on a hot day and Rowenna would think of it longingly in the afternoons when she was forced to sit reading to her father, or sewing the endless patchwork quilt.

In the early mornings, however, it was hers, and she sat for hours, gazing down at the river and thinking of Kester. Where was he now? What was he doing? Did he think of her, did he too remember how they had lain together in this little hollow? And why – why – *why* hadn't he waited?

But she knew that it had been impossible for him to stay. His work in the garden finished, for it was the trees that interested him and he refused to do the common tasks of vegetable growing or weeding the flowerbeds. That would have been too like ordinary labour, and besides he would have been under the orders of Richmond, the head gardener. The trees were his own.

And it went deeper than that, too. Once he and Rowenna had decided to go away together, and she had failed him, their relationship had undergone too profound a change for them to return to the way they had been before. The time of their tender trysts in the bluebell dell was past. They had to move on – but in what direction? What was there for them now?

And there was Molly, as well. Whatever had happened between her and Kester at the hut on that last night, Rowenna knew that it had contributed to Kester's decision to go away. And she knew that it was better for Molly that he should, for things had changed between them too, and for Kester to stay would have entangled them all in a web of pain.

At that thought, Rowenna's eyes filled with tears. Could anything have made her own pain any greater? Sitting in the hollow which seemed so filled with Kester's presence, she was gripped by an anguish which seemed to clench her body, as if in an iron fist. She rocked back and forth on the grass, curling herself up in her agony, and the tears ran hot down her cheeks as she sobbed his name. So intense was her need that several times she looked up as if convinced that her very longing would bring him to her. Surely he must sense her pain; surely he would come.

But Kester never came. And after a while Rowenna began to avoid the little dell and the wood. She walked instead in the rose-garden or amongst the vegetables. And sometimes she took a hoe or trowel and did a little work, finding comfort in the rich brown earth and the growing plants.

Always, however, she must be back in the house, clean and tidy in a fresh gown, to appear at breakfast. For although her father did not appear until ten o'clock, Mrs Oaksey would be expecting Rowenna at the table and, if she were not there, was capable of coming to look for her.

Mrs Oaksey had stayed on after Warren's illness, and showed no sign of returning to her own house. Someone must take care of the house, she said, and since there were no female relatives and she and her brother were the Mellors' closest friends, it behoved her to step into the breach. More than that, it was her pleasure.

'But I can manage perfectly well,' Rowenna objected. 'Mrs Patridge and Ackroyd run the house perfectly between them. They've done it for years.'

Mrs Oaksey chose to ignore that. 'It isn't suitable for a young girl to have such responsibilities. And you know your father mustn't be worried. Helping out at a time of need is the least my brother and I can do. What are friends for?'

Rowenna had no answer, though until then she hadn't counted Mr Boothroyd and his sister as friends. Surely the only thing he and her father had had in common was paper-making. And in that, until recently, they had been rivals.

But now Alfred Boothroyd was in and out of the mill as if he owned it. He spent as much time there as in his own

161

and he had caused a small wooden footbridge to be thrown across the river between the two properties, to make his journey easier. That meant he could be in the house within two minutes rather than the twenty or so it had taken to drive round through the village. Rowenna could no longer feel at peace, for he was liable to drop in at any hour to speak to either her father or his sister, and the only time she could be sure of his absence was in the middle of the night.

Even then she could not be free of him, for it was at night, when all else was still, that the memory of his kiss in the garden, on the afternoon when Warren had been taken ill, returned to haunt her. Her mind cringing, she would relive the moment, the feel of his lips, thin and wet against her own, the rasp of his chin against her face. What had possessed him to behave in such a way? What had he meant by it?

For a moment, she had been afraid that he was about to make some kind of declaration, even a proposal. Perhaps it wasn't his sister but he who intended to marry. But she had not, then, been concerned about such a possibility, for hadn't she been planning to run away with Kester that very night?

But she had not gone to Kester. And Kester himself had been in the garden, and had seen Alfred Boothroyd take her in his arms. What had he thought, she wondered, turning restlessly in her bed. And what had he thought later, when Molly had taken him the message that she could not come away with him?

Had that been why he did not wait? Had he thought himself betrayed, even though he'd known her true reason for staying with her sick father? Had it been that disappointment that had made him turn to Molly and take her to his bed before leaving the fells for ever?

The weeks dragged on. August turned into September

and the leaves began to turn golden. The long twilights shortened and disappeared as the sun took shorter journeys round the sky. The air had a fresh, sharp edge to it and Rowenna left the garden one morning and walked up to the fell. But Kester's hut was empty and although she sat there for a long time, it seemed that even the warmth of his presence was gone. And she knew that he would never come back to it.

Molly too was restless during that summer. With her hour off in the afternoons and the evenings more or less her own, she had more freedom than Rowenna but she did not seem to know what to do with it. She walked down to the village to visit her family, but could not sit still in the little cottage and soon left again to roam along the riverside and up through the meadows. She too visited the shepherd's hut, but it was as empty for her as it was for Rowenna, and she left it to its silence.

The weeks for her passed all too swiftly, for she had more things to worry about than Kester's disappearance, more to concern her than Rowenna's trouble. From the night that Kester and she had lain together on the heathery bed, she had known what must happen, and as time went on she became more and more convinced of it. By the end of September she knew that something must be done, and done soon.

She said nothing to Rowenna. What had happened that last night was something they did not discuss, and she was not even sure that Rowenna realised the truth of it – or wanted to. To tell her now would make it impossible for her to ignore, and would surely be the end of their friendship. And Rowenna could hardly keep Molly as her maid, once she knew.

Well, she'd have to know some time. But there was no

sense in pushing it down her throat.

Molly's mind was full as she wandered about the fields during those early weeks. The memory of that last night was strong, and she longed desperately for it to be repeated. She wanted to feel Kester's strong arms hard around her, she wanted to feel his lips on hers and his hands stroking her body. She wanted to sense again the passion and desire that had so suddenly stormed through him as they lay together on the heather bed, carrying them both to a climax that had almost torn them apart. No matter that the desire had not been for her, no matter that the passion had been born of his frustrated yearning for Rowenna. She had felt it, had known its glory, and nothing after that could ever be as great.

But against that memory was the increasing suspicion, growing into fear and finally to a certainty that thrust everything else from her mind and sent her walking about the lanes and the fields and up the fells, where she stood for a long time looking down into the depths of Potter's Tarn and wondering . . .

But life was too strong in Molly to be ended yet. And when she finally turned from the deep black pool and started to walk back down the green lane to Ashbank, she knew what she must do.

'Well, Mellor,' Alfred Boothroyd said, settling himself in Warren's study. 'I think it's time we had a talk, don't you?'

He had chosen the best armchair, Warren noticed, and fitted into it as if it had been made for him. He stretched out his long legs and took a cigar from his pocket. Warren watched as he clipped the end and lit it, waiting until there was a good head of ash on the end before putting it between his thin lips.

'I'd not say no to a cigar myself,' Warren said suddenly.

Since his illness, the doctor had advised him not to smoke, but there was something about the way Alfred Boothroyd sat there, almost as if he were in his own home, that made him want to assert himself.

'Oh, d'you think that's wise, my dear fellow? After all, Dr Cooper—'

'Cooper's an old woman. I'm perfectly fit now. In fact, I've been thinking it's time I got back into harness. Sitting around like an invalid doesn't suit me, and I've a mill to run.'

Boothroyd waved a hand airily. 'Oh, no need to bother your head with that, my dear chap. I've got everything under control. You take things easy for a while longer. No point in taking risks with your health.'

'I'm not taking risks,' Warren snapped. 'Sitting around at home with nothing to do is far worse for me than taking a walk into the mill of a morning and keeping my eye on things there. I'm bored, Boothroyd, bored and frustrated. It's time I got back to work.' He made an impatient movement of one hand. 'And I want a cigar. Pass me that box on the desk, if you don't mind.'

Alfred Boothroyd shrugged and did as he was asked. Warren took out a cigar, sniffed it and nodded with satisfaction. 'Ah, that's good. This is what I need – a smoke and a glass of brandy, after a good meal. I've been kept on pap for too long.'

'You ate heartily enough tonight.'

'Aye, because I told Partridge to give me something solid for once. They've been starving me, Boothroyd, you know that? I've lost flesh these past few weeks, too much flesh. Well, I'm not having it any longer. I'm not ill now and I want to get back to normal. I've had enough fussing and I've had enough of sitting in the parlour of an afternoon watching that daughter of mine struggle with her needle.

165

Dammit, I've been within an inch of tearing the thing out of her fingers and doing it myself And she *reads* to me, just as if I'd lost the power to read for myself. I tell you, it's driving me insane.'

'I'm sure Miss Mellor is doing her best,' Boothroyd said smoothly. 'She's simply carrying out the doctor's orders. And my sister agrees – '

'Your sister means well,' Warren said tersely, 'but she doesn't seem to have any idea how a man wants to conduct his own household. She ordered rice pudding three times last week. Three times! Look, Boothroyd, you've both been a tower of strength since my collapse, but I think it's time we all went back to our normal way of life. You in your mill, me in mine and Mrs Oaksey back at Staveley. I'm grateful to you both, but the plain truth is that I don't need help any longer.'

'I think my sister would be deeply upset to hear you say such a thing.'

'But why? Doesn't she *want* to go back to Staveley? It's her home, for God's sake – there must be a hundred things she wants to attend to there. What does she want to hang around here for? Is she expecting me to *marry* her, or something?'

There was a brief silence. Alfred Boothroyd looked at him hard and Warren caught his gaze and flushed deeply.

'My God,' he said slowly, 'is that really what's in her mind?'

'I'm astonished at you,' Boothroyd said. 'Surely it was in your mind as well. You invited us here often enough. And since she's been living in the house – taking care of you – well, it would look extremely odd if she were simply to return to Staveley now and take up the threads of her old life. I think she would find it quite humiliating. People do notice these things, you know. They talk.'

'Well, let 'em,' Warren said robustly. 'I've never bothered myself with idle gossip.'

'Of course not. Why should you? But a woman – especially a sensitive woman like my sister, who has already been through enough troubles of her own and must have thought she was in a safe haven at last – well, such talk could be very hurtful to her. She has to live with her neighbours, you see, and people can be very cruel.'

'But I thought she was just staying here out of the goodness of her heart—'

'She was. Of course she was.'

'—with no expectations,' Warren finished desperately. 'I never said or did a thing to lead her to think that . . . Boothroyd, can't you explain to her? Tell her I'm truly grateful but there's no question of – of marriage. I couldn't contemplate it, not at my age. I've lived alone too long.'

'Not alone,' Boothroyd pointed out. 'You've had your daughter's company.'

'Aye, such as it is. And that's not changed. She'll still be here when I need her. She's not bad, after all, as daughters go. Good enough company of an evening – it's just the afternoons that I can't tolerate, because that's the time I'm accustomed to working. I don't *need* a wife, Boothroyd, and that's the truth of it.'

'But what of when Miss Mellor isn't here any longer?'

Warren stared. 'Isn't here? What the devil d'you mean, man? She's not proposing to run away, is she?' He gave a bark of laughter. 'I'd like to see her try!'

'But she'll be getting married herself. Have you forgotten our talks a few months ago, Mellor? When we discussed merging our two businesses? And my marriage to your daughter?' Alfred Boothroyd smiled his sharp-toothed smile. 'You'll be alone then, my dear fellow, and glad of a comfortable wife to keep your house in order and sit with

167

you of an evening.' His smile widened. 'I'm sure my sister will be more than willing to accommodate your wishes over rice pudding!'

The silence this time was longer. Warren took his cigar from his mouth, looked at it and then put it back. He had not forgotten Boothroyd's proposals over Rowenna and the mill, but he had put them to the back of his mind. His illness had shaken him, especially coming so soon after Haddon's death, and he was less willing than ever to let go of the things he considered his. And Mrs Oaksey irritated his nerves. Plump, ever-smiling, anxious to please, she was like a fawning lapdog and he had the same urge to kick her as he had felt for a cringing little hound his wife Dorothy had once had. He had always preferred a little more spirit, in both man and beast. Rowenna, argumentative minx though she might be, had at least some fire about her. She needed taming but, by God, she was *worth* taming!

'Well, I've been thinking about all that,' he said slowly. 'I'm not so sure about Rowenna. I'm none so keen on marrying her off just yet. She's still a child.'

'She's turned twenty. Plenty of young women are married and bearing their first child at that age. And their fathers only too glad it should be so.'

'Aye, but those fathers have probably got a quiverful of daughters on their hands. I've only the one – and she's all that is left to me. I'm not too willing to give her up, if the truth be told.'

'That's a pity. A great pity.' Boothroyd waited a moment, as if debating something, then said, 'I wonder if you ought to consult your daughter over this. She may have her own expectations – '

'Then she's no right to,' Warren said sharply. 'Unless *you've* given her cause?'

Boothroyd coughed. 'Well – as to that – '

168

'You mean you've *spoken* to her?' Warren demanded, outraged. 'Dammit, man – '

'No, no – not exactly spoken to her.' Boothroyd held up his hand. 'It was on the day of your illness. You may recall suggesting that your daughter show me the garden. She seemed pleased to have the opportunity and we spent a long time out there, walking about and chatting of this and that. We were getting along famously and I had asked her to show me the little woodland, and – well, I'm afraid that having her company to myself for the past hour or two, and in such romantic surroundings – well, I rather forgot myself.' He looked apologetically at Warren Mellor. 'It didn't go *very* far, I assure you – but I think Miss Mellor can have been left with no doubt as to my feelings, no doubt at all. And I'm sure she's been waiting only for you to make a full recovery – which you now say you have – for me to make a full declaration.'

Warren stared at him. His face flushed and he put a hand over his heart, as if to hold it still. He took a deep breath.

'Are you telling me you've taken advantage of my daughter?'

'No, no, not at all. I do assure you, my dear fellow, there was no impropriety, none at all. A kiss or two . . . little more than that, really. And she raised no objection. I would never have presumed if I had thought she would dislike it.' He gave Warren a man-to-man smile. 'You must know how it is, Mellor. A man has his needs. And when he's been thrown for the whole of a summer's afternoon into the company of the young woman he loves – and by her own father, moreover – why, he can't be blamed if those needs overcome him. Of course, if you'd prefer me not to press my suit any further, I'll abide by your wishes. But I am rather afraid that poor Miss Mellor may experience just the same kind of humiliation I expect for my sister.'

Warren sighed. His head was swimming and he needed to be alone to grapple with the ideas Boothroyd was putting into his head. Kisses in the woods! Expectations! Humiliation! What sort of a tangled web had he got himself into, for God's sake?

'And then there's the mill, of course,' Boothroyd remarked, as casually as if he were mentioning that the teapot was empty.

'The mill? What about the mill?'

Alfred Boothroyd looked at him keenly.

'My dear fellow, I wonder if you're as recovered as you think? Your memory does seem to be somewhat affected. We talked about it a few minutes ago. Our plan to merge the two businesses – when Rowenna and I are married, of course. It makes so much more sense. We already share the water, and you must recall how we planned to build our own pulpmill and process the wood ourselves. One man alone couldn't do it, but the two of us . . . why, we could produce newsprint to satisfy all the leading newspapers in this part of the world. As well as other papers if we'd a mind to. And what an inheritance to pass on to your grandchildren – remember, you're to name our first son. Boothroyd and Mellor – '

'Mellor and Boothroyd,' Warren interrupted, and Alfred Boothroyd smiled.

'If you wish, of course it shall be Mellor and Boothroyd. Yes. It has a fine ring to it.' He tapped the silver ash from his cigar. 'So I may proceed with my courtship of your daughter? And you'll speak to my sister? It seems to me that now you're well again, these matters might as well be dealt with as soon as possible.'

'Wait a minute!' Warren was feeling alarmed again. 'I've never said . . . I'd like to think it over a bit longer. I don't know that I want to go into partnership. I've always got

170

along well enough on my own. I'm an independent sort of chap – '

'I know and I respect you for it. But I don't think you quite appreciate the position you're in.' Boothroyd shook his head regretfully. 'I've been able to look quite deeply into your affairs during these past weeks, Mellor, while I've been helping you out. And I'm afraid you're really in no condition to carry on alone. In fact, if you do I'm very much afraid you'll be bankrupt before the year ends.' He paused. 'I did warn you about this before, if you recall.'

Warren sat dumb. Yes, Boothroyd had told him he would be in Queer Street – or Carey Street, as he put it in his old-fashioned way – if nothing was done to save the business. He'd known even then that Warren was on the verge of losing the contract to supply Titus Wilson with paper. And Warren had said he must have time to think it over.

He had thought about it. He'd even begun to look at figures with Boothroyd and consider his proposals. He'd accepted invitations to dinner with the man and had him back to Ashbank, along with his sister. But he'd never quite agreed.

There were good enough reasons for the merger, but there were reasons against it too. Warren was as jealous of his independence as of all his other possessions. He hated the idea of giving it up even though, as Boothroyd pointed out, if he married Rowenna the firm would still be 'in the family'. 'In fact, it will be more as if *you* take over *my* business, along with my services as manager and son-in-law,' Alfred had said, showing those sharp white teeth. And there would be the boy to take it on when he and Alfred were both too old. Young Haddon. Warren had even doodled his name on a scrap of paper once or twice. Haddon Mellor Boothroyd. It had, as Boothroyd would say, a fine ring to it.

'Well,' he said at last, 'it looks as if you've got me in a box. I want to go over the figures again with you, but if it's as you say I don't seem to have any choice. Mellor and Boothroyd it'll have to be.'

'And your daughter Mrs Boothroyd.'

'Aye,' Warren said, 'that seems to be the way of it. But as to your sister – '

'Oh come,' Boothroyd said smoothly, 'you'll not distress her at this stage, surely? You'll not deal her the blow of watching me and your daughter find happiness while she's turned out of the house and sent back to Staveley? After all she's done for you! All she wants is to take care of you when Rowenna's left and ease your loneliness a little. And I'm sure she'll be more than happy to sell her house and put the money into the business, just as a small wedding present. She has some shares of her own too, you know, and we'll need all the help we can obtain to start up the new part-nership.'

Warren said nothing. The man had twisted him in knots. But he knew well enough that as far as the business went, Boothroyd was right. Another few months and he'd be facing bankruptcy charges. And was this solution so bad, after all? He'd stay in his own home, still taking a major part in running his own business. His daughter would be just across that little bridge Boothroyd had had built. Her son would bear the name he chose, and grow up in his grand-father's shadow. And all he had to do to pay for this, appar-ently, was to put a ring on the finger of a woman who was already living in his house and treating it like her own.

And that's where it'll end, he told himself. We're both too old to make anything else of marriage, even if we wanted to. But if I can't tame a soft, smiling little creature like Matilda Oaksey, my name's not Warren Mellor.

It wouldn't be much of a challenge – more like taming a

cushion. But all he wanted now was a quiet life, and to hold on to whatever was rightfully his. And in his mind, Matilda Oaksey was already becoming just another possession.

Molly slipped out of the kitchen door and walked swiftly down the path to the walled vegetable garden. It was late afternoon and the hour when the gardeners would be breaking off for the day and going home to their supper. They were there now, stacking their tools in the shed, kicking the mud off their boots. They nodded at Molly as they came out and Mr Richmond stopped for a word.

'Young John's coming along. He went over to the woods for some kindling for his mother's fire. I daresay it is him you're waiting for, and not a cabbage or two for the kitchen?'

Molly blushed and nodded. She had taken to coming down here most afternoons for a few minutes with John Richmond. They met in the evenings too, when they could, and walked along the riverbank or across a field or two. The nights were getting dark early now, and there was nobody to see them if they stopped under a hedge for a kiss and cuddle.

There'd been more than a cuddle too, just lately. Johnny Richmond had had a fancy for Molly for the past year or more, and until Kester had come along she had been encouraging him. A girl could do a lot worse than take up with the head gardener's son. A nice little cottage and plenty of vegetables for the table . . . But the arrival of the dark-eyed gypsy had pushed Johnny into the shade, even though she'd soon realised it was Miss Rowenna that Kester Matthews had been interested in.

Johnny had kept faith, however, and his devotion was now being rewarded, for once again Molly welcomed his kisses and nestled like a bird into his arms. And found

173

herself happy enough to do so, for John Richmond's arms were as strong as any gypsy's, and could hold her as tightly, and in his kisses she found all the passion and desire that she had known in Kester that last night. And knew that this time they were for her.

'My stars, Molly, you're a wholesome piece,' he murmured as they lay in the grass, looking up at the harvest moon. His hand covered her breast and she could feel her heart beating against his palm. 'The prettiest girl in Burneside, aye, or Kendal too at that. And the best little armful.'

'And how would you know that?' she teased him. 'How many armfuls have you held, Johnny Richmond?'

'One or two,' he answered with a grin that she could see shining in the silver light. 'But none as sweet as you, Molly.'

Molly was silent. She felt a little ashamed of what she was doing, for wasn't she deliberately leading Johnny on? But he wanted her bad enough and had done for years, so where was the harm? And no doubt he'd take her just the same even if she told him the truth. And for a few moments she wondered whether that was what she ought to do.

No. It would only hurt him. And if things turned out as she believed they would, it would be there between them always, and especially when he looked at the child's face. Better for him not to know; better even to wonder, so long as he never knew for sure. Then, if he wanted to, he could shut out the doubts.

She stroked his chest. 'You're a handsome lad yourself, Johnny. And when you kiss me under the moon, the way you did just now – well . . .'

'Well what?' he whispered.

'I don't think I ought to say.'

'Go on. Say it.' He kissed her now and she felt the excitement in him. 'Tell me how it makes you feel, Molly. Tell me – please . . .'

174

'It makes me feel I want you to do it again,' she breathed against his lips. 'More and more. It makes me feel I want you to love me, Johnny.'

'I want to love you too. Oh Moll, I've wanted you so bad for such a long time.' His hands were tight on her body now and he gripped her buttocks and pulled her hard against him. 'There. That's how bad I want you.' He moved against her and she felt a tingling deep inside. 'You're not going to say no, Molly, are you? Not now.' He slid his hands up her body to fumble at her bodice and her breasts spilled into his hands. He buried his face in them, kissing the softness, and Molly felt a sudden rush of desire for him. He wasn't Kester, but he was a man, and he loved her as Kester never had. And he was her salvation. 'Let me love you now,' he whispered, and she felt her body grow soft against him.

Since the night, she had walked with Johnny a good few times, but she had not allowed him to make love to her again. 'I don't want to take risks,' she told him as he held her close and slid his hands over her breasts. 'You know what'll happen to me if I fall for a baby. I'll be out on my ear. Miss Rowenna might put in a word for me, but the old Grouse wouldn't and Mr Mellor'd not have me in the house another night. I can't take chances.'

'But there's no need for you to take chances, Molly. We'll get married. I've talked to my dad and he says we can have the back room in the cottage till we can get a place of our own. What's the sense in waiting? We'd get along fine, Molly. Say yes.'

But Molly shook her head. She wanted to be sure, she said. And with the waiting, John's impatience had grown, and she knew at last that the moment had come.

She strolled along the path between the vegetables, waiting for John to come with his mother's kindling. The garden was empty when he came, and that suited her purpose. She walked forward to meet him and saw the smile that broke over his face.

Once again, she felt a moment of shame. But the moment passed, for wasn't she giving Johnny what he wanted? Wasn't she about to tell him what he wanted to know?

'Molly! I thought maybe you couldn't come out today.'

'Old Grouse made me to help with tammying tonight's soup. Me and the scullerymaid, we've been standing nigh on three-quarters of an hour, pushing stewed vegetables through a cloth with wooden spoons. It's right hard work, and when all's done half the goodness is left behind on the cloth, at least I reckon it is. But Mrs Oaksey wants smooth soup at the table, so smooth soup is what she gets.'

'She's got her foot in the door proper, hasn't she?' John remarked, walking with Molly towards the gate set in the high wall.

'Oh aye, and not just in the door, she's got both of 'em right under the table. I don't think we'll be shot of her in a hurry. But I didn't come to gossip about the family.' She stopped. They were on a path that wound between high rhododendron bushes, concealed from all sight. 'It's us. I've got to talk to you, Johnny.'

'Well, all right. Talk. No time like the present, my mum always says.' He gave her a sharp look. 'Important, is it?'

'Aye.' Molly looked down at the path. Now that the moment had come, she felt frightened. Suppose Johnny refused her? Suppose all his talk of marriage had been no more than talk? Suppose he guessed the truth and turned her away?

John laid a hand on her shoulder and his voice was gentle as he said, 'Come on, Moll, out with it. Is it some sort of trouble?'

'I don't know,' she whispered. 'It – it depends on you . . .'

'On me? I see.' He was silent for a moment, then he said

176

quietly, 'Are you in the family way, Moll?'

She looked up and met his eyes briefly, grateful that she had not had to speak the words herself. But she could not look into his eyes for long.

'That night under the hedge,' he said wonderingly. 'The first time.'

'The only time, Johnny.'

'Aye, though not for want of trying,' he said with a grin, and his voice was exultant as he added, 'Well, Moll, that settles things, don't it? We'll have to get wed now. And the sooner the better, don't you reckon?'

'Yes, but – but – ' She looked up at him, her eyes swimming with tears. 'Only if you want to, Johnny.'

'If I *want* to? Haven't I been begging you this past month?' He gave a little crow of laughter and pulled her towards him. 'This calls for a kiss! The best girl in Westmorland's just said she'll marry me. Molly, I'm the happiest man in the county!' He held her and kissed her soundly. 'In the county? In the whole world!' And he kissed her again.

Molly clung to him, half laughing, half crying. Her mind was a tumult of emotion. Shame for the deception she was practising, relief for the escape he had offered. And a deep gratitude that was already beginning to turn to love.

She would never have gone away with Kester. His life was not hers, and she had known it from the beginning. And perhaps that meant that her feeling for him was not, after all, love. Not as she loved Johnny, in a quiet way that looked forward to a simple life in a gardener's cottage, with a bevy of children about her feet.

The first of those children would be Kester's. But all the rest would be Johnny's. And her love, and Johnny's, would be shared between them all, equally.

Rowenna received Molly's news almost with indifference.

Her own brain was numbed and she could comprehend no more, even that the maid who had been her friend for so long was leaving her. She did not ask, or even wonder, why the wedding was being arranged so quickly, and Molly felt hurt that her departure seemed of so little importance.

'We'll have to find you a new maid,' she said. 'I'll help. I know what you like and don't like, and I can talk to anyone you interview and see whether I think they're up to it. You deserve the best, Miss Rowenna.'

'Oh, I shan't bother,' Rowenna said drearily. 'Sarah will do. She's looked after me often enough, when you've had a cold or been poorly. She knows my ways.'

'Sarah? But she's almost a simpleton. She won't do, miss. Why, what will you do when you need someone to talk to? I suppose you can always run down to me at the cottage, but it's not what you might call private there.'

'Oh, I'll manage. You can come and see me sometimes, can't you?'

'Well, I suppose I could,' Molly said doubtfully. 'But I don't know what the others'd say, me coming calling like a lady. Anyway, that's not the point. You need a proper maid, who'll look after your clothes and dress your hair nice and be company for you. And Sarah won't be *that*, I can tell you!'

No, Rowenna thought, she probably wouldn't. But what did it matter? In the past few months her life had changed turn and about, and this was barely more than a ripple. The news her father had just given her was far more terrifying.

She had gone into the study at his request shortly after luncheon. Normally they sat in the drawing room of an afternoon, but Warren's restlessness had driven him to starting work again, though he had not yet begun to go regularly to the mill. This afternoon he had declared his intention of working almost before they finished their fruit, but when Rowenna looked up with a gleam of hope in her eyes, he had said abruptly, 'And don't think this means you can go sneaking out into the garden, miss. I shall want to see you in half an hour, so stay at hand if you don't mind.'

In fact, it was a full hour before he sent for her. And when she went into the study, Rowenna found to her surprise that Alfred Boothroyd was there too.

She stopped and looked at the two men. There was an air of expectancy that disturbed her.

'Shut the door,' Warren said. 'And sit down. We've got something to tell you.'

Something to tell her? Rowenna looked from one to the other. There was a queer glint in Alfred Boothroyd's eyes and she was suddenly reminded of the time he had kissed her in the bluebell hollow. It was a memory she had thrust out of sight in her mind, along with the other memories of that day, but now it came rushing back and she shuddered.

She sat down, resting uncomfortably on the edge of the chair. Both men had stood up as she entered but now they seated themselves again. Her father was behind his desk, a pipe in his hand, while Alfred Boothroyd was in an armchair, his legs stretched out before him. He looked oddly pleased with himself, she thought, almost smirking, and her uneasiness grew.

Was her father about to tell her of his engagement to Mrs Oaksey?

Rowenna had been expecting such news for some time now. There was still no sign of Mrs Oaksey's leaving, and every day she behaved a little more as if the house were hers. For a time, Rowenna had tried to assert her own authority in the house, going into the kitchen of a morning to give orders for the day's meals. But more and more often, she had found a different meal being served and on enquiring had been told that it was Mrs Oaksey who had countermanded her. Remembering that her father must not be upset, she had kept quiet, but her irritation had grown on finding the maids cleaning unused rooms on Mrs Oaksey's orders and even, a week ago, putting up curtains that Rowenna had never seen before.

'Mrs Oaksey ordered them,' she was told. 'She chose the material and everything. Didn't you know, miss?'

No, she had not known, but she knew very well what it all meant. And she had given up trying to fight it. If Mrs Oaksey was to be mistress here, there was nothing she could do about it.

She looked at her father and Mr Boothroyd. Why didn't they get on and tell her? It had been plain for all to see for weeks now. Let's get the wedding over with, she thought, and perhaps then I'll have time for my own life.

Her father cleared his throat.

'Mr Boothroyd and I have been discussing this for some time,' he said. 'There are various business matters which are no concern of yours, but you may as well know that our two businesses are to be merged. It will be better for us all. The new firm will be called Mellor and Boothroyd.'

He stopped and Rowenna stared at him blankly. Her father going into business with Alfred Boothroyd? This was something she hadn't expected, though she supposed it made sense. But couldn't he have found someone more congenial? It was only in the past few months that the two had begun to see so much of each other, after years of living and working on opposite sides of the river. They had never been friends.

'Well?' Warren demanded. 'Have you nothing to say?'

'What do you want me to say?' Rowenna asked. 'You've always told me that the business is no concern of mine. You repeated it a moment ago. I wish you well, Father, and you too, Mr Boothroyd. And if that's all—?'

She made to rise but her father said sharply, 'No. That is not all. There's something else, Rowenna, something that concerns you directly and that you may find of slightly more interest than you seem to show in the business that brings you your livelihood. Please sit down again and listen.' He waited a moment, then said without any further preamble, 'Mr Boothroyd has asked me for your hand, Rowenna, and I have accepted on your behalf.'

'My—?' Stupidly, Rowenna looked down at her hands. Then she lifted her head again quickly and stared at the two men. Her father was looking belligerent, as if daring her to object. And Mr Boothroyd was sitting back in his armchair, one finger stroking his moustache, his thin face complacent as if he already owned her.

'My *hand*?' Rowenna echoed. 'You mean he wants to *marry* me?'

'That's the usual interpretation,' Warren said stiffly, and Alfred Boothroyd broke in, his voice smooth.

'Miss Mellor, I shall be delighted if you'll do me the honour of becoming my wife. There.' He smiled. 'I know every girl longs for a proposal, and I've no intention of depriving you of anything you desire.'

Rowenna looked first at him, then at her father. Her eyes were wild. 'A proposal? But you say you've already accepted, Father. How did you know if it was what I desired?'

Warren glanced at Boothroyd. His voice was annoyed as he said, 'How your husband chooses to treat you after you are married is up to him. He may well wish to give in to your every whim, and good luck to him if he does, for he'll need it. But while you are still my daughter you do as *I* say, and I've accepted Mr Boothroyd's offer and think you should be glad to get it. It's a better chance than I ever foresaw for you.'

'But I thought you didn't want me to marry! I thought you wanted me to stay here as your companion.'

'And precious fine company you turned out to be,' Warren said bluntly. 'But Alfred Boothroyd thinks you'll prove a better wife than daughter and who knows but what he's right? Most women want marriage, though by all accounts when they get it they don't like it. We'll see. As to my own companionship, well, Mrs Oaksey will provide that. We're to be married next month.'

'Next *month*?' Although she had been expecting it, the announcement nevertheless came as a shock. Her head swam and she found herself clutching at the arms of her chair. 'Father, are you sure? It all seems so sudden.'

'It isn't at all sudden,' Warren retorted. 'The whole matter has been under discussion for months. If I hadn't been ill, it would have been done by now. And I'll thank you not to question me, miss.' He turned to Boothroyd. 'That's the sort of impertinence you'll have to put up with, I'm afraid. An unruly tongue in an unruly head.'

'Oh, I don't think so,' Boothroyd said silkily. 'I'm sure Miss Mellor and I – but mayn't I call you Rowenna, now that we're engaged? – I'm sure we'll very soon have an excellent understanding. After all, everyone knows that, while children may be rebellious, a man is *always* master in his own house.' He stood up and came across the room to Rowenna, lifting her by both hands. 'And now I'm sure your father will permit a kiss, my dear. As an engaged couple, we may indulge in what we've only tasted before, mayn't we? Let me see your face, my dear, and look into those beautiful eyes.' With one hand he raised her chin so that she was forced to look up at him. She saw his eyes, full and dark, as cold as marble even now in his ivory-pale face. And then he bent his head to hers and she felt his lips, thin and wet and writhing like worms upon hers.

And she remembered, as if she were seeing it again, the afternoon when her father had had his attack and Alfred Boothroyd had kissed her in the bluebell grove. And she had stood helpless in his arms and, over his shoulder, caught sight of Kester standing frozen as a statue beneath the trees.

Chapter Nine

'How could you do it?' Rowenna demanded passionately. She paced across the study and turned to face her father. 'How could you give me to that – that *monster*? Don't you know what my life will be? I'll be his slave. I'll never have a moment's freedom. I shall *die*!'

'Nonsense,' Warren retorted. 'You're hysterical, Rowenna. Die, indeed. Of course you won't die. You'll forget all this talk of freedom and settle down to marriage like any other young woman, taking care of your household and bringing up your children in a proper manner.'

'Children? I shall never have children – not if you force me to marry Mr Boothroyd. Never!'

'You'll have what God sends,' her father stated. 'And let's pray there'll be a quiverful, for a large family is what every man needs. I should know – I only got two out of your mother, and one died and the other's been nothing but a burden.'

Rowenna felt tears spring to her eyes. As little as she had loved her father, he was nevertheless her *father*, and she had tried her best to please him – particularly since his illness. Even now, as she stared at him, she felt a pang of guilt, for hadn't the doctor said that he mustn't be upset? But did that give him the right to ride roughshod over her life? Must his illness overrule everything?

'I'm sorry if I've been a burden to you, Father,' she said shakily. 'Perhaps it would be better if you just gave me an allowance and let me go my own way. Then you need never have the bother of seeing me again.'

'And now you're talking hysterical nonsense again. You're going to marry Mr Boothroyd, and we'll have no more argument about it.' He closed his mouth firmly in the manner that had always signalled the end of an argument and turned away. But Rowenna would not be silenced.

'I won't,' she said. 'I won't marry him – nor anyone else who is chosen for me. This is my life, Father, and I don't believe you have any right to dictate how I should live it. If you won't give me an allowance, I'll leave anyway. I can find work – '

'You?' he sneered. 'Work? And what as, may I ask? A gardener's labourer?'

'I can think of many worse occupations,' she retorted. 'Yes, perhaps that's exactly what I would become. Or a teacher, or a governess – after all, I've had an education – '

'Which I'm beginning to think is one of the biggest mistakes I've ever made,' he interrupted. '*No*, Rowenna' – he held up a hand as she opened her mouth again – 'I'll listen to no more of your ranting. There's more in this than you know. If you don't do as I say, there'll be no money for either of us. The business is in a bad way and has been for months. If I don't go into partnership with Boothroyd it'll be the end of Mellor Papermaking and we'll both finish up in the workhouse. D'you want that? Well, do you?'

'No, Father,' she said, staring at him with frightened eyes. 'But – what does my marrying Mr Boothroyd have to do with the business? Can't you go into partnership without my having to do that?'

'No, I can't,' he snapped. 'It's the condition Boothroyd has laid down. He wants you as his wife, Rowenna, though

186

God knows why when he must know by now what a little spitfire you are, and if he doesn't get you the partnership is off. And the rot's gone too far to be saved any other way. What's more, Mrs Oaksey won't marry *me*, either, and she's got assets too. That house in Staveley will fetch a pretty penny, not to mention her shares in Boothroyd's business. You're not the only one to have to make sacrifices,' he added a little bitterly.

But you'll not have to make the sacrifices I shall make, Rowenna thought, staring at him. You'll not have to share Alfred Boothroyd's bed and suffer his revolting wet lips and his repulsive body that looks as if it's been dead for the past five years. You won't have to bear his grotesque children and call them your own. You won't have to look ahead to a lifetime – thirty or forty years, perhaps even more – shackled to a man you'll never love, a man who doesn't know what love is.

You won't have to spend the rest of your life yearning for the man you really want, and knowing that because you missed one chance happiness can never come your way again.

'And if I say I won't do it?' she said dully. 'If I refuse to marry him?'

'You can't refuse,' Warren said brutally. 'A father does have some rights over his daughter. You'll do as you're told, Rowenna, or suffer for it. And as I've already told you, you'll suffer in the workhouse. And so shall I.' He held her gaze with his, and she saw him sag a little in his chair, and lay his hand over his heart. 'If I live so long.'

'So you see,' Rowenna said to Molly, 'I won't need a new maid. Mr Boothroyd already has enough servants and I would have had to leave you here anyway.' She kissed the girl's cheek, feeling sorry that she had not given her news the attention it deserved. 'I'm glad you're going to be happy. John will make you a good husband.'

'I know, miss.' Molly hesitated. 'I wish there was something I could do – '

Rowenna smiled ruefully. 'There's nothing anyone can do. It seems that a father can order his daughter to marry whom he pleases, and without money of my own I'm helpless to refuse. I can't leave him to go to the workhouse. It isn't just my father who would suffer if the mill failed – it's all of you. John and his father, the other gardeners, Mrs Partridge, Ackroyd – all would lose their positions. How could I do that to you all?' She shook her head, and added in a voice that tried hard to be cheerful, 'And perhaps life as Mrs Boothroyd won't be so bad after all. A wife must have some authority and freedom.'

But she spoke without conviction and at night she lay awake, staring out at the winter sky in dread for what must come.

The two weddings were planned to take place on the same day, in a double ceremony. Mrs Oaksey had returned to her own house in Staveley in the interim, but was back almost every day, fussing about the place, ordering new carpets for this room, new curtains for that, and talking incessantly about her trousseau. One would think she were a young bride, Rowenna thought distastefully, and where was the money coming from to pay for all this? Wasn't her father supposed to be in financial difficulties?

But even worse was when Mrs Oaksey turned her attention to Rowenna's wedding. There, she really allowed her imagination to run riot and spent hours discussing lace and satin. And bridesmaids! Did Rowenna really mean to say that she didn't know six little girls who could act as bridesmaids? Well, some must be found. And she scoured the neighbourhood, seeking out friends and acquaintances, until she had found the necessary six small girls.

It's a nightmare, Rowenna thought as she stood for hours while the elaborate wedding dress was constructed around her. Really, she thought, it was more like a building than a dress. Of striped cream satin with a low-necked and sleeveless bodice, it fitted Rowenna's slender waist and softly moulded breasts exactly, while showing off the creamy skin of her arms and bosom. From the dropped waist, the full skirt was gathered back and draped over steel half-hoops and a bustle pad, so that it stood out behind her and exposed at the front a richly embroidered net underskirt, with plain satin beneath.

'So lovely,' Mrs Oaksey breathed as the dressmaker and her assistants crawled around Rowenna, their mouths filled with pins as they worked to get the frilled hem exactly right. 'Dear Alfred will be in transports of joy when he sees you.'

'But it's so expensive,' Rowenna objected. 'Surely the money would be better spent at the mill. I really don't think Father can afford – '

'Rowenna! Really, my dear, it's most unbecoming for a young girl to question her elders in the way you do. Of course you must have a wedding suitable for your station in life. Why, Mellor and Boothroyd will be the foremost papermaker in the country before long and Alfred will require a wife who looks well by his side. He intends to become a big name in the county, you know. I wouldn't be surprised if he is Sheriff before he finishes.'

Rowenna's heart sank. She had only just begun to realise how ambitious Alfred Boothroyd was. The acquisition of Warren Mellor's mill – for Rowenna had no doubt that that was what it was, rather than the partnership it was supposed to be – was only the beginning. There was a fanatical gleam in Mr Boothroyd's eyes that alarmed her, and his sister's assumption that he was aiming for the most prestigious

189

position in the county came as no surprise.

With a feeling of doom, she submitted to the wedding dress and the other clothes that Mrs Oaksey insisted were necessary: the day-dress of dark blue satin and velvet with its frill of ecru net at the collar, the grey flannel winter dress with its pink tartan pattern and matching tartan jacket, the fine white cotton negligée with its lace sleeves and trimming, which must be worn at breakfast. And the night-gowns, frothy affairs of lace and cotton which flowed from only two or three buttons at the high, demure neck, leaving the rest of the front loose.

Rowenna looked at the nightgowns, and her dread grew. Would she really have to get into bed with Alfred Boothroyd, wearing one of these concoctions? And what would happen next?

'You'll find out soon enough,' Molly said. 'It's not a thing to be talked about. But I'll tell you this – it can be beautiful, with the right person.'

'And with the wrong person?' Rowenna asked, feeling that this was more relevant to her case.

Molly hesitated and shrugged. 'It depends. If he's kind and caring and wants to make you happy – well, it's nice in a different sort of way.'

'And if he's not? If it isn't . . . nice?'

Molly looked at her with pity. 'Let's hope it don't come to that, Miss Rowenna.'

But Rowenna feared that it would come to that, although Alfred Boothroyd certainly seemed at present to want to make her happy. He was assiduous in his attentions, visiting her every morning with some small offering – a rose, an embroidered handkerchief, or perhaps a box of chocolate dragees. He asked her about her trousseau and listened courteously while she attempted to describe the latest gown, though Rowenna was convinced that he was no more interested than she. He took her over the bridge to Meadowbank, where he showed her the latest improvements and asked her advice on decoration. Rowenna remembered the night when she and her father had first come here to dinner, and wondered if he had already decided to marry her then. And she shuddered, feeling that she had been marked down months ago, and had never had a chance of escape.

And yet, if she had gone away with Kester one day earlier . . . Or even just a few hours. If he had said 'come with me now' rather than 'come tonight' . . . Where would they be today? And how would it have been, lying under the stars with Kester on a bed of heather while he loved her without the benefit of frothy lace nightgowns or silk and satin?

Beautiful, Molly had said. With the right person, it could be beautiful.

Molly and John Richmond were married quietly in the little village church of St Oswald in November, only a month before Rowenna and Alfred Boothroyd were to stand in front of the same altar with Warren Mellor and Matilda Oaksey. Rowenna went to the church and sat near the front with Molly's parents, watching as the girl came up the aisle wearing her best dress of brown wool and carrying a bunch of golden leaves. She looked at John Richmond, who had turned to see his bride approach, and saw the look on his face, the love and admiration that shone from his eyes, and a heavy sadness weighed upon her heart.

Molly was as slender as a reed. She had lost weight lately and often looked pale in the mornings, but her glowing skin belied any concern that she might be ill. Rowenna knew that she had for a time been unhappy over Kester's departure but, once she had announced her plans to marry, she seemed to have shrugged away such thoughts and her step

191

was light and her eyes merry again. If only I could shrug it away like that, Rowenna thought, but knew she could not. Kester's memory would be with her always, both precious and painful.

She walked slowly out of the church and watched Molly and John run laughing from their friends and back to the little cottage where they were to live for a while with John's parents. They would be happy, she thought, and their loving might even be beautiful. At the least, it would be what Molly had described as 'nice'.

And her own marriage?

The day was set for Christmas Eve. As it drew nearer, so Rowenna's desperation grew. And finally she went to her father in his study and told him outright that she could not go through with it.

'Not go through with it?' Warren repeated, his face immediately darkening with anger. 'What are you talking about, child? Of course you'll go through with it.'

'I can't,' she said, twisting her fingers together. 'Father, please don't force me to do this. I don't love Mr Boothroyd and I'm sure he doesn't love me – '

'*Love*?' Warren broke in. 'Whoever said anything about love? Mr Boothroyd has a very high regard for you, Rowenna, a regard that in my opinion you don't in the least warrant. You're an extremely fortunate young woman, let me tell you. I'd thought to see you an old maid and instead you'll be making one of the best marriages in the county. Boothroyd's mill is doing very well indeed. You'll never want for a thing.'

I shall want for everything that really matters to me, Rowenna thought. 'But Father – '

'As for love,' he want on dismissively, 'that's no more than a foolish, romantic idea that you get from those penny novelettes the maidservants read. Why anyone should think that the lower classes ought to be educated is beyond me! All they do is waste their time filling their heads with rubbish. Nothing but fairytales and silly nonsense. You'll do well to forget such things and make up your mind that life isn't like a trashy story. You're marrying an astute businessman, and you'll be living in clover for the rest of your life – what more can you ask than that? And you'll also be keeping your old father out of the workhouse.' He laid his hand over his heart and sat down, his jowls sagging a little.

Rowenna looked at him. She was fairly certain that her father's illness was now quite over and that he was as well as ever. He was back at the mill full-time now and his voice could be frequently heard berating workers who had made some small mistake. He made no attempt himself to remain calm, depending on other people to avoid upsetting him, and when he did lose his temper – which seemed to be as frequently as before – there were no apparent ill-effects. Indeed, he seemed to enjoy giving vent to his rage.

But any dispute with Rowenna, no matter how small, was invariably ended with this sudden fatigue, a sagging of his jaw and this gesture of placing his hand over his heart, as if he felt again the pain of his collapse. And Rowenna could never be quite sure that it wasn't genuine.

'But Father, surely Mr Boothroyd won't give up the partnership now? You've done so much work on it – he knows so much about your business – and with you and Mrs Oaksey marrying – '

'Rowenna, please don't delude yourself. I've told you before, the partnership depends upon your marriage. Without it, I shall be bankrupt within a month and we shall lose everything – this house, the carriage and horses, aye, even your fine wedding-dress – everything. And do you suppose that Mrs Oaksey will wish to marry a pauper? I imagine she will stay just where she is, in comfort. You may talk fine words of love, Rowenna, but there are few women who will abandon a comfortable life for that of a penniless wanderer.'

I would have done, Rowenna thought, gazing at him. I would have gone with Kester to sleep in a ditch and thought it as fine a bed as any in the land.

But she could not bring her father to such a fate. And even though she might be able to find work for herself, as a governess or teacher, she would not be able to earn enough to support him too. And she knew that all his knowledge of papermaking, all his business experience, would not find him work once he had been declared bankrupt – other than work of the lowliest kind, as a clerk perhaps, living in poor lodgings and half starved.

How long could he stand up to such a life? How long before he had another attack and, without the care he had received last time, died from it?

'Let's hear no more of this, Rowenna,' her father said quietly. 'You'll marry Mr Boothroyd and be thankful for it.'

And she bowed her head and left the room. But inside, she was seething with misery.

Yes, she thought, going to the window of her room and staring down at the wintry garden, I shall marry Mr Boothroyd because there is no other course open to me. But be thankful for it?

No. Gratitude was an emotion she would never feel, for Alfred Boothroyd was giving her nothing. This marriage and this partnership were all to serve his own ends. And she, her father and perhaps even Mrs Oaksey, were all no more than puppets dancing to his strings.

Christmas Eve brought snow, and Rowenna went to church wearing a fur-trimmed cloak of heavy brocade over her cream satin wedding-dress. She discarded it in the porch and it was hung carefully to wait the moment when she would emerge, as Mrs Boothroyd, and need its protection against the blizzard again.

She felt as cold as if she had walked to church naked. She looked at Matilda Oaksey, who was beside her in rich brown velvet with a shoulder cape of brown fur. It was less richly decorated than Rowenna's dress, with a plain skirt and tightly buttoned bodice, but it gave her plump body a regal look and she swept up the aisle with a grandeur that was almost intimidating. Not for the first time, Rowenna wondered if her father would find his new wife as pliant and biddable as he expected.

But she was more concerned at this moment with her own future. Alfred Boothroyd, arrayed in a dark jacket and trousers and a waistcoat of cream figured brocade, was waiting beside her father at the head of the aisle. The two men turned as she and Mrs Oaksey approached, with the six small bridesmaids behind them, and Rowenna saw their faces.

For a brief moment of astonishment, she felt the first touch of rapport with her father since Haddon's funeral. He was looking at her with what seemed to be almost regret. And then, as his eyes fell on Mrs Oaksey in her majestic brown velvet, his expression changed to apprehension.

Rowenna felt a flash of pity. Did he know what their lives were going to be? But her pity vanished as she looked from him towards the man who was about to become her husband.

Alfred Boothroyd looked as if he had been carved from marble. He stood, tall and pale, his dark eyes smooth and hard, his face without expression. His mouth was set in a straight, thin line, his nostrils slightly flared, and his chin was lifted into a jut of arrogance. He looked like a man who was gloating over a bundle of new possessions. And that's just what we are, Rowenna thought.

Her step faltered. What would happen if she turned now and ran from the church? But the pews were filled with watching people, business acquaintances and friends of her father and Mr Boothroyd, a few distant Boothroyd relatives, other businessmen from the area – the Somervells whose 'K' shoe factory was becoming known all over the country, the Wilsons whose printing business was so important to the papermakers, and other millowners from up and down the river. And outside were the villagers who had gathered to see the wedding and who had gasped with admiration as Rowenna stepped down from the carriage in her billowing cream satin and cloak.

To retreat at this point would create a scandal that would rock the whole area. But more than that, it would ruin her father and end, one way or another, in his death. And Rowenna would feel herself a murderess for the rest of her life.

She walked on up the aisle and Alfred Boothroyd stepped forward to take her hand. She felt it close around her own fingers, colder even than her own, with a clammy dampness that sickened her. She looked into the marble face with its marble eyes and wondered whether his heart was of marble too. And then the vicar stepped forward and the service began.

'*Therefore if any man can shew any just cause why they may not lawfully be joined together, let him now speak, or else hereafter for ever hold his peace.*'

Kester, she thought, Kester, come and save me for no one else can do it now. But the prayer, which seemed in her desperate need to fly from her heart, did no more than beat itself on the roof of the church, fluttering like a benighted sparrow against the beams. And although the vicar paused, as if he too were waiting, it went unanswered and the sonorous voice went on, as if prophesying doom rather than conducting a wedding.

Within moments, Alfred Boothroyd was making the responses that made him her husband. *To love, comfort, honour and keep her, in sickness and in health, so long as they both did live* . . . How long could she live, bound to such a man? And then, with a sense of horror, she heard her own voice, repeating steadily her own vows. *To obey him and serve him, love, honour and keep him* . . . How could she be saying these things? How could she be making such promises? God forgive me, her heart cried, I don't love him, I cannot honour him . . . But the words were said and the ring on her finger, and she looked at it as if it were an iron chain and then lifted her veil for her husband to kiss her.

The register was signed and the two couples proceeded from the church, followed by their guests. The wedding breakfast was to be held at Ashbank and after that Rowenna and Alfred Boothroyd would cross the little foot-bridge to Meadowbank, to begin their new life.

She still could not believe it. She looked at the gold ring on her finger and wondered whether it was really true, that a few words spoken in a church on a cold winter's morning could make her the property of a man she so much disliked, even feared. From now on, Alfred Boothroyd had all legal rights over her. He could force her to go where he wanted, to do as he wished. He could use her body as he desired. If she ran away, he could set the police to bring her back. She was his, body and soul.

Mrs Oaksey – now Mrs Mellor – was moving about the room like a queen, smiling and nodding, clearly revelling in her new position. Rowenna looked at her with envy. The marriage between her and Warren was clearly one of name only, for both had agreed from the outset that she was to have her own suite of rooms – a bedroom, a boudoir and a new bathroom and water-closet. She seemed to have no difficulty in taking over the house and was already behaving as if it were her own – which it now was, Rowenna thought, for her new stepmother had contributed handsomely with the price she had got for her own house, and she had been left comfortably off by her first husband.

'Being a widow is all very well in its way,' she had confided to Rowenna. 'One does have freedom and of course one has control over one's own money. But it isn't like having a husband to take care of things. And there are so many more social opportunities for a wife. Local functions, soirées, balls and so on. Much more satisfactory to have one's own husband to take one about.'

'I hope Mr Boothroyd doesn't expect me to appear at such affairs,' Rowenna said with a shudder. 'I've never enjoyed that kind of thing – people chattering about nothing, and all the ladies comparing each other's clothes.'

'Oh, but I'm sure he will. He'll expect you to be a credit to him.' Mrs Oaksey looked her over critically. 'And there's no reason why you shouldn't be, once you've got a good wardrobe together and done something about your hair. You're really quite good-looking, Rowenna, when you put your mind to it.'

Most of the wedding guests were known to Rowenna but some were strangers. She walked round the room on Alfred's arm, smiling through tight lips, offering her cold hand and nodding at names she would instantly forget. One or two men, clearly acquaintances of Mr Boothroyd, looked at her knowingly and made jocular remarks that she only half understood. Beneath her hand she could feel the bones of Alfred's arm. It was like walking with a skeleton. She looked up into his face but there was no warmth in it, only pride, and she knew that it was the pride of possession, not of happiness and love.

At last he declared that it was time for them to go home to Meadowbank. Rowenna's cloak was brought, and Alfred's top hat. Amidst much jocularity, the whole crowd went out through the front door and round the garden, passing the little woodland where Rowenna and Kester had lain together in the summer that seemed so long ago now, and as far as the footbridge. There, they fell back, and Alfred and Rowenna went on alone.

At the far side of the river, she turned and looked back. The faces on the other side of the river were blurred by her tears. But as she blinked, her vision cleared and she saw, at the edge of the crowd, a few faces which were like family to her.

The servants. Mrs Partridge, her homely face crumpled as if she too were crying. Ackroyd, looking stern and stiff. The housemaids, the footman, the boot-boy, the gardeners. And, beside her John and, looking plumper now and rosy with contentment, Molly.

Their faces were solemn. And Rowenna, lifting her hand in a wave of acknowledgement, felt as if she were saying goodbye for ever.

Chapter Ten

Rowenna's twenty-first birthday fell on the first of May. By then, she had been married for just over four months.

She sat at the breakfast table, looking out at the garden of Meadowbank. Alfred had already left for the mill, having given her his gift of a small gold brooch. The presentation had been both formal and casual – a mere observation of ceremony. He had handed her the box as they sat down, wishing her a happy birthday, and she had opened it and thanked him. Alfred had then retreated behind his morning copy of *The Times*, and Rowenna had busied herself with the coffee-pot and tried to keep the tears from stinging her eyes.

Why did he bother? There was no love behind his gift, no careful thought about what she might like, what would express his feeling for her. She doubted if he had done any more than glance at the brooch to make sure it was worth the money spent on it. Probably his sister had chosen it for him, and he had never even seen it until Rowenna took it out of its box that morning.

A far better gift, she thought, would have been an expression of tenderness. A kiss that told her he loved her. A touch that woke in her the warm desire she had felt for Kester.

But she was never likely to have these from Alfred

Boothroyd. And nor do I want them, she thought with a flash of her old spirit. Why should I want him to love me, when I despise him? It would be even worse than it is now, for at least we both know quite well what we think of each other and at least we can be honest about it!

She toyed with her breakfast. She wanted little enough to eat these days, for her interest in food had left her and her figure was growing rapidly more slender. At this rate, she thought, I'll be as thin and bony as Alfred, and she tried to eat more to avoid such a fate. But after the first few mouthfuls her throat refused to swallow any more, and her stomach felt too full to receive it.

The first of May. The bluebells would be appearing in the little grove by the river. It was a year now since she had slipped from her room one evening, after the quarrel with her father, and walked up the fell to Potter's Tarn. She remembered how she had sat there, gazing over the dark waters, and been startled by Kester's voice behind her. He had stood proudly beside her and told her his name and that he would call no man master. And then he had sat down beside her and held her as she wept against his shoulder. She could feel that shoulder now, warm and strong under her cheek, and hear the tenderness in his voice as he bade her cry.

And then he had taken her back to the hut on the edge of the fell, and warmed her with strong, sweet tea and let her talk about her father and her dead Canadian mother, and the brother who had been his friend too. And from that night, it had all begun – the meetings in the bluebell grove, the kisses, the loving.

Oh Kester, she thought, where are you now? And what would my life be now, if we were together? And why – why did you not wait for me?

She thought of the nights they would have spent under

the stars, cushioned by heather, the love they would have shared. How different from what she knew now.

From that first night, the night of Christmas, she had understood what Molly had meant when they talked of the marriage bed. With the right person, the maid had said, it could be beautiful. Even with someone else, if he were gentle and caring, it could be pleasurable. But with the wrong man . . . Rowenna remembered her words. *Let's hope it'll not come to that*, she had said, and looked at her with pity. She had known then, Rowenna thought. She had known that Alfred Boothroyd was not the man for Rowenna, and she had pitied her.

She thought again of that afternoon, with darkness already creeping over the sky as she and Alfred walked across the little footbridge. A path had been cleared through the snow to lead them to the house, and they walked between dark trees, as gloomy as a forest. Rowenna looked about and shivered, drawing her cloak more closely around her.

'I've ordered a light supper, and a fire in our bedroom,' Alfred said. His hand was under her elbow, striking cold even through the thickness of her cloak. 'We'll not want to be up too late tonight.'

Rowenna's body was taut with fear. She still had only a vague idea of what was to be expected, born of a few glimpses of dogs coupling in the streets, or a bull mounting a cow in a field. Did men and women really do that? She tried to imagine it but failed. And yet, with Kester, she had been conscious of strange yearnings. She had wanted him to touch her body, to press himself against her. She had felt his hardness and known a tingle of excitement. She had been filled with a longing she could scarcely describe, and when she begged Kester to love her, it was as if her body had some age-old wisdom that her mind had not yet acquired, as if her instincts would guide her in this most ancient of rituals.

But with Alfred . . . Even now, Rowenna shuddered to recall it. The supper had been laid in the dining room, where they had sat one at each end of the long table. Afterwards, Alfred had filled two glasses with wine and handed one to Rowenna. He had then guided her up the stairs.

She already knew which room was theirs. Alfred had asked – no, commanded – that she choose the furnishings herself. As if aware that her wishes would never be consulted again, she had picked all the colours of spring and early summer – primrose yellow for the walls, a deeper gold for the curtains, and a green carpet, splashed with deep red roses. The effect was startling in that house where everything was dark, and she knew that Alfred didn't like it. But he had acquiesced, and this was the first time she had seen it since it was finished.

But this evening she barely noticed it. She walked in and set her glass of wine on the dressing table. The light of the fire turned the gold velvet curtains to bronze and the old four-poster bed loomed in the middle of the room, like a huge animal about to pounce. She felt as if she had somehow strayed into a jungle, with a predatory beast by her side.

'There's warm water here, for your wash,' Alfred said, indicating the jug and bowl that stood on the washstand. 'I shall go into the dressing room while the maid helps you with your dress. Perhaps you would be so good as to ring the little bell when you are ready.' He gave her a small bow and went through the door.

Rowenna stood helpless in the middle of the room. She longed for Molly to come, but Molly was back in her cottage with John Richmond and his parents, preparing to celebrate Christmas. The maid who did come was called Annie, and although her fingers were nimble enough, her hands were rough from housework, so that her skin caught on the delicate satin and pulled threads from the embroidered net.

'It doesn't matter,' Rowenna said. 'Just hang it up in the closet and unlace my corset. I shall never wear it again.'

'Oh, mum, that's a shame,' the girl said, and Rowenna realised with a shock that this was how she would be addressed from now on – 'mum' or 'madam'. Never Miss Rowenna again . . . 'It's a lovely dress,' Annie went on, stroking its folds with her roughened fingers. 'Couldn't you use it for a ball-dress or something like that?'

'Perhaps.' Rowenna wanted only to get rid of her, though heaven knew she was in no hurry to ring the little bell. 'Thank you, Annie. I can manage now.'

'Oh, but don't you want me to help you with your nightgown?' The girl cast a longing glance at the confection of white lace and cotton that lay across the bed. 'I'm sure it'll look lovely on.'

'Another night,' Rowenna said, wondering as she spoke whether Annie would go back to the kitchen and report that the mistress 'couldn't even wait to put her nightie on'. Well, it couldn't be helped. She must have these few moments to herself. She must have time to think of Kester – to tell him she was sorry. To hold him in her mind.

Alfred was back in the room almost before the last ripple of sound from the little bell had died. He stood inside the door, clad in a striped nightshirt that showed his thin, hairy legs, and surveyed her.

Rowenna was already in bed, with the sheets pulled up to her chin. Her heart was hammering in her chest and her body was like ice. She watched as Alfred crossed the room, and looked up at him with large, dark eyes.

'So now you are my wife,' he said softly. 'At last . . .' And he reached down and jerked the sheets away from her.

205

The movement was so sudden that Rowenna cried out. Instinctively, she crossed her arms over her body, as if in a last attempt to protect herself. With a strange, guttural noise that came from somewhere deep in his throat, Alfred reached down again and pulled her arms away. As he did so, the nightgown opened and revealed her nakedness to his greedy eyes.

'My wife,' he said again on a low note, and fell upon her. '*My wife . . .*'

His body was, as Rowenna had feared, skeletal. The bones crushed and ground her soft flesh as he thrust himself against her. She cried out again in pain and he instantly quietened her with his mouth upon hers, his sharp teeth nipping and bruising her lips. His hands were on her body, gripping and pinching, squeezing her breasts. As she gasped and cried out beneath him, he jammed his knees between her legs, forcing her thighs apart, and then butted himself hard against her, again and again and again.

Rowenna struggled frantically, convinced that he was killing her. His breath scorched her cheeks, hoarse grunts wrenching themselves from his throat. Her body felt as if it would split apart with his angry thrusting, and when his mouth moved away from hers she begged him to stop.

But it was as if he was past hearing, past all knowledge of the world other than his own frenetic desires. Clutching with bony hands at her soft buttocks, he dragged her against him, holding her so that she could not escape his onslaught. She felt her flesh strain and tear, like a web giving way under a hammer, and then she felt his entry, his thick, hard organ ramming into her dry, cringing body until suddenly its passage was eased and it slid more smoothly, though the pain was still as acute and each movement brought a fresh sensation of bruising and outrage.

It was soon over. Alfred's movements grew faster and

deeper, and Rowenna flung back her head, reaching up with both hands to claw the air. At the same time, he too raised himself above her, his eyes wild and staring. A loud groan broke from his throat, and his body stiffened. For a moment that seemed an eternity, he hung there, as if frozen. And then he dropped upon her body and lay heavily across her, panting as if he had just crossed three fields at a gallop.

Rowenna lay still. She was shaken, bruised and deeply distressed. Whatever she had expected, it was not this assault, this brutality. Beautiful, Molly had said. Or if not beautiful, at least tender and caring. But there had been nothing beautiful, nothing tender or caring about what Alfred had just done to her. She felt sore and injured, her thighs bruised, as if she would never walk again. How could such a deed masquerade under the name of love? How could it ever be anything but unpleasant and painful, a duty to be performed because men decreed it and what men decreed women must accord?

And yet . . . wouldn't it have been different with Kester? Would Kester have flung himself upon her in that manner, bruised her body with seeking, clutching fingers and intruded himself with such brutal passion? She had felt the passion in him, had known he was holding himself back – was it from this that he restrained himself? Was it always so?

Beautiful . . . caring . . . loving . . .

She turned her head from side to side on the pillow and the tears ran down her cheeks.

It was never again as painful as it had been that first time, but Alfred's approach to her never varied. He would come to her, his eyes as blank as those of a statue, his thin lips wet and loose, and thrust aside all her clothing to make way for his bony body. He never took more than a few minutes, and in this she found her only cause for relief. Afterwards he would fall heavily asleep, his arm across her like a prison band, and Rowenna would be trapped there until he turned over and away from her. Only then could she slide out of the bed, steal across to the washstand and bathe her soreness away.

She learned to use a cream to make it easier for him to enter her. The sudden ease of passage that first night had been caused, she discovered, by her own blood as the web of flesh tore. Plucking up her courage, she asked Alfred if it had been uncomfortable for him too, and was frightened by the look in his eyes.

'How dare you speak of such things?' he rasped. 'I'll not have such whores' talk in my house. Go and wash your mouth, and in future keep a decent tongue in your head.'

Very quickly, she learned that what happened at night was not to be spoken of. It was almost as if Alfred wished to pretend she was not involved; as if it were something private for which she was necessary but had nothing to do with her. Certainly, it seemed, she was not expected to find it pleasurable.

'Only whores expect to enjoy a man's satisfaction,' he snarled. 'You'll do your duty to me as a wife, Rowenna, and leave it at that, do you understand?'

Beautiful, she thought bitterly, and knew that there would never be any beauty in her life with Alfred Boothroyd.

And now, four months later, it was her twenty-first birthday, and the bluebells were flowering in the grove where she and Kester had whispered words of love. After breakfastshe would walk across the little footbridge to see her father, and then she would go through the garden to the Richmonds' cottage, where Molly was expecting her first baby.

She rose from the table. Alfred would be leaving for the mill soon and, although it was only a step away through the yard, he expected her to be in the hall to wish him goodbye as if he were setting out for the city. She went through the door, and as she did so heard a slight commotion, as if some unexpected visitor had arrived.

Alfred was standing in the hall with a man Rowenna had never seen before. He turned at her approach, looking slightly disconcerted, and made as if to order her back to the breakfast-room. But the visitor, a short, elderly man with a cheerful red face and white whiskers, lifted a hand to prevent him.

'This is Mrs Boothroyd, I take it? My dear Mrs Boothroyd. Charmed to meet you. Delighted.' He bent over the hand Rowenna held out to him and glanced up at her with roguish blue eyes. 'I apologise for calling at such an early hour, but it isn't often my pleasure to bring such good news to a charming young lady on her birthday. No, indeed. Such very good news. And such a *charming* young lady!'

Rowenna glanced at her husband in bewilderment. Alfred was looking annoyed, a small muscle jumping in his pale cheek. He spoke tersely to the visitor.

'I hardly think there's any need to bother my wife with this matter. She has the affairs of the house to see to. As her husband, I deal with all such concerns, so if you like to follow me we'll just go into my study—'

'By all means, my dear fellow, by all means.' The red-faced gentleman had a voice like a jar of rich strawberry jam. He looked at Rowenna and she could almost have sworn that he winked at her. 'A capital idea. Let's all go into your study. It's a splendid place for breaking such news, a splendid place.'

Alfred's annoyance grew. 'I don't know what you're talking about,' he snapped, 'nor what news you can have to break to my wife, but I've already told you she leaves all legal matters to me. Rowenna, my dear, I'm sure you're anxious to be about your own business. If you'll just leave

209

me and Mr – I'm sorry, I don't seem to recall your name—'

'Abercrombie,' the man said cheerfully. 'James Wilson Abercrombie, of Abercrombie and Wilson, Solicitors of Repute, Stricklandgate, Kendal, at your service. Or rather, at your wife's service. I must insist, I'm afraid, that I do give her this news in person. Can't be done any other way. So – shall we go into your study? Or shall I tell her here, in the hallway?'

Alfred glanced around, his irritation plain to see, but there was no more to be done about it and, with an ill grace, he led the way into his study. Mr Abercrombie stood back for Rowenna to precede him and she did so, wondering what he could possibly have to tell her that had brought him out from Kendal so early. She sat down and looked up at him expectantly.

'Ah. That's better.' He had an attaché case with him and he laid it on Alfred's desk and opened it, revealing a sheaf of papers. 'Now, there are just one or two formalities to be gone through . . . You are Rowenna Mary Boothroyd, *née* Mellor, born on the first of May 1865, I take it? I shall need to see the appropriate certificates, of course, but all in good time, all in good time. Well, Mrs Boothroyd, I have some good news for you.' He paused and beamed at her while Alfred tutted impatiently from behind the desk. 'Some *surprising* news, I believe. Your mother was Dorothy Mellor, *née* Tyson, of Penrith, is that correct?'

'Yes, it is,' Rowenna said, beginning to feel excited. 'But—'

'Please. Allow me to finish. Her family emigrated to Canada, I understand, where they settled quite a large parcel of land, and did well – prospered, it may be said. And when she died – when was it, let's see – yes, here it is, eleven years ago, in 1875 – she was the owner of quite a large tract of forest. Did you know that?'

'Forest? No, I didn't. But—'

'Mrs Mellor left a will.' James Wilson Abercrombie was plainly enjoying himself. He paused impressively, turning his bright blue eyes from one to the other. 'She left instructions that you, Rowenna Mellor – now Boothroyd – should inherit this land and all that is on it, on your twenty-first birthday. Along with a certain sum of money. And it's my very pleasant duty to see that you do!'

He stopped with an air of triumphant delight, his face wreathed in smiles, looking for all the world as though he were about to break into a jig. Anyone would think he'd inherited it himself, Rowenna thought bemusedly. She gazed at him dumbly, lost for words.

Alfred, however, had plenty to say.

'Land in Canada? *Forest*? You say my wife's mother left this to her in her will? But why did Mr Mellor not tell me? And why—' He stopped, but Rowenna could almost hear his next words hanging in the air: *Why did he not want to keep Rowenna – and the forest – for himself*?

Silently, she echoed his question. Why had her father allowed her to marry Alfred Boothroyd, when he must surely have realised that the value of the land in Canada was enough to save his business?

'Mr Mellor knew nothing of it,' Mr Abercrombie said, answering both questions. 'You may know better than I why his wife wished to keep this from him, but my impression was that she felt that fathers and husbands had too much control over women and their possessions.' He gave Alfred Boothroyd a passing glance of apology. 'I'm sure this doesn't apply to you, my dear sir, but there it is. In fact, her original instructions were that Miss Mellor was to be given this news in absolute private – with no other person present.'

'So you said when you arrived,' Alfred said curtly. 'And I

211

think I made it clear that such a procedure was completely out of the question.'

'Oh, you did, my dear sir, you did. And of course, it doesn't really matter now, does it.' He paused again and beamed at them both. His bright blue eyes and chubby red cheeks looked so innocent, Rowenna thought, staring at him, and yet she was beginning to detect a certain underlying shrewdness, as if those eyes saw more than one thought; as if their brightness illuminated more than was on the surface.

'What do you mean, man? What are you talking about?' Alfred Boothroyd said testily. 'Naturally, any instructions that the late Mrs Mellor gave about her husband are now rescinded. I am Rowenna's husband and, as I've told you several times already, I deal with all our legal affairs. So now that you've carried out your instructions and broken the news to her, the rest may be left to me.' He glanced at Rowenna. 'I think we need detain you no longer, my dear. You may go about your own business.'

Rowenna opened her mouth to protest, but the look in Alfred's eye told her that any objection would be punished later. She half rose from her chair, but Mr Abercrombie waved her back. With another glance at Alfred's face, she sat down again.

'I'm sorry, Mr Boothroyd. We can't let your charming wife leave us just yet. You see, Mrs Mellor seems to have had quite strong reservations regarding our sex. She wanted to be very clear that the land and the money would go to her daughter, and to nobody else. I have to have Mrs Boothroyd's signature to that effect.' He gave Alfred a charming smile. 'I remember when she came to my office to give these instructions. A delightful lady, but with a mind of her own – the transatlantic influence, I've no doubt. She was very definite about it.'

'Well, well, so she may have been,' Alfred said impatiently. 'Let's deal with the matter as quickly as possible.' He turned to Rowenna. 'Sign whatever papers need to be signed, my dear, and then run along. You don't want to bother your head with such tedious matters on your birthday.'

'Oh, but it's not tedious at all,' Rowenna said. 'Do you really mean to say, Mr Abercrombie, that this land actually belongs to me? To do as I like with?'

'Certainly,' the lawyer beamed, but again Alfred intervened.

'That's a matter for discussion at a later date. Now, Abercrombie, I'd be grateful if you'll just show Rowenna where to put her name. I'm a busy man and have a mill to run – I can't waste all morning on these petty affairs.' He snorted. 'A few acres of scrubland several thousand miles away! Why, I daresay it's of no value at all – but whatever's to be done with it will be decided by me.'

Rowenna threw a glance of appeal towards the little solicitor, but he was not looking at her. He was watching her husband and his bright blue eyes suddenly narrowed.

'I'm afraid that isn't so,' he said, and the jollity had disappeared from his voice, leaving it as hard and cold as Alfred Boothroyd's. 'Not unless Mrs Boothroyd herself wishes it.'

There was a moment of complete silence. Alfred Boothroyd stared at him. His face was white and Rowenna saw the tiny muscle jumping in his cheek.

'I beg your pardon?' he said at last. 'Would you care to explain yourself?'

'I'll be glad to,' James Abercrombie said, and he sounded as though he spoke no more than the truth. 'You see, Mr Boothroyd, apart from Mrs Mellor's very definite instructions, there is the little matter of the Married Women's Property Act of 1882 – only four years ago. An Act of which the late Mrs Mellor would have wholeheartedly approved, I may say. This gives married women the right to hold their own property, including land and money, and to use and dispose of it as they wish. I daresay you've heard of it, though Mrs Boothroyd may be too young' – he bowed in her direction – 'to have taken much notice of it, even if anyone had taken the trouble to apprise her of its existence.'

The silence this time was even longer. Rowenna sat very still, hardly daring to believe in the implications of what she had just heard. Land in Canada? Money of her own? Possessions in which Alfred had no right, over which he had no control? It seemed incredible.

And yet, of what use could it be to her now that she was married? Alfred still had his own rights in her. She was still his possession, his chattel. If only it had come a few months earlier!

'You mean that my wife is legally permitted to retain this – this scrap of land at the back of beyond?' Alfred said nastily. 'And whatever pittance her mother scraped together – out of Warren Mellor's pocket, I have no doubt – and do with it whatever takes her whim, without reference to me?'

'Exactly, my dear fellow!' James Abercrombie cried, with as much apparent delight as he would have congratulated a rather dull clerk on grasping a difficult point of law. 'That's it in a nutshell. What concise way you have of putting things into words – I couldn't have done it better myself. Except' – and his tone grew suddenly stern – 'in the matter of how Mrs Mellor came by her money. Certainly not through her husband, I can assure you. It was money held in trust for her by her father, Jacob Tyson, to be passed on *only* after her death and *only* left to her daughter, should any said daughter attain the age of twenty-one. All perfectly clear and legal, and nothing whatsoever to do with Mr Mellor –

who, as I've already said, knew nothing at all about it.'

Alfred glared at him, then turned to Rowenna. She watched as he stretched his lips into a smile, showing those sharp white teeth. He came across the room and took her hand.

'Well, my dear, it all seems rather complicated, but I'm sure it can be straightened out without any difficulty. All we have to do is have Mr Abercrombie draw up whatever papers are necessary for the transfer, and there will be no more problem. So I suggest you go now and do whatever you were planning to do, while we men discuss what steps need to be taken. It's a shame for you to miss this beautiful bright sunshine, on your birthday.'

'Papers?' James Abercrombie said, his eyes very bright. 'Transfer? I'm sorry, Mr Boothroyd, I don't quite understand.'

'Why, it's simple enough, surely. Mrs Mellor's instructions were made all in good faith, I'm sure, but whatever reasons she may have had for making them bear no relevance to the present situation. We don't know her relationship with her husband, of course' – he coughed delicately – 'but she could not have known that her daughter would, by the time she was twenty-one, be blessed with a caring and financially astute husband. Clearly the best course now is for my wife to transfer all the property into my care. Otherwise we shall have the constant complication, whenever any legal quibble arises, of needing her agreement and signature. The land will still be yours, of course, my dear,' he said to Rowenna with another of his wolfish smiles, 'but its management will be simplified, that's all.'

'That would be one way of dealing with it, certainly,' Mr Abercrombie said slowly. 'But it can only be done with Mrs Boothroyd's full agreement.'

'Oh, naturally, naturally.'

'And even supposing we have that agreement, the papers will take time to draw up. Transfers of this kind must be effected with the greatest care – every tiny point considered to make sure that nothing is overlooked. You'll understand that, of course, Mr Boothroyd, being an astute businessman.'

'Of course,' Alfred said, sounding a little less enthusiastic. 'Of course. But—'

'And I'm afraid I must have Mrs Boothroyd's signature on the existing documents today,' Mr Abercrombie continued. 'That's my legal duty. Once the property is hers in law, then of course we can take whatever steps she wishes regarding its management or disposal. And I would of course be more than happy to advise her of all the many options then open to her.' He paused, then repeated almost absentmindedly, 'All the many options. Yes.' He seemed to wake from a short reverie and smiled at them both. 'Well, I think that makes everything clear. So Mrs Boothroyd, if I may just go through the documents with you ... Mr Boothroyd may be permitted to be present, if you wish it.' He gave her a bright, enquiring glance.

Rowenna gazed at him. Again, she could scarcely believe in what he was saying. The documents to be signed by her, and her alone! Alfred to be permitted to be present only if she said so! And the land in Canada and the money, however little, to be hers, to do whatever she liked with – however hard Alfred tried to persuade her to transfer it to him. It was hers. *Hers*!

My freedom, she thought as the truth slowly sank into her brain. My *freedom*!

Chapter Eleven

'Well, my dear,' Alfred said as they walked in the garden later that morning, 'you seem to have had quite an outstanding birthday present.'

Rowenna did not answer at once. Alfred had not gone to the mill after all. He had waited while she went through the papers with James Abercrombie – for she had not had the courage, after all, to order him out of his own study – and demanded to see each one. Then, white with suppressed anger, he had shown the little lawyer out and returned to where she sat, waiting with some trepidation. Alfred might have been bested, legally speaking, but he was still capable of making life as unpleasant as only a husband could.

But he had said nothing at first, only told her that he was taking the rest of the day off. 'A little holiday, my dear, to celebrate your birthday.' And then had suggested this walk in the garden, his arm firmly clasping hers against his bony side.

'Yes,' she said at last. 'It's really a great surprise. I'd no idea—'

'And nor had your father, apparently. It's a strange way for a wife to behave, don't you think? Very secretive. I wouldn't like to think that *you* might act in such a furtive manner, Rowenna.'

'I don't think "furtive" is the word I'd apply to my

mother,' Rowenna began stiffly, and he immediately hastened to placate her.

'No, no, I'm sure it isn't. I'm sure she must have had very good reasons for what she did. Or what seemed to her to be good reasons. We have to remember that she probably did not think as we do. The Americans have a rather freer attitude, I believe.' He spoke disdainfully.

'My mother was Canadian,' Rowenna reminded him, and he shrugged.

'It's the same thing. Colonials. Once people leave their own shores they seem to acquire this rather distasteful desire for independence. Why, I was reading only the other day of a woman in New Zealand who has actually formed a society to demand the enfranchisement of women! And she's not the first to suggest it, either. Fortunately the Government has too much sense to countenance such nonsense. But it's a straw in the wind.'

Again, Rowenna made no answer. To argue this point with Alfred would only make him even angrier, and although so far he had not expressed his anger to her, she knew it was simmering only just below the surface.

They walked for a few moments in silence. Rowenna had, since her marriage, managed to spend quite a portion of her time in the garden and had begun discreetly to make changes. A few of the darker trees here and there were cleared, to make little patches of sunlight. An overgrown flowerbed was pruned and tidied to display treasures that had been almost suffocated out of existence. Someone had once loved this garden, she thought, and wanted it to be a place of peace and beauty. It could be so again.

Alfred seemed to recollect himself. He dismissed women's suffrage and returned to the matter more closely concerning his thoughts.

'I was quite surprised myself, to discover the extent of this woodland in Canada.'

I'm sure you were, Rowenna thought. She had been frankly astonished. Two thousand square miles seemed an immense tract of land, and the money that came with it a sizeable sum. Her bemused mind had still not fully taken it in, but she knew that she was tolerably well off. Not rich, but certainly not poor either.

'Of course, you'll let me take care of it for you,' Alfred said casually, as if the matter had already been thoroughly discussed and agreed upon. 'It's a complicated business dealing with land in another country. And I'll invest the money for you too.'

'Thank you, Alfred.' Rowenna spoke cautiously. She did not want to antagonise him any more than was necessary. 'But I think I'll consider it for a while, if you don't mind. And I may take up Mr Abercrombie's offer of advice. I'd like to know exactly what I might be able to do.'

'Consider it? But there's nothing to consider. And you don't need Abercrombie's advice. You have me to look after your interests.'

'I know that, Alfred, and I'm grateful. But I'd like to hear what he has to say, all the same.'

'Well, you must do as you think fit, of course,' Alfred said coldly. 'But if you must consult a lawyer, though I can't imagine why you should think it necessary, you'd do better to go to my own man, Andrew Sinclair. He's sound enough. I don't think Abercrombie's at all suitable. A slippery customer, that's my impression of him.'

'I thought he was an extremely nice man.'

'Oh, I daresay you did, I daresay you did. Covered in charm. All that bowing and scraping over your hand, and all that kow-towing! He summed you up in a glance, that's plain to see. A little old-world gallantry goes a long way with impressionable young ladies, and he knows it. Fortunately, I know it too, and I'm not prepared to stand by and see you rooked, my dear.'

'Rooked? But—'

'Rooked,' he repeated firmly. 'Why, the man came here determined to twist you round his little finger – and seems to have succeeded, too. Don't you realise, Rowena, that you'll pay, and pay through the nose, for every minute of that man's time? He knows just how much money you've got. Of course he's willing to advise you what to do with it! He'll advise you as much as you like, until you've spent the entire amount sitting in his office being advised. Lawyers are all the same – out to separate fools from their money.'

'Including your man Andrew Sinclair, I suppose,' Rowenna said with a flash of sarcasm. 'I'm sorry, Alfred, but I didn't think Mr Abercrombie was like that at all. He seemed a very genuine man to me, and I trust him—'

'More than you trust me?'

The question hung on the air. Both had stopped and were standing on the path between two rows of tall, dark conifers, facing each other. Rowenna looked up into her husband's face. She was conscious of her own anger, rising as they had talked, and of her fear of him and his power over her.

'Are you saying, Rowenna,' Alfred said, his voice as cold as an Arctic wind, 'that you trust a fly-by-night solicitor more than you trust me – your own husband?'

Rowenna felt the colour leave her cheeks. His black eyes bored into hers. His hand was still on her arm, gripping it with fingers of bone. The muscle was flicking rapidly in his cheek, and she could see his nostrils flaring slightly as he breathed.

'It's not a matter of trust,' she said at last. 'I just want to know what options Mr Abercrombie has to suggest.'

'Options!' He spat the word out as if it were some noxious medicine. 'A fine, grand-sounding word! And with no meaning whatsoever.'

'It means choices.'

'Exactly. And let me remind you, Rowenna, that you *have* no choices. You're a married woman, and as your husband I have certain rights over your conduct, never mind some footling little Act of Parliament passed to protect a few trinkets and gewgaws. Don't let a bumbling country lawyer like Abercrombie bamboozle you. That Act was never intended to be applied to large sums of money and land in foreign countries—'

'Canada is hardly a foreign country.'

'It's not Britain,' he returned with undisputable truth. 'People there think and behave differently from us, as we've had amply demonstrated this morning. Nobody would expect a young inexperienced woman like yourself to deal with the problems that are bound to arise, particularly when she has a husband to take care of them for her. And now let's hear no more of the matter, Rowenna. Let's enjoy this beautiful sunshine instead.'

He drew her hand through his arm again and began to walk on along the path. Unable to resist without using real force, Rowenna walked beside him. But her anger was still smouldering and after a moment or two, she said, 'I'm sorry, Alfred, but I believe that I do have a choice. So far, all I know is that I have land and money. I can't just leave it at that. I shall go and see Mr Abercrombie and ask his advice. There must be some good use to which it can be put.'

'Well, of course there is!' he expostulated. 'Don't you understand, you little fool? It's right under your nose. We have a business to run, don't we? A paper mill! Or had you forgotten that that was where your livelihood came from? The money will be invested in the new pulpmill. And the forest in Canada will provide the timber.'

Rowenna stopped. She dragged her hand away from his arm and stared at him. The warmth seemed to have fled from the sun, leaving her as cold as ice, and for a moment or two she seemed to have lost the ability to breathe. Then her lungs dragged the air back into her body and she felt the blood surge through her veins.

'So I'm a little fool, am I?' she said, her voice ragged. 'And you want my money and land for your mill? And how much would I see of it then? What would you allow me? A trinket or two for my birthday and at Christmas? And the freedom to walk in the garden of a morning – provided you don't require me for anything else? No more, in fact, than what I have now.'

'And what more do you require?' he demanded. 'You have every comfort here, Rowenna, everything a woman could desire. What do you need money for? What else could you ask?'

'My own bedroom, for one thing,' she retorted, past caring now what she said to him, nor what the consequences might be. 'My own bedroom, as far away from yours as possible, and with a good stout lock on the door!'

Alfred Boothroyd drew in a sharp breath. His eyes narrowed and his nostrils flared wide. He looked like a bull about to charge. He even lowered his head slightly, and Rowenna took a step back, suddenly afraid. But he did not move. Instead, he said in a voice like broken glass, 'I don't think you know what you're saying, madam. You're hysterical. It's not to be wondered at – it's that damn fool lawyer's fault, bursting in here and blurting out such news without warning me first and giving me time to prepare you for the shock. I think you had better return to your bed – *our* bed – and rest. That will give you time to think over what has happened and then no doubt you'll wish to apologise for your ill-considered outburst.'

'I shan't,' Rowenna said flatly. 'I shall never apologise for what I've just said. I meant it, every word.'

'I think not, Rowenna,' he said warningly.

'I did. Every word.' She lifted her head and faced him challengingly. 'Especially the ones about the lock. I don't want to share my bed with you any more, Alfred. I never did, but I thought it was my duty. Now—'

'And so it was your duty!' he thundered. 'It was your wifely duty, the duty you promised before God and a church full of witnesses to carry out. And it's your duty still, and will remain so for as long as I have use for you . . . My God, if this is what a little money can do to a woman . . . ! It's gone straight to your head, Rowenna, that's plain to see. No wonder men have always sought to keep power out of the hands of women!'

'Yes,' she said quietly, 'no wonder. But that will change, Alfred. You spoke of the movement to enfranchise women in New Zealand. And Mr Abercrombie told us this morning about the Married Women's Property Act. I wonder just how many women know about that Act – and how many men have made sure they wouldn't find out. But we *shall* find out, Alfred, and we shall keep control of what is right-fully ours. And as long as there are men like you in this world, we shall need to!'

His normally pale face was suffused with blood. She saw his hands clench and unclench at his sides, and felt another tremor of fear. But Alfred Boothroyd would surely not attack her here – not in the garden, where they might at any moment be interrupted. As for later, she would face that when she came to it.

'You forget yourself, Rowenna,' he rasped. 'You are quite out of your mind. I wonder if I oughtn't to call Doctor Cooper. Perhaps he would be able to persuade you to behave in a more rational manner. I'm sure he would agree with me that bed-rest is the best thing for you in your present state.'

'I doubt it,' she said, though she felt a twinge of disquiet at the suggestion. 'I'm as strong as a horse and he knows it.'

'Well, that remains to be seen. There's more than one kind of illness. I should hate to see you deteriorate until there was need for more drastic treatment—'

'What do you mean? What kind of treatment?'

'Well, I'm hardly qualified to say, my dear,' he said, showing his teeth. 'But I've heard that hysteria in young women – particularly young women who have suffered a sudden shock – can rapidly degenerate into — well, what can only be described as lunacy. And it's a sad thing, but there's often no cure—'

Rowenna gasped. '*Lunacy*! Alfred, you can't possibly be suggesting—'

'Of course I'm not suggesting anything, my dear,' he said soothingly. 'You've simply become a little overwrought. It's your birthday – your twenty-first birthday, too – you've had a considerable shock this morning and somehow or other we've got ourselves involved in a silly argument over nothing. I'm quite certain that with some peace and quiet and proper care, you'll be as well as you've ever been. Now, let's finish our walk and then you can have your rest, and we'll have no more talk of doctors, hmmm? And no more talk of separate rooms, either.'

He took her arm again. Rowenna followed at his side, her mind reeling. How had they ever managed to argue themselves into this dizzying circle? Doctors – lunacy – what had she said or done to warrant such terrible suggestions?

Only wanted to be myself, she thought miserably. Only wanted to be allowed to own what is rightfully mine. But it seems that husbands still have the upper hand. An Act of Parliament still has no power compared with the act of marriage.

Was this what her mother had suffered? Was this why she had gone to such lengths to make sure her daughter inherited the land and the money – enough to grant her freedom from Warren Mellor? But she didn't know I'd be married by now, Rowenna thought sadly. She didn't know I'd be in the same dreadful trap.

'Why, look who's come to visit us,' Alfred said suddenly as they rounded a corner. 'Matilda, how pleasant to see you. Have you come to wish Rowenna a happy birthday?'

Matilda Mellor was walking towards them. She wore a grey cotton dress, its fullness gathered back into ruching that swayed behind her as she walked with small, restricted steps along the path. Her bonnet had a large brim that shaded her plump face from the sun, and she carried a grey silk parasol.

'Good morning, Alfred. I thought I heard your voices. It sounded almost as if you were arguing! But I'm sure that couldn't be so, not on such a beautiful morning.' Her small eyes stared inquisitively at them. 'And how are you this morning, Rowenna? Your father tells me you're to be congratulated on becoming twenty-one.'

'Yes, Matilda. Thank you.' Rowenna glanced at Alfred. He was smiling urbanely. 'Is my father well this morning?'

'Oh yes. He's gone to the mill as usual. He thought you might have called over to see him before he started. I think he was a little disappointed that you didn't. Perhaps you'll come at lunch-time. I don't like him to feel neglected.'

'Yes. I will.' There was a tiny silence, then Rowenna said politely. 'Well, I think I'll go indoors now, Alfred, as you suggested. I've a hundred things to do.' She gave her stepmother a small, tight smile and walked rapidly away along the path, leaving brother and sister together.

And now they'll talk about me! she thought with irritation. She knew that they discussed almost everything, and

225

Alfred would certainly tell his sister about Mr Abercrombie's visit and the inheritance. His cold fury would be fuelled by her sycophantic concern, and by the time she had gone back to Ashbank he would be more than ready to vent it. And Rowenna knew that he was quite capable of taking her straight upstairs to her bedroom to give her the punishment that he no doubt believed she deserved.

Well, that must be faced later. For now, she was determined not to go indoors at all, but to stay outside, out of reach of his anger. She needed time to think about all that had happened, time to assimilate it and decide what to do next.

If only she could have spoken to Mr Abercrombie alone. In that tubby, rather comical little man with his bright, shrewd blue eyes, she had felt she had an ally. More than that, he had actually known – and obviously liked – her mother. And he had kept her secret for eleven years and more.

I'll go and see him in Kendal, she thought. Alfred can't keep me locked up. Next time I go shopping, I'll find his office and ask him what I should do.

Heartened by this decision, she walked rapidly on until she came to the little footbridge across the river. She paused. Her father had expressed a wish to see her. It was not a visit she would have made altogether willingly, but it would keep her out of Alfred's way a little longer. And after all, he was her father, and it was her birthday. Why not call and see him? It might even be a chance to mend the breach between them.

Quickly, she stepped across the bridge and into the mill yard. Matilda had said he was in his office. Very well, then, she would visit him there. She had never done so before, for he had been positive in his assertion that it was not a fit place for a young girl. But I'm not a young girl now, she thought. I'm twenty-one years old and a married woman. I can decide for myself.

But before she could turn along the path which led to the mill yard, she heard a voice call her name.

'Miss Rowenna – I mean, Mrs Boothroyd! Oh, I'm glad to see you.'

Rowenna turned quickly. John Richmond was walking swiftly towards her, his face wreathed in smiles. She stared at him and then remembered Molly's baby – but it wasn't due yet, surely? Another month, at least.

'It's come,' he said breathlessly, coming to a standstill. 'The babby – it came last night. And Moll's been fretting about you ever since. Would you have a moment to step in and see her, d'you think?'

'Why, of course.' Her father, Alfred, even her inheritance, were momentarily forgotten. 'I'll go down to the cottage at once. Is she well? Is the baby well? Surely it's early – is it very small?'

John grinned a little shamefacedly. 'Well, no, it's not too small. Pretty big, as it happens, considering . . .' He gave her a quick glance and she realised to her surprise that he was blushing. She felt her own cheeks colour. 'And they're both doing fine,' he continued hastily. 'It's just that she seems to hev got summat in her head about you – can't seem to rest proper.'

'Oh, poor Molly.' They were at the end of the vegetable garden now, approaching the cottage. 'But – John – you haven't told me what it is. What have you got – a son or a daughter?'

'It's a boy,' he told her, his smile breaking out again. 'A fine, lusty little boy.' He glanced back through the garden. 'Look, I'll hev to go back to me work now, you go in, miss, Ma's there and she'll take you up to see Moll.'

Alice Richmond opened the door, her face lighting up

with pleasure at the sight of Rowenna.

'Miss Rowenna – Mrs Boothroyd, I mean – come in, do. Molly's bin wondering when you'd come. I told her you'd be here as soon as you could manage it, but she's bin fretting herself something sorry.'

She led Rowenna up the narrow stairs to the tiny bedroom, where Molly lay in a double bed. At the sound of the door opening, she sat up and brushed her hair back from her face. She gazed at Rowenna and the colour flooded her cheeks.

'Oh, miss.' Molly had never accustomed herself to calling Rowenna by her correct title, and Rowenna would have disliked it if she had. 'It's so long since you bin down here. I was afraid summat was up.'

'I'm sorry, Molly. I didn't mean to neglect you—' Rowenna began, but Molly brushed aside her apology.

'It don't matter about me, miss. It was you I was worried about. Sit down on that chair there, and tell me how you are. It's your birthday today, innit.'

'Yes. But that's not important.' Rowenna leaned over and kissed the girl who had been her maid and friend for so long. 'You've had a baby. Aren't you going to let me see him?'

Molly hesitated. 'Oh – yes. He's out in the garden just now. John's mum believes in fresh air and a bit of sunshine, and I reckon she's right about that. I just wish she'd let me get up and go out there too – I don't want to be laying about in bed, I feel as fit as a fiddle.'

'You stay there and rest while you can,' Rowenna advised her. 'There'll be more than enough to do once you're up. You won't get another rest like this for a while!'

Molly grinned. 'That's just what John's mum says.' She hesitated again, looking down at her fingers which were pleating the rough cotton sheet. 'Before you see the baby, miss—'

Mrs Richmond's step sounded on the narrow stairs and both girls turned their heads as the door opened. The older woman stood there, beaming at them both, and in her arms she held a bundle of white.

'Here he is,' she said, her voice filled with pride. 'I knew Miss Rowenna would want to see him so I brought him up for you to show off yourself. He's bin awake these past five minutes, and quiet as a lamb, the little treasure.'

Molly gave Rowenna a swift glance. Then she pulled back the shawl which covered the baby's face. Rowenna bent and gazed down at it.

The baby had black, curling hair and dark brows. Its face, quite uncrumpled, was brown, almost suntanned. But he's only been outside an hour or two, she thought foolishly. And then he opened his eyes.

Rowenna stared at him. The eyes that looked back at her, steady and unwinking, were not blue, like those of most new-born babies. They were brown. Dark brown. They were eyes she had seen before, looking into hers, with love and passion.

Kester's eyes.

Kester's baby.

She turned her head and met Molly's gaze. The girl's face was full of sorrow and pity and apology, but there was a hint of defiance there too, as if she were telling Rowenna that there was little use in anger or pain, that this was the situation and nothing could change it. And Rowenna remembered that last night, when she had sent Molly up to the shepherd's hut with the message that Rowenna was not coming away with him. And Molly had tried to tell her what had happened, but Rowenna had been too full of her own troubles to understand.

Molly and Kester had conceived this child on that August night, when it should have been Rowenna who lay in his arms, and Rowenna who conceived his son.

* * *

The mill was busy as she walked through the doors, and she stood for a moment sniffing the damp atmosphere and covering her ears against the sudden roar of the machinery. The great fourdriniers were in full production, sending their giant, everlasting paperchain the length of the building. Steam rose in clouds and water dripped on the floor as the web of pulp was pressed between the hot rollers, and she remembered how she had stood here with Haddon, feeling the excitement of watching huge vats of porridge-like pulp turn into smooth sheets of paper. She looked up at the gallery that ran along the upper floor where the vats stood open, blinking away sudden tears at the thought of her brother. It was over a year now since they had stood here together, yet she missed him still. Surely if he had lived, she would never have been forced to marry Alfred Boothroyd; if he had lived, her father's business would never have foundered.

And would she have found Kester again? Would he have returned? Even if not, when she came into her inheritance, would she have left her father and gone to search for him?

Everything happens too late, she thought. And now Molly has Kester's child, and I – what do I have?

She turned abruptly, determined to put her troubles behind her. She had come here to see her father. Perhaps there was a bridge to be mended here, a way into his heart. Nodding and smiling at the men who turned to watch her in astonishment, she walked quickly along the building until she came to the door of her father's office. Here, a row of clerks on high stools scratched busily away at their ledgers. They too looked up as she entered, and Grandison slipped off his stool and came forward. But Rowenna waved him aside and he went back to his place.

Everyone was busy, as usual. But when she walked into Warren Mellor's inner room, she saw to her surprise that he was sitting morosely at an empty desk, a bottle of brandy and a half-full glass the only items before him.

'Father!' She stopped abruptly, then recollected herself and closed the door.

He started and looked up, and she saw that his eyes were already bleary. At eleven in the morning! She stared at him dumbly.

'Rowenna? What are you doing here?'

Rowenna sat down in a chair. She leaned her arm on the desk and searched her father's face. He looked pale and haggard, with red-rimmed eyes, and his whiskers were unkempt and straggling.

'I came to see you, Father. Matilda told me you were expecting me. It's my birthday.' She gazed at him in concern. 'Father, what's the matter? Are you ill again?'

'Ill? No, I'm not ill. Never better.' Almost as if he were too weary to raise his arm, he slid his hand along the desk to his glass, picked it up and drank. 'Ah, that's good.'

Rowenna looked at the bare desk. 'Haven't you any work to do, Father? You used to have papers everywhere—'

'And how would you know that?' he demanded with a return of his old fire. 'You weren't supposed to come here. I suppose you tormented Haddon into bringing you. Well, whatever my desk was like it was nothing to do with you, d'you understand?'

'Yes, Father, of course I understand,' she said placatingly. 'And I never pried into your papers, I promise you. But now there's nothing. Surely Alfred hasn't taken over the running of both mills?'

'Both mills?' he said with a short, bitter laugh. 'Don't you realise, Rowenna, there's only one mill now, and that's his. This building' – he waved his arm and almost knocked the brandy bottle off the desk – 'this is all part of his little empire now. He's got us all tied up together. You, me, that

231

sister of his – the three of us. Hamstrung.' He took another long swallow of brandy.

Rowenna watched him in alarm. How much had he drunk that morning? How much did he drink each day? What was happening to him?

'Father, are you sure you're feeling quite well? You know what Doctor Cooper said—'

'Cooper's an old woman. I've said so before. Anyway, how else am I supposed to pass my time? That husband of yours won't let me do a thing.'

'If he doesn't, it must be for your own good,' Rowenna said, wondering uneasily if she could believe this. 'He knows the doctor told you not to overtax your strength. Obviously he's taken on some of your work in order to spare you. Wouldn't it be better if you stayed at home and rested, instead of coming in here?'

'Stay at home? *Rest*?' Again, Warren gave that short, bitter laugh. 'Rowenna, you don't know what you're saying. How can I rest at home, with that woman forever nagging at me and chivvying me about from one room to the next?' He put on a high, falsetto voice. ' "Don't sit in that chair, Warren, your clothes will dirty the cushions. Don't take your clutter in there, Warren, the maids have only just cleaned it." Or are about to clean it,' he said in his ordinary voice. 'Or else visitors are expected – or have only just gone. No matter what time of day it is, or what's going on, there's always some damned reason why I can't go into the rooms in my own house. And when I am permitted to sit in a chair I bought and paid for, it's no better. "Sit up straight, Warren. Please don't put your feet up in that unmannerly way, Warren. How *can* you come into my presence looking like that, Warren?" It's do this, don't do that, from morning till night, till I think I could strangle her. No wonder her first husband died early – it was probably the only way he could think of to get out of reach of her everlasting nagging tongue!'

Rowenna gazed at him. How did a woman managed to gain such mastery over her husband, she wondered. Particularly such a husband as Warren. But perhaps it was more to do with Alfred and the mill than the force of Matilda's personality. If what her father had told her before was true, only their intervention had saved him from the workhouse. And Matilda had made her own quite substantial contribution. Perhaps that was enough to bring even a man like her father to heel.

She wondered fleetingly whether her own sudden good fortune might have the same effect on Alfred, then quickly dismissed the thought. No. Living like that, having power over her husband and watching him degenerate into a whining creature such as Warren Mellor was turning into, would give her no pleasure at all.

As if her thoughts had triggered a memory in her father's brain, he looked at her with sudden sharpness across the desk.

'There was a man looking for you this morning,' he said abruptly. 'Lawyer feller. Didn't know you were married. I sent him over to see Alfred.'

'I know. He's a Mr Abercrombie, from Kendal. He – he brought me some good news.' She hesitated, wondering whether to tell her father. He was bound to find out, of course, but she was uneasy about the effect it would have on him, especially in his present condition. But he was frowning interrogatively now, and she knew she would have to tell him. 'Father, I've inherited some land and some money from Mother.'

Warren gaped at her. 'Land? Money? You've inherited land and money? From your *mother*?'

'Yes, Father.' She hesitated, reluctant to tell him how

233

much. But there was little point in keeping it secret. He would hear anyway, from Alfred. 'It was held in trust for me by my grandfather, until I was twenty-one.'

'A thousand a year? But – but—' Warren seemed to be having difficulty in speaking. He gulped down some more brandy and coughed. 'But that's enough to live on! Quite comfortably, too.'

'Yes, I suppose it is,' Rowenna said wonderingly. Events had taken place so quickly that morning that she had not yet had time to reckon up the value of the money she was to receive.

Warren was frowning again. The surprise seemed to have cleared his mind and there was a calculating look in his eyes.

'That's a useful sum,' he said musingly. 'A very useful sum.'

'I've already discussed it with Alfred,' Rowenna said quickly. 'Mr Abercrombie has offered to advise me on what to do with it, and I want to consider all the possibilities—'

'Possibilities! I would have thought Alfred would have known exactly what you should do with it. What does *he* think of your going to see this lawyer feller?'

'He thinks I should take advice from Andrew Sinclair,' Rowenna said. 'But he really wants me to give it to him to use for the mill.'

'I should just think he does!' Warren said with a short bark of mirthless laughter. 'I should just think he does . . . And he's your husband, so of course that's what you'll have to do. The money may have been left to you, but in law it belongs to him.'

'It belongs to me,' Rowenna said stubbornly. 'It was left to me. And it belongs to me *in law*. There was an Act of Parliament four years ago, Father, which said that married women *could* have their own money and property. Mr Abercrombie told me about this morning. Alfred can't use it unless I give him permission.'

234

'Which, of course, you'll do. Parliament might have passed a law but that won't affect a husband's rights. You promised to "obey", didn't you? Well then.' He paused and stared gloomily at the brandy bottle. 'Not that that has much effect on some women!'

'I shall have to see Mr Abercrombie about it,' Rowenna said hesitantly. She had not thought of this aspect and she didn't think Alfred had, either – but she knew it would occur to him sooner or later. His mind was too sharp and devious to miss something like that.

Warren was sunk in thought. She looked at him and wondered again what was happening to him. For a moment, she felt a pang of her old pity, but it faded at once. Wasn't it his own fault? He had let the business slide so that Alfred Boothroyd could take it over, he had virtually sold her to his neighbour as part of the deal, and if he had made a disastrous mistake in his own marriage, he had nobody but himself to blame. And at least he didn't have to suffer the brutalities and humiliation of the marriage bed.

'That money,' Warren said suddenly. 'That money was left to you by your mother.'

'Yes.' She spoke warily, sensing something unwelcome in his tone.

'She must have made her will before 1875. You say this new Act was passed only four years ago?'

'Yes, but—'

'Well, then,' he said triumphantly, 'by rights it belonged to me! And if anyone has the right to decide how it should be used, I do. Your mother never had any right to keep that money from me, let alone make a will about it. Why, that damned lawyer ought to be prosecuted for taking such instructions! He must have known very well they were unlawful! I'll see him in court, damned if I don't!'

Rowenna stared at him, sick with horror. Could it be right? Could the money and the land still be taken from her,

235

if not by Alfred then by her father? She saw her one chance of freedom slipping away from her and knew that she must see James Abercrombie and find out the true situation.

'Father – you can't do that. The money's been left to me. You can't prosecute Mr Abercrombie simply for drawing up a will.' She had no idea whether she was correct, but she spoke only from her own ideas of rightness and logic. 'In any case,' she added, grasping at what might be no more than a straw but could be a trump card, 'it would cost too much. All the money would be used up in the lawsuit.'

Warren's small, bleary eyes narrowed with calculation. He stroked his whiskers thoughtfully. I wish I hadn't come here, Rowenna thought. I wish I hadn't told him. But he would have had to know. There was no way in which it could have been kept from him.

'Rowenna.' His tone had changed. It was soft, almost wheedling. 'Let's not argue about this. You're my daughter. The money belonged to your mother – to my wife. One thing's certain, it was never Alfred Boothroyd's, and neither of us wants him to get his hands on it – isn't that right?'

'Yes, but—'

He reached a hand across the desk and laid it over hers. 'Tell me, Rowenna, are you happy in this marriage? I've thought once or twice that – well, I'd find it hard to forgive myself if I'd made a mistake over your life, as well as over my own.'

Rowenna looked at him uncertainly. Never before had she heard her father admit to a mistake. And had he really been worried over her marriage? Had he really been feeling guilty over his behaviour? She felt a softening, a sudden hint of warmth.

'Are you unhappy, child?'

Tears came into her eyes. She looked down at their hands and whispered, 'Yes. Oh, Father, I'm so unhappy!'

236

'Then isn't our way clear before us? You have this money and this land, left to you by your mother. Enough to live on. Enough for us both to live on. We could go away together – buy a small house somewhere, far away from here, where Alfred will never find us. You'll have your freedom, and you'll be able to look after me.' His wheedling tone changed gradually to a whine. 'You were right, Rowenna – I'm not well. I'll never be as well as long as that woman's living in my house. She's killing me, Rowenna, killing me. But you can save me now – you can save your old father.' His hand was clutching hers tightly, almost crushing her fingers. 'You're a good daughter, Rowenna, you've always been a good daughter to me. And I've been a good father, too, haven't I? I've always looked after you as a father should, I've fed and clothed and educated you, I've done my best for you always. You'll look after me now, won't you? Say you will. Say you'll do it . . .'

The sick horror returned and gushed over her so violently that she thought she would actually retch. She dragged her hand away and leapt to her feet, backing away from the desk as if it harboured a venomous snake. She stared at him, at the pitiable figure he presented as he slumped over his desk, half drunk, his skin bloated and pasty, his eyes wet with self-pity, and she felt nothing but repugnance.

'You don't care about me at all,' she whispered. 'You ask me if I'm unhappy, but you don't really care. All you're thinking about is yourself and the mess you're in. Well, that's not my fault. You threw me to Alfred Boothroyd as if you were throwing me to a den of lions and you never cared what happened to me, so long as you got what you wanted. I had to marry him to save you from the workhouse, remember? And now you're drinking yourself to death instead. You say Alfred's taken the mill away from you – well, much as I hate him, I don't blame him for you'd have dragged him into bankruptcy along with yourself if he'd given you the chance. And you'd drag me there too. No, I won't use my money to keep you in comfort while you sit slobbering over a bottle of brandy! Mother left me that money because she'd lived with you long enough herself to know that I'd need it – although she didn't know how badly I'd need it. And I'll use it as I believe she meant me to use it – to go to Canada and see my land, and my family there, and make my own life.' She lifted her head proudly, feeling a sudden rush of excitement and power. 'That's what I'll do – and neither you nor Alfred nor anyone else will stop me!'

Without waiting to see the effect of her words, she turned on her heel and stalked from the room. Outside, the clerks hastily bent their heads and began to scribble furiously. Grandison looked at her, his face burning. She realised that they must have heard every word.

It didn't matter. They could all come crowding into the room to listen and it wouldn't have mattered. She gave them a brilliant smile and marched through the office, past the fourdriniers with their endless procession of paper, and out into the fresh morning air.

Warren's pony and trap were standing in the mill yard. Thomas, his driver, stood leaning on the shafts and chatting to one of the grooms. They looked up as Rowenna strode towards them, and jumped to attention, touching their caps respectfully.

'Good morning, Thomas, good morning, Samuel. Thomas, I need to make a visit to Kendal urgently. Will you take me in the trap? My father won't be needing you this morning.'

'To Kendal, miss – I mean, Mrs Boothroyd? It'll be a pleasure.' The driver, who had known Rowenna since she was a baby, gave her a friendly grin. 'It's a long time since I've had the pleasure of driving you anywhere, miss – oh, there I go again – and might I be permitted to wish you a happy birthday? Where do you want to go?'

'Thank you, Thomas.' Rowenna clambered up into the trap and settled herself at the front, where she had sat so many times with Haddon and often been allowed to take the reins herself. Well, this morning she had reins of a different kind to handle – the reins of her own life. And she was determined not to relinquish them.

She sat proudly in the driving seat and lifted the reins in her hands. Thomas grinned at the groom and climbed up beside her. Rowenna gave the pony his order and they clattered out of the yard.

'We're going to Stricklandgate,' she said. 'To the offices of Mr James Wilson Abercrombie.'

Alfred was, as might be expected, coldly furious.

'I told you go to indoors and rest,' he said. 'Instead, you go careering off to Kendal without my permission and hobnob with a lawyer I have already advised you to have no more to do with. And I gather you were over at your father's mill, interfering with his work and upsetting him too. It seems to me that you've completely taken leave of your senses, Rowenna. I shall have to consider again calling Doctor Cooper.'

'There's no need,' she said crisply, 'I'm perfectly well. And I'd already told you that I intended to consult Mr Abercrombie over my inheritance—'

'We discussed the matter fully,' he interrupted. 'I thought I'd made it quite clear to you that a husband's rights—'

'You told me what you wanted me to believe. I wanted to find out what the situation really was.'

'Are you calling me a liar?' he demanded in a terrible voice, beginning to rise to his feet.

'I think you may have been mistaken. After all, you yourself said you hadn't heard of the Married Women's Property Act until this morning—'

'I said no such thing! I told you, it was intended merely to apply to a few personal possessions, not major items—'

'And you were mistaken,' Rowenna said quietly. 'It applies to *property*, Alfred. Money, land, houses, jewellery ... property. It applies to the inheritance my mother left me. It's my money, Alfred, and my land, and nobody can take it away from me.'

He stared at her in silence. The tic was jumping in his cheek. She sensed the repressed violence in him and trembled a little. What would happen if he lost control? Brutal though he was in bed, he had never struck her. But neither had she ever made him angry.

'Is this what that slyboots of a lawyer has told you this morning? I thought I told you to go to Andrew Sinclair if you needed advice. I'd have willingly taken you to his office myself, or better still had him call on you here. There was no need to go rushing off in that deceitful manner, giving your father's servants food for gossip. And paying for bad advice.'

'Mr Abercrombie didn't ask me for a penny.'

'No, he'll send the bill to me. And a very pretty penny it will be too, I've no doubt,' he said grimly. 'Well, you'd better tell me exactly what he said. Provided you have done nothing silly, such as signing more papers, there shouldn't be too much harm done.'

Rowenna looked at him. James Abercrombie had said a good deal that morning as they sat in his office with its windows looking out towards the mountains of Langdale. But she wasn't prepared to tell Alfred all that they'd talked of.

Mr Abercrombie had been surprised to see her, but ushered her into his office with a beaming smile and an order to his clerk to bring fresh coffee at once. He had brought forward a chair, dusted off its seat, and urged Rowenna to make herself comfortable. Then he returned to his own chair behind his desk, placed his elbows on the leather-covered surface, laced his fingers together and gazed at her with bright, interrogative eyes.

'You were very prompt to take up my offer of advice, Mrs Boothroyd. Very prompt indeed. I confess, I did not expect to see you again for some time.'

'I decided it was essential,' Rowenna said, and accepted a cup of coffee from the clerk, who bowed and withdrew. 'My husband and my father both have very definite ideas as to what I should do with my inheritance. Or even if I have a right to it.'

'Oh, you have a right to it, there's no doubt about that. From the moment you signed my documents this morning, the money was yours. You can spend it all before lunchtime if you like – though I wouldn't advise you to do such a thing!'

Rowenna smiled. 'But my father says that as my mother made her will before 1875 – that's when she died – the property would have been his. He says she had no right to leave it to anyone. And he says my husband will tell me that, as I promised to obey him during the marriage service, I will have to do what he tells me with it.' She gazed helplessly at the lawyer's rosy face. 'One tells me this and the other tells me that, and I don't know which is right or what I should do. I'm almost beginning to wish that Mother had never left me the money!'

'Oh, come, you don't mean that,' Mr Abercrombie said soothingly. 'Why, if all you say is true, it seems to me that this inheritance is just what you need.' He paused and added delicately, 'Ladies sometimes have to look after themselves, you know. One can't always rely on those we feel should have our best interests at heart. And if you're fortunate enough to have the kind of income that will give you a measure of independence . . .'

241

'But have I? Are they right? Could my father make a legal claim on my inheritance? And if not, can my husband insist that I put it into the business or at least allow him to invest it for me?'

'Please, please.' The little lawyer held up his hand. 'One question at a time, my dear. Now let's take them in order.' He ticked them off on his fingers as he spoke. 'One: yes, you do certainly have an income which would enable you to live independently if you so chose. Two: I can't tell you if your father and husband are right in what they claim unless I know exactly what those claims are. We may discover that in due course. Three: your father can definitely *not* make a legal claim on your inheritance. You see, even if he were correct about that, your mother was very careful to make provision against such a claim. The money and the land were never actually hers. They were held in trust for her by her father, in Canada, and passed on to you by him. There is no question of that property ever being part of your father's estate.' He paused again and looked straight into Rowenna's eyes. 'I drew up the documents myself,' he said, 'and both your mother and myself were most careful – *most* careful – to ensure that it was so.'

Rowenna read the message in his glance and bit her lip. 'My mother must have been very unhappy, to have been so anxious to do that,' she said quietly.

'She never discussed her happiness or otherwise with me,' James Abercrombie said, 'but I was concerned to do whatever she wanted.'

No, Rowenna thought, looking at his kindly face, she wouldn't have needed to discuss it. But you knew. And you know now, about me.

Mr Abercrombie looked at his hands. One finger was still held out and he stared at it for a moment, then recollected himself.

'As for your fourth point, that your husband can still order you to hand your inheritance over to him, to use as he thinks fit, I would maintain that the law of the land applies even over the demands of the marriage service. God,' he said sententiously, 'is not especially interested in finance.'

Rowenna stared at him and then burst into laughter. Mr Abercrombie maintained his serious expression for a moment longer, then allowed his face to relax into a thousand smiling creases.

'There, that's better!' he exclaimed. 'I've made you laugh. I was quite sad, my dear, to see such a pretty face solemn, and on your birthday, too. Especially when I'd brought such very good news. Now' – he leaned forward over his desk – 'tell me if I've disposed of all your worries, and we'll think about what you should do next.'

Rowenna hesitated. Alfred's suggestion in the garden seemed so outrageous that she felt hardly able to bring herself to mention it. But it was also so horrific, so terrifying, that she knew she must.

Mr Abercrombie was watching her keenly.

'There's something else troubling you, my dear. Tell me what it is.'

'It seems so silly—'

'It's all the sillier to keep it to yourself,' he said firmly. 'And if it's indeed silly, it will take no more than a moment to deal with it. What's the matter?'

Rowenna looked down at her hands. Her wedding ring gleamed dully. She opened her mouth to speak, but found her lips too dry. She licked them and tried again.

'It's just that – can you tell me, Mr Abercrombie, is it easy for a husband to have his wife certified? As a – a lunatic?' The word was out and she raised her eyes and gazed at him.

The lawyer stared at her. For a moment all humour left his face and he looked appalled. Hastily, Rowenna added,

'My husband hasn't suggested that he would do such a thing – only that I might be a little *overwrought*, or hysterical. But I – I—' She could not finish and looked down again at her hands, feeling the tears hot in her eyes.

'My dear,' James Abercrombie said gently, his voice filled with compassion, 'I cannot believe that any doctor would declare any such thing. And it could not be done without a doctor's consent. Nor without my knowledge.' There was a note in his voice which assured Rowenna that only over his dead body would she be declared insane. 'You have nothing to fear in that respect, nothing at all, you may be quite certain of that. But if ever you have reason to think otherwise – you'll come straight to me. Is that understood?'

Rowenna nodded thankfully. And her feeling that here was a friend in whom she could place complete trust was confirmed during the next hour, as they sat together in his sunlit office, drinking coffee and discussing her future. James Abercrombie, while never directly denigrating her husband, made it clear that he was perfectly well aware of what kind of man Alfred Boothroyd was, and what her life with him must be. He also knew Warren Mellor by repute (and presumably from Dorothy Mellor, twenty years earlier) and shook his head, tutting, when Rowenna told him of her father's plea that she should use her money to rescue him from his disastrous marriage.

Eventually, gathering up all her courage, she asked Mr Abercrombie if it was possible for her to use her money to go to Canada.

'Canada?' he said, looking at her sharply. 'Well, of course, there's no reason why you shouldn't use it for that as well as for any other purpose. In fact, it seems an excellent plan. You have relatives there, after all, who no doubt would be pleased to see you, and you have land. Er – would you be planning to ask Mr Boothroyd to accompany you?'

'Oh, no!' Rowenna exclaimed, and he smiled a little, then grew serious again.

'I could not, of course, advise you upon any course which might be construed as suggesting that you actually *leave* Mr Boothroyd. Not unless you have certain provocations. And so far you've given me no intimation of such things.'

Rowenna hesitated. What kind of provocation did a woman need, to leave her husband? More than Alfred had given her, she had no doubt. He had, after all, acted only as she supposed all husbands must. He had housed her, fed her, claimed his own conjugal rights . . . 'No,' she said reluctantly, 'I don't have the sort of provocation you mean. But—'

'I understand,' he said gently. 'I simply don't want to see you making your life more troublesome. Now, let's see . . . I don't think there could be any objection – in law – to your taking a long holiday to visit your family and see your land. In fact, it seems an eminently reasonable thing to do. And once at such a distance – well, you would have to assess the situation as you saw it then, wouldn't you?' He beamed again. 'Yes, I see no harm in that, no harm at all.'

'But how do I go about it? I've never travelled anywhere on my own. How does one buy tickets? Where do the ships go from – Liverpool, I suppose, but how would I get there?' Rowenna shook her head. 'Mr Abercrombie, do you think you could possibly find out for me—'

'But of course I can! Now, don't worry about a thing, Mrs Boothroyd. I can see to all that for you. And if you would prefer to communicate with me here, rather than my waiting on you at Meadowbank, why, that can easily be arranged.' His rosy face was wreathed in smiles. 'I'll assume you'll discuss all this with your husband, of course – I couldn't possibly advise you to do anything against his wishes – but that taken for granted, I'll do all I can to assist.

Anything you wish to know, anything at all, don't hesitate to let me know. A note dropped through my letter-box is all I need. And if you'd like to call in at any time when you're in town, I can let you know how things progress. Sailing times, what clothes and luggage you need – all that kind of thing. How does that seem to you?'

'It sounds wonderful. But — oh, Mr Abercrombie' – Rowenna twisted her hands together – 'how am I to do all that – buy new clothes and luggage – without my husband — I mean, without being troublesome at home? I don't want to annoy my husband when he has the mill to think of . . .'

'Of course not. Of course not.' The rosy face was creased with thought. 'I have it! You can order all deliveries to be made at my house. No' – he held up his hand again – 'it's no trouble at all, I assure you. Much more convenient for you. After all, you'll be leaving on the train from Kendal, I've no doubt, so why have everything taken out to Burneside only to be brought back again? And we've plenty of room for it, plenty of room. Yes, that's the answer.'

'Oh, Mr Abercrombie.' Rowenna's eyes filled with tears. 'Why are you being so good to me? You've only known me a few hours.'

It had not seemed possible for the ruddy cheeks to grow any redder, but redder they certainly became. The little lawyer coughed and turned his head aside for a moment. Then, wiping his own eyes with a large and spotless white handkerchief, he muttered, 'Not good at all. Not at all. Daughters of my own, all happily married, thank the good Lord. And a wife who's worth all the riches of Arabia. Besides, I knew your mother. Grew to admire her. She asked me to take care of you when the time came and I promised I would. Now it's come and I'm doing as she asked. That's all.'

'Well, I appreciate it very much,' Rowenna said sincerely. 'And I know my mother must have appreciated you too.' She got up and held out her hand. 'I'm really very grateful. And now I mustn't take up any more of your time. I'll have to go back home. I'll call in the next time I'm in Kendal, and see what news you have for me.'

'Yes, my dear. Do that. If I'm not here, my clerk will give you any messages I have, and you can always leave instructions with him, of course.' James Abercrombie took her hand and bent over it. He glanced at her again and seemed to think for a moment, then plunged his hand into his waistcoat pocket. 'Here, my dear, take this. It's my card, with my home address on it. If you're in any kind of trouble – or any doubt, any doubt at all – then you must come straight to us. My wife will be as pleased to receive you and give you any help as I will. Now, promise me that you won't hesitate.'

'Thank you,' Rowenna said, taking the card and looking at it. The letters blurred and swam before her eyes and she looked up at the kindly little lawyer again, her mouth trembling. 'Thank you very much indeed.'

James Abercrombie saw her out into the street and she climbed back into the waiting trap. Thomas headed the pony towards home and she twisted in her seat once to wave to the lawyer before they turned a corner and out of sight.

She did not relish the thought of facing Alfred or her father when she arrived home again, but at least she was certain now, both of her own ground and of her plans for the future. And her certainty was all the more because she believed that this morning had brought her a birthday present as valuable as the one her mother had left her.

She had found a friend.

* * *

247

Rowenna said nothing at first to Alfred of her plans to go to Canada, and for some time nothing could be done, as Warren was once again taken ill. This time, he took longer to recover and it was early in the spring of next year before she felt that she could carry out her intention.

Several times, he demanded that she go with him to see Andrew Sinclair, his own solicitor, before making any decisions. 'I'm sure Sinclair will advise you to allow your money to be invested sensibly in the family firm. It is, after all, exactly what I should do myself with such a windfall. I don't imagine many wives would stand by and see their father's and husband's – not to mention their own – livelihood ruined for want of a little extra capital. And the land may be useful too. A new source of timber, to provide wood for the pulpmill – it could be just what we're looking for. But Sinclair will tell you all this, since you insist on troubling yourself with such things.'

'I'm quite happy with Mr Abercrombie's advice, thank you, Alfred,' Rowenna said composedly.

'You may be, but I'm not!' His control was perilously near snapping, she thought with a thrill of fear. 'And you still haven't yet seen fit to tell me what advice he did give you on that madcap trip to his office on your birthday. I daresay he's got some high-falutin' scheme to part you from your money that seems more attractive to you!'

'Mr Abercrombie doesn't want to part me from my money. He wants to help me keep it.'

Alfred glared at her.

'And just what do you mean by that? Are you implying that I intend to steal it from you? I'm simply suggesting you *invest* it, Rowenna. It will still be yours.'

'Will it? I doubt if I'll ever see it again, once it is swallowed up by the mill.' She gazed at him steadily. 'I'm sorry, Alfred, but I am not going to let you invest my money. Nor am I going to visit Mr Sinclair. My mother intended me to keep my inheritance and use it as I wished, and that's what I mean to do.'

'And just how is that?' he demanded witheringly.

Rowenna met his eyes. Well, he'll have to know sometime, she thought. And the last time she had seen Mr Abercrombie, during a hasty visit made while on a shopping trip a day or two ago, he had told her that he thought he would be able to get a ticket for a berth on the next ship to leave Liverpool for Canada. It might be no more than a few days before she was away from Burneside, perhaps for ever.

'I'm going away,' she said, and then, recollecting Mr Abercrombie's warning, 'for a holiday. I thought I might visit some of my relatives.'

'Your relatives?' he said sharply. 'I understood you had no relatives in this country.'

'I haven't.'

There was a brief silence.

'Do I take it,' Alfred asked slowly, 'that you intend visiting *Canada*? Alone?'

'I thought it might be pleasant, yes.' Her heart was beating quickly. 'I know you're too busy to leave the mill to accompany me, Alfred, but it's not unusual for ladies to travel alone these days—'

'Not unusual? It's extremely unusual for a young married woman, especially one married for only a few months, to go gallivanting off to the other side of the world without her husband. I would advise you most strongly, Rowenna, to forget this ridiculous scheme.'

'There's nothing ridiculous about it,' she answered, keeping her voice calm. 'I simply want to go off on a holiday to see my relatives. I've a grandfather I've never met – uncles, aunts, cousins. I'm not asking you to pay for it, Alfred.'

At once, she saw that she had made a mistake in referring to her own financial independence. His nostrils flared again and small muscles contracted beneath his eyes.

'Then if you refuse to take my advice,' he said icily, 'I shall have no other course open but to refuse. I forbid you to go, Rowenna.'

'Forbid me?'

'You seem to have forgotten,' he said silkily, 'that as your husband I have the right to determine what you shall do and where you shall go. You are my wife. I require you here, at my side, and I will not have you rushing about all over the world, getting into God knows what kind of scrapes, on your own. It's quite unthinkable. And now I wish to hear no more of it.'

He stood up and prepared to walk out of the room. Rowenna leapt to her feet and rushed to stand in front of the door.

'No, Alfred! You can't forbid me. I may be your wife, but I'm not a prisoner, to be locked up in a cage and kept there. Even you don't have the right to do that. I shall go to Canada – and I shall probably stay there.' Her eyes blazed defiance at him. 'I can live without you, Alfred, and I know I shall live a great deal more happily!'

He took a deep breath and blew it out through his nostrils. His eyes showed white. His jaw tightened and he said in a voice in which the control was stretched as thin as a piece of fine elastic, 'I shall call Doctor Cooper to examine you, Rowenna. You're either mad, entranced or . . .' His eyes narrowed suddenly with calculation '. . . or perhaps in some other state. Is there anything you haven't told me?'

'Anything I haven't told you?' She looked at him, bewildered. 'Why, what do you mean?'

He snapped his fingers impatiently. 'You must know what I mean! There are certain functions of a woman's body, aren't there, certain *regular* functions. Have they been taking place?'

Rowenna's mind spun. Regular functions? He was talking about her monthly periods – what the girls at school had called the 'curse'. Blankly, she tried to recall when the last had been. It must have been during the last month. She racked her brains. And then remembered that it had been due a week before her birthday – almost a fortnight ago. And then, with dawning horror, that she had missed the one before that . . .

'I see they have not,' Alfred said, watching her face. 'You realise what this means, don't you, Rowenna?'

'I'm going to have a baby,' she whispered, appalled.

'A child,' he said coldly, as if the word 'baby' sounded too sentimental. 'You're going to have a child. *My* child.' He smiled, and she turned her face away from the sharp white teeth. 'There is no question, you realise, of travelling anywhere while you are in such a condition. And you will not have time, of course, once the child is born.'

'I'll go then,' she said, grasping at straws. 'I'll take my baby with me.'

'*My child*,' he said again. 'And you will not be permitted to do any such thing. No court in the land would allow it. In this case, at least, common sense still prevails. Wives who desert their husbands are not deemed to be fit mothers, Rowenna. And if it came to a court case, you would lose everything.'

Chapter Twelve

Pregnant.

Pregnant with *Alfred's child*.

Rowenna laid her hand over her flat stomach. Could it be true? Could it possibly be true? Surely I'm too thin, she thought. There can't be a baby in there. But she remembered Molly at her wedding, slender as a reed, and yet a month later her waistline was already noticeably thick, and then, in May, her baby had been born. Clearly she had been a good three months pregnant when she and John Richmond had gone to the altar, yet there had been no outward sign of it.

And if Rowenna were pregnant now . . . she looked at her calendar. She had missed twice – though even before that, the flow had been only scanty – so she must be approaching three months. But I've had no hint at all, she thought in panic, no sickness, nothing. Only, at times, a terrible fatigue. Molly had told her once that could be a sign.

Molly. Molly was the only person who could help her now. She could confide in Molly, tell her the fear that Alfred had put into her mind – perhaps even tell her how she had planned to run away, to Canada – and ask her if it could really be true that she was expecting a baby.

Rowenna had been lying on her bed since Alfred had gone back to the mill after dealing her his shock. He had told her to go and rest and for once she had felt like obeying his command. She had been shaking so much that she could barely climb the stairs, and when she had reached her room she had fallen on the bed and lain there, dry-eyed, too numb with horror to find the tears she knew she must weep.

Alfred's baby. Alfred's baby, growing inside her like a homunculus, a tiny replica of its father. Another Alfred, formed specifically to draw her back into the trap from which she had so nearly escaped, to keep her here for years – for the rest of her life.

For it wouldn't stop there, she knew. Once a woman began to conceive children she continued to do so for as long as her husband wished it, until she either grew too old to conceive again, or died. And many women died.

And Alfred had expressed a wish for children. Sons, who would follow him into the business. Now that he knew she was capable of conception, he would want what her father had described as a 'quiverful'. It was only common sense, when so many children died in infancy. Rowenna herself, when she visited her mother's grave in the little churchyard by the river, looked every week at the little row of head-stones that belonged to her own baby brothers and sisters.

Her father too was looking forward to his first grandchild. He had declared already that the eldest was to be named Haddon and he would want a say in the upbringing of the child who would inherit the business from both sides of the family. He would not now, she thought, encourage her to leave Alfred, even to keep himself comfortable in his old age.

The trap was closing its jaws around her more tightly than ever and she laid her hands on her stomach again. Who are you, she wondered, and what are you? What are you doing in my life?

254

And, as if it were answering her, the thought came clearly into her mind: *I am your child. Your baby. I shall need you more than I need anyone else in the world.*

Rowenna lay quite still. Until now, it had simply not occurred to her that the baby she might be carrying was not solely Alfred's. He had been so positive about it – '*You're going to have* my *child*' – that her own part in it had been swept aside. After all, she had felt no pleasure in its conception, no love or closeness for its father. But it *was* her child. It was growing inside *her* body, it would suckle at *her* breasts. Until now, she had thought of it as a miniature Alfred, like him in every respect. But in some respects it would resemble her. It might even look like her.

It might be a girl, she thought, and wondered if it would dare.

With a swift movement, Rowenna sat up and swung her legs over the side of the bed. She could not stay here a moment longer, wondering and worrying. She must have someone to talk to. And that someone must be Molly, the only close friend and confidante she had ever had. Molly, who would be able to tell her all about it . . .

During the past few months, when Rowenna's life had once more seemed to be set aside while others took precedence, the two girls had drawn even closer together. It had seemed at first, when Rowenna was faced with the evidence of Kester's betrayal, that things could never be the same again. But Molly had insisted that he had not betrayed her. 'It wasn't me he was loving that night,' she said over and over again. 'It was you. He wanted it to be you.' And Rowenna had come to believe her, though she still sensed a tiny reserve in the other girl's manner, as if there were something else that had never been said. But through the months of her father's illness and her husband's increasing demands, she had needed Molly's friendship too much to jeopardise it with further questions.

Nobody was about as she hurried over the little foot-bridge to Ashbank. She passed through the garden with scarcely a glance at the plants she had tended with such care, and went straight to the gardener's cottage.

Molly was alone with baby Jack, now nine or ten months old and beginning to stagger about, his strong, brown little hands clutching at chair legs to keep himself upright. He beamed at Rowenna and she lifted him into her arms, feeling the pang she always felt at the sight of his dark, gypsy face.

'It's good to see you, miss,' Molly said. 'I was just saying to John's mum, you hadn't bin round for a bit, and I wondered if there were anything up.' She looked critically at Rowenna's face. 'You're looking a bit peaky, if you don't mind me saying so.'

'There's something I want to ask you, Molly,' Rowena said. 'It – it's rather important.'

'There! I knew, soon's I saw you, there was summat up. And I've bin thinking about you this past fortnight.' Molly stretched out her hand and laid it on Rowenna's. 'Tell us all about it, love.'

Rowenna looked down, suddenly unable to speak. The warmth of Molly's hand was a painful reminder that she was seldom touched in that way these days, with affection and comfort. Alfred's body was cold and bony against hers, and when her father reached out his hand it was as if he were trying to grasp at something inside her, as if he were trying to draw out her essential self.

'It's your marriage, in't it?' Molly said softly. 'I've known for a long while there were summat not right about it.'

'Oh, Molly,' Rowenna said, her eyes filling with tears, '*nothing*'s right about it. I don't love Alfred and I'm certain he doesn't love me. And now – now—' Her voice broke and she covered her face with her free hand. Molly waited while she sobbed, stroking the hand she held and murmuring softly. At last Rowenna lifted her wet face and said, 'Molly, I think I'm going to have a baby.'

Molly sighed and nodded, as if this was what she had been expecting.

'And you're none too happy about it, is that it?'

Rowenna shook her head. 'I don't know how I feel about it. When Alfred first told me—'

'*Mr Boothroyd* told *you*?'

'Yes,' Rowenna confessed, realising how strange this must sound. 'We — we were talking about my going away and he said I must be either mad or entranced or — or pregnant.'

Molly stared at her.

'Miss Rowenna, you're not making any sense. Why did he say you'd got to be either mad or' – she stumbled over the word 'entranced' and dismissed it as unimportant – 'or expecting? What did he mean – and where are you going?'

'I'm not going anywhere now,' Rowenna said drearily. 'Not if I'm having a baby.'

Molly shook her head.

'I don't understand. Tell me from the beginning. Tell me what's been happening.'

Rowenna took a deep breath. She had never told anyone, other than her father, about her unhappiness with Alfred. And she had only told Warren because he had shown a moment of apparent sympathy, quickly revealed as self-interest. It was, she felt, disloyal for a wife to confide the secrets of the bedroom to another person.

But did Alfred have a right to her loyalty? Had he earned it? She had been trapped into marrying him, into making promises she did not want to make. Did that give him the rights that love would have given without question?

If it were Kester, she thought, I would never have had a

257

moment's doubt. And I would have been filled with joy to think that I was carrying his baby.

But Kester was far away and she did not expect to see him ever again.

'Tell me all about it,' Molly urged in her soft, comfortable voice.

'Oh, Molly – it's so dreadful. Being married to Alfred.' The first few words were hesitant, but as Rowenna continued they poured forth, describing to Molly the misery of Alfred's coldness, his rigid domination of her and, worst of all, the demands he made on her at night.

'It isn't a bit what I expected,' she confessed. 'You told me it could be beautiful, Molly. You said that even with the wrong person, so long as they were kind and caring, it could still be a pleasure. But I don't think it could ever be a pleasure with Alfred. He does it almost as if he hates me.'

'I think he hates himself,' Molly said. 'He don't know what anything else feels like . . . But oh, miss, you poor, poor soul. What you must have bin going through . . . It *ought* to be good. How else can men and women spend their lives together and be happy like God meant?'

Rowenna shivered. 'A whole lifetime of it, Molly! I can't bear it. I really think I will die.'

'Maybe that's why so many women do,' Molly observed. 'But it's not going to happen to you, miss. Here, what were you saying about going away?'

Rowenna told her about the inheritance from her mother and what she had planned to do with it. She told her about Mr Abercrombie and the help he had offered. 'He said he would see to everything for me – the ticket for the ship, my luggage, everything. And now I won't be able to do any of it. I won't be able to go to Canada after all. Perhaps never.'

'But why not? You can have a babby over there as good as here.'

258

Rowenna shook her head. 'I can't. Alfred threatened to pursue me wherever I went. He would claim the child back and probably take all my money as well. He says women who abandon their husbands are not fit mothers and the law would take everything. And' – she touched her stomach again – 'it *is* my baby, Molly. At first, I thought it was just Alfred's, as if it were something he had given me to hold for a while. But it's mine as well. *More* than his, because it's in my body it's growing, it's my body that will feed it. And I don't believe I could give it up.'

'No,' Molly said, 'you couldn't. There's not many mothers that could. But are you sure it's true? You said *he* told you.'

'He said it must account for my condition. And he asked me when I'd last seen blood. Molly, it was almost three months ago! I've missed twice – I *must* be expecting a child.'

Molly gazed at her thoughtfully. Her eyes travelled over Rowenna's slender body, over the small breasts outlined by the sprigged muslin dress she wore, over the tiny waistline and flat stomach, the narrow hips unencumbered by a bustle.

'That's not the only sign,' she said. 'And you know you've never bin that regular, Miss Rowenna. Is there owt else makes you think it might be so?'

'Anything else? But I don't know what other signs to look for.'

'Well, your bubbies ought to be getting fatter and feeling a bit sore, and tight, like. And the teats going dark. Has that happened? And you might have bin feeling a bit sick in the mornings, like I did. And tired, more'n usual. And you might've gone off some foods you liked before, or started craving summat you wouldn't usually eat.'

Rowenna shook her head. 'I can't eat much. I can't swallow. But there's nothing I really don't like, nor anything I crave. And the other things you speak of – no, I don't think

259

any of those have happened. Do – do you think Alfred might be mistaken, Molly?'

The other girl sighed. 'I dunno, miss. It could be just too early to say. Some people never feel sick nor nothing. But you oughter get some sort of sign soon, I should think.'

'And in the meantime?'

'Well, I suppose you'd better go on as if there's a babby there. After all, you wouldn't want to harm it, would you? So don't go standing on any chairs or jumping off things. And don't lift your arms up above your head, or you'll get the cord twisted round its neck. And come down here as soon as you know for sure, and we'll reckon on what to do next.'

Rowenna looked at her. The tiny gleam of hope that Molly's doubts had lit in her flickered and grew dim. She does think I'm pregnant, she thought. And if I am, there'll be nothing we can do next. I shall be trapped more securely than ever before, because I shan't be able to help loving my baby and love itself can make the tightest trap of all.

I am carrying Alfred's child, and will never, never know what it is to be truly loved.

'You mean you are forbidding me from my own bed?'

Once again, Alfred's voice was terrible, but Rowenna faced him unflinchingly. Her chin up, dark blue eyes steady, she said calmly, 'It seems best to be careful, don't you think, Alfred? I believe any slight disturbance can be enough to dislodge the baby. My own mother had several miscarriages. I should not want to take any risks with our child.'

He stared at her suspiciously. 'Hm. Well, I shall see what Cooper says. I'll call him out immediately.'

'Oh, no,' Rowenna said quickly, 'I don't think there is any need for that yet. Even the doctor can't know for certain at this stage. In a month or so, perhaps . . . and meanwhile, we simply take all the precautions we can.'

'Well, you seem to know a good deal about it. And I'm pleased to see that you're taking your condition seriously, anyway. As you say, there's little the doctor can do at this stage and he certainly knows how to charge for his visits . . . We'll wait until there's something definite that he can say. And you'll take care of yourself. No grubbing about in the garden or long walks up the fell.'

'Oh, but I think walking is a good thing to do,' Rowenna said. 'The exercise and fresh air are very beneficial.'

'Very well. But not alone – take one of the maids with you. And definitely no gardening.'

'No, Alfred,' Rowenna said meekly, with a small sigh. But the loss of a few hours in the garden was a small price to pay for peace at night. And if she had to take one of the maids out walking with her, well, there was little harm in that. At least he had agreed that she could go.

She went upstairs to the bedroom – her bedroom now! – and stood by the window, stretching her arms up luxuriously until she remembered Molly's warning and hastily lowered them again. Still, it probably didn't matter. The baby – if there was one – would be too tiny yet to have a neck around which a cord could be twisted. What cord, anyway? Rowenna was, she realised, still very ignorant about the process of having a baby.

She sat down and gazed out into the garden, feeling suddenly depressed. The dark trees that crowded around the house were like jailers pressing in on her. Beyond and above them the fells rose in a swoop of freedom, but it was a freedom curtailed. How far could she walk in a day? Ten miles, twelve, perhaps fifteen? That meant less than eight away from this house. Eight miles, and she had dreamed of going to Canada!

Now she would never be able to go, for if she were not

261

pregnant now Alfred would soon see to it that she was. In fact, she had been surprised not to have had the signs sooner than this. And then she would be tied to a family, a new baby every year or two – children she would love, no doubt, but children who would keep her here simply because of that love.

Children who would have part of Alfred in them.

May ended, and Rowenna was still not sure that she was pregnant.

She had grown no fatter, but Molly told her that women often lost weight at the beginning. 'You'll soon start to show,' she said, adding, 'if there's anything *to* show,' for she was still not certain. The other changes she had spoken of had still not occurred, though Rowenna examined her breasts every morning, sometimes believing that they must be larger and darker, at other times that they were actually shrinking. But as Molly said, it was a case of a watched pot never boiling. 'You hardly notice it at first, but suddenly you'll know.'

The major sign that she was *not* pregnant had not occurred. And unless it did, Rowenna must continue to be careful not to stretch her arms above her head, nor to bend to pull out weeds in the flowerbed. And to try to swallow the food that almost choked her, for she was now 'eating for two' and must think of the baby.

At least she could sleep alone at night. But although she rejoiced in the privacy and in the relief of being free from Alfred's assaults, Rowenna did not sleep well. Instead, she lay awake hour after hour, watching the late northern twilight and the early dawn that kept the summer nights so pale, and trying to see into the future.

What would her life be like now? Was there nothing she could do to restore the independence that had been so nearly hers?

No more had been said about her inheritance. Alfred had stopped trying to persuade her to let him invest it in the mill – in fact, his whole manner towards her had changed. He was almost repellingly considerate, begging her to rest, to put up her feet, to try the most delicious morsels of her food. Clearly he did not intend to take any risks with her pregnancy, and believed that any emotional disturbance also could be dangerous. She did not imagine that he had forgotten it, or that he would not return to it later.

She had been to see Mr Abercrombie again and told him that she would again have to abandon her plans for going to Canada, at least for the time being.

'I'm not quite certain yet,' she said, looking across the desk at the rosy face, 'but until I am, I'm sure you understand I can't make any plans for travelling. So I'm afraid my ticket will have to be returned.'

'Yes, yes, of course, my dear lady,' he said, looking distressed. 'I'm sure another opportunity will arise. And when it does, you must take it. Meanwhile, I'm here at your disposal should you need me. And remember,' he added as he saw her to the door, 'my wife and I would be more than happy to give you any other kind of help you may need. You still have my card?'

Rowenna assured him that she had, and he showed her out to Stricklandgate where the trap was waiting, with Molly inside for they had come to Kendal together. And as they trotted home through the lanes Rowenna had felt that she had just closed another door in her own face.

Another opportunity will arise... Could it possibly happen? How many chances were you allowed to miss? I must have had my allowance for a lifetime, she thought ruefully. There will surely be no more.

And if there was – just one – would she be able at last to take it?

I shall have to, she thought. I shall have to, for both life and sanity's sake.

'We must consult the doctor,' Alfred declared. 'You're looking thinner than ever. If you don't put on some flesh soon, you'll lose this baby. I believe you're starving yourself on purpose, so as to rid yourself of it.'

'No, Alfred! How can you say such a thing?' Rowenna folded her arms across her stomach. 'If I am to have a baby, I shall love it as—'

'What do you mean – *if you are to have a baby*? Is there any doubt? Is there something you haven't told me?' His black eyes bored into hers. 'I trust you have not been deceiving me, Rowenna,' he said dangerously.

'No, indeed. But I have never been completely certain. There was only the one sign – and that needn't mean a pregnancy. There could be other causes–'

'All the more reason to consult Dr Cooper. If your body isn't functioning as it should, you need treatment. And then we need waste no more time. I'll send for him at once.' He frowned at her. 'I warn you, Rowenna, I intend to have a son, indeed I intend to have several children, and if I find you have been using this as an excuse to delay this . . .' He stopped, glowering at her, then turned abruptly and walked out of the room, leaving Rowenna trembling.

Suppose there was no baby! She touched her stomach, as flat as ever. Her breasts were small and her hips bony. The last time she had seen Molly, the girl had looked at her with doubt in her eyes and said she really ought to be showing soon. There had been nothing else, no sickness, only this terrible choking feeling whenever she tried to eat. And the anxiety and fear that kept her awake night after night, wondering what she could do next.

When Dr Cooper came, she looked at him with wide,

dark eyes, and he took her into the bedroom and instructed her to lie on the bed. Alfred followed and stood by the window, watching sombrely.

'Sensible girl,' the doctor said. 'You've worn loose clothing. 'Now—' he produced a small doll and set it on the table beside her pillow. 'I want you to look at this and if you have any pain, point out to me on the doll where you feel it.'

'I don't have any pain,' Rowenna said. 'But wouldn't it be easier if I showed you on myself?'

He gave her an odd glance and she heard Alfred make a sound of disapproval.

'Possibly. Certainly. But many ladies find it easier this way. Now, are you sure there's no pain anywhere at all? Not even the slightest discomfort?'

'No. Only when I eat.' She told him about the lump that seemed to fill her throat whenever she tried to swallow. 'I think it's why I've got so thin.'

He examined her throat, resting his fingers against it while she swallowed, holding her tongue down with a spatula while he peered inside.

'I can find nothing wrong. Now, about this pregnancy—'

Rowenna gave her husband a quick glance. 'I don't know if that's what it is, Doctor. It's only that my periods have stopped. I haven't been sick or anything else. Molly told me what I should expect – none of it has happened.'

He looked at her speculatively. 'And how long is it since you last saw blood? March? Then there should certainly be some sign. Lie back, my dear, while I examine you.'

Rowenna lay on her pillows, her heart beating fast. She was acutely conscious of Alfred, watching from the window. The doctor lifted her loose skirt and placed his hands flat on her stomach. She felt his fingers moving gently, then probing more firmly. He watched her face.

'Any discomfort? Does this hurt? Is this tender? This?'

Rowenna shook her head. 'None of it hurts, Doctor. Should it?'

'No,' he said, frowning a little. 'Oh no, it shouldn't hurt.'

'Then what's wrong? Why are you looking like that?' Her eyes flicked towards Alfred, who was leaning forwards, his head slightly lowered in the way that frightened her most. 'What have I got wrong with me, Dr Cooper?'

The doctor closed his bag. His face was thoughtful. He too glanced at Alfred.

'Perhaps it might be better if I discussed this alone with your wife, Mr Boothroyd. Such delicate matters—'

'You can discuss it with me. My wife and I have no secrets between us.'

Alfred's voice was coldly implacable. He met the doctor's eye steadily and the doctor shrugged.

'As you wish.' He turned back to Rowenna and spoke apologetically. 'I'm very sorry to tell you this, my dear Mrs Boothroyd, but you are not pregnant, nor ever have been. Nor can I find any physical cause for whatever ails you. The only—'

'*Not pregnant*?' the words seemed to burst from Alfred Boothroyd's throat. He started forwards, and for one terrifying moment Rowenna thought he was about to attack the doctor. 'What in God's name do you mean, man,' he snarled, 'by saying that my wife is not pregnant? Explain yourself'

'I was about to do that.' Dr Cooper spoke mildly, but he had edged around the bed, putting it between himself and Boothroyd. 'Naturally, the cessation of the monthly period is normally the first sign, and such a sign might confuse anyone. I would have taken it so myself, had you called me earlier. But at this stage there should be more to guide us. Some swelling and tenderness of the breasts – a darkening of the aureoles – and, of course, marked changes in the abdomen. None of these signs is present. Therefore, I cannot deduce that your wife is expecting a child.'

Alfred stood quite still, and Rowenna saw his hands clench and unclench at his sides. She licked her lips and asked desperately, 'Then why can't I eat, Doctor? Why am I getting so thin? And why have my periods stopped? There must be *something* the matter.'

'As to that,' he said, looking at her with some sympathy, 'you have partially answered your own question. If you cannot eat your food, you will lose weight and grow thin. And that in turn can interfere with menstruation. But as to *why* you can't eat – yes, that's another matter, and may be more serious.' He hesitated, glancing again at Alfred Boothroyd. 'Is there anything worrying you, my dear? It often happens that serious worry can result in loss of appetite and all the other effects you've mentioned. If that's the case, something can be done about it – indeed, *must* be done about it.'

'My wife has nothing in the least to worry her,' Alfred Boothroyd said curtly. 'She has a free hand in the house and garden. There is no question of this being caused by worry.'

'There must be some reason,' the doctor pointed out. 'And I can find nothing physical—'

'Then it must be mental.' Alfred turned to the bed where Rowenna still lay, watching the two men with frightened eyes. 'I warned you of this! I told you I was beginning to fear for your reason. And I daresay you thought to divert me with this pretence of a pregnancy—'

'But Alfred, it was *you* who thought that I was pregnant—'

'*I*?' He gave a harsh, incredulous laugh. 'And why, pray, should I make such a suggestion – *you* are the one who is in charge of the workings of your body. Well, I shall not be duped again.' He turned back to the doctor. 'I shall want a full examination by a doctor who is versed in such matters. Naturally, I shall give my wife all the care necessary, but I shall need advice as to whether she can be kept at home or will have to be confined to an asylum. I take it that these conditions are often degenerative?'

'My dear sir, I've made no suggestion—'

'But I have. And I require a full investigation. It's possible, I hope, that the condition may have been caught in time and can be arrested? Perhaps a long rest—'

'Yes, indeed,' the doctor said quickly. 'A rest may be just what Mrs Boothroyd needs. And I would be happy to provide a tonic. That, and a richer diet to provide the sustenance she needs, may well be quite enough to set her on the road to recovery. I'm sure your housekeeper will be able to help. Butter, eggs, cream – such foods have all been effective in these cases. I'm sure you have no cause to fear for your wife's mind, Mr Boothroyd.'

'I hope not,' Alfred said in a tone that boded ill for Rowenna if he had. 'And I'll see that your suggestions are carried out, Cooper. But I'll be gratified if you'll give me the name of the most accomplished doctor there is in the matter of the mind. I shall call him for consultation.'

Dr Cooper shrugged. 'If you insist, my dear sir, but for myself I have little confidence in such ideas. People do go mad, I agree, but they usually exhibit very different symptoms from those your wife displays. In my opinion, she has merely overtaxed her strength and needs rest and sympathetic treatment. These conditions are not at all uncommon in young women and I have always found such measures to be effective.' He gave Rowenna another look in which she read both comfort and helplessness, and then turned away. 'I'll see that a tonic is sent round immediately. Goodbye, Mrs Boothroyd.'

Alfred gave the bell-pull a sharp tug and a moment later

the housemaid appeared. The doctor left the room with a sigh and Rowenna, alone with Alfred, gave her husband a look of uncertainty.

'So,' he said, in his deepest and most terrible voice, 'so you are not expecting a child after all.'

'Alfred – I swear to you, I did not know. I—'

'All this time,' he said in a voice like the growl of an enraged bear, 'you have kept me from your bed for the good of our *child*. And now there *is* no child.'

'Alfred – please—'

'All these months wasted.' He was fumbling with his clothes, ripping at the buttons of his shirt, jerking at his trousers. 'All this time when you could have been carrying my child – all wasted, lost. Well, madam, we'll have no more of it, do you hear?' He was over her now, looming like a black and repellent shadow, like a cloud of evil intent. He rested his hands on the pillow, one on each side of her head, and she felt his legs between hers, already forcing them apart. 'We'll waste no more time,' he snarled, and lowered himself so that his face was only inches from hers. 'If you aren't pregnant now, you will be soon.' She felt his body hard against hers, bone on bone only thinly covered with flesh. 'Open your legs, damn you!' he thundered, and she flinched beneath him. 'I'm your husband, do you hear, and you'll keep me out of your bed no longer with your lies and your pretences. Spread yourself wide, you sloven, and give me what you swore before God would be mine. Aye, and give it to me again – and again – and *again* . . . until I'm satisfied . . . Or until you can give me a son . . . *My* son!'

'*No!*'

All the misery and anger which had been smouldering inside Rowenna for so long was suddenly ignited. She reached up with both hands and thrust against his shoulders, at the same time bringing her knee up hard into his groin.

With a yelp of pain, Alfred toppled sideways and collapsed beside her on the bed, groaning and clutching himself. Rowenna wriggled free and swung her feet to the floor. Her eyes on the crouching body of her husband, she backed over to the washstand and lifted the heavy china jug.

'You infernal bitch!' he snarled through his teeth. 'You spiteful little vixen! Wait until I get my hands on you – I'll teach you a lesson you'll never forget. I'll whip you until your body bleeds, aye, and then I'll take you and throw you into the nearest ditch. I'll tear you apart and make you beg for mercy, and by the time I've finished with you, you'll be *glad* to lie with me and take my seed, glad I tell you, for it'll be nothing – *nothing* – to what I'll make you suffer first!'

'No, Alfred,' Rowenna answered in a trembling voice. 'No, you won't. You'll never lay hands on me again, never. I'll suffer no more at your hands, for I'm leaving you now and I shall never come back. You may be my husband but you've no right to treat me as you have done, none at all. Wife I may be, woman I may be, but I'm a human being and I have as many rights before God as you – and no man is ever again going to use me the way you have.' She saw from his movements that he was beginning to recover, and she lifted the jug higher. 'Don't move, Alfred. Don't move. Or I swear I will throw this at you, and I will not miss.'

Still with her eyes on him, she thrust her feet into a pair of slippers which lay on the floor. Moving slowly, she backed to the door and reached behind her to open it. The jug was heavy in her hand. She stood in the opening, took a firm grip on it and faced him for the last time.

Alfred was still on the bed but she knew that the moment she closed the door he would be after her. She could give herself a start of no more than a minute or two. She took a deep breath, hurled the jug towards him, slammed the door between them and turned the key in the lock.

There could only be moments, she knew, before Alfred recovered his wits enough to ring for a servant to let him out. She ran into the little room next door which she had used as her own, for reading and sewing, and snatched up the photograph of her mother and the shell Haddie had given her. A cloak she had been mending lay on a chair, and there were one or two other garments which she stuffed into a bag. There was no time to gather more. With a swift look round at the room that had been her only haven in this dark and oppressive house, she ran out and down the stairs.

The front door was standing open. Rowenna flung herself through it and out into the air. Thanking God for her loose clothes and light slippers, she ran like a hare through the garden and over the little footbridge to her own garden, the garden she had grown up in, had worked in and loved – the garden she knew like the back of her own hand.

Rowenna left the main path and took the narrow track that ran along the top of the riverbank, past the trees that Haddon had planted, the grove where she had lain with Kester, the pool where he had first seen her bathing naked. Past the house where Matilda now reigned, past the kitchen garden and the roses whose scent wafted on the summer breeze. And she came at last to the Richmonds' cottage, where Molly was in the garden, bending over the cradle where Kester's son lay crooning and waving his tiny brown fists.

'Miss *Rowenna!*' Molly exclaimed, straightening up to stare at her. 'What in the world—'

'Molly – I need your help.' Rowenna stopped, her loose dress flying about her, and glanced back the way she had come. 'Go to the stables and have the trap made ready for me. I have to go to Kendal at once. I've left my husband, Molly. I'm free. *Free!*'

Chapter Thirteen

The main street of the little town of Appleby, running down from the castle to the church of St Lawrence, was thronged with horses. They grazed the wide grass verges in the shade of tall trees, they tossed their heads and stamped their hooves as they were led through the town, they drew brightly painted wagons to the riverside and fields where their owners would camp. The sun shone warm, for it was early June and the start of the annual Horse Fair.

Kester Matthews and his father Kieran were amongst the first to arrive. They had been on the road for a fortnight, for the fair that Kieran normally travelled with had been working down in the Midlands, and he had left them to come with Kester and a few others to trade and barter horses. It was his annual holiday and had become the main pleasure of his life for, like Kester, he was tired of the noise of steam roundabouts and organs, and wanted nothing more than the peace of the old way of life. But there were plenty still to live it, and those who did were all at Appleby for June. It was here that every traveller and gypsy in the north gathered, to exchange news and gossip as well as horses.

Since leaving his shepherd's hut near Burneside, Kester had wandered far and wide, unable to settle in any spot. His burning disappointment had been like a sickness from which, if he stood still, he could not recover; it drove him

273

on, from meadow to moor, from wood to field, from the fairgrounds of his family to the forests where he felt most at home. But even they could not hold him, for they reminded him too vividly of the trees Haddon Mellor had planted and the little bluebell grove where he had lain with Rowenna.

Where was she now? What was happening to her? He had gone down to her garden that last morning, hungry for the sight and sound of her, and stood in the early dawn staring up at her window. Once, for a brief moment, he had thought he saw her face at the glass; but if it had been there at all, it was quickly gone, and he turned away and melted back into the shadows of the trees.

What was happening in that house? He knew by now that Warren Mellor had been struck down with an attack of the heart, and Rowenna could not leave him. How long would the old man hold her at his side?

And if he recovered? Kester could not rid his mind of the image of Rowenna, standing in the bluebell grove with Alfred Boothroyd. Standing within his embrace, allowing him to kiss her with his serpent's kisses, running away across the lawns with him, hand-in-hand. He could not forget her eyes as she had looked past Boothroyd and into Kester's shocked face. There was no joy in her expression, rather a shock of her own. But she had not stopped the kisses.

What was happening between her and Alfred Boothroyd?

Kester touched the bark of one of the trees he and Haddon had planted. And then he lay down in the little grove and wept like a girl for the love that had been denied him. For he knew that Rowenna was trapped; that she would never be able to leave Ashbank while Warren Mellor kept her bound. And that Alfred Boothroyd was a part of that trap.

And he had got up at last, taken one final look at the

window, and walked slowly out of the garden and away over the fells.

He had heard nothing of Rowenna after that, for he had tried to close his mind to his despair. Instead, he wandered and kept on wandering, taking work here and there for a few days, a week or two, perhaps even a month before the ache inside drove him on. He shunned all company at first, living alone wherever he could find shelter; then, when the haunting memory of her face and body became too much for him to bear, he found himself hungering for new faces and voices, and he sought the company of others and even found other girls to replace her. But none could. And in the last moment of lovemaking, he would look down and see the face beneath him and know that it was not hers, and he would be washed with pain and guilt, until at last he gave up seeking solace in the arms of other women.

Finally, he returned to his own people. They were still travelling the roads with the fair, and his brothers were working the steam merry-go-rounds with their gaily painted, cantering horses, and the swing-boats which needed no power other than that of their occupants. There were coconut shies as well, shooting-galleries, cheap jacks, sparring-booths and the usual array of oddities – tattooed ladies, skeleton men and, if the travellers were lucky, two-headed calves and lambs.

There was plenty of work now for a strong young man who wanted to keep himself occupied. All the wagons and trailers needed horses to draw them, and there were still one or two old-fashioned dobby-set roundabouts, with a pony running round inside the circle of wooden horses to keep them moving. The entire travelling community numbered about a hundred animals to be fed, watered and looked after. And there was always something in need of repair – a wheel to be mended, a wagon roof that had sprung a leak, a roundabout horse that had lost an ear or got its pole damaged. Everything must be kept bright, shining and in good order, for a scruffy fair would soon lose its good reputation – and its customers.

'There's plenty here for you to do,' Kieran Matthews said when his son returned. He was seventy years old now, still tall and straight with plenty of hair, though it was now more silver than black. He gave Kester a sharp look when he first walked into the camp, but asked no questions. It was only later, as they settled in his wagon over a pipe one cool, rainy evening just before they arrived in Appleby, that they began to talk.

'So what brings you back to the travellers? It's not a whim, I can see that – you've got a look about you, a sadness in your eyes. Is it shelter you want?'

Kester hesitated. He had spoken to no one, save Molly on that last night, of his love for Rowenna. He had kept it to himself, as if he were guarding a precious jewel. But his father was looking at him with eyes that saw beyond his closed expression and into his heart, and he knew that his secret must be shared.

'Shelter?' he said thoughtfully. 'Perhaps it is a kind of shelter that I've been looking for. But I've discovered in these past months that there are some things you can't hide from.'

'Yourself,' Kieran said, and he nodded.

'Myself, aye. And the sorrow I take with me, wherever I go. It won't let me alone. It goes with me through woods and fields and over the hills. It haunts me at night and stays beside me through the day. I thought it would fade in time, but it don't. It's a torment, yet it's a torment I can't be without, for without it I reckon I'd be only half alive.'

'It's a woman,' his father said. 'Only a woman can do that to a man.'

'Aye, a woman. And I thought she was mine and lost her. She *was* mine,' he repeated passionately. 'She was and still is, always will be, even though I'll never see her again.'

'And why is that?'

Kester looked into the glowing red heart of the little stove that kept the wagon warm. If he answered this question, he must tell the whole story – the story of how he had fallen in love with the girl he had seen walking in her garden, how he had found her sitting by the tarn on Potter's Fell and taken her back to his hut, how he had watched over her as she slept. How he had come upon her, bathing in the stream, and then sat with her in the bluebell grove as she dried herself in the sun; and how they had met there, day after day, growing closer in their love, until at last she promised to come away with him.

As twilight gathered its shadows around the edges of the fireglow, Kester began to speak. He told his father all this and more; how he had lain at night, his body on fire for her loving, yet refused to allow himself any relief because the fire was for her and not for himself. And how, on that last night when she had sent Molly in her place, he had been unable to hold back the flames any longer and had taken the maidservant instead.

'She was willing enough,' he said. 'She'd been wanting me for herself, though she would never have given her life to me as Rowenna would. But I've felt sorry for it since, for there was no love in it, only an easing for us both.'

'And that was a good thing,' Kieran said gently. 'It's a kind of loving itself, to give another ease. And if you can both give it, where's the harm?'

'I don't know. I only know it was Rowenna I should have been loving that night. With her, I would have been giving my heart; with poor Moll, it was no more than my body.'

There was a silence. Then Kieran said, 'And so you came

away next day, not knowing if she would have come with you.'

'She wouldn't. Molly told me that quite plain. The old man was sick, and she had to stay with him. And he would have kept her there for ever. He had a queer sort of hold on her. And besides, there was Boothroyd sniffing round. I'd seen him a few times, coming through the mill yard to talk to the old man, and calling at the house with his mealy-mouthed sister. There was something going on there, I'd no doubt of that, and when I saw him kissing her in the bluebell grove I knew what it was.'

'He was after marrying her, you think?'

'Aye, no doubt of it. And the old man'd be all for it. There's the mill, you see.' He sighed. 'Once they'd got Rowenna tied down there'd be no escape for her. It was too late – it was always too late for us.'

'And you just accepted that? You just walked away and never stayed to find out? You left her to the mercy of those two men, who wanted to use her for their own ends and would bend her life to suit their plans? *And you say you love her*?'

Kester stared at his father. The firelight glowed on his face, casting strange dark shadows around his smouldering eyes. And it seemed to burn in his voice as well, with a fervent intensity that threatened to break into flame. He felt as if he were about to be devoured by scorching white heat.

'I—'

'Did you never remember my advice?' Kieran demanded. 'Did you never remember my telling you to take your chances when they came, for they may only come once?'

'Yes, I remembered that. But what can you do when the chance is snatched away from you just as you reach out your hand? Are you saying I should have waited? I might have waited for ever. I might have had to watch her marrying that snake—'

'You should never have allowed it.'

'But how could I prevent it?' Kester cried desperately. 'What could I do against all of them?'

'You should have done something. You should have waited until the old man was better – or dead – and you could have taken her then. Even if she protested, you should have taken her anyway, because you said you loved her and then you left her to a living death. She deserved better of you than that.'

'You don't understand. Girls like that – they're brought up to do as they're bid. Rowenna had a mind of her own, but even she was caught in the trap old Mellor had set for her. It's all duty and repayment – they've got naught of their own, it's all given them, and they're expected to pay it back in service. Service to their fathers, service to their husbands. And if there's no father or husband there'll be a brother or two, or a cousin or uncle they can go and keep house for and pander to. It's like they're caught in chains.' He shook his head. 'But you wouldn't know about that, you've never had to do with these people.'

Kieran sat silent for a moment. Then he said quietly, 'You're wrong, son. I do know about it. I know more than you think. And I understand just how it was for you and your Rowenna.'

'How can you? Nobody can understand, unless they've been through it too.'

'Aye,' Kieran said, 'that's the truth of it.'

Kester sat looking into the fire, his father's words sinking into his brain. Slowly, he turned his head and stared at the shadowed face.

'What do you mean? What are you telling me?'

Kieran sighed heavily. He shifted in his wooden armchair and reached into his pocket for the shabby tobacco pouch he had carried for as long as Kester could remember. He refilled his pipe, puffed at it for a moment or two, then began to speak. His voice was low and there was a thread in it that Kester had never before heard; a thread of pain, of regret, of wisdom, that came directly from experience.

'I told you about chances,' he said slowly. 'How you should always take them when they come, for they may not come again. I had a chance once, and hearing you talk has been like living that chance all over again. Your story – you say I couldn't understand, but I tell you I can and do, for it's my story too. Word for word, it's the same.'

He stopped. Kester waited, for he knew that his father must tell his story in his own time, his own way. But – his story too? Could it possibly be so?

'It was fifty years ago, and more. I met her down near Duddon. She'd run away from her family – only for the afternoon, for she was just a young girl then, but she'd heard there were gypsies about and she wanted to see us for herself. She'd heard tales of how we'd steal children and stain them brown with walnut juice!' He smiled in the firelight. 'I think she'd half a wish we'd steal her, for she wasn't too happy at home. And we became friends, she and I. I'd take her guddling for trout or gathering bilberries on the hill. It was her taught me to read.'

'Her!' And because of her, Kester thought, that his father had taught him and his brothers to read. Few travellers could, and it had made a difference to the whole family – but most of all to him. For reading and the thirst for knowledge had driven him to seek a different kind of life, and had brought him finally to Ashbank and to Haddon Mellor, who had talked to him of trees and lent him books.

And from Haddon to his sister Rowenna . . .

'Aye, her. We learned a lot of things together. And in the end we learned to love.'

'So . . . what happened?'

'You've already told me,' Kieran said. 'When you told me

your story . . . It was like living it over again. The plans to go away together – the last night, with me waiting at the gate. And then hearing that her father had been taken ill and she couldn't leave him . . . It was like a ghost coming back, listening to your tale.' He gave a wry smile. 'Perhaps it's none so uncommon after all – perhaps it happens to a main of gypsy lads who're fool enough to set their caps at *gauje* girls!'

'And did you ever see her again?'

Kieran shook his head. 'The tribe moved on then – didn't go back to that area for a long while. And then . . .' He was silent for a moment. 'And then I married your mother, and we had a good enough life. She was a good woman, your ma. But I never forgot that bright-haired girl hiding in the bushes, half longing to be stolen by gypsies. And wishing in the end that she had been, I reckon.'

'Why? What happened to her?'

'What happens to all women of that kind? You've told me yourself – they live the lives their menfolk map out for them, they wed and have children, and then they die. I'd missed my chance – and it never came again. That's why I always gave you boys that advice, in the hope that you'd not have to suffer the same way. I might have known we can never learn by other people's mistakes, only by our own.'

Kester said nothing for a few moments. He thought over his father's words, seeing in them the answers to questions that had plagued him all his life. The look in Kieran's eyes at times, the way he would suddenly get up from the camp fire and walk away into the darkness, even the strange tenderness he had sometimes shown towards their mother, as if he were trying to make up to her for some lack. Had he been thinking then of the girl who had run away from her family to see the gypsies, the girl he had taught to guddle trout, who had loved him and lain with him?

281

The girl who had been caught in the end by the same trap that had been set for Rowenna – a trap of duty and obligation, set for her on the day she had been born?

'Are you telling me I should go back?' he asked at last. 'Should I go and find her – and bring her away with me? Is the chance still there?'

Kieran shrugged. 'Who can say? It's for you to decide now. I've told you all I can. Our stories may the same always, or they may go a different road, and who am I to tell you how to live your life? Perhaps after all, you can learn from my mistakes. But don't forget that she's living her life too, all this time – nothing stands still.'

'She may be married by now, to Boothroyd. Or someone else.'

'And may need you all the more because of it,' Kieran said sombrely.

Kester turned his head again, but the fire had died down now and his father's face was darkened by shadows, his expression hidden. It was as if the story had been told and there was no more to be said. Only Kester himself could decide what was to be the next step on the road he trod through life.

Take your chances when you have them, for they may not come twice.

Or make your chances for yourself, he thought. Go out and create them. I don't have to sit here and wait – Rowenna will never come looking for me. How could she? She's no idea where to find me. But I can go back to her. I can go back and take her away, away from that selfish old man and that snake Boothroyd. I can make our chance, all over again.

And as the thought took shape in his mind he felt a new restlessness, and a wonder that he had not seen the answer before. Why had he left her, without a word? Why had he believed the trap closed for ever, when he was the one who must open it?

He stirred in his chair. A powerful urge was overcoming him, a need to go out and make all speed for Burneside, to discover for himself what had happened to Rowenna during the months of their separation, and how she fared.

He reached out to light the lamp and looked at his father's face. There was all the strength and experience of seventy years in that face, all the joy of living and all the sadness and grief. He knew that nobody else had ever heard the story Kieran had just told him; nobody else understood the shadows that sometimes passed across those dark features, nor the root of the wisdom so famous throughout the tribe. As Kieran had said, every man had to make his own mistakes. But if he could not learn from the wisdom of those who had gone before, of what use was that wisdom?

'I'll go and find out,' he said. 'I'll go and find her and I'll take her away from there, for I know – I *know* – she can't be happy. I know she needs me.'

James Abercrombie's drawing room was large and spacious, with a high ceiling and a tall, curved bay window that took up almost all of one end of the room. Deep red velvet curtains hung at the side of the window. The walls were papered in pale green, and the elaborately carved cornices and ceiling rose painted white like the woodwork around the rich mahogany of the doors. The fireplace was surrounded by tiles painted with scarlet poppies, and above the mantelpiece hung a portrait that looked uncommonly like Mr Abercrombie himself.

'My father,' Mr Abercrombie explained when he saw Rowenna looking at it. He regarded the benevolent features with approval. 'A wonderful man. I've always modelled myself on him.'

283

Rowenna smiled. It was plain to see that Mr Abercrombie had indeed grown and trimmed his bushy whiskers to resemble those of his father, but had he actually bleached them too, or had he been forced to wait patiently until nature came to his aid? There was no doubt, however, that the bright blue eyes were the same, and the twinkling smile. Either the artist who had painted the portrait had not subscribed to the view that the sitter should be represented as eternally solemn, or he had been unable to stop the old man smiling.

'And now,' Mr Abercrombie said kindly, 'perhaps you feel ready to tell me what brought you here in – if I may express it so – such a deplorable condition.'

Rowenna turned her eyes reluctantly away from the portrait. For the three days since she had arrived, she had been treated with the utmost gentleness. Mrs Abercrombie had welcomed her with as much warmth and concern as her husband, and had promptly taken her to a comfortable bedroom, where she had been put to bed without any fuss. She had fallen asleep immediately, waking only once or twice to find a maid beside her with a warm drink, and had finally struggled back to reality a good twelve hours after her arrival at the house.

'Poor child, you're exhausted,' Mary Abercrombie said, and took her to a room where an immense bath with clawed feet stood like a beast in its lair, clouds of steam rising like dragon's breath from the water. But it was scented breath, and the bath enclosed her like a womb as she sank into it, and when she finally climbed out again it was with a feeling of having been reborn.

Even then, no one had bothered her with questions. In her room, she had found clothes laid out and a maid to help her dress, but the clothes were simple ones – a comfortable wrapper, a loose muslin gown – and there was neither a crinolette nor a bustle amongst them. They were the kind of clothes to wear at home, when visitors were not expected, soothing clothes that allowed the body to move with ease and freedom.

Rowenna dressed and then sat at her window for a while, looking down into the garden. It was small but pretty, with a curving lawn and flowerbeds filled with colour. Shrubs and low, blossoming trees grew against the wall that surrounded it and at one side of the lawn there was a small pool, bright with waterlilies, and beside it a small round white table and some chairs.

Mary Abercrombie was sitting in one of the chairs, sewing, and after some hesitation Rowenna went down to her.

'My dear, how pleasant to see you.' Mrs Abercrombie gestured to one of the chairs. 'Sit yourself down and be comfortable. Now, tell me, are you feeling stronger?'

'Oh yes, much.' Rowenna looked at the other woman. She was exactly the kind of wife one might expect James Abercrombie to have, she thought – small and round like her husband, with curling white hair and smiling eyes, though hers were dark brown. Her skin was like rose-petals, soft and faintly pink, and her hands were constantly busy as she added the colourful stitches to her embroidery. 'I can't thank you enough for taking me in as you did,' Rowenna went on. 'I don't know where I would have gone if you'd turned me away.'

'Turn you away! What an idea. It was plain you were in desperate trouble, my dear. No' – she held up her hand – 'you aren't to say a word until you feel quite ready. Then you must ask for whatever help you need. And meanwhile, you are to stay here and rest. Nobody will bother you.'

'But suppose my husband—' Rowenna began, and heard the fear tremble in her voice.

Mrs Abercrombie looked at her with kindness.

'You are quite safe here,' she said. 'Quite, quite safe.'

And for the next two days, Rowenna had stayed in the house or garden with its peaceful atmosphere, taking her meals during the day with Mrs Abercrombie and listening to her gentle conversation. In the evening Mr Abercrombie joined them and kept them amused with small anecdotes of his day. And until this afternoon, neither had put a single question to Rowenna.

But now, as she sat in the airy drawing room, so unusually bare of the ornaments and photographs beloved of so many people, Rowenna knew that she must tell Mr Abercrombie all that had taken place.

It was easier than she had expected. Mary Abercrombie sat at her elbow and laid her hand over Rowenna's, conveying her comfort and support. When the story came to the moment of Rowenna's final bid for freedom, her eyes were wet and she felt for a handkerchief.

'You poor child! Of course you cannot go back to him. Men like that should not be allowed to have wives.'

'Hush, my dear,' Mr Abercrombie said. 'One should never judge hastily.' He questioned Rowenna more deeply, probing into every aspect of her marriage. 'I'm sorry to have to ask you these questions, but a court would undoubtedly do so and I would rather save you such embarrassment if at all possible.'

Rowenna felt her cheeks colour but answered steadily. 'But do you really mean I will have to go into court? I've done nothing criminal, have I?'

'A good many people would like to consider it so, your husband included. But no, you've done nothing for which you can be prosecuted, in the legal sense. Civil law is different, however, and if your husband sues for divorce—'

'Divorce! But surely very few people take such a step as that.'

'Few indeed,' he agreed. 'But one never knows who they may be . . . Did you tell him you intended going to Canada, my dear?'

'Yes. I said I wanted to go for a holiday.'

'Good, good,' he approved. 'And I think I would suggest that you do just that. Go to Canada, but write to him – from the ship, before you sail, or soon after your arrival – to tell him again that you are enjoying a long holiday with your mother's family. He can't then accuse you of having deserted him.'

'But what should I do then? I can't go back to him.' She shivered.

'Well, then it depends largely on what happens to you when you are there. You may find your relatives welcome you and want you to stay. And after a period of time, it's possible that your husband will realise that pursuing you would be useless and agree to a separation.' He frowned a little, ruefully. 'I'm afraid I can't give you any more useful advice than that, my dear. Marriage is a very binding contract, you see. And escaping from it an expensive and very upsetting business. But a number of people live contentedly enough apart, and if there is enough money to do so, it seems to me to be the best course.'

'I think I have enough money,' Rowenna said. 'My father said it was enough to live on.'

'Oh, certainly. You need have no worries on that score.'

'Then that's what I'll do,' Rowenna decided. 'I'll go to Canada. But' – she looked at the lawyer and his wife and lowered her eyes, feeling the colour in her cheeks again – 'there's something I must do first. Someone I need to find. And I'll need your help again, for I haven't the least idea where to look.'

When Alfred Boothroyd was released from his bedroom he was in the most vindictive fury that any of his servants had ever known. His face was distorted in a grimace of bitter rage, his thin lips drawn back from his yellowing teeth, his eyes like black pits in his marble face. His hands were curled, the fingers hooked into claws, and he held them as if he wanted to tear Rowenna's eyes from her head.

The footman who had unlocked the door and let him out took one look at him and scuttled down the back stairs as fast as his legs would carry him. But Alfred barely noticed. He came down to the front hall as if stairs did not exist, and snarled when he saw the door still standing wide. Then he turned and yelled for his servants, who came in a huddle, staring at him with terrified eyes.

'Your mistress has taken leave of her senses,' he told them in a terrible voice. 'She has run mad, and God knows what she'll do next or where she'll go. If any of you see her or hear of her, you're to tell me instantly, but you'll say nothing – *nothing* – to anyone else of what's gone on in this house, today or any other day. Nothing, d'you hear me? Or it'll be the worse for you all.'

He glowered at them and they gazed back, stuttering. Impatiently, he dismissed them and then marched round to the stable. To the grooms and stable-boys, who knew nothing of Rowenna's departure, he gave the same curt orders, and then stormed across the bridge to question his sister and Warren.

'It'll be that lawyer,' Warren said when he understood at last what Boothroyd was telling him. 'She'll have gone to him for help. And he'll have given it her, slimy rascal that he is! God knows where she is now – halfway across the Atlantic, I dare swear – but it'll be he who knows if anyone does.'

Boothroyd agreed, but his pride would not allow him to go at once to James Abercrombie and ask for Rowenna's whereabouts, and it was not until she had been gone for a week that he finally took himself surlily to the sunny little office in Kendal and demanded to see the solicitor. By that time, Rowenna was in Manchester, buying clothes with Mrs Abercrombie, and Mr Abercrombie was able to assure Alfred in all honesty that she was not in Kendal.

'In any case, she's my client,' he said, unperturbed by Alfred's fury. 'I couldn't possibly divulge her movements to anyone without her express permission. It's my legal duty to honour her confidence.'

'For God's sake, she's my *wife*—'

'And my client,' Mr Abercrombie repeated calmly. 'I'll let her know you were enquiring, of course – should she contact me. More than that, I'm afraid I cannot say.'

Boothroyd stared at him and for a moment looked likely to make an attack, but James Abercrombie was well used to such threats and sat quite still, exuding a smiling certainty that the other man would do no such thing. And after a minute or two, Alfred turned away, muttering his rage. At the door, however, he swung back to face the little lawyer.

'Very well. She's not here. But don't imagine you've seen the last of me. I know she's been here – I know you've helped her in whatever hare-brained scheme she's devised. And if I find you've sheltered her or helped her in any way more than your *legal duty*, I'll sue you for enticement. I'll take you through every court in the land if necessary, and I'll see you in the gutter for it before I've finished. As for my wife – you may tell her this. I shall find her. I shall find her wherever she's gone, and when I do, I shall make her sorry that she ever was born. I shall make her sorry for the rest of her life that she ran away from me, and I shall make her sorry she was never the wife I thought to have. If she regrets marrying me now, she'll regret it a thousand times more by the time I've finished with her – a *thousand* times more.'

He gave Mr Abercrombie one final glare, then slammed out of the room. Mr Abercrombie listened to his feet pounding down the stairs and took out a large white handkerchief with which he mopped his brow.

'A thousand times?' he murmured. 'Well, then, Mr Boothroyd, we shall just have to make sure that you don't find her, shan't we?'

Mr Abercrombie took everything in hand. He arranged Rowenna's voyage on the ocean liner from Liverpool, leaving at the end of June. He sent her off with his wife to spend a few days in Manchester – the days during which Boothroyd came raging to his office – buying the clothes and luggage she would need. He even made enquiries and found a respectable middle-aged couple who were also travelling to Canada and would be happy to look after Rowenna during the voyage, and he helped her write to her Canadian relatives to announce her arrival.

Only after all this was done did he turn his attention to her request to search for Kester, and here she found his sympathy a little less wholehearted.

'A gypsy?' he repeated doubtfully when she explained. 'Are you quite sure, my dear? It seems a little hazardous. What do you know of this man, after all?'

'Enough.' She hesitated. This was something she had never told the Abercrombies, but clearly she must do so now. 'We loved each other. I – I was going to run away with him.'

'*Run away with him*?' Mr Abercrombie was scandalised. 'You're not serious! You, a well-brought-up young lady, leaving everything to run away with a *gypsy*? Why, I can hardly believe it.'

'But I was.' Rowenna looked from him to his wife, trying desperately to think of a way to explain. 'You forget,' she said a trifle bitterly, 'what my life was like with my father. Well-brought-up? I was trained from the beginning to believe that his word was law in everything. While my mother was alive, she protected me, and while I was at school I barely saw him. Even Haddon took care that I had some life to call my own. But with both of them gone, and nothing to do all day, it was unbearable. You know that, Mr Abercrombie. You knew what my mother's life was, when she came to you to make her will.'

'Yes,' he said, 'I knew. But – a gypsy!'

Mary Abercrombie glanced up from her embroidery. 'Still a man, James. And a tender, loving man by Rowenna's account – and I think she has met enough of the other sort to know the difference. As for her running away with him – well, if my father had forbidden me to see you, don't you suppose I'd have done the same?'

Her husband looked at her and his rosy face grew a little ruddier. He cleared his throat and turned away for a moment, then flourished his large white handkerchief. 'Well – hrrrmph – be that as it may, gypsies aren't the easiest of people to find, you know. Have you any idea where he might be?'

'None at all,' Rowenna said sadly. 'Except that he told me his family ran a pleasure fair, and he once mentioned going to Appleby Horse Fair.'

'Applcby!' the little lawyer cried. 'Why, that's this very week – it always ends on the second Wednesday in June. We must go there at once.'

'You mean you *will* help me find him?' Rowenna asked, dazed by his sudden change of heart.

'I'll help you *look*,' James Abercrombie corrected her. 'And if it's possible to find this young man, then we'll certainly find him. But don't be too disappointed if we don't succeed. The place is full of gypsies – we'll have our work cut out to find just one, if he's there at all.'

Would he be there? Rowenna's heart beat fast at the

thought of seeing Kester again. And what would she say to him, if they did meet? What would he do?

She did not know. She only knew that she could not leave for Canada without at least trying to find him, if only to wish him a last goodbye.

Appleby was crowded with people when Rowenna and the Abercrombies arrived. Leaving the railway station, they walked through the narrow streets to the square and stood for a moment looking up the hill towards the castle.

'I've never seen so many people and horses together in my life,' Rowenna said.

Mr Abercrombie laughed. 'Nor I! This is the biggest horse fair in the north and every gypsy who can comes here to barter and trade. Over the years, it's turned into a kind of Romany festival, with harness racing in the evenings, a pleasure fair and every sideshow and cheapjack you can think of. But the horses are the main attraction, of course, and the gypsies take their buying and selling very seriously.'

They walked up the main street. Rowenna looked at the houses and shops, almost hidden behind the throng of stalls that had been set up, and wondered if the people enjoyed having their lives disrupted by this invasion every June. But probably they set out to make the most of it – a good many of them were offering teas or accommodation to visitors. It was a meeting place for others besides gypsies, it seemed, for there were country folk who had clearly come in from miles around, gathered in little knots on the pavements to exchange news.

And there were surely as many horses as there were people. Of all colours – black, grey, chestnut, and the skewbald that was a mixture of all – they were tethered to graze on the verges, or led along the street. Here and there, they were being examined by dark-skinned gypsies who were holding up the animals' hooves to inspect them, or peering into their mouths. Rowenna watched the brown hands running over silky skin, assessing the muscles beneath, and thought of Kester's touch. Was he here somewhere, looking narrow-eyed at some pony, pursing his lips over the price demanded and shaking his head before making his own offer?

Her heart quickened. This was surely the nearest she had been to finding him since he had left Burneside nearly two years ago. How much had happened since then! Her father's illness, her marriage to Alfred. The pregnancy that had never been, and Alfred's fury that had caused her at last to abandon him. Less than two years, yet she felt so much older.

What had happened to Kester during that time? Had he too changed? Would he want her to find him – or would he turn away, believing that she had rejected him, soured and embittered by the promise she had broken?

Mr Abercrombie set off again up the hill and his wife and Rowenna followed him. Every few yards they were stopped again by another cluster of gypsies, arguing over another horse. The men were laughing, yet there was a seriousness behind their banter and when it came to money changing hands they were narrow-eyed and careful. Rowenna watched in surprise as an elderly man, with bow legs and a battered bowler hat, bought a piebald horse from a young gypsy and then, within minutes, sold it again to another. Almost before the horse was out of sight, he had repeated the procedure with a skewbald and was looking about him for another when the Abercrombies moved on.

'It's a way of passing the time,' Mr Abercrombie said. 'He can feel part of the fair without ever spending a penny. I daresay he may end up with a horse, when it's all over, but he might just as well end up with no more or less than the money he began with. Whatever happens, he'll have enjoyed himself.'

Mr Abercrombie was enjoying himself too, Rowenna thought. His blue eyes sparkled as he looked about him, and he stopped at every sideshow to see what was on offer. By the time they reached the castle walls at the top of the hill he was carrying several fairings, won in the shooting galleries or on the penny roll-'em-downs. But at every stall he also enquired about Kester Matthews.

'His name's known,' he reported to Rowenna, handing her a piece of ruby glass which looked as if it ought to have a function though it was impossible to decide what. 'But nobody will say if he's here or not. I suppose they think I'm a policeman. They're a tight lot, these gypsies, they'll never give one of themselves up to the law.'

Once again, they walked down the hill, and turned to stroll along to the riverside. Here, every morning, the horses were washed with soap to make their coats soft and shiny. Boys and young men rode them thigh-deep into the water and scrubbed them. Then the crowds would gather to watch them being paraded at a run through the streets, showing off their paces.

'Perhaps if we went to their camp,' Rowenna suggested, beginning to feel that Mr Abercrombie was right when he said it would be like looking for a needle in a haystack. But if the needle was there and you searched long enough ... 'There must be someone who would tell us.'

'Well, we could try, but we might not find ourselves very welcome.' He looked doubtfully at his wife. 'I think it would be better if I went there alone. You take Rowenna back to our hotel, my dear, and rest before dinner.'

Rowenna protested, but the lawyer was firm. There was no knowing what one might find in a gypsy camp, he declared, and he would prefer to see for himself before taking the risk of exposing her to sights a young lady ought not to see. He went off in the direction of the fields where the wagons were standing in long rows, and Mrs Abercrombie and Rowenna went back to the hotel where they had booked rooms for a night or two.

Mrs Abercrombie declared her intention of doing exactly as her husband had suggested and retired for a rest. Rowenna, alone at last, prowled about in her own room for a time, and then snatched up her hat and ran down the stairs. It might be discourteous to the couple who had been so kind to her, but how could she possibly stay indoors on a fine afternoon such as this, when Kester might at any moment walk past the door!

The gypsy encampment was thronged with wagons of all kinds. Many were bow-tops made of canvas stretched over huge steel hoops, their doors and windows set at the ends, some plain, some gaily decorated. But the most elaborate were the square-built wagons with their bright red or blue wheels, their yellow and green panelled walls with their carved and painted scrolls. Gathered together along the old Roman road or on the grass verges, they made a bright splash of colour, and the gypsies themselves added to the atmosphere of holiday, with their song and laughter, and their camp fires sending thin spirals of blue smoke into the air.

Rowenna wandered amongst them, searching each face for the one she knew. At every wagon there seemed to be a group of people gathered round a fire, tending large pots from which enticing aromas drifted across to her nostrils. Mostly, they were women and children, but the men were wandering back now, leading the horses they had bought or tried to sell – perhaps both! Rowenna thought, remembering the old man in the square – and settling themselves on the wagon steps.

As she walked, Rowenna was conscious of the curious

stares which followed her. Eyes, some friendly, some hostile, followed her progress. Eventually, having seen no one who resembled Kester in the slightest, she gathered her courage and approached the nearest group.

'Is there summat you want?'

Rowenna looked from one face to another. Two or three young women with babies on their laps, a couple of older ones stirring the pot, a white-haired grandmother in a wooden armchair. A man, detaching himself from his seat on the driving platform of the wagon to drop lightly to the grass and confront her.

'Yes,' she said bravely, meeting his eyes. 'Yes, I'm looking for someone I know. Kester Matthews.'

'Matthews?' the old woman asked in a surprisingly deep voice. 'Is that one of Scarth's lot?'

Rowenna shook her head. She had never heard of anyone called Scarth.

'*Dinilow*!' the man said with a snort. 'Scarth's been dead and gone these past ten years. The Matthews went off with their own fair – they run a merry-go-round and such now.'

'Yes, that's right,' Rowenna said eagerly, remembering that Kester had told her how he disliked the steam round-abouts that had replaced the old dobby-sets, and how he had preferred the old way of life, making baskets and selling lavender and herbal potions as the family made its way about the countryside. 'Kester's brothers did that. Are they here now? They might know where he is.'

'Aye, they're about somewhere. Over the other side of town they'll be, where the pleasure fair is.' He looked at Rowenna, his eyes narrowed. 'But what'd a lady like you be wanting with a Matthews? Ordinary travellers, they be, like the rest of us.'

'Kester's not ordinary,' she said softly. 'Will you show me the way?'

296

'Hold on a moment,' one of the young women said suddenly. She came over to the wagon, holding a large baby against her hip. 'Ain't Kester the lad that left the travellers and went off on his own? I heard he'd gone back to his old dad.'

'Aye, that's right,' someone else chimed in. 'But not for good – he comes and goes, like. I dunno if he's here in Appleby.'

'He is,' another woman asserted, and Rowenna's heart leapt, only to sink again as an argument broke out. 'No, he went away again.' 'I seen him, I tell yer, down by the river.' 'No, that wasn't Kester, that'd be his brother, like as two peas they are.'

'Please,' she begged them at last, 'if you could just tell me where his father's wagon is. Or his brother's. They must know where he is.'

The gypsies turned and stared at her, almost as if they had forgotten she was there. Immersed in their argument, they had become embroiled in a discussion of the Matthews family, recalling old names and faces and reminding each other how this one had lived and that one died . . .

'You mean you want to find him? Kester Matthews?'

'Yes,' she said, 'that's who I'm looking for.'

'Oh, aye,' the man said. 'Well, old Kieran's camped just down the road here, about twenty vans away. That's Kester's dad, see, Kieran Matthews. He don't stop too near the fair, independent old *mush*, he is. He might talk to you, and then again he might not.'

Rowenna set off again, her heart beating fast. Could she really be so close to Kester? Was he here now, only a few hundred yards away from her? She counted the wagons as she passed them. Five, six, seven . . . twelve, thirteen . . . eighteen, nineteen, twenty . . . She paused and gazed about, searching each face again.

A red wagon stood at a short distance. At the foot of its steps the usual fire burned, with an iron pot hung above it. And beside it stood two men.

One was old, seventy at least, yet still straight and broad-shouldered. His face was dark, but the hair that must once have been black now curled iron-grey over his head.

The other man was James Wilson Abercrombie.

Mr Abercrombie turned as Rowenna approached. He looked surprised and disconcerted to see her, then his face broke into its usual smile and he held out his hand in welcome.

'Well, my dear, I see that it's impossible to keep you from your search! And you've done as well as I, for we've both found Mr Kieran Matthews. Mr Matthews, this is Rowenna Boothroyd.'

Kieran turned. His eyes were dark brown, looking straight into hers. And as Rowenna stared at him, she knew that this must be Kester's father, for this was how Kester would look in fifty years' time.

But there was a slight look of puzzlement in the dark eyes that looked so directly into hers, and a hesitation in the clasp of his hand.

'Boothroyd?' he said. 'Boothroyd? I understood you were called Mellor.'

'I was,' she said quietly. 'I was married a year ago last December.'

Kieran looked at her a little longer, then let her hand go.

'Aye,' he said. 'I feared as much. And so did he. He saw you, you know, that last afternoon.'

Rowenna stared at him.

'That last afternoon? When I was in the garden with – with Mr Boothroyd? He's told you about that?'

'I reckon he told me most things,' Kieran said quietly. 'Some he understood, some he didn't. Like that last day.'

'I know. I've wished so often I could have explained. I had no idea, you see – it was so unexpected, I hardly knew what to do. And I would never have married Alfred if – '

'No,' he broke in. 'Stop. It's not me you should be telling this. It's my son. He's the one who's yearning for you.'

Rowenna's heart leapt. 'Yearning? You mean he – he still loves me?'

'A year or two's none so long to keep on loving,' Kieran said. 'It'd not be worth much if it had died already.'

'No. And I still love him.' She spoke frankly, knowing that nothing less would do for this man. Meeting his eyes again, the eyes that were so like Kester's, she asked, 'Where is he now? Is he in Appleby?'

Kieran's head shook slowly and her hope began to fade. Had she lost him after all? Had he gone too far away? Was it even now too late?

'He was here,' Kieran said. 'He was here until a few days ago. And then he went.' He paused, as if thinking over his next words. 'He went to find you.'

'To find *me*? But – ' She turned to Mr Abercrombie. 'Did you hear that? He's gone to look for me – while I was coming here to look for him!'

The lawyer's face was wreathed in smiles. 'I did indeed hear it, my dear. And it's clear what we must do. We must make all speed back to Kendal. We'll leave first thing tomorrow morning. And then we'll see what else the good Lord sends!'

But what was sent to Rowenna when she returned to Kendal was another surprise. For Kester had been to Ashbank to look for her, as might have been expected since he knew nothing of her marriage. He had encountered one of the maids, who had told him that Rowenna was now Mrs Boothroyd. But when he crossed the bridge to Meadowbank he saw no sign of Rowenna, and finally one of the gardeners told him that she had gone away.

'We don't know where she've gone,' the man said. 'The master don't tell us nothing. And we don't ask him, neither. Walking about like a bear with a sore head, he is, and a face like thunder. Wherever she've gone, he don't like it much, but I reckon she's a lot better off. Pale as a ghost she was those last few weeks, aye, and as thin as that old rake over there.'

Nobody knew about James Abercrombie. And there was nothing Kester could do but go back to Appleby, where the fair was packing up and the gipsies making their goodbyes before setting off on their own routes. It would be another year before many of them met again.

'It doesn't matter,' Mr Abercrombie said when they discovered from Molly what had happened. 'It's a great pity he didn't ask Molly, since she's the only person who knows you're here, but how was he to know she was married to young Richmond? But his father will tell him when he arrives in Appleby, and he'll be back again, soon enough.'

But before Kester could return, a further shock came from Meadowbank. Alfred Boothroyd had discovered where Rowenna was, and appeared in Mr Abercrombie's office one morning. It was only with the greatest difficulty that Mr Abercrombie managed to send a message to the house, where his wife completed Rowenna's packing in great haste and set off at once with her to Liverpool, to sail on the first ship available for Canada.

'But I can't leave now!' Rowenna cried in agony, as the train steamed out of Oxenholme station. 'Why, Kester might arrive at any moment – '

'And so might your husband.' Mrs Abercrombie patted her hand. 'My dear, you must look after yourself. If Alfred Boothroyd catches you now, he'll have you committed to an asylum – you know he's threatened it, and he's capable of doing it, just to punish you. And there would be nothing any of us could do to save you. And if the young man wants you badly enough, he'll follow you – to Canada or to the ends of the earth. But you'll be better to think of making your own life, amongst your own family, in a new country. Put the past behind you, all of it, and start afresh. And tell yourself that whatever happens, it will turn out for the best.'

The best? Rowenna stared out at the fleeing countryside and wondered. How could all the things that had happened to her be 'for the best'? Her mother's death, and Haddon's. Her father's possessive greed. Alfred's cruel brutality. And the anguish of her love for Kester.

Shall I ever see him again? she wondered as the tall masts of the ships in Liverpool docks came into view. Is this the end of our story? Or will it continue, somehow, in a different place and time?

And what will I find in Canada?

Part Two

Chapter Fourteen

'I suppose,' Fay Tyson said with a smile, 'that you thought we were all pioneers here in Ontario, living in log cabins and fighting off bears every time we stepped outside the door.'

Rowenna coloured a little. She had indeed been surprised by the grace and comfort in which her Canadian relatives lived, but hoped she had been able to conceal it. She looked around the large, airy drawing room. It could have been part of the home of any prosperous merchant or manufacturer in England, yet there was something about it that set it apart. A different way of hanging the pictures, perhaps, or draping the curtains. But the furniture was just the same – richly upholstered in deep red, with fringes of gold – and each surface was scattered with family photographs and bric-à-brac.

'It's a beautiful house,' she said sincerely, thinking of her first glimpse of it a couple of weeks ago. A little near to the road, perhaps, and open to the gaze of all with no more than a wide strip of lawn between it and the road, but elegant in a way that was certainly different from anything she had seen at home. It was larger than Ashbank and built of stone, and it looked as if it had been built with casual artistry, with turrets and corners being stuck on almost as an afterthought, while the verandah which ran round two sides was an invitation to sit out in the warm summer air.

Fay shrugged carelessly. 'I guess it's not bad. I keep telling my father, we ought to find somewhere better, but he's an old stick-in-the-mud and likes it here. Imagine,' she said, rolling her eyes, 'wanting to stay in the same house all your life! Can you think of anything duller?' She stretched her body lazily, showing off the dress she wore. It was at least as fine as anything Rowenna had seen in England and Fay, though a year or so younger than her cousin, had a poise that would have been envied by quite a few of the society ladies of Kendal. People, as well as houses and furnishings, were turning out to be a great deal more cosmopolitan than Rowenna had expected.

'I can't think of anything nicer, if it's a house you like and you're with the right people,' she said.

'The right people! Who are they? Oh, I guess you mean a handsome husband and a crowd of children.' Fay laughed. 'Well, I'd go along with the handsome husband, but I'd want a nurse or someone to look after the children. And between you and me, I wouldn't mind too much if they didn't just happen to come along. They don't have to, you know. There are ways of preventing it – sponges, syringes, even pieces of sheep's intestines, though I think that sounds quite grue-some!' She laughed at Rowenna's shocked face. 'Didn't you hear all the scandal a few years ago, over that book – "The Private Companion of Married People", it was called. It told you all about it, in the most graphic detail!'

Rowenna shook her head. It was not a matter that would be discussed in the drawing rooms of Kendal, and she would never have dreamed of suggesting such a thing to Alfred.

'But surely gentlemen are always anxious to have children,' she said, wondering how she and this girl had come to have such an intimate conversation so soon after meeting. Fay had been away, staying with a friend, when Rowenna had arrived, and only returned yesterday. 'It's a wife's duty.'

Fay stared. 'Well, *you* may think so, but I'm of the opinion that a woman should be able to decide for herself whether she wants to put her life in danger. *And* whether she wants to lose her figure.' She got up and preened herself in front of a large mirror, running her hand down the long, golden waves that streamed down her back, and moving her body a little to show off its slender curves. Her dress was the same sky blue as her eyes, with white lace on the bodice and running down the skirt, and she wore little blue boots to match.

She turned and looked down at Rowenna, her eyes bright with curiosity. 'You're married – why haven't you had any children?'

'No reason at all,' Rowenna answered, feeling her cheeks colour as she thought of the false pregnancy. 'It doesn't always happen immediately.'

Fay laughed. 'That's not what I've heard!' She studied Rowenna speculatively. 'If you haven't been married long, why have you come to Canada on your own? Wasn't your husband loth to let you go? Didn't he want to come too?'

Rowenna looked at her helplessly. She did not want to answer Fay's questions but sensed that if she didn't the other girl would probe mercilessly until she was satisfied. To her relief, at that moment the door opened and her Aunt Ruth came in, followed by a maid wheeling a trolley laden with sandwiches and cakes.

'Don't quiz the poor girl,' she admonished her daughter. 'Why, she's scarcely got her feet on dry land! I daresay she just wanted to come over and see us all, didn't you, child? Now, are you hungry enough for a turkey sandwich, or will a cookie be enough?'

Rowenna was hungry enough to eat some of everything. Since leaving Alfred, her appetite had returned and, with it, some flesh and all those bodily functions which had begun to dwindle or even disappear. She no longer found it impossible to swallow and the taste of ashes, which had been in her mouth whenever she tried to eat, was replaced by all the flavours she had thought lost for ever. On the sea voyage across the Atlantic, she had been the envy of her fellow-passengers, for she never suffered the slightest twinge of seasickness and was sometimes the only passenger in the diningroom. Her only fear now was that she would put on too much weight and be unable to wear the dresses she had brought with her.

Her Aunt Ruth was her mother's sister, and she had told Rowenna several times already that they'd been 'as like as two peas'. As soon as the family had received news of Rowenna's visit, she had declared that the girl must stay with her and John, her husband, and their daughter. Especially as her father, Jacob, lived with them now and would be wanting to see as much as possible of his granddaughter. Fay, too, was only a year younger than Rowenna and would be company for her.

It had all worked out well. Ruth welcomed her niece with effusion and made sure she had every comfort. Her husband John Davis welcomed her equally in his quiet way, and old Jacob Tyson had been almost overcome with emotion, holding her hands in both of his and repeating her name over and over again, calling everyone to come and see how much like Dorothy she was.

'She was my favourite daughter,' he said, regardless of his other daughter's feelings as she stood by to hear this. 'My Dorothy. Just like her ma, she was pretty and sweet as the day is long. It was a crime what that man did to her.'

'Father!' Ruth protested. 'You're talking about Rowenna's father.'

'Well, that doesn't alter the truth of what he was,' Jacob said uncompromisingly. 'A surly old curmudgeon too mean even to give himself the time of day. He drove my daughter to her grave. There's no reason why I have to be polite about him, even to his daughter.' He looked with sharp blue eyes into Rowenna's face. 'I daresay you know him pretty well anyway, ain't that so?'

Rowenna felt her face break into a smile. 'Yes, I do, Grandfather.'

'Hm. And you'd rather I spoke the truth, I daresay. No more time for mealy-mouthed cant than I have, if there's a scrap of Tyson about you.'

There is, and more than a scrap, Rowenna had thought, looking at the bewhiskered old face, strong even though he was over ninety. From what he had said, she knew that she resembled her grandmother, his wife Jemima, but she felt a rapport with him that told her that such resemblance was only skin deep. In character, she was like him.

He came in now to eat tea with them. He was not often in the house during the day, for he worked as long hours as he ever had at the sawmill he had built on Chaudiere Island, in the middle of the Ottawa River. Here the massive Falls provided water power for several mills, including those of the two great lumbermen Ezra Butler Eddy and John R. Booth.

The careers of these two men, Jacob had told Rowenna, had followed almost parallel paths. Both born in 1827, they had worked their way up – Eddy through making matches, Booth through building railroad bridges and carpentry – and into the logging industry. Both were now important figures on the local scene. Ezra Butler Eddy's new sulphite mill was already in its first stages of construction and it was said that he would follow it with a papermill. He was tipped to become Mayor of Hull, across the river from Ottawa, that year. And J. R. Booth, who had supplied all the wood for the great Parliament Buildings which stood so proudly on their wooded promontory looking up and down the river, now owned more timber limits than anyone else in Ontario.

Jacob Tyson was thirty years older than these two and had come to Canada as a settler, with only a small parcel of land. He and his wife had worked like slaves to clear their land and grow enough food for themselves and their family to live on. They had been fortunate enough to be near a waterfall and Jacob had quickly realised the need for mills – a grist mill for grinding the wheat they grew, and a sawmill for building. Once these had been erected, other settlers began to arrive. Jemima Tyson ran a small general store at the end of the mill and, with the timber Jacob was now felling and cutting, the settlement grew rapidly. A blacksmith arrived, then a butcher. A school was built for the children, a church, and a hotel for travellers. A distillery was set up on the banks of the river, using up surplus products from the grist mill, and a tannery took advantage of the high tannin content of the bark of hemlock trees. A tavern was essential for all the men now working at Penrith, as Jacob had named it, and bigger houses for the doctor, the teacher and the minister. Jacob and Jemima too extended their farmhouse, turning it into a long, rambling building which was by now filled with children. And gradually they ceased to harvest wheat, and instead harvested trees, which grew in profusion and were there for the cutting.

'Millions and millions of 'em, stretching as far as the eye could see,' he told Rowenna. 'Aye, that was a sight and no mistake. And the men going off into the bush in September to start work, and not coming out again till spring. They still do, but it's easier now – they live in log cabins and shanties instead of tents, and they use horses to draw the timber down to the water. In my day we used oxen, and they're stupid great beasts, you have to drag them about to make 'em do what you want. Horses, now, they get to understand, they know what the job is and they make sure it's done right. I've had teams wouldn't move till their tackle was fastened right. I might forget, but *they* never would!'

Rowenna listened, fascinated, as he told her tales of the bush. He had been one of the early loggers, going into the forest during the summer to inspect the trees and see if they were suitable. He scorned the old 'timber-lookers' used by some settlers.

'Charlatans, they were! Why, they knew nothing about trees – they'd just go paddling up the rivers in their canoes, look at the trees from the water and guess how much there was. Never used their legs. Now *I'd* land where it looked good and walk – two, three miles sometimes, I'd walk through thick bush – I'd get up on a hill or climb a big tree and see what there was to be seen for miles beyond that. And you know what, sometimes I'd see that there'd been a bush fire, a big one, spread almost down to the water, and not a tree left living. And any feller employed one of these guys, he'd be wasting his money buying nothing but burnt wood. I never did that. Anything I bought was good stuff, still is.'

He had a strange accent, half Cumberland, half Canadian. But he had all the astuteness of a northerner, and Rowenna guessed that he had never wasted a penny in his life. But he wasn't mean. His house was comfortably furnished and, she guessed, kept warm in winter. Nobody would shiver over a meagre dinner in Jacob Tyson's home. And even though Ruth was now in charge of the house-keeping, it was obvious that it was still run on very much the lines that Jacob decreed.

'Mind you, we knew hard times, Jemima and me,' he told Rowenna. 'It wasn't easy, coming here back in the twenties

311

to virgin forest. We had to cut it back ourselves, build our own shanty – we lived the first three months in a tent, and Jemima expecting our Eliza most of the time – and while we were doing that we had to grow our own food or starve. There were times that first year or so, before the garden got going, when I thought we would, too. And a day's journey to go to the nearest trading post for supplies – aye, it was a cruel time. It was a good few years before we were really on our feet.'

Rowenna was half admiring, half envious. A hard life it certainly had been, but how exciting, coming to this new country to carve out a new life.

Some of the settlers hadn't survived, her grandfather said. Unable to get their homes weatherproof in time for the winter, they had almost died of cold in the bitter snow-storms. They had run out of food and starved, or their gardens had not grown as they should. Some were over-whelmed by problems and returned, bankrupt, to the city. Some women died in childbirth, leaving families of small children for a father to look after; some men were killed by accidents or illness, their wives forced to sell their homes for whatever they could get.

'But if you were canny and ready to work hard, you could get by,' Jacob said. 'Jemima and I – we were lucky, coming from Cumberland. It's not an easy life on those fells and we were used to cold – though it was never as cold as it is here. You'll see what I mean, if you stay the winter.'

Part of their early success had been due to their obtaining the postal franchise for the store that Jemima ran. This meant regular visits from every settler for miles around to collect mail and buy supplies. And soon the sawmill was expanding and Jacob was looking further afield.

'I wanted to build a mill at Chaudiere ever since I first came to Ottawa,' he said. 'Why, it wasn't even *called* Ottawa then – Bytown, it was, after its founder. But when the Queen, God bless her, chose it for the capital of the Province, she decided on Ottawa, thought it was more fitting.'

'But what does it mean? It's such a strange name.'

Jacob smiled. He still had his own teeth and they gleamed through his snowy whiskers. 'Aye, that's because it's Indian. "City of the Big Ears", it means – because the local Injuns, them from Algonquin who lived in all this part, wore earrings so big their ear-lobes reached their shoulders!'

Rowenna laughed, hardly knowing whether to believe him or not. In such a strange country, almost anything was believable – but shoulder-length ear-lobes? Surely not.

'And so you built your mill at Chaudiere.'

'Aye, that's right. There was all that power there, y'see, tumbling over the rocks and going to waste. I was one of the first – there's others there now – Bronson's & Weston, A. H. Baldwin, Levi Young, Ezra Eddy – and young JR himself, of course. Him and Eddy, they're rivals, one on the north of the river, the other on the south. The Civil War gave us a few problems – the Americans stopped buying our lumber – but young Booth had done well out of the contract for the Parliament Buildings and he bought out his partner and kept going. And once it was over, business picked up for all of us. And he and I and one or two others saw that the way ahead was to buy up as much good timber as we could lay hands on.'

'So that's what you did next.'

'Aye, and borrowed heavily to do it, too. Just twenty years ago this was – a lot of timber limits reverted to the Government at that time, and the Department of Crown Lands decided to auction it off. Well, we weren't going to let that chance slip through our fingers so JR went to his bank and I went to mine and a couple of others did the same. The banks took a bit of persuading, I can tell you, but we had good standing and they knew if they didn't take a risk on us they could lose a lot of money too, so they gave us good credit.

'JR and me, we went to the auction together. He was interested in the Egan limits, up on the Madawaska River, and I was after some more land around Penrith. He'd sent his cousin from Pembroke up to have a look, and he'd said it was so good he ought to buy at any price. He reckoned the pine was standing like grass up there.' He smiled and stroked his whiskers with a strong forefinger. 'You'd have laughed to see us that day. We went dressed as rough labourers, just looked in to gape at the fun, like. JR stood with his bank manager and I stood with mine. Well, the bidding started for the limits I wanted and I let it go on for a bit before I joined in. Most people reckoned the limits would fetch about twenty or twenty-five thousand dollars but it went on past that and they started dropping off like flies. Up and up it went, and just me and some city guy left in it. And then it got to forty thousand. The auctioneer looked at us both – the city feller all dressed up in his best, and me in my working clothes. He shook his head – and I nodded mine. And that was that!'

'And Mr Booth?' Rowenna asked, picturing the scene as the roomful of men watched the battle between the sleek city man and her grandfather, big and burly in his working clothes. 'Did he buy the land he wanted?'

'Aye, he did. Paid five thousand dollars more'n I did, but he was well pleased. Mind you, they all thought we were mad. Said we'd lose all we'd got. And I reckon our bank managers had a few sleepless nights over it, too. But d'you know, six months hadn't gone by before one of the big timber barons offered me another ten thousand dollars on what I'd paid, and last year I turned down over a hundred thousand. And the same thing's happened to JR. Those limits had some of the best standing timber in the whole of the Ottawa valley. I don't reckon we've ever taken out less than a hundred and fifty thousand logs in a season, and sometimes it's been nearly double that.'

'But how can you keep on doing that?' Rowenna asked. 'Surely you'll run out of trees some time.'

Her grandfather shook his head.

'Not in my lifetime, nor yours, nor your children's children's lifetimes. There's timber in Canada for everyone. You'll see for yourself when you go up to Penrith. Trees stretching for thousands of miles – why, if you walked into the bush and kept on going, you wouldn't see another human being till you got to Hudson Bay, and then it'd be Eskimos! That's if you lived long enough. It'd be a long walk. There's plenty of men died through getting lost in the forest.'

Rowenna listened to her grandfather's tales for hours on end. Not only were they fascinating to hear but, as he shared his experience with her, he was giving her something she had unknowingly craved all her life: he was taking the place of the father she had never truly had. For although Warren had figured largely in her life, he had always been a frightening figure, dominating his wife and daughter. He had never shown Rowenna any softness, never taken her on his knee and crooned to her, never given her any more than a duty kiss with his bristling whiskers.

Jacob Tyson was a hard, tough man, who had toiled hard for all of his ninety-odd years and still rose at five every morning to ride to work on his favourite horse or in a buggy driven by an old employee who had lost a leg in a forest accident. The labourers' clothes he had worn to the auction were no fancy-dress – they were his normal costume, for he was as likely to be found in the lumberyard, piling timber or repairing the buildings, as in his office.

315

'I'll not rust away,' he would say. 'I can sit at my desk when the daylight's gone. And good manual work never did anyone any harm – it's worry that kills men off. Working with his hands keep a man fresh. And there's nowt better than being amongst the trees.'

He was fond of saying that he never asked any of his employees to work harder than himself – though more than one of them would ruefully attest that it would be a difficult thing to achieve. But he was as generous as he was demanding, and frequently filled his buggy with scraps of wood to deliver as kindling to the poorer homes during the cold winters. Sick men were paid as if they were at work – 'they still have families to keep, don't they?' – but he did not, as a few other timber barons did, pay pensions to old employees. Instead, he gave them easier jobs, as watchmen or general helpers.

'I don't believe in retirement,' he told Rowenna as she poured him another cup of tea. 'I don't intend to retire myself and I won't pay anyone else to sit at home with nowt to do. A man's better with something to occupy himself with. I've worked hard all my life for what I've got and I'm working still – why should I hand it over to men who are healthy and strong, and twenty-five years younger than me!'

Rowenna laughed. She looked at her grandfather, who had been up since five that morning, piling timber with men not just twenty-five but fifty, even seventy, years younger than himself, and thought of the difference between him and her father. No wonder Dorothy had asked his help in making provision for her daughter.

'Aye, I knew she wasn't happy,' he told Rowenna. 'He let her come over here once on a visit, but never again – scared she'd not go back, I guess. And I reckon that's what would have happened, if she hadn't died. But she made sure you'd be all right first, and I was glad to help her do it.' He gave Rowenna one of his sharp glances. 'Still am. Don't see any reason to change my mind over that.'

He set down his cup and wiped his mouth with a large handkerchief. 'Well, I've got work to do. Can't sit gossiping with a pack of women all day. Ruth, we'd better make plans to take Rowenna up to Penrith. I'll be going up myself in a week or two, to plan out next year's harvest with young Serle, she can come with me then.' He glanced at Rowenna. 'You'd like that, I guess.'

'Oh yes,' Rowenna said at once, but Fay cut in quickly.

'Penrith? Oh, what a good idea. May I come too, Grandpa?'

Ruth looked at her daughter in surprise. 'But you don't like the forest. You said you wouldn't care if you never saw Penrith again.'

'Oh, Mother, really!' Fay moved her shoulders impatiently. 'That was years ago. I was just a child. Of course I'd like to see Penrith again. Why, it's beautiful there. Anyway, Rowenna will need some female company – there's nothing but rough men at Penrith.' She waited a moment, then added casually, 'It will be pleasant to see Serle again, too.'

Ruth glanced sideways at her but said nothing. Jacob shrugged.

'Come along if you want to. But don't expect home comforts. And you'll have to pull your weight, take care of yourself. There's no room for frills and furbelows.'

He got up and left the room, still tall and sturdy, and Ruth disappeared on some household concern. The two girls were left alone.

'Let's go and look at your clothes,' Fay suggested.

'My clothes?' Rowenna could think of no duller pastime, but Fay was clearly interested and she wanted to get to know this new cousin, so she led the way up to her bedroom and opened the big closet.

Fay lifted out the dresses on their hangers, eyeing them

317

critically. Rowenna had the impression that she was disappointed and was amused when Fay said in slightly scornful tones, 'Why, I thought you'd be real fashionable, coming from England. Is this the sort of thing they're wearing now in London?'

If I said yes, she'd probably exclaim over them and want her own made in the same style, Rowenna thought, but she said equably, 'I shouldn't think so. I don't really take much notice of what they're wearing in London – or even in Kendal. I just have things made to suit me.'

'*Do* you? But don't you care about such things at all?'

'Not much.' Rowenna put her hand up to her head. Before sailing from Liverpool she had paid a visit to a hairdresser and had her hair cut short, cropped almost like a boy's. Without a maid to help dress it, she could never have coped with the long mane that had been growing ever since she was a baby, and since it was always worn up at the back of her head, it made little difference whether it was long or short. But she was aware of other people's curious glances, although she could see that some of the women envied her.

'Is *that* a fashion?' Fay asked dubiously, and seemed relieved to be told that it was not. 'Why did you have it cut?'

'Because it would be easier to look after. It used to be longer than yours.'

'Long enough to sit on?'

'Yes. But I don't find hair convenient to sit on, and it was such a nuisance in bed. I'm much more comfortable without it.'

Fay shrugged. 'Well, you're obviously one who would rather be comfortable than stylish, and since you've got a husband I suppose it doesn't matter. But I like to lead the fashions around here. I'm always first with anything new.' She didn't seem displeased that Rowenna was unlikely to oust her from this position, and Rowenna realised that her cousin had probably not looked forward to the arrival of this visitor from England. Well, she has nothing to fear from me, Rowenna thought. I've no desire to be one of the fashion leaders of Ottawa.

'Who is Serle?' she asked, remembering Fay's interest when their grandfather had mentioned visiting him. 'Is he one of Grandfather's lumbermen?'

Fay's eyes widened. 'Don't you know? Surely Ma has given you a complete family tree of all of us here in Canada? Serle's a sort of cousin – he's not really related, not by blood, but Uncle George and Aunt Phyllis kind of adopted him when he was about six years old. His ma was Aunt Phyllis's cousin. She got killed somehow in a riding accident and his pa went off west and couldn't look after Serle any more, so they took him over. He works for Grandpa now, up at Penrith. He's in charge of the whole operation up there.'

She spoke with a kind of half-possessive pride, as if Serle were of more than ordinary interest to her, and this impression was confirmed when she gave Rowenna a sharp look and said, 'I've known Serle since I was a baby. He's twelve years older than me but we've always been real good friends – specially since I came home from school. I daresay we'll get married some time, when I'm ready.'

Well, that's a clear enough notice to keep off the grass, Rowenna thought. She said, 'Are you engaged?'

'Oh no! There's nothing official – I won't agree to that yet. I want to have a little fun before I settle down. Of course, it would be nice to have a diamond ring on my finger and for all the other girls to know not to bother setting their caps at him – but I'd have to be so dreadfully *good*!' She wrinkled up her nose. 'It would be no fun at all to go to balls and such, with Serle away up at Penrith, and not able even to flirt a little. No, I'm not ready to tie myself down yet – but when I am, Serle will be there.'

'Tell me about Penrith,' Rowenna suggested. 'I gather it's not so comfortable as Ottawa.'

'It's not comfortable at all,' Fay declared. 'Serle lives in the home Grandpa and Grandma built for themselves. It's quite big, but really it's no more than a shack. Quite plain and bare, you know. Of course, it's been improved – Serle's put in a water-pump so you don't have to go to the well any more – but I shall insist on a better house when we're married. Not that I intend to spend much time there. I want a new house in Ottawa, where I can see my friends.'

'But how can you be married if you don't want to live with your husband?' Rowenna asked, bewildered, and Fay gave a little trill of laughter. Her voice was light and silvery, almost babyish at times.

'Who said I didn't want to live with Serle? Of course I do – why, he's the handsomest man this side of the Ottawa River. He'll move down here, of course – he doesn't have to be up at Penrith all the time. I tell him, there's no use in being boss if you can't leave the work to someone else.'

Rowenna wondered what her grandfather would have to say to such a philosophy, but said nothing and after a few minutes Fay announced her intention of going to get ready for dinner. Apparently some friends of her parents were coming and they had, she said, the most *wicked* son. 'He looks at me as if he'd like to *eat* me, and he always manages to snatch a kiss somehow or other.'

Rowenna went to the window. Below her, the lawn stretched to the quiet road and beyond that she could see trees spreading down to the banks of the river and, on the far side, the swell of the Gatineau Hills. She had never seen such forests before, for on the hills at home in Westmorland and Cumberland the trees had gone, grazed out of existence

320

by sheep. Fascinated, she gazed at the thick, varied green of the leaves which she had been told would turn in the autumn to brilliant golds, bronzes and reds. And this was in the city! Wherever there was spare land, not yet built upon, there were trees. What must it be like in the real forest?

How Kester would love it here, she thought, and pressed her forehead against the glass, thinking of the dark-eyed gypsy and wondering once more if she would ever see him again.

She had received no word from England since her arrival for, even had there been any news to tell, there had been barely time for a letter. Daily, she looked for the post, but none came with her name upon it. But at the first opportunity, she had sat down to write to Mr Abercrombie and she knew he would reply soon.

What would Kester do when he learned that she had been looking for him? Would he write to her? She wondered if he had even gone back to Appleby – his father, Kieran, had told her that he came and went almost like a shadow in the sun, appearing without warning and vanishing again as soon as the mood took him. He was restless, unable to settle anywhere, and as likely to take ship and go to sea as to return to the travelling life. Fairgrounds, with their noisy steam roundabouts and organs and bawling cries, were not for him. He preferred to work with living things – horses, plants, trees.

But plants and trees took time to grow, and Kester could no longer stand still to tend them.

Rowenna could feel his torment, for it was hers too. The journey to Canada, with almost two weeks at sea, had satisfied some of her need for movement and action. Each day she had walked the decks, watching the waves that rolled endlessly by and gazing at the vast circle of the horizon. The sky rose in a huge dome above, sometimes entirely blue, sometimes scudding with clouds that grew to an ominous black shadow, bringing rain and wind that tossed the waves to gigantic walls of green glass with crests of broken white foam. Such storms, driving most passengers below to their cabins, filled Rowenna's yearning breast with excitement, and she watched with rapt eyes, turning away only when one of the ship's officers persuaded her that she would be safer below decks.

Her arrival in Canada, too, had distracted her a little from her longing. The excitement of a new country, with so many different sights and sounds, had driven much else from her mind. It had all been so much more foreign than she had expected, for Quebec, where the ship had docked, was more French than English. On every side, she had heard voices she would have associated more with Paris, and even notice-boards and signs were in French. She had been forced to dredge her mind for the words and phrases learned at school, though she had been assured that even the French Canadians could speak English perfectly well, when they chose. It's just that they don't always choose, she had been told with wry humour.

From Quebec she had travelled by train to Montreal, and from there, on the newly opened Canadian Atlantic railway – built, her grandfather had since told her, by J.R. Booth to carry his lumber more quickly down to the seaports – to the Canadian capital. The journey took less than three hours, for the train travelled at a mile a minute, and Rowenna had not even had time to accustom herself to dry land before she was being welcomed by her Aunt Ruth and Uncle John and whisked away by buggy to the elegant house on Elgin Street.

But thoughts of Kester could never be far from her mind and in the fortnight since her arrival she had been in a ferment of wondering and longing. What was Kester thinking and doing? Where was he? Did he know she had come to Canada – and what would he do? Would he write to her – might he even follow her?

But he knows now that I'm married, she thought with a clench of her heart. He was told when he went to Ashbank, while we were looking for him at Appleby. Suppose he didn't go back to his father. Suppose he never finds out about Mr Abercrombie, or hears that I've come to Canada.

Suppose he thinks I'm happy with Alfred Boothroyd . . .

The thought of her husband's name made her shiver. What was he doing, now that she had left him? And what of her father, who might not know even yet that she had fled to Canada? Would they combine, the two of them, to bring her back, perhaps even to follow her here?

Was she truly safe?

Warren Mellor swayed unsteadily as he made his way through the mill yard. He had not been into the mill for some while, and the noise of the machinery struck his befuddled brain as he entered the doors and stood for a moment looking down the steam-filled paper hall. The four-driniers were working steadily, paper moving along the length of the hall in a great, endless sheet, from the huge open vats on the upper floor where the pulp was stirred into a thick porridge to the reels where it was wound ready for slicing.

The office door was closed as usual but he opened it and went through the main office to the little room which had been his sanctum. Here, through the glass panel, he could see that Alfred Boothroyd was at work, his head bent over a desk laden with papers.

Warren pushed open the door and Boothroyd looked up. The irritation on his face was quickly deepened to annoyance, tempered with wariness. He got up.

'Mellor! What are you doing here?'

'I've come to work.' Warren stared at him truculently. 'In my own office. Is there something strange about that?'

'You know you're not fit to work,' Boothroyd said curtly. 'You should be at home, taking it easy.'

'Taking it easy! There's precious little ease for me at home, since that nagging shrew of a sister of yours moved in and took over. Why, she – '

'I'll thank you not speak so of my sister,' Boothroyd warned, and Warren snorted.

'She's my wife and I'll speak of her how I choose.' He stared around the office. Boothroyd had altered the position of the desk. He had put up racks for paper samples, and shelves for files and ledgers. 'You've changed it. You've thrown out all my things.'

'Personal possessions only,' Boothroyd said coldly. 'Brandy bottles, glasses, a decanter. They're packed in a box and will be sent to your house immediately.'

Warren started forwards. He raised his arms threateningly.

'You're not throwing me out of my own office! This is *mine* – in *my* mill. What right d'you think you've got – '

'It's *ours*,' Boothroyd said. 'And that in name only. I knew you were a sinking ship when I entered into partnership with you, but I didn't realise you were a complete wreck.' He gestured at the papers lying on the desk. 'I found an even worse mess after I married Rowenna than there was when you were ill. God knows what you'd done in those few weeks! Orders ignored, deliveries not met, entries not made in the ledgers . . . We're lucky to have kept our heads above water, Mellor, and if I hadn't been able to inject a good deal of assistance from my own side of the business, you'd have gone down and sunk without trace.'

'I don't believe it – '

324

'It doesn't matter to me whether you believe it or not.'
Boothroyd pushed a chair round the desk for him. 'Sit your-self down and rest, then I'll get someone to see you safely home. Meanwhile, I have work to do . . .' He bent his head again over the ledger he had been working on.

Warren stared at him. He was trembling, and he put out a hand to steady himself against the door jamb. His knees felt weak and there was a roaring in his ears. He raised his voice, trying to achieve the threatening bellow he had used so often in the past to intimidate his family and his employees, but instead he heard the shrill complaint of an old man.

'Haven't you taken away enough, Boothroyd? You've taken away my mill, my daughter and most of my money. You've taken away my office and my work. And all I've got in exchange is that scold of a wife, who won't even let me into my own drawing room, let alone what she's now pleased to call *her* bed. For pity's sake, can't you even leave me somewhere to sit of a morning?' He waited a moment, but Boothroyd did not look up, and Warren suddenly lunged forward and banged his hand on the desk, so viol-ently that a pile of papers flew into the air and scattered themselves over the floor, while the ledger itself trembled.

'For God's sake,' Boothroyd said in irritation, bending to pick up the papers. 'Control yourself, man, or I'll have to call someone in to throw you out.'

'*Throw me out*? Of my own office?' And this time Warren did achieve his old belligerent roar. Filled with sudden energy, he started forwards again, both hands held out like claws, as if to throttle his tormentor. 'Do you dare to threaten me like that? Why, I'd see you in hell first – aye, and be glad to welcome you in. And maybe there you'd tell me what you've done with my daughter, for there are no secrets in that place, I can tell you that!'

There was a moment of total silence. Then Boothroyd

gave a quick glance towards the outer office. The clerks all had their heads bent, scribbling away furiously, but he knew that their ears must be pricked up like rabbits'. Swiftly, he came round the desk and thrust the door shut, then pushed Warren into the chair he had put ready for him.

'Sit down, Mellor, and calm yourself. Now, what in God's name do you mean by that?'

'By what?' Warren asked, but his tone was little more than truculent again now, and he stared up at Boothroyd with bleary, reddened eyes. His lower lip worked and he plucked at it with nervous, shaking fingers. 'I just want to know where my daughter is,' he whined. 'She's not been across to see me lately. I miss her.'

'I told you the other day, she's gone away for a short holiday.'

'The other day? It must be a fortnight ago, even longer. Where's she gone, and why did she go without coming to say goodbye to me?' He stared suspiciously at Boothroyd. 'People are asking me where she is. What am I to tell them?'

'The same as I've told you. As for when she's returning, why, she doesn't even tell me that – as and when she pleases, I suppose. She's enjoying herself too much to think of returning to her dull life at home.' He seemed to detect a note of bitterness in his own voice and changed his tone quickly, giving Warren a crooked smile, as if to invite him to share a complicity of men faced by the vagaries of their womenfolk. 'You know what these young women are when they get a notion in their heads. And you must admit, your daughter has always been a little headstrong.'

'Headstrong? She's never been allowed her own way. If she's breaking out against discipline, it must be your doing.' Warren was not to be mollified. He had come here with one thought in his blurred mind, and he would not let it go. 'I still want to know where she is, and so do other people.'

'Then they must continue to wonder,' Boothroyd said crisply. 'It's none of their business anyway.'

'And I suppose you're telling me it's none of my business. I'm the girl's father – '

'And I'm her husband. What she does is my business and nobody else's. Not even yours.'

'Dammit, I was responsible for her for nearly twenty-one years – '

'And I'm responsible for her now. If there's anything you need to know, you'll be told. Now I'd be grateful if you'd go home and leave me to get on with my work.'

Warren's face was puce. 'Are you telling me I have no right to know anything about my own daughter? Are you really trying to tell me – '

Boothroyd slapped his palm on the table.

'She's not your worry any more, Mellor. Can't you be grateful for that fact? God knows she's given me enough headaches – and I'll tell you this, if I knew where she was now, I'd be glad to let you go and bring her home, so that I can deal with her as she deserves – ' He stopped and closed his mouth tightly, his eyes snapping with fury.

Warren stared at him.

'You don't know where she is? You *don't know* where she is?' His voice rose to a shout. 'My God, man, what's been going on in that house of yours? What have you been doing to her to drive her away? She was my daughter – my companion – and you took her from me, just as you've taken everything else I possessed. And now you've *lost* her! Where is she, for God's sake, where is she?'

'I haven't lost her,' Boothroyd snapped. 'She isn't a parcel, for heaven's sake. She's simply taken it into her head to go off for a few weeks' holiday with that money your damned wife left her. I've no doubt she'll be back with her tail between her legs, having spent or been relieved of the

327

bulk of it, and be glad enough to resume married life. And if I may say so, none of this would ever have happened if she had been brought up in the way a young lady should. You let her have far too much of her own way, Mellor, and that's the truth of it. And now I'll send for someone to see you home. You're in no fit state to be wandering about, no fit state at all.'

Warren's head shook violently, as if he were attacked by the ague. He tried to speak, but his words were incoherent, little more than a babble, rising to a shrill scream. He came to his feet, his whole body shaking, and lunged again across the desk. And his babbling suddenly became clear, a demand that refused to be ignored.

'Gone away? I don't believe it. What have you done with her? If you've harmed her, Boothroyd, I'll – I'll kill you. I'll kill you, that's what I'll do!' His hands were claws again, reaching for Boothroyd's throat. *'Tell me what's happened to my daughter!'*

Alfred Boothroyd thrust back his chair, the legs scraping on the stone floor. He lifted an arm to ward off the demented man, but before Warren could touch him the door had burst open and two clerks rushed in and grabbed his arms, holding him back. Boothroyd waited a moment, still leaning back against the wall, until they had the struggling man under control, and then he stepped forwards, breathing hard and wiping spittle from his face.

His voice shaking a little, he said, 'Take him home. Put him up in his bedroom and tell my sister to keep him locked in. I'll send for Dr Cooper at once.'

The quarrel with Warren left Alfred Boothroyd in a state of cold fury, its intensity if anything even greater than the anger he had felt when Rowenna locked him into his bedroom and fled.

It was difficult to know whether his bitter wrath was due more to Rowenna's desertion or to the indignity of Warren's attack. Being virtually forced into admitting that his wife had left him – and admitting it to her father, over whom he had always kept the upper hand – was too bitter a pill for Boothroyd to swallow. After Warren had been dragged away, he sank back into his chair, his body shaking, feeling again the humiliation he had suffered on the day she had locked him into his own room and run from his house.

To be forced to summon a servant to release him from his own room! To know that they must all have heard his quarrel with Rowenna, that they were all well aware of the fact that she had run away from him! His imagination cringed at the thought of what they must be saying below stairs, the sniggers and sly innuendoes. He had never made any effort to win the liking of his servants; now, he was certain that they all hated him and – worse than that, for he cared nothing for their feelings – were laughing at him.

From that day, he had masked his anger with a forbidding iciness which dared any person to approach him and threw himself into his work, giving out that Rowenna had gone off for a short holiday. None of his servants had the courage to refute this, and all kept up the fiction, letting no mention of Rowenna pass their lips. After that first day, they dared not speak of her even to each other, for fear the master might overhear, and within a week it was as if she had never been in the house.

But none of them had forgotten her, and Alfred least of all. And now, leaning his elbows on the desk and resting his head on his hands, his thoughts were filled with images of his wife.

Dressed in black in the churchyard on the day of her brother's funeral, when he had first desired her; walking in the garden in the violet silk she had worn to supper at his

329

house; grubbing amongst the plants in her holland overall. Standing in the little wood, her body pressed lightly against his in their first embrace, her face turned shyly away as he kissed her for the first time. And then in bed, lying beneath him, her eyes tormented as she stared up at him, withdrawing from him even as he thrust into her, driving him on to a greater violence in his desperation to possess her utterly.

He had never possessed her. He knew that. He had used her body to satisfy his appetite, he had striven to make her submit to his will, he had strained to make her look at him, just once, with that look which would tell him that he had won, that she was his, totally subjugated, totally dominated. And he had failed.

Never before had Alfred Boothroyd tasted failure. And the taste of failure and its accompanying humiliation were more bitter to him that aloes. He burned to punish the woman who had dealt him such bitterness.

Chapter Fifteen

The settlement of Penrith was now a healthy township, with the timber limits stretching, as far as Rowenna could see, to the very limits of Canada. She sat in the buggy on top of the hill, at the head of the main street, and stared over the endless forest, trying to comprehend an enormous scale, beyond any of her previous experience. It's like being at sea, she thought, remembering that encircling horizon. There, on calm days, it had been as if the ship was in the middle of a huge blue disc. Now the disc was of thick green vegetation, and although her grandfather had talked of hundreds of thousands of trees being removed, it was difficult to see where there had been any cutting at all.

'But where are the logging camps?' she asked. 'It looks like dense forest everywhere. And we've come through so much already!'

The road from Ottawa had been rough and stony, cleared through forest that grew thickly on either side. Now and then they had passed through small townships like Penrith, or little settlements where families still lived in rough log shanties. The great river had wound along its wide valley on their right, with the dense forests of Quebec apparently untouched on its distant bank. There too logging was steadily removing the great white pines and balsam, yet there was no sign of any depletion. It seemed that taking trees from the

331

Canadian forests was like trying to empty the ocean of water.

Surely it must destroy them eventually, she thought. Even great forests like these can't last for ever. But her grandfather had shaken his head.

'Trees seed themselves. They grow again – that's how they got here in the first place.'

Now, he told her that the camps themselves were further up river. 'We're working on a good stand of pine up there. Come spring, you'll see the rafts coming through here, fifty thousand dollars' worth of logs all bound together, with men living and cooking aboard 'em on their way down to Ottawa. That's what they do, see, they fell the timber all winter and drag it down through the snow to the river, build the rafts on the ice and wait for the thaw to take 'em down. Of course, it's a rough trip – there's plenty of spots higher up, where the river's not so wide, where a raft can't get through and the logs have to be sent down singly. You see 'em all jammed up together in places, piling up by the dozen, and then some poor devil has to go in and sort 'em out. Lost a few good men that way, we have, and a lot of timber too, but plenty of men learn to ride 'em, and that's another sight to see.'

Fay, who had been growing restive on the back seat of the buggy, leaned forward and pulled her grandfather's sleeve. 'Can't we get on now, Grandpa?' she pleaded. 'We've been in this buggy for three whole days. I'm tired of looking at the back of a horse!'

Jacob Tyson laughed and flicked the reins. He took turn and turn about with his driver and had sent the man on, to walk down to Penrith House and warn them of the impending arrival. The buggy moved forwards and the pony broke into a trot, as if it could smell a familiar stable and were as eager as Fay to have done with this journey.

Rowenna looked about her with interest. Fay had spoken disparagingly of Penrith, and she had expected a rough shanty-town, with shabby buildings mostly built of logs. But to her surprise she found a neat village, a good deal larger than Burneside, with rows of white clapboard houses on each side of the road, many with gardens planted gaily with flowers, and a small church with a wooden spire on a grassy mound. There were several stores, each with a covered walk-way in front and a rail where horses could be hitched, and a saloon with glass doors. The road was wide enough to turn a horse and cart, so that the little town had a spacious air, and the people on the sidewalks were dressed as tidily as anyone in England. Several of them waved as the buggy went past, and Jacob lifted his whip in answer.

'Known most of 'em all their lives,' he said to Rowenna. 'Knew their parents when they first came here, and watched 'em grow from babbies. Aye, it's a happy place, Penrith, everyone knows everyone else and we're all good neigh-bours. Have the occasional ding-dong, of course, but that happens in the best of families. It's a good place for wives and families to be while their menfolk are away in the bush.'

Fay wrinkled her nose. 'It's all right for a holiday, but I shouldn't like to live anywhere but Ottawa. There's nothing to *do* in a place like this.'

'Nothing to do?' her grandfather snorted. 'Why, there's everything you could want. Plenty of work, plenty of fun. Socialising, if that's what you want – tea-parties for those that have the time, square dances, whist . . . Why, your grand-mother used to say there was too *much* to do! Let yourself get involved in all that, she'd say, and there was no time for bringing up your family. And that's enough to occupy a woman, no matter where she is.'

Rowenna gave Fay a sideways glance. She didn't agree with all that her cousin said, but she was inclined to feel that Fay was right when she said there was more to a woman's life than bringing up children. Her ventures into her father's papermill with Haddon had given her a taste for what was usually defined as 'man's work'. But why shouldn't a woman do such work too, she argued. Plenty of women slaved in factories. If they could do that, why not enjoy some of the more interesting tasks? And hadn't her grandmother run a store and post office of her own?

After her own experiences at a girls' boarding school, she knew that one of the stumbling blocks was education. But again, her brother had proved to her that a girl could do exactly the same work as a boy. If girls received the same schooling, there was nothing they could not do. And she knew that there were already a few women doctors and even one who practised as a surgeon, while the new colleges at Cambridge were educating girls to the same degree standard as the men.

But all that was a long way from Canada, and at this moment she was more interested in seeing the farmhouse her grandparents had built when they had first settled here and which had grown with their family. It was now occupied by Jacob's adopted grandson, Serle, who managed the Penrith timber limits.

'I only had the two boys,' Jacob had told Rowenna. 'Daniel, sixty-one he is now, and he and his boys are working over in British Columbia – my, there's some timber over there, trees we never see the like of here. Douglas fir, now there's timber for you, only grows over there where it's wet but a good Douglas will make a coupla hundred feet tall. Why, I've seen one out near Chemainus, the Westholme it's called, and it's getting on for three hundred feet high, over forty round its base and must be a good thousand years old. A thousand years? Can you imagine that?'

There were no such vast trees around Penrith but the forests were awesome just the same. They came close to the settlement, their great crowns shading the houses. Fay shivered as the buggy came to a halt in front of the long, low farmhouse with its white-painted picket fence and green lawns.

'They look as if they're just waiting to take over again,' she said. 'When Serle and I are married, we'll have them cut down. I hate them, crowding in the way they do.'

'I suppose they were left to provide shade for the house and garden,' Rowenna said, for she had already found the summer much hotter than she was accustomed to in England. She climbed down from the buggy. Jacob had gone ahead, calling for his grandson, and now he came out of the house with a tall, broad-shouldered man whose dark grey eyes moved over Rowenna with interest.

'This is Serle,' Jacob told her. 'He takes care of the forest while I'm not here. Serle, meet my granddaughter Rowenna, over from England.'

Serle's face broke into a smile and he held out his hand. She took it, feeling a little dazed. He had deep gold hair, almost the same shade as her own though without the fairer streaks that had caused Kester to liken hers to honey and cream, and his eyes were the colour of deep riverwater under a cool sky. They rested on her with appreciation and he held her hand warmly.

'Good morning, Mr Tyson,' she said, wondering if this was the right way to address him. Already she had noticed that Canadians were just as meticulously polite as people at home, calling each other Mr and Mrs or Miss. But Serle was a kind of cousin, wasn't he? She tried to work out their relationship in her head.

'Oh, come,' he said, smiling. 'Surely we don't have to be so formal. I know I'm no blood relation, but we're family all the same, aren't we? And Rowenna's such a pretty name, it seems a shame not to use it.'

Rowenna smiled back at him, but before she could speak Fay broke in, her voice high and pettish.

'Well, aren't you going to say hello to me, Serle? I'm here as well, you know! And I'm hot and thirsty too – aren't you going to ask us in or do we have to stand here on the sidewalk here all afternoon and fry?'

Serle laughed and reached out for Fay, giving her a light kiss on the cheek. He winked at Rowenna.

'Now I shall be kept in order. Fay won't let me get away with a thing. But she's quite right. We forget our manners up here. Come inside and let me offer you some fresh lemonade. Mrs Hutty makes it and sometimes I'd swear it's the only thing keeps me alive in this heat, especially during the black-fly season.'

Rowenna followed him into the house. Fay had told her about the blackflies that swarmed in July and sworn she would never go near the forest when they were about. 'They're so tiny you can hardly see them,' she said, 'but they make big black clouds all the same, and they get *everywhere* – in your ears, your eyes, your nose, down your throat – ugh, they're horrible! I don't know why people don't go screaming mad with them.'

There were plenty of other insects too, Rowenna had discovered during the three-day journey, notably the mosquitos and other biting creatures that came out mostly in the late evening, although there were always a few about during the day and she'd learned to listen for their high-pitched whine. But to compensate, there were the fireflies, little dancing flames that made bright swirls of light in the darkness, and the hummingbirds that looked no bigger than bees, darting like jewels in the sun and hovering over flowers as if held there by invisible cords.

'And how was your journey?' Serle asked when his house-keeper had furnished them all with glasses of cool lemonade and a large plate of cookies. 'Did you enjoy it, Rowenna?'

She nodded. 'Yes, it was beautiful. I've never seen any-thing like your forests. I can't wait for the autumn – *fall*, I mean! – to see all the colours. And it was so interesting seeing all the little villages along the way and stopping overnight.'

'Interesting!' Fay exclaimed, wrinkling her nose. 'Why, it's one of the things that puts me off coming. Those places are disgusting. How families like the Dowlers can put up with living there, I can't imagine.'

'Their home is decent enough,' Jacob said, sounding a little annoyed. 'And the accommodation they offer is quite adequate. We're not looking for luxury.'

He turned away and Fay made a face, as if to say that he might not be looking for luxury, but she certainly was. Rowenna bit her lip to keep from smiling. It had taken her only a very short time to realise that Jacob did not relish his other granddaughter's company, nor she his. The sparks had not flown during the journey but there had been several moments when they had trembled in the air.

'And how did you find the accommodation, Rowenna?' Serle asked, offering her the cookies. 'Was it up to the standard of English hotels?'

'I've no idea,' she said, laughing. 'I've never stayed in one. But I was comfortable enough. As a matter of fact, I enjoyed the Dowlers' settlement at Buchanan most of all. The log houses and barns were fascinating – especially the tiny one they lived in while the main house was being built. How they all squeezed in! But I'm sure they thought it worth waiting – the main house is very nice.'

'Well, it's useful to have such places to put up overnight and stable the horses. They feed them well too, for only twenty-five cents a night.' He turned back to Fay. 'And how many hearts have you broken since I saw you last? A good few, I've no doubt.'

337

Fay gave him the quirky smile that showed off her dimples. 'Really, Serle, what a thing to say! Anyone would think I was a flirt.'

'Oh, surely not,' he murmured, and Rowenna gave him a quick glance. But his face was perfectly straight as he refilled Fay's glass from the tall iced jug. Before anything more could be said, Jacob, who had been growing restive, cut in abruptly.

'It's only three o'clock, Serle. You hadn't planned on taking the whole day off, I guess? Shall we walk down to the yard and you can tell me what's been happening the past few weeks?'

Serle uncoiled himself and stood up, graceful as a cat. He was broad and muscular as well as tall but, Rowenna noticed, he was also very lean. He looked hard and fit, lithe enough to ride logs on the liveliest stretch of water. She thought of the men she knew at home, mostly manufacturers or professional men such as doctors or lawyers. None of them looked like this, as if they spent their lives exercising the muscles that had grown flabby through under-use. None of them looked as if they could survive the life her grandfather had described, living rough in the forest, working in the bitter cold of winter and riding logs down torrents of water unleashed by the thaws of spring.

Except for Kester. But Kester was different from any man she had ever known.

'So,' Serle remarked a day or two later as he drove the buggy out along the forest road, 'you're a woman of property.'

'My timber limits, you mean? Do you know where they are?'

'I certainly do. Deep in the bush – too far for you to make a visit, I'm afraid.' He looked sideways at her and gave her his lazy smile. 'No place for a lady, a loggers' camp.'

'I'm not afraid of travelling,' she said. 'And I'm used to wild places.'

Serle laughed. 'Wild places? Grandpa's told me about Cumberland – why, it would fit into a backyard here! And what kind of wild animals do you have there? Wolves? Bears? Cougars?'

Rowenna shook her head, smiling. 'None of those. Just foxes, badgers and deer.' She glanced at the trees they were passing, clustered thickly beside the road. 'Are there really bears and wolves in there?'

'Why, sure. And moose, like we saw a few minutes ago, and raccoons, and porcupine. Not to mention the odd rattlesnake ready to nip your ankle.' He grinned at her. 'You don't go for a Sunday afternoon stroll in these woods, not without keeping your eyes skinned and a gun at the ready.'

'But surely most animals hide from humans. They don't deliberately attack – or so I've heard.' She remembered tales she had heard of wolves following sledges through the snow and dragging off their prey. She was beginning to feel slightly uneasy. The road was wide enough, but the trees pressing closely to its edges looked as thick and untamed as if they were at the centre of a jungle. Already, as Serle had said, they had seen several moose crossing from one side to the other, huge, burly animals with spreading antlers. Might there even now be a couple of bears or a pack of wolves lurking in the undergrowth?

'Not unless they're cornered, usually. Or particularly hungry in the winter. But I'd never risk a bear's good temper – they can be savage for no reason at all. And their claws can rip a man from top to bottom with one swipe.'

Rowenna shuddered.

'Well, it's true we don't have animals like that in England. But even our hills can be quite dangerous places, especially in winter.'

'Winter!' he exclaimed. 'Why, you don't know what winter's like. It reaches twenty or thirty degrees below here, and that's mild weather. You don't get cold like that in England.'

'I don't know what it goes down to,' Rowenna said, 'but we have a lot of snow, and the lake freezes over some winters.'

'The lake? What lake's that? How big is it?'

'Windermere. It's the biggest one we have. It's about nine miles long and – oh, half a mile wide, I suppose. It freezes hard enough to skate on.'

Serle roared with laughter. 'Nine miles long and half a mile wide! Why, that's just a puddle. It'd take no more'n a hard frost to cover that with ice.' He transferred the reins to one hand and patted her hand with the other. 'Don't take any notice, Rowenna. I'm not really laughing at you. It's just that we're so different.' He looked at her, suddenly serious. '*You're* different.'

'Am I? How?'

'Oh, in lots of ways,' he said. 'I don't know whether it's because you're English or because you're you. But you're not like Fay, for instance. She's all buttons and bows, and curls and lace. You don't seem to care about those things.'

In other words, I'm not feminine, Rowenna thought. 'I just don't think they suit me,' she said, a little defensively. 'I like to look my best, of course—'

'Oh, but you do.'

'—but I've never felt happy dressed up in frills. And anyway, I think there are plenty of things more interesting than clothes.'

'Such as?'

'Well, trees, for instance. My brother Haddon was fascinated by them and he told me a lot about how they grow. He bought seeds from plant-collectors and grew them in our garden. Some of them are quite large now, others are still tiny.' She was silent for a moment, thinking of the seed-bed

340

she and Haddon had been so proud of and nurtured with such care. Kester too had known every baby tree by name and had made the whole wood his own special province.

Who was looking after it now?

'You look sad,' Serle said gently. 'Does the thought of your garden bring back memories?'

Rowenna looked at him, startled. His eyes were pewter-grey, warm and smiling. He gave her fingers a small squeeze, then returned his hands to the reins.

'I don't like to see you looking unhappy. Won't you tell me what's troubling you?'

'Nothing's troubling me,' she said instantly, but knew that she hadn't convinced him. He tilted his head slightly and gave her a slanting look.

'Rowenna, may I say something? You've come to Canada all alone. You've never met any of us before in your life. We may be your relatives, but you don't have any real friends here – not people who have known you and watched you grow up, who really care about you. It would be surprising if you didn't feel lonesome at times, and I want you to know that when you do, or when you want a friend at all, for any reason – well, I'm here. That's all. A friend to laugh with or a shoulder to cry on – whatever you need. Is that okay?'

Rowenna felt the sudden sting of tears in her eyes. She nodded, unable to speak, and Serle smiled. He put her hand back in her lap and took the reins again.

'Tell me some more about your life in England,' he said.

Rowenna hesitated, then began to tell him about Burneside and Potter's Fell. She described the mountains of the Lake District, the bareness of the hills and the little rocky outcrops sticking up through the purple heather. She told him of the bubbling cry of the curlew, as wild as the keening note of the Canadian loon, and the birdsong in the garden on a summer dawn. She told him about the garden, the plants

341

she and Haddon had grown, the azaleas and camellias and rhododendrons, the wild daffodils and primroses that carpeted the meadows and woods.

'It sounds delightful,' he said. 'But what about your family? You only mention your brother. I know your mother died a few years ago, but what about your father? Doesn't he miss you? And your husband – you've been married such a short time, how could he bear to let you come away without him?'

Rowenna had written to Warren since arriving in Canada, to tell him where she was, and also – on Mr Abercrombie's advice – to Alfred. She had received several furious letters from Alfred, but did not think that he would pursue her to Canada. If he did she would enlist her grandfather's help – even Alfred wouldn't be able to outface that commanding old man.

Was Warren missing her? More probably, he was furious that she had eluded him, particularly since he had seen her inheritance as a chance to escape the clutches of his nagging wife.

'My father married again,' she said. 'He has a wife to take care of him now. And since Haddon died—'

'Ah yes, he died too, didn't he? I remember Aunt Ruth mentioning the fact. Your closest friend, I'd guess – no wonder you look sad when you think of your garden. Well, Rowenna, I know I can never take the place of your brother – indeed, I wouldn't wish to! – but as I said just now, I hope you'll look on me as a friend.' He smiled at her again.

They drove for a while in silence. Rowenna looked about her. They were passing beside the river and she could see a few rafts, the last of the winter harvest, drifting down the river. It took almost the whole summer to get the crop away from the camps where they had been felled, and then it would begin all over again, the chopping and sawing, the hauling along snow-covered skid roads, the piling up on the ice. For a few weeks, the lumbermen could come home to their wives and families, or spend their dollars roistering about the towns but, with the colouring of the trees, back they would go into the bush, where there was no drinking and no female company, only months of bitter cold and hard toil.

Fay had developed a sick headache that afternoon and announced her intention of going to bed, and Serle had offered to bring Rowenna out for a drive to look at the countryside. The instant he had made the offer Fay had looked as if she regretted her decision, but the headache was obviously genuine and she could not possibly have accompanied them. She had seemed inclined to accept Rowenna's offer of staying in the house in case she needed anything but Mrs Hutty, who was standing by, had said quite sharply that she was perfectly capable of looking after Miss Tyson, since she'd done it often enough before, and Jacob had approved the outing. Serle had brought the buggy round to the front of the house at once, as if determined not to risk any change of mind, and within a quarter of an hour they were bowling off down the road.

'Tell me about your husband's mill,' Serle said suddenly. 'He makes paper, doesn't he?'

'That's right. And my family have owned our mill for a long time. It's hundreds of years old – it started as a cornmill, then it made bobbins for a while. My grandfather turned it into a papermill and now my father and my husband have gone into partnership.' She bit her lip. Since leaving Alfred, she had been strongly reluctant to talk about him, even to mention his name. It was an acknowledgement of her marriage, of the fact that she was still bound to him, and brought back all the misery of the months when she had been trapped in his house, in his bed. 'It's quite a large business now,' she said at last.

'Is that so?' Serle studied the road ahead. 'And didn't I

hear that your pa had been pretty ill lately? Being in partnership must've been quite a relief to him then.'

'Well, that was just before they did it,' she said. 'But my
husband was a great help to him then. He took over the mill
completely.'

'And does your husband have any other family? I believe
he's quite a lot older than you. Was he married before –
does he have sons to follow him?' Serle gave her a quick,
apologetic glance. 'I'm asking too many questions, aren't I!
Don't answer if you don't want to.'

Rowenna smiled, though she would have much preferred
to talk about something else. But she shook her head and
said, 'No, he was never married before. He says he never had
time. And he has just one sister, who is now my father's wife.'

'So you're heir to everything,' Serle said thoughtfully, his
eyes on the track ahead.

'Yes,' Rowenna said with some surprise, 'I suppose I am.'
But the thought seemed unreal, as if the thousands of miles
that separated her from her old home could also separate
her from the person she had been, from the Rowenna Mellor
who had bathed naked in the river and run in frenzy from
her husband's arms. She looked about her at the trees, so tall
and thick, stretching as far as the eye could see. 'And I have
my property here too, of course.' It seemed much more real
to her now.

'So you have.' But Serle didn't seem very interested
now. He reined in the pony and pointed across the river.
'See those forests? That's the province of Quebec. It's wild
country over there, even wilder than here. Dense bush,
hardly touched. It's being logged of course – timber's too
valuable to be left standing – but it's French Canada and
they do things a bit different there.'

'But surely it all belongs to Britain?'

'Oh, sure. You just try telling that to the Quebecers, that's all!' He laughed. 'They hang on to their Frenchness, I can tell you. Speak the language and all. I reckon it'll be the same a hundred years from now, too. They're a stubborn lot – but then I guess we all are. That's what makes a pioneer.'

Rowenna laughed. She was enjoying this outing, she discovered. It was the first time she had ever been alone with a man – apart from Kester and Alfred. Nobody like Serle had ever paid her any attention. She watched as he flicked the reins over the pony's back. He had long, well-shaped hands with tapering fingers. They looked smooth and well cared for – not at all as if they spent a lot of time in the forest, working with trees.

The sleeves of his white shirt were rolled up and the sunlight glinted on the golden hairs that covered his muscles. He wore his collar loose, revealing a brown throat, and his face was tanned a deep gold. Today, his eyes were silver, and there was a smile in them as he turned his head towards Rowenna.

'You're looking thoughtful again. Has life been so very hard for you?'

The gentle, almost idle, question brought tears to her eyes. She shook her head, unable to prevent one or two falling on to her cheeks, and his smile turned to concern. He reined the pony in by the side of the road and drew her into his arms.

'Hey. What's all this? Tears, on such a lovely day? What is it, Rowenna? What's making you cry?' He took a large, clean handkerchief from his pocket and wiped her eyes, as gently and delicately as if she had been made of finest porcelain. 'Why not tell me about it?' he whispered. 'Remember, I'm your friend. You can trust me.'

Could she? For a moment, she was tempted to tell him everything – all about her father's possessiveness, the way he had virtually sold her to Alfred Boothroyd; about Alfred's brutal, unthinking treatment of her; most of all, about Kester

345

and her love for him, her despair at losing him, and her growing conviction that she would never see him again.

But talking about it all would bring back the pain she was trying so hard to bury. And instead, suddenly startled by the realisation of their position – the sheer intimacy of it – she sat up and brushed back her short hair. She pressed his handkerchief against her face and took a deep breath, then smiled rather shakily at him.

'I'm sorry. I don't know what came over me. It was thinking about home. I suppose – I suddenly felt an awfully long way away from everything. Silly!'

'Not silly at all,' he returned. 'You *are* a long way away from home. It's my fault for reminding you about things you'd maybe rather forget – your brother, your father's illness – why, you've been through a lot in the past couple of years, it's no wonder you feel a bit sad at times. I promise I won't say another word.' He gave her a slow smile. 'Except to remind you that I *am* your friend, and if you ever need any help, I hope you'll come to me right away and ask.'

'Thank you,' Rowenna said quietly. 'I'll remember that, Serle.' And she smiled tremulously into his silver eyes.

Serle flicked the reins again. The pony, which had been grazing quietly on the grass at the roadside, lifted its head and moved on. Rowenna gazed across the river at the dense forest of Quebec.

Perhaps she would try again to persuade Serle to take her up to her own property. It was only right that she should see it, after all. And then she could decide what to do with it.

The forest stretched away into the distance, over low rolling hills, into deep folds, until it touched the far horizon. Somewhere in there were her own trees – the white pine, balsam, hemlock and spruce that were so valuable to the timber and paper trades, the sugar maple, which she had been told turned such a deep, rich red in the fall and which produced the delicious syrup she had already sampled. Trees as yet untouched, set aside by her mother and grandfather, kept for her should she ever need them.

I do need them, she thought. I need what they will do for me. With those trees I can bargain for my freedom, or I can set up my own business. Those trees can give me my life.

But she would have to see them first. She needed to stand beneath them, to touch their friendly bark, to look up into their great crowns. She needed to know them as trees, not merely as dead logs floating down the river, logs like any other log, logs that could have come from any part of the forest.

That, she felt obscurely, would seem a betrayal.

Betrayal . . . the word haunted her. It seemed a summing-up of her life so far. Her father's betrayal of her when he had sold her to Alfred Boothroyd. Her husband's betrayal, when he had promised to cherish her and then used her body as a possession, a vessel for his own bitter frustration. Her own betrayal of the man she truly loved, and his betrayal of her with Molly.

Was it a betrayal, or simply a mistake   an urge born of disappointment and frustration, to be regretted as soon as it was done?

Where was Kester now? Did he know she had come to Canada? Did he believe that she had abandoned him for ever?

She had hurt him bitterly, from the moment she had stood in Alfred Boothroyd's arms in the bluebell grove, unresisting as he kissed her; from the moment when she had stood at the altar in St Oswald's church and promised to love, honour and obey a man she loathed; from the moment she had allowed her husband the knowledge of her body, a moment that ought to have been Kester's, for it was he who had awakened her desire, he who had brought her trembling womanhood to life, he who had the right to consummate it.

I couldn't help it, she told him silently. It was never in my hands, never under my control.

But she knew that there had been moments when she could have taken matters into her own hands, when she could have assumed control.

She could have walked away from her father when he was ill and gone to Kester, as they had planned. She could have left her husband at the altar and fled to the gypsies. She could have waited at Appleby, until Kester returned, or she could have refused to flee to Canada until she had seen him.

With hindsight it all looked so easy, even though at the time each course had seemed impossible. And sorrow and regret were eating into her heart like a canker for which there was no cure.

No cure. Unless, in this new, strange country, she could make a fresh start. And begin, perhaps, with the friendship offered her by the man who sat beside her now, who had told her she could trust him.

Chapter Sixteen

To Kester, the discovery that Rowenna was married had come as a bitter blow.

He had stood in the back drive of Ashbank, after the housemaid had closed the kitchen door on him, feeling as if the world had suddenly twisted sideways on its axis and was about to topple out of control. Despair roared in his ears and his legs were weak. He turned and stumbled away, putting out his hand blindly for support from one of the trees that lined the drive. He looked up at it, into its green crown swaying in the wind, and tried to understand what he had just been told.

Rowenna married. Married to that slimy snake Boothroyd. He remembered seeing her in the garden that day, standing in the man's arms, letting him kiss her. Had she known then? Had he just proposed to her and been accepted? On the very day when she had promised to come away with Kester?

He remembered how he had stood in the garden on that last dawn, gazing up at her window. Was it her face he had glimpsed, pressed against the glass? If he had walked out on to the lawn then and called to her, would she have come to him? Or was it already all over, her promise given instead to that man, her life planned to take her in a different direction?

349

Take your chances when they come ... But had he ever really had any chance?

Dazed, Kester wandered on through the garden where he had so often worked. He came to the bluebell grove where he and Rowenna had met, and stood at the top of the bank, his hand resting against the friendly bark of one of the trees he knew so well, gazing down at the tumbling beck. Here he had seen her bathing, almost naked, in the bright water; here they had lain together, her breast beneath his hand, and she had begged him to love her.

Why didn't I do it, he asked himself. Why didn't I take her then, when she was eager and loving in my arms? Why did I leave her for that snake to take his pleasure?

He was willing to swear it had been no pleasure for Rowenna, and once again guilt and anger and misery rose in him, a flood of anguish that cracked afresh his already shattered heart.

He removed his hand from the tree and saw the pattern of the bark imprinted on his palm. There were tiny spots of blood where he had pressed against its roughness.

Married to Boothroyd ...

He raised his eyes and noticed the little footbridge across the beck. Of course, they would have put that there to make it easier for her to come to see her father. Perhaps even now she was wandering in the garden on the other side. Perhaps he would look across and see her there, watching him.

His heart suddenly thumping, he started across the bridge. If he could just see her, be sure that she was well, that Boothroyd was treating her as he should, perhaps then he could be at ease.

But he knew now that without Rowenna at his side, there would never be ease for him in this life. And he remembered the story his father had told him, of the woman he had loved and of the regret that had haunted him down the years.

She's my woman, he thought with sudden passion. Mine. I'll find her, wherever she's gone.

Kester caught up with his father on the road out of Appleby into Yorkshire, where a few wagons were camping in a small wood by a murmuring beck. The gypsies were sitting around their camp fire, watching the pot in which a rabbit stew was gently simmering and, as always, he was welcomed into their midst as if he had been away for no more than a few minutes.

It was much later, when the others had disappeared into wagons or tents, that his father told him of Rowenna's arrival in Appleby.

'She was with a lawyer – a comical little fellow, but goodhearted and honest enough, I reckon. And he's fond of the girl. He and his wife, they seemed to have taken her under their wing. They'd been looking after her since she left the man she married—'

'*Left* him? The man I spoke to just told me she'd gone away.'

'Oh, she's left him, right enough, though he might not admit it. And off to Canada, too. He'll not pursue her there.'

'*Canada*?'

Kester stared at his father. The firelight was dying down, a spatter of stars giving the only light. Canada. She had talked of it, and so had her brother Haddon. But he'd never really believed she would have the opportunity to go.

'Aye,' Kieran said. 'She's got land and money there, by all accounts. And family too. She'll be going to them.' He glanced at his son, who was sitting hunched in an attitude of despair. 'But she came looking for you first,' he reminded him.

'And what use is that? Why did she come looking for me? To say goodbye? To tell me she'd never be back?' He lifted his hands and dropped them again, hopelessly. 'She's

351

married, for all she's left him, and she's going halfway across the world to get away. It's plain enough to see she's got no more use for me.'

There was a short silence. Then Kieran said quietly, 'That's not how it struck me. Seemed she was proper disappointed you weren't here. I reckon if you go back to Kendal now, you'll be in time to catch her, and I reckon she'll be waiting for you to do just that. As for her being married—'

'There's only one true marriage,' Kester broke in. 'And that's between two hearts and souls that are meant to be together. I knew as soon as I saw Rowenna in the garden that she was meant for me. It's a shame against nature for her to be tied to another man – especially that skunk Boothroyd.'

'So why did you let her go?' his father asked.

Kester sighed. 'I was a fool, I know. But now – I don't mean to let her go. I feel like tearing the world apart to get her back.' He looked at his father, his eyes burning with passionate determination. 'Aye, I'd tear the world apart. So what's a small matter of an ocean to stop me? And a man who should never have had her in the first place? She needs me, I could see that when I first looked into her eyes. And I – by God, I need her.'

He stood up suddenly, an immense shadow blacking out the stars. He felt a surge of strength, of power. Why wait any longer for chances to come to him? He would go out and make them happen. 'I'll find her. I'll go back to Kendal – aye, and to Canada, even to the moon if that's where she's gone. I'll find her again, and this time I'll keep her. She's *my* woman, and no man is going to take her from me!'

It came as no surprise to Mr Abercrombie to find Kester on his doorstep as he locked up his office a few days after Rowenna had sailed for Canada. He stood for a moment regarding the young man, then nodded and put out his hand.

'Mr Matthews, I believe.'

Kester blinked.

'Aye. Kester Matthews. But how—'

'You're like your father,' Mr Abercrombie said. 'The same eyes and features. And the same hair, though his is white now. And, I'd guess, the same kind of character.'

Kester shrugged. 'Perhaps. I'd not be sorry to think so. And you must be Mr Abercrombie.'

'James Wilson Abercrombie, at your service,' the lawyer said with a small bow. His bright blue eyes twinkled a little, and he added, 'I daresay you find it difficult to imagine how I might be useful to you. Gentlemen of your kind rarely seem to need lawyers.'

'Except to get us out of jail,' Kester said with a grin. 'But I don't think I'm in any danger of that at the moment. I like to steer the right side of the law – prison's too uncomfortable.'

'Very wise, very wise.' Mr Abercrombie nodded and laid his hand on Kester's shoulder. 'Well, now, you'd better come along home with me. There's rather a lot to discuss.'

Kester backed away a little. 'Discuss? But – I just want to see Rowenna. My father told me she was with you and—'

'And so she was, so she was.' Mr Abercrombie sighed. 'But events have rather taken us by surprise since we returned from Appleby.' He thought of the unpleasant scenes with Alfred Boothroyd, when the man had come storming into his office, demanding again and again to know where Rowenna was, demanding to have her returned to him at once. He had accused Mr Abercrombie of abduction, of wife-stealing, of illegal practices such as the lawyer himself had never heard of. He had threatened to bring lawsuits against him, to have him struck off the legal lists and barred

353

ever from practising again. It had taken all James Abercrombie's not inconsiderable control to sit quietly under this tirade, waiting for the storm to blow itself out, and then he had pointed out that Rowenna had left England of her own free will, and finally handed Boothroyd the letter she had written before her departure, ready for just such circumstances as these.

There had been little that Alfred Boothroyd could do after that. His first visit had caused Rowenna's hasty flight and it was clear that she had no intention of returning. He could only go back to Meadowbank and pretend, for the sake of saving his own pride, that she had simply gone away for a holiday.

'I think you really should come home with me now,' Mr Abercrombie told Kester. 'That's the best thing. I'm sure you need a good meal after your travelling, and a bed for the night.'

'A bed?' Kester stared at him. 'But – what about Rowenna? Where is she? Has – has anything happened to her?' Fear seized him. 'She's not gone back to that devil, has she?'

'No, no, no indeed,' Mr Abercrombie reassured him. 'But I'll tell you all about it on the way home. Come with me now and we'll fetch my pony and trap.'

Bewildered, Kester allowed himself to be led through the archway that led off Stricklandgate into one of Kendal's many yards. These formed a maze of small alleyways and courts behind the buildings of the main street, and here most of the life of Kendal was lived. Tiny houses, shops, mews and stables all jostled for space in the cobbled yards, thrown in higgledy-piggledy as if by a giant baby playing with bricks. Horses' heads looked out of stable doors, women sat on broken-backed chairs in front of their cottages, and there was little difference to be seen in either. Children, their faces grimed with the dirt of days, or even weeks, dressed in tattered clothes, played half-heartedly in the dust and mud and looked up as Mr Abercrombie passed by, some holding out their hands in the hope of being thrown a farthing or two.

'And townsfolk have the gall to look down on us travellers,' Kester commented as he climbed up into Mr Abercrombie's trap. The lawyer gave the groom a halfpenny and the pony moved out of the yard and into the main street. 'Our *chavvies* are cleaner than these, and look stronger, too. And no wonder – the air's foul in there.'

'Yes, such places do Kendal no credit. And it's the same in most towns and cities, I fear. Too many people and not enough money going around.'

'The money's in the wrong pockets,' Kester said.

'Some of it, indeed, that's true. What's the old saying? "*It is the duty of the wealthy man. To give employment to the artisan.*" And to pay them a proper wage for doing it, too, I would add. There are far too many people working twelve or fourteen hours a day, even more in some cases, and still not earning enough to support a family.'

'And that's why I'll call no man my master,' Kester said warmly. 'Why should I sell myself to men such as that, who are not fit to lick my father's boots?' He was silent for a moment and then, as the pony's head turned towards home, said quietly, 'And now you may tell me what's happened to Rowenna.'

'Yes.' The lawyer reflected for a moment, as if deciding how to begin. Then he said, 'I think you might as well know the most important thing to begin with. Rowenna is no longer with us. She has gone to Canada.'

'She's gone already? But my father—'

'Your father saw her only a few days ago. I know. She had no intention of going so soon. But a day after we arrived back here. Alfred Boothroyd – you know who Alfred Boothroyd is, I take it—'

'Her husband, the bastard. I know.'

355

'He discovered that she had been with me and came demanding to know where she was. It would only be a matter of time before he came to my home and accosted me there, so it was imperative that she leave at once. I sent a message to my wife and she and Rowenna set off for Liverpool immediately. They were fortunate in securing passage on a ship that was leaving for Quebec the very next day, and Rowenna took it.' The lawyer turned his head and gave Kester a kindly glance. 'She was most upset. She wanted to wait for you. But we felt that if she did not escape at once, Boothroyd might well catch up with her, and the law would be on his side, you see. There would be nothing we could do to prevent him from taking her home again. And once there—'

'She would find it all the harder to get away again,' Kester said.

'Worse that than, my dear boy. He had already threatened to have her committed to a lunatic asylum. I feel sure he would have done that. It would have kept her under his control – and given him the use of her money and property in Canada as well, you see.'

Kester was silent. Then his nostrils flared and his eyes narrowed. He shuddered slightly, and seemed to swell, and Mr Abercrombie glanced at him and thought that in a physical battle this man would be terrifying. And invincible.

But physical battle was not the way to deal with a man like Alfred Boothroyd. Particularly when he had the law on his side. A wife was a piece of property, and possession nine points of the law.

Mrs Abercrombie welcomed Kester with as little surprise as her husband, for both had known he would come. She took him into the comfortable drawing room and sat him down without fuss, then went to tell the cook that there would be another mouth to feed at supper and another bed

356

needed. She brought him tea herself, and a large slice of her own fruit cake, and while he ate and drank – and neither could help noticing that he seemed famished – she took up her sewing.

'So she's gone to Canada,' Kester said at last. 'And she's got family there – d'you think she'll have need of me?'

The Abercrombies looked at him thoughtfully. The question was almost an appeal, as if he had lost confidence in Rowenna's feelings for him. Yet he seemed as certain as ever of his own, and he was not looking for her money, the lawyer and his wife were convinced of that. You only had to look at the expression in his eyes, as Mrs Abercrombie said later, to see that he truly loved the girl.

'She needed you when she left, certainly,' James Abercrombie said at last. 'It was only her fear of the asylum that drove her away in the end. But as to when she starts a new life, thousands of miles away – who can say? Nobody can make promises in this world; we can only hope.'

Kester looked at him broodingly. 'So if I want her, I must follow – yet be prepared for her to refuse me.'

'And you must remember, she is still married,' Mrs Abercrombie put in.

'Dammit – I'm sorry, ma'am – that's no true marriage!' Kester exploded. 'She was forced into that, I'll swear, and never happy. How could she be, with such a man? And now she's left him. Doesn't that say enough?' He paused, then added, 'It's for her to say, anyway. I'll go to her and offer her what little I have – myself, there's nothing more – and if she refuses me, I'll be her servant, if only I can stay nearby.'

Her servant, and he the man who had always sworn he would call no man master. But he would call Rowenna mistress, if she would not be wife, and even that in only the ordinary sense, if that was her decision.

'I'll give you the money for your passage,' Mr Abercrombie

began, but Kester shook his head fiercely and said he would take no charity. 'I'll lend it, then.'

'No. That's another thing I've been taught. *Neither a lender nor a borrower be.* We may be travellers, my people and I, but we have our pride. And our independence is like gold to us. Why should I live idle on board ship? I'll not make it easy for myself. I'll earn my passage, and then she'll know I'm in earnest.'

She'll know you're in earnest anyway, Mrs Abercrombie thought, looking at the burning eyes. And she turned her head towards her husband and saw that he was thinking the same.

He looked towards her and they smiled at each other. Once, the same fervour had burned in them too, and even now it lay smouldering. But better still was the warm contentment that they had reached, like a safe harbour after the storms of life.

She hoped and prayed that Kester and Rowenna would come one day to the same safe harbour. Though how it could happen, she did not know, with a marriage and several thousand miles lying between them.

Chapter Seventeen

Fay had returned to Ottawa alone. To her annoyance, there had been several engagements in the city that she could not miss without deeply offending some of the most important members of society. For a while, she was torn between her desire to be a leader of the city's fashionable set, and her determination to become engaged to Serle. A telegram from her mother, requesting that she return at once, had settled the matter.

'I don't know why she dithered so much,' Jacob remarked after they had waved her goodbye. 'She don't enjoy being in Penrith, after the first few days. Too rough and ready up here for her, and the women not fashionable enough – though they're interested enough in *her* clothes. But I suppose all young girls like a bit of competition, to make 'em feel good.'

Rowenna smiled. She had known girls at school whose lives seemed to revolve around a frill here and there, a scrap of lace or an extra ribbon, but such concerns had never interested her. And she was thankful not to have to endure any more of Fay's constant chatter about fashions, or about her marriage to Serle.

'But you aren't exactly engaged to him, are you?' she asked one day in an effort to put a stop to these outpourings. She had noticed that Fay never talked in such a way when Serle was present – her conversation then consisted of arch hints and coy innuendo, never a direct reference.

'Not *engaged*, no – not in the way that most people understand it,' Fay said loftily, as if the situation between herself and Serle went a good deal deeper than that. 'Of course, it will be pleasant to have a ring to wear, but it won't actually mean anything different, you know – not to us.' She gave Rowenna a patronising smile. 'Being married, you've probably forgotten the delights of first love.'

I never knew them, Rowenna thought bitterly – not with Alfred. But she had known them well enough with Kester – and her heart yearned again for the presence of the tall, dark wanderer who had captured her heart and then abandoned her. Oh Kester, Kester, she thought, why didn't you wait?

She looked at Fay, fussing now over a hem that needed trimming, and wondered if what she and Serle felt for each other bore any resemblance at all to the passion that had existed between herself and Kester. How could it? There was never any desire in their eyes, never any tension between them. How could they sit in the same room, making banal conversation? How could they walk together through the woods without wanting to touch each other, live in the same house without being overpowered by their need?

But these were forbidden thoughts. She had made up her mind that when she came to Canada it would be to start a new life, far from all the unhappiness and pain that she had suffered in England. A new life as herself – Rowenna Mellor – free from the traps set by marriage.

After Fay had gone, Rowenna felt more at ease in the clapboard farmhouse her grandfather had built. She slipped into the simple routine of the household, walking down to the few shops each morning for groceries, helping Mrs

Hutty with the cooking. There was a small kitchenmaid too, and a groom, but no other servants were kept. Serle, coming in from the lumberyard one morning to find Rowenna with a feather duster in her hand, apologised for this.

'Grandfather reckons we ought to be self-sufficient, like him and Grandma when they first came here. I tell him it's not a museum, but he won't listen. He just says everyone ought to be able to shift for themselves.'

'Well, I rather agree with him.' Rowenna had moved the few ornaments and photographs to a table in order to polish the sideboard, and now she began to put them back. 'Why should we sit idle while a child like Suky slaves for us? And it's so much easier here, without all the clutter most people have in their rooms.'

'Oh, it's necessary out here, I guess, but I feel like Fay sometimes – I like the elegant life. And you don't find that in a place like Penrith, right over in the middle of Algonquin! Still, I suppose the old man'll hand over the reins eventually. He can't go on for ever.'

Rowenna looked at him, slightly disturbed by his casual tone. 'Do you mean you'd go back to Ottawa and run the mill there?'

'Why, of course.' He grinned at her. 'You wouldn't expect me to hide myself away in the backwoods for ever, would you?'

'Why not? It's a good life here.' Rowenna was feeling more and more at home in the little town. Already she knew quite a few people and would stop to chat as she went about her daily shopping. She had been to tea with two or three young matrons, and – best of all – had started to work in the garden.

And each day, she deepened her relationship a little more with her grandfather. Most days he went down to the yard with Serle, but when the two men came back to the house for tea in the afternoon Jacob would stay on, talking to Rowenna. She found that he was able to reach out to her with his wisdom, wrapping her about with a security that gave her the confidence to confide in him as she had been able to confide in no one else. I could have told Kester, she thought – but turned her thoughts abruptly away. Kester had gone, left her, and she had to go forward through life without him.

But did that mean she must always be alone? Her marriage to Alfred had precluded her from taking a husband. Did it prevent her from any sort of friendship?

Several times, Serle took her out in the buggy for an evening drive. They would go to one of the lakes and leave the pony while they walked through the great trees. Serle would point out beaver-dams and Rowenna marvelled at the industry of the animals, gnawing at the trunks of huge trees to fell them, dragging branches into the water to build their lodges. She saw how their work had actually changed the countryside, making new lakes and swamps where the standing trees died and stood like stark skeletons in the water.

The floor of the forest was thick with the fallen leaves of centuries, creating a deep mould that Rowenna would have liked to carry back for the garden. Here and there trees had fallen and lay rotting slowly into the ground, a haven for birds and small animals. She watched in delight as chipmunks scampered through the bushes, stopped quite still as a woodpecker began to hammer into a trunk just above her head and leapt back in alarm as a snake slithered suddenly from nowhere across her path.

'It's all right,' Serle said. 'It's not a dangerous one. But you have to watch out for rattlers.'

'Rattlesnakes?' Rowenna glanced around nervously, reluctant to linger where there might be dangerous snakes.

'Oh, it's all right now. They don't hang around when there's people about.'

Rowenna looked doubtfully at the bushes. Did snakes always behave as they were supposed to?

'Shouldn't we be going back?'

'Oh, there's plenty of time.' He glanced up at the trees. 'It's too beautiful here to hurry. Look – the colours are beginning to turn.'

Rowenna looked up. The canopy of the sugar maples hung high above, and she saw that their big, splayed leaves were beginning to turn red. Soon, the cool green forest would be a blaze of fiery colour – reds, golds, bronzes, yellows and browns.

'It's like being in the heart of a sunset,' Serle murmured. 'When the light tries to break through and the colours glow . . . You'll be here to see it, won't you, Rowenna? You won't go back to Ottawa just when the Algonquin is at its best?'

She shook her head slowly, dazed by the picture he was painting in her mind. She thought of the garden at home, the trees Haddon had planted and the autumn colours they would be showing now. But memories of the garden brought back memories of Kester, who was far away, and then of Alfred and the day he had kissed her for the first time. The remembrance made her shudder, and Serle looked at her with concern.

'What is it? What's frightening you? Have you seen another snake?'

She shook her head, unable to speak, unable to tell him of the nightmares that still haunted her nights. Alfred, coming to search for her. Alfred, forcing her to go back to him . . .

'Oh, Rowenna, don't be afraid. I shouldn't have brought you here – you're not accustomed to it. It's too big, too wild—'

'No. No, I love the forest – I love its wildness.'

He smiled.

'I believe you do. I believe there's a touch of wildness in you, Rowenna – more than a touch. You'd have made a good wife for a pioneer.' His eyes half closed, as if he were seeing a vision. 'I can just imagine you, striding out across the hills, helping to fell the trees to build your log cabin, tending the garden, cooking whatever your man brought home for supper – why, Rowenna, what's wrong?'

Rowenna turned away abruptly, staring up into the trees. How could she tell him how she had planned to run away with Kester, to live with him under the stars, to make a home somewhere on the hills where they would dwell simply, making a garden together and living on what they could either catch or grow?

A pioneer. Was that so very different from a traveller, save that the pioneer made the land his own? Wasn't that what Kester had yearned for? He had left his own people to wander alone, but didn't he always half settle down, working in a wood or garden and living in some hut or bothy?

Rowenna looked at the forest and knew that this was what he had craved – to carve a piece of land out of the wilderness and make it his home. If she would have made a good pioneer's wife, Kester would have been the pioneer. And together, they could have built a life that was rich and new.

But she knew that the glory that could have been was now beyond all hope, for Kester was somewhere in England and she must go through life without him.

Kester was penniless when he arrived in Ottawa.

He had found work on a steamer bringing cargo to Montreal, and worked his passage across the Atlantic. But there had been little money left in his pocket, and he had decided to spend what he had on the train fare to the capital city. A sense of urgency pervaded him, a desperate need to complete the endless journey and find Rowenna. He was convinced that if he didn't find her soon, some further harm would come to her. And his conviction that she was his, that only he could give her the love and care she needed, drove him harder. Bitterly, he regretted leaving her on the day her father had been taken ill. I should have waited, he thought. I should have stayed at her side.

In his pocket he carried the papers Mr Abercrombie had given him – Jacob Tyson's address, with a letter of introduction the lawyer had written to him, and a map showing the position of Rowenna's land in the Algonquin. He knew that she would have wanted to go there to see it, to touch and know the trees that were hers.

When the train arrived in Ottawa, he went straight to the house on Elgin Street and knocked on the door. A maid came, looking startled to see the dark young man, so roughly clad.

'You should go to the back door,' she said disapprovingly. 'Unless you're from the timberyard?'

Kester shook his head. 'I'm here to see Mrs Boothroyd.'

The maid stared. 'There's no one here. They're all away, except for Miss Fay.' She made to close the door.

'But she must be here,' Kester said desperately. 'I've got a letter—'

'From Mrs Boothroyd?'

'No – from her lawyer in England. Look, if I could just see Mr Tyson—'

'He's away,' the maid said flatly. 'Up at Penrith.'

Penrith? The name was familiar enough to Kester, but the Penrith he knew was at home in Cumberland. Surely old Mr Tyson hadn't gone to England? And where was

Rowenna? He shook his head, but before he could say any more another young woman had come to the door and was standing behind the maid, gazing at him curiously.

'Who is it, Maisie? What does he want?'

'I don't know who he is, miss. He says he's looking for Mrs Boothroyd and he won't take any notice when I tell him she's not here. I've tried to send him about his business but he won't go – I think we should send someone for the police.' She glared at Kester.

Fay's eyes gleamed. She looked Kester up and down, taking in his travel-stained appearance. Her glance lingered on his broad shoulders and curling black hair, and warmed to an approving interest.

'Mrs Boothroyd? Who sent you?'

'Her lawyer in England. He gave me this address – said Mr Tyson was her grandfather. She must have been here.'

'Very well, Maisie. You may leave this to me. And I'd be grateful if you didn't gossip about it, just for the moment.' Fay watched as the maid disappeared reluctantly towards the kitchen, then turned back to Kester. 'Now then. You're looking for Mrs Boothroyd. Can you tell me her Christian name?'

'It's Rowenna,' he said, bewildered. 'Look, has she been here or hasn't she? If she hasn't, I'll need to find out what's happened, because this is where she was heading, I'm certain of it, and if anything's—'

Fay cut him short. Her face was filled with suppressed enjoyment. She beckoned him inside the hall and shut the door.

'We don't want the whole street listening to us, do we? Now, tell me what's happened. Is there some kind of trouble?'

Kester shook his head. 'No. But I must find her. She *is* here, isn't she? Why did the maid tell me—'

'She's not here now.' Fay looked up at him speculatively. 'I don't know if I should tell you where she is or not. Who are you? Why have you come?'

'I'm Kester Matthews.' His heart sank at her blank expression. Clearly, Rowenna had never mentioned him – but then, why should she? She had probably given him up as part of her old life, a life she had left behind her. He felt again his bitter regret at having let her go, at walking away from her when perhaps she needed him most. Oh Rowenna, his heart cried, let me have one more chance. I'll not fail you again. But his cry seemed to go out into silence, into a dark and lonely space where none could hear.

'I've come from England,' he said to Fay. 'I'm looking for Rowenna. She knows who I am – I know she'd see me if she were here. Where is she? Where's she gone?'

'Why do you want to find her? Why has her lawyer sent you?'

Kester felt the slow burning of inner rage. Who was this yellow-haired girl who was taking so much interest in him? Why wouldn't she tell him where Rowenna was? She obviously knew, and equally obviously was enjoying not telling him. He wanted to take her by the shoulders and shake the truth from her, but commonsense told him that wasn't the way. She'll tell me in her own time, he thought, and schooled himself to have patience.

'Nobody's sent me,' he said. 'I want to find Rowenna on my own account. I'm a friend – I've been worried about her. It's not so unusual, is it, to want to look up a friend?'

'A friend? You?' Fay's eyes moved over him again and he was uncomfortably aware of his shabby clothes. 'You don't look the sort of person to be a friend of Mrs Boothroyd. You look more like a gypsy.'

The contempt in her tone stung, and Kester felt his anger rise further. He straightened his shoulders and looked down at the small, golden-haired girl who was so clearly enjoying taunting him. There was a challenge in her eyes, a flirtatious lift to her chin, that he recognised, for he had met it a good many times before. But he was not interested now in games. He had felt himself so close to Rowenna, only to find her yet again slipping away from him, and there was room for nothing else in his mind.

'So I am a gypsy,' he answered Fay curtly. 'And none the worse for that, from what I've seen of *gaujes*. And I've travelled too far and waited too long to be put off now by a saucy little piece like you – so tell me where Rowenna is, damn you, and if you can't do that, take me to her grandfather and I'll see if he'll talk sense to me.'

Fay gasped, but although she feigned shock her eyes danced and her mouth trembled with laughter as she said, 'But she really isn't here. And neither's Grandfather. They're at Penrith – didn't Maisie tell you that?' She moved away and opened the drawing-room door. 'Look, why don't you come in and have some tea? You must be parched. Have you really just come from England? I want to hear all about it – I've been dying to go there, only Grandfather's never allowed it, said I was too young to travel on my own. But I mean to ask Serle to take me.' She took his hand and tugged him into the drawing room, then rang the bell. 'Now, you sit right there and I'll order tea and sandwiches, and then I'll tell you all about dear Rowenna.'

Kester waited while the maid brought a tray of tea and a plate of ham sandwiches. His body was itching with impatience. He looked around the room, barely noticing the richness of the dark red curtains and upholstery, unaware of the ornaments and photographs. A stuffed owl in a glass case on the mantelpiece caught his eye but was instantly forgotten. He glanced at his hostess, registered that she was young and pretty, but immediately thought of Rowenna again. As soon as the maid was out of the room again, he burst into a torrent of questions.

'Where's Rowenna? You said Penrith – where's that? The only Penrith I know is back in England. She hasn't gone back already, has she? She – she hasn't gone back to that bastard of a husband?'

Fay pursed her mouth but her eyes still gleamed. 'My, my, such language in a lady's drawing room. But there, I guess you don't know any better. So dear Rowenna has run away from her husband, has she? Isn't that *interesting*. I wonder why she didn't tell us.'

Kester bit his lip. Had Rowenna really run away, after all – or had old Abercrombie got it wrong? And if she had, why hadn't she told her relatives?'

'Just tell me how to find her,' he said abruptly.

'But I don't know that I ought to do that. I mean, I don't know anything about you, do I? Suppose you meant my cousin some harm? I'd never forgive myself if—'

'I don't mean Rowenna any harm at all,' Kester said through his teeth, 'but by God, I'll do you some, miss, if you don't answer my questions straight away. Now, *where is she*? And how do I get there, wherever it is?'

Fay shrank back in her chair, a flicker of real fear in her eyes, and Kester found he was leaning over her, his fists clenched. With an effort, he sat back and took a deep breath.

'I'm sorry, miss – I don't even know your name. I didn't mean to speak like that. But I've been looking for Rowenna a long while and to come all this way and *know* she's been here, and not to be told . . . You've been playing games with me, that's the truth of it, and that's summat I don't like. But I'd not harm you, so don't be afraid. Only – for God's sake, tell me where she is, for I don't think I can stand this much longer.'

Fay gave him a wary glance and relaxed a little, but her hand hovered near the bell as she spoke.

'I'll accept your apology, Mr Matthews, though you deserve to be thrown out at once. But I suppose it's my own fault for inviting you in. Since you're so interested, I might as well tell you that I'm Rowenna's cousin, Fay Tyson. I live here with my parents and grandfather – he's Rowenna's grandfather too, and totally smitten with her. Just because she's new here!' She wrinkled her nose scornfully. 'And they've gone to Penrith so that she can see all the places where he and Grandma lived when they first came to Canada, and the forest and all that. I went with them but I had to come back – I've got so many things to do, I couldn't spare the time to stay longer, though Serle begged me to. Mind' – her eyes flirted again – 'I'm not really sorry I came back. I wouldn't have missed this afternoon for worlds!'

Kester ignored this. His voice tight, he said, 'And where's Penrith? How do I get there?'

'Oh, it's three days from here by buggy. There's no other way – unless you walk. But I guess you'd be used to that.'

'I am,' he said. 'A walk doesn't scare me. I just need to know the way.'

'I can tell you that,' Fay said. 'But it isn't all you need to know. There are one or two things about dear cousin Rowenna that you might find handy to be told.' She paused, her eyes narrowed. 'Like, she's making up to my fiancé. Set her cap at him the minute she arrived in Penrith. And he's as bad as Grandpa – lost his head over an English accent. I don't know how it's going to work out, what with her being already married, but it looks like trouble to me – and I'd be grateful if you could sort it out. I don't relish taking second place to a girl who's run away from one man and starts straight in stealing someone else's.'

Kester stared at her. Rowenna, setting her cap at another man? Stealing her own cousin's fiancé? Rowenna, causing trouble in her family, less than a month after her arrival? He didn't believe it. Rowenna was not a flirt, nor would she turn to another man so readily. Even if she believed he had forgotten her, she would not forget their love.

But whatever the truth of the matter, there was still only one thing to do. He had to get to Penrith – as fast as possible – and claim Rowenna for his own.

She needs me, he thought. She needs me even more than I dreamt.

Rowenna's sadness in the forest had changed the relationship between herself and Serle. He was no longer the rather insouciant cousin, eager to take her driving and visiting his friends; instead, he was attentive and considerate, treating her as if she were made of fragile china.

'I hate to see you unhappy,' he said, coming upon her in the garden, gazing up at the trees that had been left dotted upon the wide lawn. 'Isn't there anything I can do to help you?'

Rowenna turned and smiled at him. 'You do help me. But I think time is the only thing that will really do any good. And at least there's plenty of that here.'

'There sure will be if you're happy to be stuck here during the winter,' he said with a grin. 'The fall's coming fast, and once the snow starts we'll be drifted in.'

'Won't you be in the forest then? That's when most of the logging is done, surely.'

'Oh, sure. And I'll be there part of the time, to oversee things. But a good manager knows how to delegate the work, Rowenna – I don't need to be on the spot all the time.' He gave her a conspiratorial wink. 'I'm not like Grandpa, think the world'll stop spinning if I don't get up at five every morning to go to the yard. You won't find me still slaving away when I'm ninety-five!'

She laughed. 'And what will you be doing instead?

Dandling the latest great-grandchild on your knee?'

He smiled, but then his face grew sober and he said, 'That's a nice thought, but I'd need a lady to be a great-grandmother with me.'

There was a tiny silence. Rowenna turned away and looked back at the trees.

'They're lovely, aren't they? Look, the leaves are turning red. It's just that touch of cold in the air, I suppose – there was a frost last night, did you notice? It always starts the colours changing at home – not that they're as spectacular as here, of course, but lovely just the same. You must come to England some time, Serle, and see . . .' Her voice faded away. She turned her head again and found him watching her, his expression curiously abstracted, as if his thoughts were somewhere else. 'What – what is it?'

Serle's eyes snapped back into focus. He laughed and took her arm.

'Nothing, my dear. Nothing at all. I just came out to tell you that Mrs Hutty has dinner on the table and we're all starving. So why don't we go in and eat, huh?'

He led her back into the house. But to Rowenna, it was as if the changing colours of the leaves symbolised the changes in her own life. And she could not tell what might happen during the long, snow-barricaded months of winter, nor what the leaves of spring might bring.

Chapter Eighteen

With the approach of winter, the colours of the trees continued to change and Rowenna watched them with fascination, climbing to the top of a nearby hill to gaze out over the endless carpet of reds and golds and bronzes, interspersed with the evergreen of pine and the deep blue of the lakes. Outcrops of rock showed as patches of smooth grey, and the trunks of paper-bark birches gleamed brilliant white against the rich, glowing tapestry.

There must, she knew, be areas of devastation in the forest, great patches of nakedness where the loggers had passed through and taken out huge trunks, leaving their limbs and glorious crowns to rot on the forest floor. But in such vast distances, these areas showed as no more than a slight hesitation in the endless colour, no more than the lakes or beaver swamps that were also hidden in the rippling carpet.

Some of these trees are mine, she thought, staring towards a horizon that must be hundreds of miles away. Somewhere amongst these majestic trees, hundreds of years old, are the ones my mother left me. White pine, hemlock, balsam and the lovely sugar-maple. Mine to fell or to leave standing, mine to use or let grow.

Which should it be?

I ought to go and see them, she thought. I ought to see my

trees and touch them. I ought to know them, before I make any decision.

'Leave them to me,' Serle had offered a day or two earlier. 'I'll look after them for you. They're not far from where we're logging at present – it'd be a simple matter to move a few men over there, set up a camp and bring them out. There aren't so many of them, as it happens – it's a rather poor stand. But I'd make sure you got the best price.'

Rowenna shook her head doubtfully. 'It doesn't seem right to do that. They've been growing so long – and my mother left them to me. I feel I ought to visit them, just once.'

Serle laughed. 'You're a sweet and sentimental woman,' he said, touching her nose with the tip of his finger. 'But they're only trees, same as any other. And nothing more'n that, till they get to the timberyard. If you ask me, you'd be better to keep well away – you're the sort who'd take one look and say you couldn't bear to cut any of them down! And we'd not get far in this business if we all felt like that.'

Rowenna was forced to admit the truth of his words. All the same, she felt that to visit her trees, the ones her mother had chosen for her, would link her in some way with the woman who had foreseen her need and made provision for it. Simply to allow them to be felled felt almost like a betrayal of her mother's love for her.

'So what d'you think?' Serle said, breaking in on her thoughts. 'Shall I see that work starts on your limits? It's the best time to see to it now, so the men can get camp set up before the winter sets in.'

Rowenna shook her head. 'I'd still like to see them first.'

Serle looked faintly exasperated.

'But there's nothing to see! Nothing any different from what you can see here. Just trees, trees and more trees. Besides, they're quite a way from here and it's rough travelling in the bush. I doubt if Grandpa would allow it.'

Rowenna lifted her chin. 'Grandfather has nothing to do with it. I go where I please. And I want to see my trees.'

'You *will* see them, for heaven's sake! You'll see them floating down the river. What more do you want?'

'I want to see them standing,' she said stubbornly.

'Look,' he said, 'lumber camps are rough places. They're full of the sort of men a lady like you should never meet. Even their own women don't go there. They do their own cooking and washing, they live pretty near the ground. It'd take a good week to get you there, and another to get back, and you'd hate every minute of it – and all to see a few trees. We've got trees here, right beside the house! Yours aren't any different just because they're yours.'

'I didn't imagine they would be,' Rowenna said coolly. 'But if you won't take me, I suppose I can find someone else who will.'

'I doubt that,' he retorted. 'I doubt it very much indeed. Nobody's going to risk Grandpa's wrath – and that's what the man would be doing who took you off into the Algonquin, whether it was me or some other poor – well, take it from me, his job wouldn't last long.' He frowned thoughtfully. 'Listen, how would this be as a compromise? You exchange your stand for one of similar value near at hand, and you can see 'em and touch 'em and kiss 'em goodnight if that's what you want. And when we fell them you can watch the whole thing and know they're *your* trees when they go off down the river. You can even head off down to Ottawa and get there first – meet 'em coming in. How does that sound?'

'It's very kind of you,' Rowenna said politely. 'But it wouldn't be the same. You see, I want to go where my mother went and see the trees she saw—'

'She saw the trees here, for God's sake!'

'The trees she picked out for me,' Rowenna said firmly. She gave Serle a glance and said, 'Are you sure there's no

375

other reason why you don't want me to visit my own limits?'

He stared at her, his tanned face flushing red. 'Why d'you say that? What reason could there be?'

'I've no idea,' Rowenna said, shrugging. 'But you do seem very anxious to dissuade me.'

'Because I know what it's like up there, and I know Grandpa would forbid it. And before you tell me again that he can't forbid *you*, let me tell you that our grandfather rules the roost around here and nobody goes against him. He's that sort of man. And just because he's taken a shine to you, don't mean he won't put his foot down if you start giving trouble.'

'I don't want to give trouble. I just want—'

'To see your trees. I know.' Serle's voice softened. 'Rowenna, my dear, I do know how you feel. Don't think I don't understand. It's just that I know what conditions are like, and I wouldn't expose you to them, even if Grandpa did agree to it. You're too precious.'

'Very well,' she said, 'I'll go in the spring.'

'But by then the harvesting—'

'The harvesting can wait another year.' She looked at him with stubborn eyes. 'I mean it, Serle. I want to see them. And neither you nor my grandfather can stop me. In fact, I'm sure *he* won't want to. What I want to know is why *you're* so anxious to prevent me.'

Serle sighed. 'I'm not anxious to prevent you at all. I've told you, conditions are impossible in the forest during the winter. By all means make a trip up there in the spring, if that's what you've set your heart on. Of course the harvesting can wait another year. It means you won't get any money until then, but you don't have to worry about that – Grandfather's only too happy to have you staying here as long as you like.' He smiled at her and Rowenna smiled back a little doubtfully.

'I know you're only doing what you think best for me,' she said. 'But – I do so want to see my trees. You see, I've never owned anything before. It's a strange feeling and it's important to me.'

He looked at her for a long moment, then nodded his head.

'I can see that. Okay, Rowenna, how about this for a solution? It's getting close to winter now – it really is too late to take you on a trip into the forest. But come the spring, we'll go up there together, just you and me. We'll make a holiday of it. We'll go up the skid roads and watch the logs coming down, and you'll see the men riding them like horses in the river. And we'll look at your trees. There won't be much to see – I told you, it's not a specially good stand – but you'll see them and touch them, and then if you want we can harvest them the following year. How does that sound?'

'It sounds good.' She gave him a cautious look, not certain even now that he meant what he said. 'And shall we go by canoe for some of the way? And camp, like Grandfather and Grandmother did? And catch fish, and cook them on an open fire?'

'And get eaten alive by mosquitoes,' he retorted, grinning. 'Sure, we'll do all those things if that's what you want.'

Rowenna laughed, but her laughter was still tinged with uncertainty. Serle seemed open enough now, but there had been a moment during their conversation when his eyes were veiled, as if his thoughts were different from his promises. As if he were thinking that when spring came, she would no longer want to go into the forest.

Since their first meeting, Serle had shown nothing but concern for her. Yet just occasionally that concern slipped and she caught a glimpse of a different Serle, hard and ruthless as a woodsman must be. It brought a shiver to her spine and, although it was difficult to believe that he did not have her interests at heart, she could not rid herself of that slight touch of unease that lurked at the edges of her mind.

Why had he not wanted her to make the trip into the forest? Was it really because of the dangers – or did he have some other reason?

It took Kester only four days to reach Penrith, but they were the four longest days of his life. He set out to walk, unable to help marvelling at the forests despite his anxiety and impatience, and was fortunate enough to be given lifts on carts or lumber wagons for several stretches of the rough, stony road. From the drivers he gleaned as much knowledge of the bush and logging industry as he could, and also gathered a good deal of information regarding Jacob Tyson and his adopted grandson Serle. When he finally arrived, he was dishevelled, tired and almost starving, but the thought of seeing Rowenna at last and discovering the truth kept his head high and his back straight as he strode through the main street of the little clapboard town.

Fay had given him the address of Jacob Tyson's farmhouse, and he found it easily, with only one or two enquiries. Everyone, it seemed, knew old Jacob Tyson. Why, he was one of the founders of the town, he and his wife Jemima had been the first settlers here and gave it its name – Penrith, some place in the north of England, wasn't it, where old Jacob had come from? And now look at him, getting on for a hundred years old and still travelling up to the lumber camps twice a year to oversee the harvest and plan the next year's logging. They didn't make 'em like him any more.

Kester turned the last corner and stopped. Before him, at the end of the road, stood a long white house surrounded by wide lawns, with great trees left here and there by the original clearance, and the edge of the forest itself crowding up to the picket fence. The leaves were like multi-coloured silk against the clear blue September sky and their colours were mirrored by beds of brilliant flowers in the lawns and along the fence.

The door of the house opened and a tall, fair-haired man came out and strode rapidly across the lawn towards him. His eyes took in Kester's dishevelled appearance, his shabby clothes and the haversack in which he carried his few belongings.

'Who are you? What do you think you're doing, staring over my fence? If it's a handout you want, you're out of luck – get off, before I take my whip to you!'

Kester's eyes flashed. 'I've come to see Mrs Boothroyd. I'm a friend of hers, from England.'

'From *England*? You look like a common labourer! If you've come to spy on behalf of her husband—'

Kester said angrily, 'I've nothing to do with that swine. I've come on my own account, to see Rowenna. We've things to talk about.'

Serle's eyebrows rose. 'Things to talk about? And you're very familiar, calling a lady by her Christian name. I suppose you're looking for money. You've followed her here in the hope that she'll get you started in a new country – what was the matter with the old one, too hot to hold you?'

'I'm not asking for money,' Kester began tightly, but Serle lifted his hand.

'No, no, my dear fellow, of course you're not. Perish the thought. I'm sure you had no more thought in your head but to set your mind at rest about Mrs Boothroyd's health and wellbeing, and then go on your way. And why should you not? It was a kindly thought.' He nodded. 'And now, if you go round to the kitchen door and say I sent you, the cook will give you a good meal to help you on your way. You look as if you need it.'

'So I may do,' Kester said with fury in his voice, 'but I'm not looking for charity.'

Serle lifted his eyebrows again. 'Are you expecting me to

offer a bed for the night, then? A fortnight's holiday, perhaps? A common vagrant who worked his passage across the Atlantic and now looks as if he's walked all the way here from Ottawa, who quite obviously does not have two pennies to rub together and is equally obviously hoping to batten himself on my cousin's good nature and sentimentality? I'm sorry, but I can't allow her to be taken advantage of by every ruffian who wanders by and claims he knew her in England.'

Kester took a deep breath. He wanted nothing more than to smash his fist into Serle's face, to wipe that patronising smirk off his face and see him felled to the ground. But the man was Rowenna's cousin, and he hadn't come here to make trouble.

'You've got it wrong,' he said, when Serle had finished. 'I didn't come here looking for handouts, nor hospitality. I'd be glad of a meal, but that's no more than you'd offer any friend who called unexpected. And then I'd like to talk to Rowenna alone. I've got a proposition to put to her.'

'A proposition, indeed! That's bold talk. But I don't think there's any proposition you may have that's likely to interest Rowenna. She has all she needs here. Well, I'll offer you a meal, despite your insolence. Is the kitchen good enough for you? Perhaps you'd like me to lay the dining table specially? We do have some rather fine silver – no, perhaps not. Forget I said that.'

Kester's voice was coldly furious.

'Don't worry. I won't run off with your knives and forks. I won't use them – not even the tin ones. I wouldn't let myself across your doorstep.' He turned away. 'I'll be in Penrith for a while, I reckon. If you want me, you'll likely find me in the sort of places that a chap like me finds a welcome. I've heard they call it garbage in this country.' He stopped and looked back at Serle. 'But don't think you've heard the last of me. I came a long way to talk to Rowenna. I'll not leave here until I've seen her for myself.'

Chapter Nineteen

Kester turned the corner and left the long white farmhouse behind him. He was smouldering with fury and humiliation. He was in the centre of Penrith now, in the wide main street with its shops on either side with their rails for hitching horses, its saloon, its little white-spired church on a grassy mound. His footsteps slowed and he paused to lean against a rail and look around.

What should he do now? After the reception Serle had given him he was inclined to walk away for ever, to shake the dust of the little town off his feet and never come near the place again. But it was impossible to leave while Rowenna was here. After coming all these thousands of miles to find her, was he to turn meekly away and lose himself in this vast country? He shook his head. Where she was, so must he be, at least until he knew for certain that she no longer wanted him.

But how was he to live, while he waited?

His eyes roved around the town, taking in the appearance of the buildings, looking past them to the wooded hills that rose behind, flaming with the brilliance of the fall. Trees, stretching away in every direction, Millions of them, spread all over this huge country, and the greatest industry of that country the harvesting of their timber.

Well, if there's one thing I know about, he thought, it's

trees. I can work with them, and there's work to be had, for this is the start of the harvesting season. And his eyes, still moving slowly over the scene before him, settled on the boarding above the wide entrance to a lumberyard, close to the river.

J. S. Tyson & Sons.

J. S. Tyson. That was the name on the letter Mr Abercrombie had given him. The name of Rowenna's grandfather. He was here in Penrith now and, since he wasn't at the farmhouse, he was likely to be in the lumberyard itself.

Kester straightened up and pushed his cap back on his head. He lifted the haversack which accompanied him everywhere, and strode across the road.

Jacob Tyson was out in the yard, stacking timber. It was one of his favourite jobs, for he always believed that manual labour not only kept the body fit, but also refreshed and stimulated the mind. And it kept him in touch with his men. Shut yourself away in an office, he would say, and you don't know who you've got working for you. And more important still, they don't know you – and how can anyone respect a man, whether he be boss or employee, if he doesn't know him to speak to?

This afternoon he was working with two or three other men, and when the stack was finished he sent them off to start another job at the other end of the yard while he tidied up the little splinters and shards always scattered on the ground after such operations. The task done, he straightened his back and stood for a moment before returning to his office. There was no doubt about it, after the age of ninety a man did begin to slow down. Like it or not, he couldn't do the work as he had twenty years ago.

A voice spoke at his elbow and he turned with a start, frowning. The man was nobody he knew, a stranger to

Penrith. Looking for work, no doubt, yet he hadn't the appearance of the usual kind of man to come seeking work in a lumberyard. Jacob assessed the tall, broad frame, the curling dark hair and frank eyes. He looked tough, yet there was an air almost of distinction about his bearing and he met Jacob's eyes with the direct glance of an equal.

'Aye?' Jacob said. 'Were you wanting something?'

'I'm looking for Mr Tyson.'

'Mr Jacob or Mr Serle? There's two y'know.' With some interest, he noticed a change of expression on the young man's face, no more than a flicker but enough to tell him that there was some hostility there. His curiosity grew. Hostility to himself, or to Serle?

'Mr Jacob,' Kester answered shortly. 'I've already met the other.'

'Oh, aye? And took against him?'

'The other way about, I'd say, but he didn't greatly impress me. Is Mr Jacob about? I suppose he's in his office.'

'And why should you suppose that?'

'Well, he's an old man, isn't he?' Kester said.

Jacob did not answer directly. Instead, he narrowed his eyes, stroked his bushy white beard and said, 'And when's a man too old to do a day's work, then?'

Kester looked at him and grinned. 'Older than you, I'd say. But he owns the yard. He's not likely to be out stacking timber with the timbermen, is he?'

'Is he not?'

'Not in my experience of bosses,' Kester said, and then added as an afterthought, 'Not that I've had much – I've never worked for another man before.'

The shaggy brows lifted. 'And why's that?'

'Because I like my freedom too much. Oh, I'll work, and work as hard as any man, but I've never called any man master, nor ever meant to.'

'And what's changed your mind now?'

Kester glanced at the bewhiskered face and then turned and gazed out at the trees that encircled the little town, spread like a glowing silk cloak over the hills. He felt again the sense of space that had accompanied him on his journey here.

'Did I say I'd changed my mind? I'm looking for work, yes – I need to earn my living. I've never been averse to selling my labour, only myself. And I've always loved trees. I like working with them. I understand them. The place, too – it's a good place, big and open, there's *room* here – I like my space about me.'

Jacob studied him. It was the first time for years that any man had talked to him of the openness and space of Canada. He remembered when he had come here, as a young man, and first gazed out across the endless horizons. He had felt the same surge of elation that he detected in the throb of this young man's voice, in the glow of his eyes. A pioneer, he thought. There's not so many of us left now.

'Three good reasons,' he said, counting them off on his fingers. 'But unless I mistake you, there's another and it's more important than any of the rest.'

He saw the young man's eyes darken and his jaw tighten, and sensed again that hostility he had noticed when Serle's name had been mentioned.

'As to that,' Kester said, 'it's my business. Something I might discuss with Mr Tyson – Mr *Jacob* Tyson – but none other.'

'Indeed?' The bushy brows lifted. 'Well you're talking to him now.'

Kester stared at him.

'*You're* Jacob Tyson? But – but he's—'

'An old man,' Jacob said, his eyes twinkling. 'Too old for stacking logs. Isn't that what you said?'

'I heard you were past ninety,' Kester said wonderingly.

'And so I am. Well past. But that'll not stop me doing a hand's turn in the yard. So—' he gave Kester a piercing look – 'maybe now you'll tell me what business you have to discuss with Jacob Tyson and none other, and why you look the way you do when you mention my adopted grandson.'

He turned and led the way across the yard. At one end stood the office buildings, and he pushed open the door and strode inside. Half a dozen clerks were working at a long desk, but Jacob marched past them to a small office at the end. He ushered Kester inside, pushed a chair forwards and sat down.

'Well, boy? What have you got to tell me? No – give me your name first. You're English, aren't you?'

'Some might say so. Some of my people would rather call themselves Romany.'

Jacob's eyebrows climbed.

'A *gypsy*? And are the rest of your people with you?'

'No, I'm alone.'

'In Penrith alone?'

'In Canada alone.'

Jacob frowned at him. 'I thought your sort hung together. Is there some rift?'

'No, I just prefer a different life.' He told Jacob about the steam roundabouts, the noise, the changes that had taken place. 'I like the woods and the quiet. The old way.'

'Hmmph. So you came to Canada, because we had trees and space. D'you think it's quiet here?'

'Isn't it?'

Jacob gave him a long look.

'In a lumber camp? You'll find out. Now, what's this business? And you still haven't told me your name.'

For answer, Kester produced the letter James Abercrombie had given him. He handed it across the desk

385

and the old man took it and unfolded it, reading with frowning attention. He read it twice, then laid it on the desk and looked up.

'Kester Matthews. So you're a friend of my granddaughter.'

'Yes.'

'A close friend?'

'I was,' Kester said, thinking of the hours they had spent together in the bluebell grove.

'And just what does that mean? How close? Was there any impropriety between you? She's a married woman, y'know.'

'I know that. We were friends long before that bastard Boothroyd came along. More than friends,' he added, half to himself.

'So you were her lover.'

'I didn't say that,' Kester said quickly, but he could see that Jacob didn't believe him. His dark eyes flamed as he looked across the desk at the old man. 'You don't know what Rowenna's life was like with that old curmudgeon of a father, nor with the husband he foisted on her. Since her brother died there's been no one to look out for her, and I want to make sure that now she's got away from them she won't walk into another trap. Seems to me she might.'

'Does it, indeed?' The bushy brows were lowered, almost hiding the piercing blue eyes. 'And why d'you think that?'

'I've seen your grandson,' Kester said flatly.

The leonine head came up, the brows lifting again. 'Have you, by George? And so from one brief meeting you can tell just what's going on, can you? You know more than I do about my own family. Is that the famous Romany second sight?'

'It's no more than what anyone who knows people and cared about Rowenna could see with half an eye.'

386

Jacob's face hardened. 'Are you saying that I don't care for my granddaughter?'

Kester looked at him consideringly, then replied, 'No. I'm not saying that. I think you're a man who might care for a granddaughter he'd only just met, and I think you're a man she could trust. But I don't think the same of your grandson.'

'Turned you away, did he?' Jacob gave a bark of laughter. 'Well, he don't suffer fools gladly, nor hangers-on. I've seen him give short shrift to a good many men who came calling at the house, cap in hand, looking for an easy handout—'

Kester came to his feet with a jerk. His face suffused with rage, he glowered down at the old man. His fists were clenched, his whole body taut, and behind him in the outer office the clerks stopped writing and scrambled down from their stools.

'I didn't go to your house cap in hand,' he said angrily. 'I went as a friend. I didn't look for an easy handout – I've never looked for handouts – and I asked for nothing other than the right to talk to the friend I had. It was no business of your grandson's, nor is it any business of yours. And now I'll get myself out of your office and out of your way, for I see I'm no more welcome here than I was in your home.' He reached across and snatched up James Abercrombie's letter. 'But I'll not leave Penrith until I've seen Rowenna and satisfied myself no one's going to take any further advantage of her.' His eyes blazed into the old man's piercing stare. 'Very well,' he said suddenly. 'We *were* lovers, Rowenna and I, though maybe not in the sense you mean. More than lovers. She's the woman I want most in the whole world – the *only* woman I want – and I know I'm the right man for her, the man she should stand with through life. I lost her once, but now I've come for her and I don't mean to lose her again. I don't want her money – I don't give a damn for money – and I'll work like a horse for her – aye, I'll even sell my

387

labour to another man for her, if that's what's needed. But I'll not lose her again, so don't imagine you or your family has seen the last of me!'

He turned as the door opened and two of the clerks came in. They reached out to grab his arms but he shook them off with ease, his big frame dwarfing them, and they looked uncertainly at Jacob Tyson.

'It's all right,' the old man said, waving them away. 'There's no trouble. Shut the door again. And you – Matthews. Sit down and calm yourself. I've no desire to quarrel with you. I like the way you talk and I like the way you hold yourself. You put me in mind of myself when I was your age – aye, and I like the way you talk about my granddaughter. So you were lovers, whether you possessed her or not – well, I think no ill of you for that. I'd think it strange for any man not to love that girl. If you're a friend of Rowenna's, that's good enough for me, and this lawyer speaks well enough of you. Besides, I can judge for myself – I've lived long enough to know a man's straight when I look at him.' He gave a sharp nod. 'Don't imagine that because Serle Tyson – who's no blood of mine, by the way – works for me, he speaks for me as well. I make up my own mind.' He watched as Kester settled himself reluctantly in the chair. 'Now – let me have another look at that letter. And then we'll talk.'

Rowenna stared at Serle. Her eyes widened and her hands lifted to cover her throat. She shook her head slowly from side to side, as if almost unwilling to believe what she had just heard.

'He's been here?' she whispered. '*Kester's* been here?'

'Your gypsy friend, yes, I just told you.' Serle watched her curiously. 'Came here with all the cheek of the devil, asking to speak to you as if he thought he had some sort of right over you. I suppose you were soft with him back home in

England – gave him money – and now he thinks you're an easy touch here in Canada.'

'I never gave Kester money,' she said, her voice still little more than a whisper. 'I never gave him anything.' *Except my heart*, her mind added.

'Well, he seems to think you'll give him something now. Anyway, you needn't worry – I sent him off with a flea in his ear.'

'You did what?'

'Sent him packing,' Serle repeated. He looked at her in surprise. 'You surely didn't want him hanging around?'

'Don't you think you should have asked me first?' Her voice rose more strongly and Serle lifted his eyebrows.

'Why, what's so special about a common labourer? Look, Rowenna, I know his type, they're always hanging about looking for easy pickings. I don't want 'em here. All right, so he was someone you knew in England, did a bit of work for you on and off perhaps, but that don't give him the right to come calling here, demanding to see you like some young lord. Anyway, I'm the one who gives the orders around here, and if I say he's not welcome, that's it!'

'Even if I told you he was my friend? Am I not to be allowed to have my friends here?' Rowenna's voice shook with anger and Serle moved towards her, holding out both hands.

'Rowenna, Rowenna,' he said, his voice conciliatory. 'Let's not make too much of this. Of course it never occurred to me that he was your friend, or that you'd actually want to see him. Why should it? But if you really want to see him, why, I daresay we can find out where he went. But I'd really much, much rather you took my advice and left it alone. Whatever he was like in England, he looked a shifty beggar to me now. Been drinking, I'd guess too. I wouldn't want him causing you any trouble, my dear.'

Rowenna looked at him uncertainly. Kester, looking shifty? Kester, drunk? She could not believe it, would not believe it. And Serle had sent him away! Where had he gone?

Serle left to go back to the timberyard and Rowenna went up to her room and sat by the window, gazing out. The sun had left the flowerbeds where she had been working, and the sharpness of autumn chilled the shade. She shivered a little, thinking of the coming winter, thinking of Kester.

Why had he followed her to Canada? Was it because he truly loved her, or had he come simply because he wanted to explore a new land, and had decided that as she was here he might as well renew their relationship? She shook her head. That did not sound like the Kester she knew. And she did not believe for one moment that he had, as Serle suggested, come looking for charity, for help. *That* was certainly not the Kester she knew!

What would he do now? What should she do now?

She leant her head on the cool windowpane, thinking of the days when she had met him in the garden at home. Days which would have been long and hard, had it not been for those hours they had spent together under the trees, talking, exploring each other's minds, and touching each other with a tenderness that grew into love.

I did love him, she thought. And I believed that he loved me – until he made love to Molly that night and would not wait for me.

But now . . . She felt the familiar ache in her throat and the hot sting of tears in her eyes. She thought of him, waiting in the old shepherd's hut on the fell, waiting and wondering. He had seen her in the grove – their grove – with Alfred Boothroyd. And then Molly had come to him, and given him her message. Molly, who had been her friend – but who wanted Kester for herself. Rowenna thought of how he must

390

have felt. The sharp pain of betrayal, which she knew so well herself. The torment of frustration. And the girl, so willing and ready, pressing herself against him, whispering in his ear . . .

Must she blame him for what he had done? Could she not forgive that sudden wild response as his body stormed its way to desire? She thought of him, when it was over, gazing at Molly and knowing that it should have been Rowenna he held in his arms, she thought of his remorse, his self-disgust. No wonder he had walked away into the night, no wonder he had thought her lost to him.

During all these months, through her father's illness, through her marriage to Alfred, she had carried that same pain of betrayal in her own heart. Lying awake with Alfred beside her, she had thrust away the memories of Kester's touch and kisses, had suppressed the ache of longing. He was a man, and men took what they wanted of you and then let you down. Her father had done it, Alfred had done it. Even Haddon had done it, by dying when she needed him still. It was only to be expected that Kester would do it too.

But he hadn't. He too had ached and yearned, he too had lain awake at night, and now he had come to Canada to find her.

I did love him, she thought. And he loved me. And nothing has changed.

She looked down at the shadowed garden and beyond it to the forest. Somewhere out there were her trees. Trees that she and Kester could harvest together, to start their new life. As her grandfather had done with his wife, so they too could go together into the vast timberland and clear their own garden, build their own home and become pioneers.

Chapter Twenty

'You've given him work?' Serle echoed. He stared disbe-lievingly at Jacob. 'But the man's a charlatan! He's come here simply to batten on to us, because he and Rowenna had some – some sort of friendship in England.' He flicked a glance at Rowenna. 'You should have sent him packing at once, just as I did.'

'He had a letter of introduction,' Jacob said, 'from a respected solicitor.'

'Respected by whom?' Serle jeered. 'You've never heard of the man – what was his name, Absalom, Abraham—'

'Abercrombie,' Rowenna supplied quietly. 'And he *is* much respected. He was very kind to me.'

'Because he knew you had money. That sort always—'

'I knew him too,' Jacob interrupted. 'I met him when I was back in England, when Dorothy had the misfortune to meet Warren Mellor, and I've corresponded with him over the past twenty years. My daughter knew and trusted him as well. I have no doubts about him at all.'

Serle looked disgruntled. 'Well, he can still make mis-takes. He's old enough now, I suppose—' He caught his grandfather's eye and stopped abruptly. 'Not everyone's as hale and hearty as you, Grandpa. Anyway, what can he know of this gypsy? The man's an itinerant – he never stays in one place long enough to become known. Why, he probably makes a career out of working in country-house gardens and seducing—'

'*Serle!* That will be enough!' Jacob's eyes flashed beneath the bushy brows. 'I'll thank you to remember there's a lady present and keep a civil tongue in your head. I'll hear no such talk at my table, nor anywhere in this house. Apologise to Rowenna at once.'

Serle's jaw tightened, but he turned to Rowenna and after a moment regained sufficient mastery of himself to give her his usual charming smile.

'I'm sorry, Ro,' he said wryly. 'That was unforgivable. I should never have said such a thing and of course I never intended it to be applied to *you*. Can you *possibly* forgive me?' He reached out and touched her hand, still looking boyishly rueful, his head tilted appealingly to one side.

There was little she could do but nod. Jacob watched, his brows still gathered in a frown. He said, 'And I'll not have this continual questioning of my actions, either. I'm still in charge of this business, Serle, and if I decide to employ a man it's not for you to tell me I'm a fool.'

'Grandpa, I never said—'

'Not in so many words, perhaps, but you certainly implied it. Calling him a charlatan, telling me what I ought to have done. I might remind you that I've had over seventy years' experience of working with men and reckon I'm a pretty good judge.' He lifted his brows, and his eyes flashed, a piercing blue. 'Matthews struck me as a good man – he's tough, he's got a mind of his own, he's determined. If he takes on a job, he'll see it through, and he's not scared of responsibility. That's the sort of man we need in the timber.'

'He's English,' Serle said. 'He doesn't know a damned – sorry, the *first* thing about trees. He'll be worse than that pair of city fellows we had through here last fall, thinking they could do timber work in thin shoes and summer suits.'

'He knows a lot about trees,' Rowenna said. 'That's what he did at home – he worked with the trees. And Haddie lent him his encyclopedias—'

'God give me strength,' Serle said, staring at her, and this time not apologising for his language. 'A few trees in an English garden and a couple of books! The Canadian forests aren't like that, for G – for heaven's sake. He'll be useless.'

'Well, we'll see, won't we,' Jacob said equably. 'I'm sending him out to take a look at Rowenna's timber stand. See what he has to say about that – that'll tell us what he's made of. Should be interesting.'

Serle turned his head slowly. His face paled, and the skin around his eyes tightened. There was a tautness in his nostrils and mouth.

'You're sending him out to look at *Rowenna's* stand?'

'That's what I said.'

'But that's not necessary. I was out there in spring. I told you what those trees are like.'

'So we'll have something to compare his report with. We can see if he knows what he's talking about.'

Serle snapped his fingers impatiently. 'He *doesn't* know! How can he? He's only been in the country five minutes – he knows *nothing*. He'll come back with some cock-eyed idea of what the trees are like and we won't even know if he's looked at the right ones. That's if he comes back at all!'

'Why shouldn't he come back?' Rowenna asked sharply.

Serle looked at her again. 'I've told you before – those aren't just woods, like you get in England. They're more like the jungle. We have *animals* in there – wild animals. We don't stop at rabbits and foxes – we have bears, bigger'n a man, and wolves and cougars. You don't mess with them. And if it's not them it's snakes – rattlers. And—'

'Stop!' Rowenna begged him. She looked at her

grandfather, her eyes dark. 'Did you tell Kester that? Does he know how dangerous it is?'

'Calm yourself, child. I'm not sending him to be mauled to death and eaten by bears and wolves. He'll be all right. I'm sending one of my best men to act as his guide.' He glanced at Serle. 'We'll know he's been to the right place. Abe McKenna's going with him.'

There was little chance for Kester and Rowenna to meet before he set off into the forest. The winter would be closing in soon, and if he were to make the journey to Rowenna's timber limit and return before the blizzards began, he would have to make good time. But he came the next afternoon, having spent the day with Jacob and Abe McKenna, and stood at the picket fence. And there, in one of the beds, he saw someone working. A young woman, wearing an old brown smock, her face hidden by a shady hat.

'*Rowenna,*' he breathed.

She could not have heard him, yet she looked up instantly. Their eyes met across the green lawn, and slowly, staring at him, she straightened and came across to him. He gazed at her, needing to see her reaction, but the brim of the hat hung over her brow and her face was in shadow.

'Kester?'

Her voice was wondering, only half believing. He nodded his head and took a step towards the fence, both hands held out. As if in a trance, Rowenna laid her hands in his and they stood, one on each side of the fence, gazing at each other.

'I've come so far,' he said at last, his voice little more than a whisper. 'I've come so far to find you. Tell me you're still mine. Tell me you're still my woman.'

Rowenna stiffened. Her eyes flashed and she answered him indignantly.

'*Your* woman? By what right? A few kisses in a garden, in another place, another lifetime? That's how it seems to me. Not much more than a dream. If I had truly been *your woman*, you would have waited for me, as I asked you to do.'

'As you asked me to do?' Kester repeated, bewildered. 'But you never asked me to wait. Molly told me you had said I should go, your father needed you and you had to stay with him. Don't you think I would have waited, if I'd known you wanted me?'

'You did know. You knew I wanted you, every time we met in the garden. I wanted you more than you wanted me.'

'No,' Kester said quietly, 'never more than that. And I did *not* know, that last afternoon when I saw you kissing Alfred Boothroyd in our place, and then sent that message to say you'd not be coming after all.'

'I didn't kiss Alfred – he kissed me.'

'There was precious little difference,' he said, 'from where I was standing.'

Rowenna was silent. Then she said, 'Did Molly really tell you that I'd said you must go away?'

'Aye, she did.'

'She lied,' Rowenna said sadly. 'She lied to you. And then you – you made love to her. Yes,' she said as the scarlet colour flooded his face and began to speak, 'yes, you did. I know you did.'

'Did she tell you?'

'Not in so many words. Not then.' Rowenna paused. 'But her – her son is very like you.'

'Her . . . *son*?' Kester let out a long breath. 'Is this true, Rowenna?'

'I've seen him myself.'

'I never knew,' he said, and then wonderingly, 'A son . . .'

Rowenna felt a swift flash of jealousy. 'He should have been our son, Kester,' she said roughly. 'It should have been me you lay with that night, not Molly. You believed her lies and you made love to her—'

'I didn't want to! I didn't *mean* to!' He stared at her, then ran one hand through his thick black curls. 'Rowenna, my love, how can I explain it? The torment of wanting you all those months – did you never have any idea, when you lay in my arms and let me caress you and begged me, aye, *begged* me, to make love to you – did you never realise what it was doing to me? I was in a fever for you, yet I always held back. For *your* sake I held back. But that night – you were coming to me at last, there was to be no more holding back. I was like a volcano ready to erupt. And when you didn't come, when she said you would never come, and I knew that I'd lost my chance, that I'd never be able to love you – and there *she* was, ready and willing . . . What was I to do, Rowenna? I wanted you – but if the world was coming to an end, what did it matter any more?'

Rowenna gazed into his eyes. She saw the tears in them, the dark anguish that had tormented Kester through the eternity through which they had both passed since that night. And she took his hands and lifted them to her lips, knowing that nothing more need be said or done than that.

They stood silent for a few moments, each recovering a little, then Kester asked quietly, 'Tell me about Molly's baby.'

Rowenna smiled. 'He's called Jack. He's a little monkey, always into mischief, but he has the most enchanting smile.' Her voice shook as she added, 'Like his father. He – he looks very like you, Kester.' Tears fell on to the backs of her hands as they clasped his on the fence, and she shook her head.

'And she still works at Ashbank? Even after—'

'She married John Richmond, the head gardener's son.'

'John Richmond? Well, I can think of many worse to

bring up my *chavvy*.' He glanced at Rowenna. 'Does *he* know?'

'I don't think so. If he does, he hasn't said. He loves Molly, you see.' She looked him straight in the eye. 'Far better than you ever did.'

'I never pretended to love her,' he protested. 'That night – it was just disappointment and misery, all mixed up together, and Molly was there. She knew it didn't mean a lifetime. But I didn't reckon there'd be a *chavvy* out of it.'

'I understand it's always possible,' Rowenna said drily, and his mouth twisted wryly.

'Aye, it's always possible, and always more so at the wrong time, or with the wrong woman!' He caught her startled look. 'No, my sweetling, I don't have a pack of *chavvies* yapping at my heels. No more than the one. I've never been a man for making love to any girl who happens along, and then going on to the next. For me, it's summat important, to be shared with the right one.'

'And Molly was the right one that night?'

'No! No, she wasn't, but – I thought I was never going to see you again. And all the waiting and the longing and the loving . . . And afterwards I looked at Molly and I wanted to hate her, but how could I do that? It was myself I hated.'

Rowenna was silent. She had thought so often of that night, of her own unhappiness and despair at losing the chance of Kester's love. And the bitterness of his betrayal had seared her heart. She thought of the first time she had looked at Molly's baby, of that moment of recognition. It had been like looking into Kester's eyes, and she had known then why Molly had been evasive, why nothing had been the same between them again.

Molly, in Kester's arms, sharing the love that should have been hers. Molly, with Kester's baby – the child that should have been hers.

'I tried to hate you too,' she said honestly. 'But it was impossible. I couldn't stop loving and wanting you. I just thought you would never – we'd never—' She shook her head, the tears too close for speech, and he clasped her hands more tightly and lifted them to his lips.

They stood silent for a few moments. Then Kester said, 'You'll come with me now, won't you? We'll not miss another chance.'

His voice softened and he stroked her fingers with a tenderness that sent waves of desire storming through her body. 'If you come with me, we'll both be free. We can go where we like – do as we will – and nobody to follow or deny us. Isn't that what you want? Isn't it what we both want?'

Rowenna could feel her body melting towards him. She wanted him to take her in his arms and kiss her as he had done in the bluebell grove, she wanted to feel the contact of his body, hard against hers yet a haven of warmth and comfort and sustenance.

She thought of walking away with him now, leaving everything – the tools she had brought out into the garden, the clothes and belongings in her room, everything she possessed both in Canada and in England. None of them mattered a jot.

She thought of leaving her family. Her aunts and uncles, so newly discovered. Her cousins. Her grandfather.

'We have to talk,' she said softly. 'We have so much talking to do. I'm married to Alfred—'

'Boothroyd!' he said scornfully.

'—and you've promised to do a job for my grandfather.'

'Aye, and I'll do it too. But it's for you, Rowenna, not for anyone else. But when I've done that – when I've been to the forest and seen your trees—'

'Then I'll come with you,' she said, and looked into his eyes.

Kester drew her closer to him. The fence stood between them, hard and unyielding, and he looked at it with impatience.

'Come into the forest with me now, Rowenna. Come walking with me, as we used to do. Will you do that?'

She pulled off the old gloves she used for gardening and dropped them on the grass. He gave her his hand and she climbed over the low fence. For a moment, they stood close, looking into each other's eyes.

'Oh, Kester,' Rowenna said, her voice shaking, 'I've missed you so much.'

'Aye, and I've missed you.' His voice was quiet. 'It's been a long time since I could touch you, except in my dreams.'

They turned and walked along the road towards the forest. The canopy of leaves, a blaze of scarlet and gold, swayed high above their heads as they came to the edge of the trees and followed the path between the soaring trunks. Beneath their feet, a thick carpet mirrored the colours above, as if in some fashionable drawing room with the pattern of the ceiling the same as that on the floor. A scuffling and angry chittering voice betrayed the presence of a squirrel, and on the smooth grey boles of the beech trees Rowenna saw the great slashing marks made by the claws of bears as they clambered up.

The sight reminded her of Serle's words and she gripped Kester's hand.

'Grandfather's told me where you're going. You will take care, won't you? These woods aren't like those at home—'

'I know.' He grinned at her. 'Bears and wolves and cougars. And if that's not enough, the odd rattlesnake. What are you doing, walking in such a dangerous place, Rowenna?'

She gave him a quick, startled glance. 'You mean they could be here? This close to the town?'

'Why not? The forest goes for hundreds of miles. And

401

they could get away fast enough. I've heard the bears actually come down the streets some nights, looking for stuff people have thrown out. And one of the men in the timber-yard told me you can hear the wolves howling at night. So aren't you too scared to come walking here?'

She thought for a moment, then shook her head. 'No. I think it's safe enough, so long as one keeps a careful watch. And I know enough not to get near a bear if we do see one. Grandfather's told me what to do – you just back away, very carefully, and don't run. And never get between them and their cubs.'

'And they might chase you just the same,' he said. 'It doesn't matter whether you're in the middle of the forest or on the edge, Rowenna. People get killed by bears in both places. Same as they get drowned in rivers or run over by carriages or fall out of trains. We can't live charmed lives and we can't stay at home in the parlour all day in case we have an accident.' He grinned. 'I've heard of people falling in the fire from their armchairs, anyway. It isn't safe anywhere!'

Rowenna smiled. 'No. I know. And I know you can look after yourself in the woods, Kester. I'm not really worried about you. Except—' She paused.

'Except what?'

Rowenna stopped and looked at him. The blue of her eyes was dappled with the burning colours of the flickering leaves.

'We've only just found each other again,' she said shakily. 'We've been apart so long – I thought we'd lost each other, I thought we'd missed our chance. And now here you are again, I can see you, I can *touch* you, and in a day or two you're going away again. I'm just – afraid that you won't come back.'

Kester stared at her. Her eyes were wide and dark, trem-

402

bling with shadows. He put up one finger and touched her cheek, and a tear spilled on to his skin.

'Rowenna, my sweetling, my love. Of course I'll come back. Why, it would take every wild horse in the world to keep me from you. And if it wasn't your trees I was going to see, I wouldn't leave you at all.' He smiled crookedly. 'And I'm darned sure your grandfather knows that. He's a wily old character, you know.'

'You mean – he *wants* you to go away? He's doing it deliberately?'

'Aye, that's it. He knows I'd never go for any other reason. He wants you to be sure, Rowenna. He sees plain enough what there is between us but he don't want you making a mistake.'

'I've made all my mistakes,' she said, shaking her head.

'Aye, but he don't know that and he just wants to give you time. And me too, perhaps. I've got to prove myself out here, and going up into the forest with winter coming on and working for him in the lumber camps is as good a way as any of doing it. The best way, as far as he's concerned.'

Rowenna sat down on a fallen log. She looked at him with glowing eyes.

'When you come back,' she said, 'we'll go away together. We'll make our home out in the forest and we'll harvest my trees. *Our* trees. And we'll build our own home and start our own business – perhaps even build our own mill. Grandfather did it with less than we have, and we can do it too.'

'Aye,' he said, 'but your cousin's right – I've got a lot to learn about trees and the timber business. This trip will be a chance for me to make a start. When I come back, I'll be in better shape to take it on with you.' He sat down beside her and put his arms around her, looking steadily into her face. 'I've never called any man master,' he said quietly, 'but that doesn't mean I don't pay my way in this world.'

'There's no question of anyone being master,' she said. 'I just want us to be together.'

He touched her face again. His palm was warm and strong against her cheek and she turned towards it like a baby seeking milk. She could feel his body strong against hers, the power of his arms, the length and hardness of his thigh, the thudding of his heart. His chin was slightly bristled, rough against her smooth skin. His breath was sweet and familiar, though she had not felt it for so long, and when his lips touched hers she was pierced by a longing so sharp, so tender and so undeniable that she cried out and caught him to her, covering his face with wild, frantic kisses and burying her head against his shoulder as he held her close in the circle of his arms.

'Kester – Kester – don't leave me again.'

'I'll never leave you, my darling,' he whispered, his tongue touching her ear. 'I'll never be far away from you. I thought we'd lost our chance too – I thought it would never come again. But the other thing my father used to tell me was that we make our own chances – and that's why I came after you to Canada. I don't mean to let chance rule our lives any more, Rowenna – from now on, we live our lives the way we want to, the way we were made to, and the devil take any man who tries to stop us.'

He pulled her gently down to the forest floor, to the thick bed of leaves that glowed like a multi-coloured counterpane beneath the canopy of the trees. He laid her on her back and leaned over her, kissing her face and neck. His strong brown fingers as gentle as a mother's, he unbuttoned her bodice and laid her breasts bare to the sunlight and the tender breeze.

'My darling,' he murmured as he bent his head to their softness. 'My darling, you asked me so many times to love you, and so many times I wanted to. Did you have any idea how much and how often I longed to undress you, there by the river where I first saw you naked? Did you have any idea how I yearned to have your skin touching mine, to feel the warmth of your blood and flesh and muscle? Oh, my Rowenna, my nights were filled with you then, with the heat of wanting you. I thought I'd go mad with it at times, but always there was next day – until that last time.'

'Don't talk about it now,' she begged. 'It's over. We're together here, and nobody to stand between us.' She held his head against her breasts, cradling him there. 'We can love each other now.'

He lifted himself and looked down into her eyes.

'But not for the first time. That bastard Boothroyd was first, where I should have been. It was he gave you your introduction to loving, when it should have been me, and for that I can never forgive myself.'

Rowenna flinched as the memory of Alfred Boothroyd, leaning over her in just this fashion, stabbed her heart. For a moment, she closed her eyes, fighting to shut him out, to remind herself that all men's loving was not as his had been. And then she opened them again and looked up into Kester's dark, tender face.

'There was no loving between Alfred Boothroyd and me,' she said quietly. 'What he did, and the way he did it, was nothing to do with what happens between us. You will show me what loving truly is, my darling, and it will be as new to me, and as beautiful, as if Alfred Boothroyd had never existed.'

Kester bent and kissed her lips. He kissed her cheeks, her eyelids, her ears and her neck. He kissed the hollow of her throat and her shoulders and her breasts, and slowly, as he revealed them, each part of her quivering body. He rose to his feet, slid from his own clothes as if from a skin, and stood before her, brown and strong, before stretching his

405

length on the crimson leaves beside her. She felt the human warmth of his flesh, moulded against her, and pressed herself against the hardness of his thighs. Her heart was pounding and her blood singing, and her entire body tingled as if teased by a myriad frosty stars.

Kester slid his hands over her body, shaping its curves with his palms, tracing tiny patterns with his fingertips. He stroked the sensitive creases beneath her breasts and in the hollows of her thighs. He kissed her all over, slowly, ignoring her gasps as his tongue touched sensitive spots, his fingers and palms moving on her skin all the while. And then he sat over her, straddling her body, and gazed down into her face.

'You're sure about this?' he whispered, and his voice was low and deep.

Rowenna nodded her head. She reached up and laid her hands on his shoulders, pulling him down towards her. And he groaned suddenly and caught her up against him, holding her with arms that were suddenly iron bands, his kisses no longer gentle but passionate and wild, following a pathway of their own that led him to every portion of her body, to each swelling curve and each deep crevice, until Rowenna knew herself as tormented as he, her need as desperate, her desire as fierce.

He dropped her back on to the leaves and she caught his hips and held him above her. And then both moved, in a swift convulsion that brought them together, smoothly, easily, as it had never been with Alfred. And Rowenna felt a great joy surge through her, as if this at last was what she had always longed for, always needed, as if now at last she was complete.

They looked into each other's eyes with joy. And then Kester began to move gently, stroking and caressing her very depths, sometimes with slow, almost dreamy languor, sometimes with swift thrusts that took her almost to the peak of sensation. Now and then he rested, as if not wanting to complete his loving too soon, and they lay closely entwined, kissing softly. But neither could rest for long, and at last he could hold back no longer and rose above her like a victor, driving deeper and deeper until she could feel his penetration almost to her heart; and the tingle that had earlier shivered over her skin now spread from loin to fingertips, as if a star had burst deep inside and sent its shimmering particles streaming over her body.

The moment held, then faded. And they lay quiet in each other's arms on the crimson and gold bed of leaves. As Rowenna had said it would be, the loving was as new and as beautiful as if nobody else had ever existed; and the tears that slipped gently from her eyes had nothing to do with the tears she had shed for Alfred Boothroyd.

Kester left Penrith three days later, together with Serle and Abe McKenna. They were bound first for the new lumber camp, which men had been building all summer in order to start cutting a new stand. From there, Abe and Kester would go on up river to Rowenna's limit.

'I still say there's no need,' Serle had protested whenever he could get Jacob to listen to him. 'I've seen that limit and it's by no means the best in the area. In fact, I'd say it wasn't worth the labour. I'm sorry, my dear,' he added, turning to Rowenna, 'but it's better you should know the truth. It's poor land up there, and poor land grows poor trees.'

'It wasn't poor land when I saw it last,' Jacob said. 'And the trees looked pretty good to me. I've a good mind to go along with Kester and see for myself.'

'That's foolish!' Serle said at once, but subsided when he saw the expression on his grandfather's face.

'Please, Grandfather, don't do that,' Rowenna begged

him. 'Kester would feel you didn't trust him – he wants to do this job *himself*. It's important to him.'

'Aye, I understand that. Well, I'll wait for his report.' He gave Serle a frowning stare. 'I'll be interested to hear just what is up there now.'

Serle looked sullen but said nothing. He accepted Kester's company in the buggy with ill grace, and the three of them waved goodbye to Rowenna and Jacob, and disappeared up the dusty track. Rowenna watched until they were out of sight and then turned to go back into the house, her lips tight.

She still felt uneasy about this trip. Kester's reassurances about the dangers of the bush had calmed only a few of her fears. Bears, wolves and rattlesnakes, she thought, were not the only perils he would face. Accidents could happen anywhere, and there were plenty of things to go wrong in a lumber camp. Since arriving in Penrith, she had heard of men being drowned in the river, crushed to death by log jams, killed by falling timbers, or trampled by horses. Hands were broken, fingers lost almost as a matter of course, and legs sometimes taken right off by the huge crosscut saws. The harness used to shackle the horses to the huge stacks of logs on the sleigh could fly loose and strangle or even decapitate a man, and if the stack was too high and the load too heavy it could run out of control down the steep banks, killing both horses and men.

And if that were not enough, there was Serle. Rowenna had never seen true hatred on a man's face before, not even Alfred's, but she knew that it smouldered in Serle's eyes for Kester, and she shivered as she thought of them, out in the bush together.

'Don't go,' she had begged him as they clung together on that last evening. 'Please, please don't go.'

'I have to,' he said, stroking her face. 'I've promised your grandfather. He's a good man, Rowenna, and he's given me this chance to prove myself – I can't let him down.'

She leaned her head against his breast, holding him close. His heart beat steadily against her ear, and she closed her eyes, willing the world to stop, time to stand still. Perhaps if neither of them moved . . . But Kester stirred and kissed her, and she knew that time had not stood still, that the minutes still ticked by, each bringing them inexorably nearer to the moment of parting.

I can't bear it, she thought. He's leaving me again, and he may never come back. I can't bear it . . .

But she had had no choice. Kester had kissed her again, a long, searching kiss as if he were giving his heart into her keeping, and then turned and walked away. And she had watched his figure disappear into the darkness, and then turned back into the house.

Serle was standing there, a tall, dim figure in the candlelit hall. Rowenna jumped and gasped, her hand at her throat. She stared up at him with wide eyes.

'How very touching,' he drawled. 'I wonder what your husband would say if he saw you behaving like that.'

Rowenna's eyes flashed. 'That's my business.' The relationship between herself and Serle had deteriorated rapidly. He had been unable to conceal his dislike of Kester, and his boyish charm no longer had the power to win Rowenna over. But she would not let him see that she was afraid of him. She faced him in the dim, flickering light, her chin lifted defiantly. 'Let me pass, please.'

But he stood in her way, his arms folded across his chest, legs planted firmly apart.

'Aren't you going to wish *me* goodnight and safe journey?'

'I shall see you in the morning, before I go.'

'You'll see Matthews too. But perhaps you won't want to

behave like a wanton, before the whole town.'

Rowenna gasped. 'How dare you!'

'Oh, I dare easily,' he answered coolly. 'What else can it be called when a married woman, far from her husband's side, presses herself so intimately against another man's body and kisses him in such a way?' His hand shot out and caught her wrist, jerking her against him. 'A way in which you've never kissed *me*!'

'Surely you'd not want me to,' she retorted, breathing quickly as she stared up at him. 'You'd never want me to behave so *wantonly* with you.'

He glared down at her and spoke through his teeth. 'Don't be so sure. Now that I've seen what you can be like – and what a little spitfire you are—' His other arm was round her waist, a band of steel from which there was no escape. Rowenna felt suddenly afraid and twisted fruitlessly in his grasp.

'Wriggle all you please,' he hissed. 'It gives me all the more pleasure . . . Now, shall we complete this conversation in your room or in mine? We'd be far more comfortable behind a locked door, don't you think?'

'I think nothing of the kind! Let me go at once. I shall scream for Grandfather—'

'For an old man? Do you want to give him a seizure? In any case, he'd never hear you, he went to his bed an hour ago, as you well knew when you let that gypsy into the house.'

'I'd have let him in with Grandfather's blessing, if he'd been downstairs,' she retorted. 'He likes Kester, and trusts him too – as *you* well know.'

Serle's face darkened. His arms tightened painfully about her. He bent his head and his teeth grazed her mouth. She tasted blood.

'You will kiss me, you little devil,' he muttered. 'And

you'll do more – you'll give me what I'd swear you've already given that gypsy. Tonight, before we go on this damned trip into the bush – *now*!'

Still gripping her wrists, he loosened his arms and began to propel her up the stairs. Rowenna struggled, but he was too lithe and too strong; she could not even kick him. He half lifted her up the stairs and they were almost at the top when Jacob's bedroom door opened suddenly and the old man, clad in a striped nightshirt and cap, stood staring at them.

'What the devil's going on here? Serle, what are you about?'

Serle stopped at once and slid his arm around Rowenna's shoulders in a gesture of protection.

'Matthews came to say goodbye, and Rowenna's a little upset,' he explained easily. 'I was just lending her my shoulder to cry on, and seeing her to her room. I've told her he'll be perfectly okay in the bush, with me and McKenna to give an eye to him, but you know how women are – she thinks we're all going to be eaten by bears!'

Jacob stared suspiciously at him, then looked at Rowenna. 'Is this true? You're upset over Matthews – nothing more?'

Rowenna looked at him. If she told him the truth, he would believe her. He would believe her above Serle, because she was of his blood, his daughter's daughter, and Serle was no true relation. And because in recent weeks he had been increasingly suspicious of this grandson who had been wished upon him, and who was showing a marked tendency to want to take over the entire business.

But he was an old man – frighteningly old. He looked no more than seventy, a score or more years less than his true age – but even a man of seventy could be frail. She thought of her father and his attack of inflammation of the heart. To tell Jacob the truth about Serle might all too easily bring on a similar attack. And at over ninety, could he survive it?

'Yes, it's true,' she said. 'Serle was just helping me up the stairs. I'm afraid I was rather silly.'

Jacob's eyes softened. 'Not silly at all,' he said. 'Just a tender girl – as your mother was too, at your age.' He bent his head. 'Here – give me a kiss and then go off to your bed. Kester will fare well enough in the bush, you'll see. He's no soft city dweller, and he can hold his own with any lumberman. He'll be back safe and sound, almost before you've had time to miss him.'

I miss him already, Rowenna thought, but she kissed her grandfather's cheek and then turned away to her own room. Conscious of the two men watching her, she opened the door and went inside. Then she closed it, leant upon it and turned the key quietly in the lock.

Serle would not have the chance to molest her again tonight. Nor tomorrow, when he and Kester and Abe McKenna left to go to the camp.

Nor ever again, she vowed. For when Kester returned, he and she would go away, together, and this time *nothing* would stand in their way.

Chapter Twenty-One

The main lumber camp was close to the lake, on an acre or so of level ground at the top of a gentle slope. The buildings were all of logs, wedged into each other by notches, with the spaces plastered over. The floors were of adzed logs and the roofs of lumber and tarpaper, with rafters made of spruce and balsam.

'That's the cookery,' Serle said briefly, pointing his whip. 'The biggest building. Bunkhouses over there – stables at the far end. That smaller shanty is the cobbler's – there's a lot of work to be done on boots in camp – and that's the blacksmith's forge. He makes snowshoes for the horses, or shoes with spikes for dragging the logs on icy roads. We've got a bit of a store too – the men can buy socks and jackets and such.' He glanced disparagingly at Kester's clothes. 'You'll need to get fitted out yourself if you're going to be here long.'

He swung down from the buggy and disappeared. Abe and Kester looked at each other.

'He's right,' Abe said. 'You need a few things. I'll show you round and then we'll go to the store and see Norman.'

Kester hoisted his haversack on to his back and followed the other man across the camp. He liked Abe McKenna and was glad to have his company on the way up to Rowenna's timber limit. In the few days it had taken them to get here, he had seen just what the Canadian forests were like. You could step off the road and be lost within thirty paces. And there was no proper road past this camp, except where the loggers had built skids to the places they were clearing; only a track here and there, mostly overgrown.

They went to the bunkhouse first and Abe showed Kester the rows of bunks – no more than wide plank shelves, nailed to the long walls. Each was covered by a tick mattress, stuffed with hay, and had two blankets. In the middle of the long floor, on a mound of sand, a fire was burning and a boy of about fifteen was stirring a large, steaming pot.

'We used to cook over that,' Abe remarked. 'But now we got the cookery we don't need to – we just boil up a pot of tea at night. A camboose fire's good, though, keeps you warm at night, though it'd be out by morning if we didn't have a chore-boy to keep it fired. We didn't at first. And the cold then – wheew! Why, I've woke up in the morning, found my socks frozen stiff and my boots too hard to walk in. I soon learnt to take 'em to bed with me, I can tell you. And the rest of my clobber too, make no mistake.' He grinned. 'I remember one guy, he had long hair and he woke up one morning and it was all stuck on the wall! We told him it'd have to be cut off and we took it off with shears. Of course, it thawed out after a bit and he was that wild to think he'd lost his hair . . . But it's better now we got a chore-boy to do them sorta things and make us a mug of tea to drink. You need that at five in the morning in the middle of winter.'

He found a spare bunk and Kester dropped his haversack on it. The men were coming in from work and they glanced curiously at him, nodding when Abe introduced him and then going off to throw themselves on their bunks. Some of them started to play cards and the boy filled mugs with strong black tea.

'I'll show you round the rest of the place,' Abe said. 'We'll go to Norman's first, get you something to wear.'

The store was plain, with shelves stacked with heavy woollen socks and blankets, boots and moccasins. There were racks of jackets and breeches, and Kester examined them, feeling the thick material between his fingers.

'What's this?'

'That?' Abe said. 'That's mackinaw, that is – long wool, woven from the inside out. That'll keep you dry in all weathers, and warm too. You want a jacket of that, and pants. See if there's anything here'll fit you.'

Kester looked doubtfully at the breeches. 'Knee-length. Isn't that a bit cold in the snow?'

The storekeeper came over and lifted a pair from the rack, holding them against Kester to measure him. 'Cold? Never! You want to be able to pull your socks up over the top, see? Long pants make a great big leg, you can't get your sock over it and you can't tie your moccasins on. Anyway, they make your legs too hot and leave your feet to freeze.'

'That's right,' Abe said. 'Knee pants are best. Same on the drive – when you're taking logs down river. Long pants get dirty, they get hooked up on things, and they get wet. And if you do fall in the water, they're too heavy. It's easier to climb about in short pants.'

'How much are they?' Jacob had given Kester some money for his needs while he was in the bush, but he had no idea what his expenses might be. Still, he had to have the right clothes; that was a matter of survival.

'Three dollars twenty-five for the pants and five for the jacket. You'll need woollen underwear as well, and a couple of shirts. Got any mitts? I got these in, good leather they are, serve you for years. And moccasins, best deerhide, keep you warm when it freezes hard. Twenty-five dollars all told, how'd that suit you?'

415

Kester paid and took his bundle back to the bunkhouse. There was still no sign of Serle, but a few men were wandering around the camp, sitting in small groups or lying on the grass. Soon it would be too cold to stay out of doors once work was finished.

He passed the blacksmith's forge, where two men were working, and was startled to hear the shrill blast of a trumpet from the other side of the camp. He turned and saw Abe laughing at him.

'That's the cookee, that is, calling us all in to supper. That trumpet of his sounds right up in the forest, so anyone still up there knows it's time to get back. Come on. It's salt pork and beans tonight.'

The cookhouse was the largest of the buildings. Inside, it was furnished with rows of long tables and benches, with the stoves and work tables at one end. Men were already filing in and settling themselves round the long tables, which were set with big steaming dishes. Rapidly, they helped themselves, loading their plates with meat, beans and potatoes. Kester, realising suddenly how hungry he was, heaped his plate and started to eat. It was only when he had almost finished that he realised that, apart from the clatter of plates and cutlery, the big building was silent. Nobody spoke.

He glanced at Abe, wanting to ask why, but the sound of one voice in that busy silence would have seemed an intrusion, and he held his tongue. Afterwards, as they went outside again, Abe grinned at him.

'I could see you bursting to ask! The cooks don't allow no talking at mealtimes – it takes too much time. See, there's another lot of men going in for their dinner now, they don't want to hang about outside listening to the first lot chattering away. And the cooks know that once men start talking, they start in to argue and maybe fight. There's been too many good cookeries bust up over men getting too hot round the collar. Anyway, they don't want no complaints over the food!'

There was a shout from the other side of the clearing, and Kester saw Serle beckoning him. They walked over and he glanced inimically at Kester, then turned to Abe.

'I want you out in the bush tomorrow, Abe. One of the foremen's had an accident. They took him down to the hospital this afternoon – broken leg. He'll be off best part of a couple of months.'

'But I'm supposed to be taking Kester up to the far edge,' Abe objected. 'Ain't there anyone else can take over?'

'No, there's not!' Serle snapped. 'Anyway, you're needed here – I can't spare my best man to go on sightseeing tours. I don't know what my grandfather was thinking of.' He gave Kester a withering glance. 'If you were a real woodsman, you could go on your own, no trouble to anyone. As it is, I suppose I'll have to find someone else to hold your hand.'

Kester shrugged. 'I'm used to wild places. I daresay I could find it if you gave me the directions.'

'Directions? What directions? Turn left by the stunted oak, take five thousand paces east and dig beneath the giant fir? This isn't a boys' adventure story, man! You won't find a neat little pathway with signposts every mile. You need someone who can read the woods, someone who knows his way about.' Serle turned away in exasperation. 'Well, you'd better make up your mind to stop here a day or two till I get a man organised. You can go out with Abe tomorrow, see what a real job of work's all about, but don't get in the way – I don't want any more accidents.'

He strode off and Abe looked at Kester and shrugged his shoulders. 'Well, that's that. I don't get my camping trip. Pity, it's a nice place up the far edge. I went there a while ago, thought what a good place it'd be for a camp.'

'What did you think of the timber?' Kester asked. 'Serle said it was poor.'

'Did he?' Abe raised his eyebrows. 'Well, I didn't go right in, but I wouldn't have said it was poor. Not on the edges. Maybe there was a fire or summat in there some time. You get that, bush fires, lay the forest waste and it takes ages to get going again. Maybe that's what happened.'

He took Kester round the rest of the camp. A short distance off they came to another, smaller clearing and here there was a herd of pigs, roving about the forest, digging for roots with their snouts. Kester looked at them in surprise.

'Yeah, there's our meat ration for the winter,' Abe said, leaning on an old stump. 'Old Willie McGraw, he looks after them all summer and kills off all but the breeders to salt down. Means we don't hev to bring so much in each fall. Brings 'em up good and fat, he does – that's what a man needs, a good lump of pork fat to keep him warm.'

'What else do you eat?'

'What else? Why, nothing else – bit of fish sometimes, if a feller has time to catch it. Pickerel, that's nice, and the cook will fry it up for breakfast if you ask him right. Or maybe the chore-boy'll do it on the camboose. Otherwise, it's pork and beans.'

Kester grinned. 'So that's how you knew what was for supper.'

'That's it. Pork'n'beans. Always is.'

A short distance from the pigs' enclosure, they came to a small hut, built of bark stripped from felled logs and leaning against a pile of discarded timber. Kester stopped and glanced at it curiously.

'Who lives here?'

'Oh, that's the Indian's hut,' Abe said. 'We call him Grey Otter. He's a trapper – sets his traps in the late summer and fall, then spends the winter in the forest, picking up what he's caught, and sells the pelts. He'll go round the big lumber camps, that have got stores like ours, or else to trading posts. Sometimes he'll fetch up as far as Penrith. You never know where you might run into Grey Otter.'

'He lives alone in the forest – even through winter? I thought it wasn't possible for anyone to do that.'

Abe laughed 'Only Injuns! They're a different breed. Never get lost – why, old Grey Otter's brought back more than one man who got hisself lost in the bush.'

'Is he in the camp now?' Kester asked.

'Oh aye, he's around. Don't mix much, mind. And he could be gone tomorrow – just comes and goes as the fancy takes him, I guess.'

They went back to the main camp. It was growing dark now and the log cabins and shanties were lit with lamps. The windows of the cookhouse glowed with light, but the bunkhouse was solid. 'What d'you need windows for, when you're only in there at night?' Abe asked. But as they came nearer, they could hear music, and the sound of voices singing and the thump of feet.

'They're at it already,' Abe remarked. 'Stag dance. Sometimes wonder whether this is a lumber camp or a dancing school! Every night after supper, till nine o'clock, there's a bunch of 'em get singing and dancing. And the songs they know! Reckon there must be fifty or sixty of 'em, driving songs, love songs, shanty songs, war songs. You'll never hear singing nowhere else like you'll hear in a lumber camp.'

They stood in the doorway looking in, then found places to sit on the floor. The middle had been cleared and three or four men were step-dancing to the tune of a mouth organ and violin, their boots clattering on the wooden floor. The rest were singing lustily.

'Come all you lumberjacks and I'll sing you a song,
A nice little ditty, it won't take me long.
It's all about lumbering, you plainly will see.
One winter we spent down in Camp Number Three.'

The song went on for six verses, and then the musicians began to play faster. The men fell silent, watching as the dancers' feet flashed – heel and toe, heel and toe – and their legs kicked higher and higher. Kester, who had seen plenty of dancing round the camp fires of his own people, felt the music stir his blood. The rhythm pounded in his head and his limbs twitched. He folded his arms, trying to keep still, but it was useless, and suddenly he was back in the Romany camps of his boyhood, watching as the young men pranced and twisted in the firelight, some of them leaping through the fire itself, their eyes and teeth flashing as they went. He saw his father Kieran, dancing with the best of them, his brothers vying with each other to make the highest leap. And then, as the music grew even quicker, he could sit still no longer. He sprang up, jumped out on to the floor, and began to dance.

'Horroo!' the men shouted. 'Who's this, thinks he can dance better'n a lumberman?' They jeered and cheered, both catcalling and egging him on. The musicians changed their beat and Kester changed with it. He let his feet fly, let them respond directly to the music that was in his ears, in his brain, in his body. The other men danced with him, stamping their feet hard, kicking them high in the air, making leaps that took their heads almost to the rafters. And Kester matched them all until at last they began to drop out exhausted, and he was the only one left, dancing to a ring of faces.

When the music finally stopped he stood still, breathing hard. There was a moment of complete silence in the bunk-house. And then one man began to clap his hands.

The others burst into cheers. The men who had been dancing jumped on to the floor and slapped Kester on the back. They crowded around him, shaking his hand, and he grinned around at them, feeling suddenly at home. These were his kind of men, his people, and he knew that from this moment he would be at ease.

But the evening was over. The chore-boy pushed his way between them, shouting, 'Ten to nine! Ten to nine!' and the men began to prepare for bed. Within a few minutes, they were all in their bunks and the lamps were being doused. From now until morning, Abe told Kester, there would be no talking.

Kester scrambled into his own bunk and lay there, still slightly breathless. The chore-boy was attending to the fire and its light flickered over the log walls, the high rafters and the floor. It was the nearest to a house he had ever been in to sleep, except for the shepherd's hut up on the fell near Burneside.

He thought of Rowenna, back in Penrith. Was she abed yet, or was she sitting up with her grandfather? He thought of their lovemaking, the way she pressed herself against him, the way she kissed. When this trip is over, he vowed to himself, I'll never leave her again.

The door had been left open and he looked out at the shadowy trees, at the star-filled sky. And as he lay there, the space was darkened by the figure of a man, who paused to look in.

It was Serle. Kester was just near enough to see his face, lit by the glow of the fire. Perhaps it was a trick of the light, perhaps it was merely a fire-reddened shadow, but the expression on Serle's face was such that he found himself beginning to shiver.

Kester had known many men he disliked, and who disliked him. But he had never before seen one who looked at him with hate.

'This here's a chopping axe,' Abe said, hefting the big tool. 'It's different from a hewing axe, see? You don't grind a chopping axe more'n you have to, you just give it a bit of a rub with a fine whetstone now and then and let it get smooth. Then it'll go deep into the timber. Now, the hewers, they need a good tempered axe for limbing hemlock, and peeling bark, so they grind and file their axes. And you don't never touch another man's axe. Every man has his own way of handling, and if an axe ain't handled the way it's used to, it'll lose its face and be no good, see?'

Kester took the axes Abe was showing him and weighed them in his hand. He imagined swinging the long handle above his head, bringing it down into precisely the right point on the trunk, making the first cut – and then swinging it again and again, each time striking a little further into the same cut, each time driving the edge a little deeper into the timber.

'Mind you, most of us choose crosscut saws now,' Abe went on. 'It's only the oldtimers, who won't change, who go on using axes.' He lifted the end of a long saw with irregular teeth and a handle at each end. 'These started to come in about ten years ago. After the first notch is cut by axe, the two men saw the tree down together and I tell you, they can do double the work two axemen can do. A hundred logs a day ain't no trouble with one of these fellers.'

'Didn't you ever use saws before?' Kester asked.

'Yeah, sure, a few people did, but the trouble was, y'see, the teeth would catch in the sawdust once you'd started cutting, and get jammed. Well, these saws hev special teeth – rakers – in between the cutting teeth, to pull out the shavings. Mind you, they hev to be kept sharp and filed regular, or the rakers get too long as the cutters wear down. We hev to hev filers now – old Sam's ours, he's got a workshop down behind the blacksmith's forge. Take your saw

422

along to him of an evening and he'll set his gauges on it and file it down proper, and it'll be good as new when you goes to collect it. Some fellers carry their own file, but you needs the gauges or you don't get it set right.'

Kester looked up at the swaying canopy high above. Few of the trees had leaves now, and the branches showed a fine tracery of pattern against the sky. As he watched, he heard the yell of 'Timbe-er-r-r!' and saw one of the great crowns sway a little further, hesitate for a second and then topple slowly away. There was a mighty crash, a thud that shook the ground beneath his feet. And a space in the sky, where the tree had been.

Kester felt a pang. He had grown up amongst trees, in camps set up in the clearings of English woods. He had worked with them in Rowenna's garden. He had never before been present when a tree was chopped down in its prime.

But there was no time to think of that now. Abe was showing him quickly around the chopping site. Felling had only just begun, for winter had not yet set in and there were other preparations to be made first. Most important was a new skid road built to take the timber to the river. The trees now being felled were used for this road – a trackway made of logs, laid across the path with earth piled between them, to make it easy for the horses to draw the sleighs. The sleighs too had to be built, great trolleys with sliders which could carry logs stacked high in a pyramid, chained together to prevent them falling.

'Most winters there's a prize for the most logs skidded in a day,' Abe said. 'I won it last year. I did it with squared timber – you can load more on if it's squared off. I had to tell the foreman the night before, and he'd send someone out to see that nobody else hooked the chain, or unhooked it, and nobody but me swung the doubletree. It had to be all my own work. Well, there were logs everywhere, piled up on the skidway, all ready for me to take, and I could load fifty at a time. So I made it sixty – I even got sixty-five on two of my loads. Sat right up in the sky, I was, could've shook hands with the Man in the Moon. And I went backwards and forwards all day till I'd cleared that whole skidway of every log. Five hundred and twenty, that was, and there was four hundred to beat, so I reckoned I'd done pretty well. I got fifty dollars' prize money – and with wages at twelve dollars a month, that was money!'

'Why do you square the timber?' Kester asked, looking at the shreds of bark and shaved wood lying all over the forest floor. 'It looks as if you waste a lot of good wood.'

'Oh, we do, no doubt about that. Good job there's plenty here!' He laughed. 'We square it off because it's going overseas – it'll be driven down to Quebec, see, and then stowed aboard ship to go to Europe. It stows easier if it's squared. And if it's hemlock, the bark's used in the tanneries, so that has to be peeled anyway.'

He turned away to shout a command to the men in the gang, and Kester wandered off. He had no specific job to do, and soon saw that there was no place in the gang for a passenger. Each one worked smoothly with the others, part of a team. He began to think that Serle was right. Working with trees in England, and a bit of book-knowledge, counted for nothing out here in the Canadian bush.

At eleven o'clock lunch was called and the men knocked off to eat the beans and drink the tea that had been made over a small fire. They sat around on felled logs, discussing their work and reminding each other of men they had known, and incidents in the previous years.

'D'ye ever meet old Hector McCallum? Him that only had one arm. Come out from Scotland around the same time as Mr Tyson, and settled up the river a way. Felled the trees, built his own log house and a thirty-two-log barn, all with just one arm. He could use a scythe and a broad axe, well as anyone. One arm!'

'What about Mel Harris? They called him the Bull of the Bush – he was a roarer and no mistake. Fight! He didn't reckon a Saturday night was over till he'd had a fight or two. He'd fight anyone when he'd got a skinful, but he was as nice a chap as you could want to meet the rest of the week.'

'I remember him,' Abe said. 'He got lost in the bush once – took him a good two weeks to get himself out of it, and he was almost starved. Had nothing in all that time but a jack rabbit or two. We asked him why he hadn't set snares or done a bit of fishing but he said he hadn't had time! Too busy getting himself out, y'see.'

They talked on, about lumbermen who were already legends in the forest. Bill Shaker, who was said to have been too tired to walk back to camp, so rode on the back of a passing bear. Arthur Tott, who worked with a team of oxen and got so fond of them he slept in their stable at night. Jig Gibson, who could kick so high he left footmarks on the ceiling. And Grey Otter, the Indian, who was like a shadow about the camp but knew the bush better than any man alive.

By now, Kester had met Grey Otter himself. He had come upon him amongst the trees, sitting motionless with a pipe between his teeth. He had glanced up as Kester came through the undergrowth and the two men had stared for a long moment into each other's eyes, dark brown at dark brown.

It had been a moment of communication, of recognition. But there had been no word spoken and Kester did no more than nod and pass quietly on his way.

Abe stood up and looked around at the men. 'Well, that's dinner-hour over, now let's get back to work. Kes, you reckon you're good with horses?'

Kester nodded. If there was one way in which he could match these men, it was his skill with horses.

'Take this'n back to the camp then, will you? He's looking sick to me. And bring us a fresh one.'

Kester took the horse and walked it back through the trees. It was a big Clydesdale, the kind that were used as draught horses at home, and it walked stolidly beside him, very nearly showing him the way. He caressed its long nose, feeling reassured that here was something he could do. But he was also confident by now that he could, with a little practice, accomplish any of the jobs a lumberman did. He had the strength and the ability; all he had to do was learn the skill.

He thought of Rowenna's plan to start life again, as pioneers. Was it possible that they could still do that? It was a hard life, he knew, but there were still settlers coming out from England, still people clearing the bush for their own homesteads. He thought of building a log cabin with his own hands, and living in it with Rowenna. Living in a house . . . But a house made of wood, of trees you had felled yourself, that was different from one built with stone and bricks, that other people had lived in first. He could share such a house with Rowenna.

For Rowenna's marriage, he cared nothing. Alfred Boothroyd and Warren Mellor had, between them, forced her into an alliance that should never have been. Now she had left her husband, left her country, and was his again, as she should always have been. *Would* have been, had it not been for Mellor's sudden illness and Molly's deception.

He thought of his son, the baby who had been born nine months after that night. The child he had known nothing of, until Rowenna had told him only a week before. A week! Was that all it was since he had arrived in Penrith and seen

426

her working in the garden? He remembered how time had run back for him at that moment, how for a few minutes he had been transported back to the garden at Ashbank and seen her working in her holland overall, her face shaded by a floppy hat – how he had come upon her bathing in the river, and told her she looked like a water-nymph, a naiad . . .

But many things had happened to Rowenna since that day, and now here they were, thousands of miles from Ashbank, with a new life within grasp of their fingertips. A new chance, not to be missed.

A son. His mind edged round the thought like a cat stalking a bird. His son and Molly's. How had she felt when she knew she was pregnant? Had she been afraid, knowing that she risked dismissal and worse, or had she been calm and collected, finding herself a husband at once, getting herself safely wed? John Richmond had always been sweet on her, and no doubt delighted to marry her – but had he suspected? Did he know now?

Well, that was their business. Kester had never intended that a child should result from their brief madness. He had never intended to make love to Molly at all. But she had been there, and so willing, so eager . . . If she hadn't been it would never have happened. Still, he couldn't blame her, it took two to make a bargain. The *chavvy* was hers, all the same. She'd had it, kept it, given it another man's name. It wasn't Kester's child, save in blood. And when Rowenna gave birth to her first child, that would be his too, the first born to him out of love.

The horse was going more slowly now, clearly sick, and Kester listened for the sounds that would tell him they were approaching the camp. The track was plain to follow and there was no risk of their being lost, but he was anxious that they should get back before the animal sickened further.

427

And then he must go back with a fresh one, so that the team could work efficiently again.

The trees towered above him and the air was scented with pine. He touched the bark of a huge white pine, taller than any tree he had ever seen in England. These, together with the balsam, hemlock and spruce, were of a soft wood, light enough to float, and it was this fact which made them so easy to harvest. Not that *easy* was the right word, he thought wryly, thinking of the stories he had been told of the hardships, injuries and even death that had been suffered by the timbermen. But the heavier hardwoods, such as beech and maple, which would not float, must be left standing, unusable until the railroad came through.

A chipmunk skittered across his path and ran up a tree-stump, sitting at the top with its tail hanging down, its striped back a slash of brightness against the bark. It held a pine cone in its paws and was picking out the seeds with its teeth and storing them in cheek pouches already bulging with food.

Kester had already seen several wild animals – a porcupine, waddling through the undergrowth as he, Serle and Abe had driven in yesterday, a pair of moose on the track, a red fox disappearing between the trees. He had seen the jewelled flash of the hummingbird, heard the wild lament of the loon and watched as an osprey dived out of the air and smashed against the surface of a lake, rising again immediately with a large fish struggling in its talons.

He thought about bears. Did they come near the camps? He had seen the cooks store food in large tin containers, safe from marauding claws, and watched as garbage was disposed of so as not to attract them. But there was usually too much noise around a camp. Abe had told him, for such animals as bears and wolves to come sniffing about. It was when you were on your own that there might be a danger.

428

Kester was now within earshot of the camp, and a few minutes later he emerged from the trees and found himself close to the bunkhouse. A few older men and boys were sitting in front of it, playing cards. He recognised one as the chore-boy who had sent them all to bed the previous night, and several others as cookees, who assisted the chief cook. Two or three he had not seen before, but guessed that they too were chore-boys, too old now to do the heavy work of lumbering but still able to earn a living around the camp.

He took the horse along to the stable and handed him over to the man who looked after them, then set off again with the fresh animal. He was only halfway across the camp, however, when he heard his name called.

'Matthews! Here.'

Kester turned. Serle was standing outside the overseer's shanty where he lived. He shouted again, his tone peremptory, and Kester led the horse over to him.

'Where the hell are you going with that animal?'

'Back to Abe's gang.' Kester said shortly. 'I brought one of the Clydesdales back – it was going sick. He wants a fresh horse as soon as possible.'

Serle stared at him and grunted. Then he said, 'Well, you'd better find someone else to take it. You're going up into the bush.'

'What, now?' Kester said in surprise.

'Yes, now. That's what you wanted, isn't it – to see Rowenna's timber? Well, you can go – straight away. In fact, the faster you're out of this camp the better I shall like it.'

'But Abe—' Kester began.

'I've already told you, Abe won't be going. He's too good a man to be sent off on a wild-goose chase, playing nanny to you. I've found someone else to hold your hand and wipe your nose and bottom.' He turned away and shouted, 'Duffy! Here.'

One of the older chore-boys detached himself from the group and came over, eyeing Kester curiously. He looked between fifty and sixty, short and stocky, with a bald head and small button nose. His mouth and eyes were small too, and looked as if they had been bunched together in the middle of his face. His jaws moved rhythmically as he chewed a wad of tobacco.

'Here's the Englishman,' Serle said, as though it were a term of derision. 'Though I'm not sure he can even claim to be that – he's a gypsy really, isn't that right, Matthews? Thinks he's a woodsman because of it.' He smiled slightly and the man grinned. 'He wants you to take him for a walk in the woods.'

'Well, you're the boss,' the man answered. He had a thin, rather piping voice. 'But it's gettin' a bit near the back end for pleasure walkin', I'd say.'

'I'm not here on holiday,' Kester said. 'I want to see Mrs Boothroyd's stand. Do you know where that is?'

Duffy glanced at Serle. He stopped chewing for a moment. 'Yeah,' he said, 'I know where it is.'

'And you can guide me there?'

'Yeah, I can do that.'

Kester looked at him doubtfully. The man seemed confident enough, and he must have been working long enough in the forest to know his way around. But Jacob had said it was Abe who should take him.

I can't wait for Abe to be free, he thought, and if this man really is a good guide . . . Even Serle wouldn't send me off with someone who was likely to get lost. He'd want his timberman to get back safely, even if he didn't care about me!

And Kester wanted desperately to get up to Rowenna's timber limit, see what there was to be seen, and get back to her. They had been apart too long.

'Right,' he said. 'I'll be glad of your help.'

Duffy nodded. He resumed his chewing and looked again at Serle.

'Duffy'll be ready within the hour,' Serle said abruptly to Kester. 'See that you are too.'

'But what about the horse? Abe's waiting for it.'

'Someone else can take the horse.' He called to one of the younger chore-boys and rapped out a quick command. The boy led the horse away, evidently quite pleased to have the job. 'Now, get yourselves some provisions from the cook and be on your way. I want you out of here before sundown.' He gave Kester a look of pure dislike.

'Before sundown? But that's only a few hours away.'

'Scared of the dark, are you?' Serle sneered. 'Look, sonny, this isn't a picnic. We're well into October now. Winter's coming. That means *cold*. Blizzards. Ice. Snow fifteen foot deep. Anyone who's in here then don't get out till April, and I don't mean to be one of 'em. If you do, good luck to you, but you'll need to be back in camp if you want to live. It's a long walk up to those timber stands, and a longer one back if the snow's started by them, and it'd take an Indian miracle to get a man out of it. You'd be a gonner, Matthews, and I don't say I'd cry many tears over that, but I don't aim to lose one of my best men along with you.'

Kester looked at him. There was no doubt that Serle meant what he said, and he knew that most of it was probably true. Winter wasn't far off, there would be a great deal of snow, and it must be dangerous to be away from camp with bad weather looming so near. And yet . . . There was something else in Serle's face, something in his eyes, something that Kester didn't like.

Forget it, he told himself. You don't like Serle either. But he can't harm you once you're out in the forest, and even if it is bigger than any English wood, with bigger and fiercer animals, you can still look after yourself. Trees are the same anywhere.

'Right,' he said calmly. 'I'll collect my gear. I'll be five minutes.' He glanced at Duffy. 'I'll see you by the cookhouse.'

'Okay,' the man said laconically, and turned away. Kester watched him, then turned back to Serle and saw a smile play across the other man's face.

'You sure he's the best guide?'

Serle gave him a cool look. 'The best you're getting. I told you, I can't afford to send my best men out on fancy walks through the woods. But Duffy knows the forest all right. He'll do what I tell him.'

He'll do what I tell him ... Was there something sinister in those words? A threat of some kind?

'What's the matter?' Serle asked jeeringly. 'You're not scared of Duffy now, are you? Why, he's as gentle as a lamb.' His eyes raked Kester with scorn. 'First it's the dark, then it's a poor old timberman who's never hurt a fly. You're sure you wouldn't like me to call the whole thing off and go home to Mommy?'

Kester's face darkened. He narrowed his eyes and felt his body grow taut. For a moment, he was tempted to smash his fist into Serle's sneering, handsome face. Then he regained control of himself and turned away.

'I'll see you when we get back,' he said coolly, and strode to meet his companion by the cookhouse.

432

Chapter Twenty-Two

Winter came suddenly, with a drop in temperature and a flurry of early snow. The clouds gathering overhead were sullen, yellow-bellied and ominous, as if the fine snow now falling were merely a taste of what was to come. Rowenna gave up working in the garden and came indoors, and Jacob Tyson began to talk of going back to Ottawa.

'But we can't go yet,' she exclaimed. 'Kester is still up in the camp, I must wait for him to come back.'

Jacob shrugged. 'We can't wait much longer. If we're to go at all, it has to be soon. The roads'll be blocked from here right into Ottawa, and there'll be no coming in or getting out. And I want to get back to the sawmill.'

Rowenna was silent. She knew that Jacob only came to Penrith for a month each fall and spring, and that Serle was left in charge of the timberyard for most of the year, making regular visits to the camp when the weather permitted. Presumably Kester would return with him, but suppose the snow came sooner than expected and they were both trapped up there?

'Well, then, they'll wait till spring,' her grandfather said reasonably. 'But Serle's never got caught yet. He'll be back, don't you fret.'

I'm not fretting about Serle, she thought. But Jacob didn't know that. Even on that last night when Serle had attacked

433

her and dragged her upstairs, she had colluded with his explanation that he was merely helping her to bed. Helping me! she thought. But she could not have told her grandfather the truth, could not have risked what the shock might do to him. He might be extraordinarily active, clear-minded and incisive but he was still over ninety years old. And she could not forget her own father, forty years younger, collapsing from inflammation of the heart.

Serle had apologised next morning, with apparently genuine remorse.

'I can't tell you how sorry I am,' he told her, as she sat as far away from him as possible in the breakfast-room, wishing her grandfather or Mrs Hutty would come in. She had lain awake most of the night, missing Kester desperately and filled now with a new fear of the man who had promised to be her friend, wondering how she could possibly go on living in the same house. His voice was soft again now, with all its old boyish charm back in the gentle tones – yet how could she ever trust him again? 'I don't know what came over me. I guess it was seeing you with that gypsy – obviously so fond of him, wishing him goodbye as if – well, you'll forgive me saying this, but it was almost as if you were lovers. I know that can't be true,' he went on quickly, before she could speak, 'but in the darkness, and you standing so close . . . well, I guess I was just jealous. And when a man feels jealousy – it's like a knife, Rowenna, stabbing right through to the heart.'

'Jealous?' she echoed blankly, and he gave her a wry smile.

'Yes, jealous. I'm not proud of it and I'd never have said a word if it hadn't been for him and what happened last night – but maybe I should tell you now just how I feel about you. It'll help you understand why I behaved the way I did, perhaps. At the very least, you'll know the truth.'

434

Rowenna stared at him. Her heart was beating quickly and she lifted one hand, as if to stop him. Whatever Serle was about to say, she was suddenly quite certain she didn't want to hear it. Life is complicated enough already, she thought.

'Just say you're sorry and leave it at that,' she said breathlessly. 'I really don't – '

'No. An apology's not enough for what I did last night.' He gave her his wry look again. 'I'm not asking your forgiveness, Rowenna – I know I've no right to that. But I would like your understanding. I'd like to know that you can see *why* I did it. Maybe I'm asking the impossible – why *should* you understand? You're a woman – how can you be expected to understand how a man thinks and feels? But . . . I'd like to explain, if you'll let me, so that maybe you can try.'

He finished on a note of appeal, looking at her so wistfully that she could not find it in her heart to refuse. After all, wasn't every man entitled to be heard? Even the worst of murderers, being tried before a judge, was allowed to state his case.

'Very well, Serle,' she said quietly. 'Go on. Tell me why you attacked me, and why you felt you had a right to be jealous of Kester.'

'Rights?' he said. 'Oh, *rights* don't enter into it. I had no *right* at all – I freely admit that. But when a man loves a woman, his emotions and his body don't stop to think of rights.'

'*Love* – ?' she began, but this time it was he who lifted a hand for silence.

'Yes, love. I've loved you from the moment I came out of the house and saw you standing there by the buggy. I tried to hide it, of course – you're a married woman *and* my cousin, and the last thing I wanted was to stir up trouble in

435

the family. Besides, I thought you must be happy in your marriage and wouldn't look at another man.' He sighed. 'Those times when you were sad and turned to me, I thought it was just homesickness and missing your husband. I offered you my friendship, which you seemed pleased enough to have – '

'I was,' she said quickly. 'But I never dreamed – '

'What else could I do?' he swept on. 'I couldn't love you – not as I wanted to – but I could be your friend. And until the gypsy came along, that was how it was.' He was silent for a moment, not looking at her. 'But when I saw the way you were with him ... oh, can't you see, Rowenna, didn't you know? The way your eyes brightened, the way your whole face lit up – it *was* as if you were lovers! And when you came back on that first day, when you'd been in the woods with him – you looked like a bride!'

I *was* a bride, Rowenna thought, staring at him. Kester and I made love that day as if we had just been married, and it was my awakening. All the times with Alfred were wiped away when Kester took me in his arms, and I was a virgin again.

And Serle had seen their faces and understood.

If he really was in love with me, she thought, if he really had been hiding his own feelings all that time – surely I can understand his pain.

'Very well,' she said quietly. 'I'll tell you the truth. Kester and I do love each other. We wanted to go away together – oh, a long time ago now, before I was married. But my father was taken ill and I had to stay with him. And then Kester went away. I didn't think I would ever see him again. And – '

'And so you married Boothroyd.'

'I was forced into it!' she cried. 'I never wanted to marry him – nor anyone else. I loathed him, Serle. He was harsh

436

and cruel and cold – he made my life a misery. When I came to Canada, it wasn't just for a holiday; I left him. I meant never to go back.'

'My poor Rowenna,' he said tenderly, and moved as if to take her in his arms. But Rowenna recoiled and he stopped abruptly, a shadow crossing his face.

'God damn him!' he cursed. 'Look what he's done to you – you're afraid to trust any man now. My poor Rowenna, you have nothing to fear from me. I'm your friend – remember?'

'Until last night,' she said in a trembling voice, 'I believed you.'

Serle snapped his fingers, as if angry with himself for forgetting some minor point. 'My dear, what can I say? Is it so impossible for you to understand? Can you ever forgive me?' He slipped out of his chair and knelt beside her. 'Try – just for a moment – to look at it from my point of view. I was in love with you – desperately in love – and yet I knew you were married, I knew you could never be mine. I had to go on living with you in the same house, seeing you day after day, sharing meals with you, taking you for drives in the forest. Can you have any idea of how I felt – how I longed to stop the buggy and kiss you, how I yearned to take you in my arms and tell you? But you were married and I knew I must respect that. I could only be your friend.' He paused, then went on. 'And then Kester Matthews arrived. A *gypsy*. And you were like a young girl in love for the first time, your face alight, your eyes like stars. I wanted you to look like that for me. Instead, I had to stand by and watch while you went walking with *him*, and came back looking as if someone had lit a lamp inside you.'

And that's just how it was, Rowenna thought. A lamp, lit inside me. She looked at Serle with pity. How would she have felt, if it had been Kester and another woman? How had she felt when she had learned that he had turned to Molly?

'I said nothing,' he whispered. 'I did nothing. But when I saw you together last night – something snapped. My last shred of self-control deserted me. I know there can be no forgiveness for what I did. Perhaps you will never even be able to understand. But at least you've listened, and I'm grateful for that.'

He made to get up from his knees, but Rowenna stopped him. She laid one hand on his arm and looked directly into his open face. She saw the regret in his silver eyes, the appeal that softened his mouth, and she felt a deep compassion for him.

'I'm glad you told me, Serle,' she said softly. 'I'm only sorry that you feel so strongly about me. But you're right – I do love Kester. And when he comes back from the forest we shall make our lives together. My marriage to Alfred is over.' She hesitated, then added, 'I can't ever be more than a cousin to you, Serle. Go back to Fay.'

His mouth twisted a little. Then he tilted his head on one side and gave her an earnest look.

'And last night? Am I forgiven? It won't happen again,' he added quickly. 'It was a momentary loss of control – just that seeing you there, with him, brought all my longing, all my love, welling up inside me so that it was just too much to bear.' He lowered his eyes and shook his head. 'It will never happen again.' And then, with a look that went straight to her heart, 'I shall never stop loving you, Rowenna. But I'll never mention it again, unless you ask it of me.'

'And I'm afraid I'll never do that,' she said. 'Not as long as Kester Matthews walks this earth.' But she had forgiven him, for what else could she do? And Serle had left for the logging camp with Kester, leaving her alone with her grandfather.

And now Jacob was talking of returning to Ottawa, before they came back.

'But Kester was to come back here,' she said. 'He wasn't going to stay all winter at the camp.'

'Well, it'll do him no harm if he must,' Jacob said cheerfully. 'Best way to learn the trade. He'll find plenty to make himself useful with, up in the camp.'

Rowenna went up to her room and gazed out of the window. The trees were bare now, only the pines still clothed with green needles. The sky had the cold look of iron, and the ground was hard with frost. What was it like now, away in the logging camp? Had it already begun to snow?

Had Kester been to her timber stand and returned already to the camp? Was he even now on his way back with Serle? Or had some disaster overtaken him, out in those vast, cold forests?

She shivered, feeling suddenly afraid. I should never have let him go, she thought. We had found each other again, we were together, we knew at last what it was to love. I should never have let him leave me.

At last, humouring her, Jacob agreed to stay until the last minute. Watching the clouds, and the lightly falling, powdery snow, he gave it as his verdict that they had five more days before the heavy fall began. 'We've got to leave here ahead of that,' he said. 'Once it starts, it'll sweep down the country and we'll be stuck. And I've got things to see to back in town.'

Rowenna nodded. She knew that she could not ask him to stay longer and, although she was tempted to suggest that she stay alone in Penrith, she was afraid to spend the winter here with Serle. In any case, her grandfather would almost certainly not have allowed it.

It was time for her afternoon walk. She wrapped herself

in the fur-hooded coat her grandfather had bought her in the local store as the weather grew colder. The Eskimos, way up in the northern tip of the country, wore hooded coats, he had told her, though they trimmed them with the fur of wolverines. 'Don't matter how wet or frozen that gets, it's still warm. Don't hold the water, see, it just runs off. Wolverine's the best of all, but you don't want to tangle with the live animals, devils on four feet, they are.'

Rowenna stepped outside the door. She looked down the road, as she always did, hoping and half expecting to see Kester come swinging round the corner, his haversack slung upon his back. But as usual there was nothing to be seen. And then she heard the clatter of hooves and the rattle of iron wheels.

A horse and buggy! She clutched the gate, staring in heart-thumping anticipation. Were they coming at last? Would she see Kester's laughing face, feel his arms about her again? It was over a month since he had left and it seemed an age since she had been able to touch him. She swallowed, feeling almost sick with excitement and need.

The buggy was in sight now. It turned the corner and clopped along the rough, metalled road. Rowenna stared at it and frowned.

There was just one man sitting up in the little trap, one man who held the reins loosely in his hands and was looking at her now with grave, almost sorrowful eyes.

Serle.

The buggy came to a halt. He jumped down and moved towards Rowenna, holding out his hands.

Rowenna took a step back. She stared up into his eyes, her face white.

'Kester. Where is Kester?'

Serle shook his head. His face was kind, concerned. He laid his gloved hands over hers and held them closely.

Rowenna stood quite still, her eyes still fixed upon his face.

'Where is *Kester*?'

'Let's go inside,' he said. 'I'll call Jack to see to the horse – he needs a good rub down and some mash. And I want to talk to Grandpa.'

She shook her head. He made to move, but she detained him. Behind her, she heard the door of the house open and close, heard her grandfather's voice, heard the exclamations of the housekeeper. But she could make no sense of them.

'Serle, *tell* me for God's sake – *where is Kester?*'

Serle looked at her with compassion. His eyes were the soft grey of the feathers on a pigeon's back and his expression was one of both regret and concern.

'I'm sorry to have to tell you this, Rowenna my dear,' he said quietly, as Jacob Tyson came down the path and stood by Rowenna's side, watching and listening. 'But Kester got himself lost in the forest. He never came back.'

Winter had come suddenly in the forest too. The yellow-bellied clouds emptied their burden one night, after a week of bitter frost, and smothered trees and forest floor in a thick, fleecy eiderdown of white. The sounds of the forest were suddenly muted, muffled by the soft blanket, and the tracks of animals – moose, fox and wolf – appeared in hidden pathways that had been unnoticeable in the loose undergrowth. Now, it could be seen just how many animals roamed about the camp at night, though the huge clawed pads of bear were missing, for the big animals had gone into hibernation well before the snow began.

Serle had gone from the forest as soon as the great clouds appeared, hanging over the iron-hard ground and turning the freezing lakes to steel. He had done all that he could do in the camp and now left the overseer and foremen in charge. He knew that Jacob would be waiting for his report before he too left, for Ottawa, though he was also aware that he had delayed his own departure and that Jacob might well have been forced to leave Penrith before he arrived.

Nevertheless, he took his time over the journey. For once, he was in no real hurry to get back in Penrith. If Jacob had gone before he got there, it would be another five months before they met again. Another five months before he need break the news . . .

Duffy had returned alone to the camp. He had lost Kester somewhere away up to the north. Probably not far from the timber they had gone to see, he said, though they'd never got there. The gypsy had just wandered off one night, never came back. His coat had been found lying a hundred yards or so away, ripped as if by great claws. And although Duffy had searched for him long and hard, he'd seen no other sign and eventually, seeing how the weather was turning, he'd had to come back.

Serle had gone into his shanty with a smile playing about his lips. Duffy was a good enough man to send as a guide – not as good as Abe, but even Jacob couldn't have expected him to let Abe go to waste when he had a foreman with a broken leg. And he'd agree that Duffy, who knew the forest as well as any man, was a likely enough choice.

There was no blame to be attached to Duffy, nor to himself. And the gypsy might yet be found – people did survive the forest, after all. And he'd called himself a woodsman.

He glanced behind him at the clouds, massing ominously to the north like armies on the march – but in the snow, with few provisions and no shelter? Wandering far from any logging camp, with wolves prowling hungry through the trees, ready to snap up anything that moved? And what of his coat, and the claws that had torn it?

No, he did not expect to see Kester Matthews again. And with him out of the way, and a few months of the winter to help her forget, perhaps he would have a better chance with Rowenna.

She had been almost ready to turn to him, almost ripe to fall into his arms, when that damned gypsy had arrived. He knew she was married – but what of that? Her husband was far away and she had no intention of returning to him. A young, spirited girl like that would find a way out of such an unsatisfactory marriage, and meanwhile he would win both her confidence and her trust. And then it wouldn't matter about the timber stand.

Rowenna, he knew, stood to inherit more than a few trees up in the north. Jacob had taken a real fancy to her. And although the old man would not see his other children suffer, there was plenty for all, and Rowenna would take the share that had been Dorothy's.

Serle never forgot that he was not the old man's true grandson. He too would inherit but it could be no more than his adopted father's share, and George Tyson was not yet sixty years old. If he was as long-lived as Jacob, it might be a long time before Serle was anything more than manager of the Penrith timber limits.

It was a pity he'd frightened her, that last night before he and the damned gypsy had left to come up to the logging camp. But he was pretty sure he could make up any ground he'd lost. Show her some concern, give her the comfort she'd no doubt need. Apologise, give her that little-boy smile that always seemed to win women over, beg her forgiveness . . . Women like Rowenna were easy enough to handle. From all accounts, she'd never had much in the way of loving, all she wanted was someone to make her feel cherished.

Well, he could do that as well as any gypsy. And so, when he returned to Penrith and was forced to break the news on the doorstep, standing in the bitter cold, with Jacob at her elbow, he could do nothing else but take her in his arms and hold her. And swear that they'd done all they could to find him. And tell her he was sorry.

It wasn't enough, he knew, to bring her tumbling into his arms again. But it was a start, and in the months that followed he would turn it to his advantage. Instead of staying in Penrith, he would go back to Ottawa for the winter. Five months in the city, with snow like a barricade around them, ought to be enough to make her forget she had ever known Kester Matthews.

Winter was coming as well to the fells and lakes of northern England. The hillsides were brown with faded bracken, the heather had long since lost its amethyst glow, and the first frosts laced the bare twigs of the hedgerows. Sheep which had roamed all summer on the high slopes were being brought down to the patchwork fields of the valleys, and there was already a shimmering curtain of icicles clinging to some of the more sheltered waterfalls. The birds of summer – the swallows, the martins, the warblers – had long since departed and the hedgehogs had put on winter fat and burrowed into piles of leaves or the roots of trees to sleep away the months of cold weather.

Warren Mellor had not been committed to an asylum, although Alfred Boothroyd had suggested strongly to the doctor that this might be necessary. Instead, he had been kept in his room, nursed by a manservant recommended by Dr Cooper, and after a few weeks, much subdued, permitted to come out and live a more normal life.

'But you must be sure to have Godley on hand at all times,' Boothroyd warned his sister. 'I'd not like to answer for the state of Warren's mind. He's unbalanced, that was clear enough the day he burst into my office, and he could tip over the edge at the slightest provocation.'

'I'd far rather he was kept locked up,' she said, casting a

nervous glance over her shoulder as if Warren might at any moment come charging in waving Mrs Partridge's meat cleaver. 'I don't feel happy, letting him roam loose. And what am I to say if he insists on coming into my drawing room, when I'm having an At Home?'

'Let him. He's meek enough now. And Dr Cooper says he's better for being allowed to imagine he's sane. Let him live as normal a life as possible. After all, we don't want any gossip, do we? The mad husband locked away in the attic – there have been too many fanciful stories about that sort of thing.'

Matilda Mellor thought for a few minutes. It was true that Warren had been much more biddable since being unstrapped from his straitjacket and allowed out of his room. He no longer rampaged furiously about the house, no longer sat drinking late into the night. Instead, he would sit for hours, gazing blankly out of the window or even at a bare wall. He no longer wolfed down his food, demanding more meat; instead, he pushed it listlessly about on the plate, swallowed a little and left most of it on the side.

He had lost his muscular bulk and was thinner, paler, than he had ever been. He drifted about the house like a lost soul, and when Matilda did have visitors he came into the drawing room and sat silent and docile, gazing at them like a lapdog begging for some morsel of food.

'I don't like it,' Matilda said to her brother. 'He seems so strange.' But Alfred shrugged her complaints away.

'Tell your friends he's suffering from his heart complaint again. He's been told to rest, and not to excite himself. He mustn't even converse too much, though a little company's good for him. That will allay any fears they may have, and provide a good reason for his manner. And they'll all think what a good wife you are, to be so solicitous of your husband.'

Matilda considered this and then agreed. But she would

not have Warren in the room all the time. Like a small child, he was brought in for half an hour at tea-time and then sent away with his manservant. 'He likes a walk in the garden at this time,' she would explain, watching his departure with relief. 'The doctor says it's good for him.'

And Warren was sent out, accompanied by Godley – surely too burly to be an ordinary manservant – to walk in the garden until everyone had gone.

Strangely enough, it was in the garden that he felt most at home. Yet he had never before taken any interest in the garden, had kept it merely as a symbol of his position in the local community, had even been annoyed by first his wife's and then his daughter's care for it. Now, he looked at the plants as they grew and flowered and died again, and felt a kinship with them, as if he too was dying. But they'll come again next year, he thought, they'll go on living. Will I see another spring?

He sat on a rock and stared at the river as it tumbled by. The river had been the reason for his mill being built here, so many years ago. First a cornmill, then a bobbin mill, now used for making paper, endless rolls of the stuff, for sending to printing works in Kendal or even further afield – Lancaster, Manchester. And for what? To print newspapers which would be bought one day and discarded the next, half their closely printed stories left unread.

What use was it all? What use was it to be born, to struggle through life, to end in this way – half mad, a wreck of the man he had once been, tied to a wife who delighted in tormenting him, usurped from his rightful place by a man who had weaseled his way into Warren's own business and stolen it from under his nose. Aye, and stolen the daughter who was supposed to have been his companion, who would have comforted him in his old age.

Rowenna would never have let him come to this, he

thought, and tears of self-pity welled up in his eyes. Rowenna would have taken care of him, nursed him when he needed it, helped him. Why, she'd even offered to help him with the work of the mill! Why the devil hadn't he agreed? She needn't have actually gone into the building – work could have been brought home for her to do of an evening, there would have been no need for anyone else to know what was happening. But no, he'd been too obstinate to see that his daughter could be as good as a son to him. He'd rejected her help, trodden on her every effort to please him, and in the end driven her into the arms of Alfred Boothroyd. And look at the results!

During the fortnight when he had been incarcerated in his room, Rowenna's letter had come from Canada, telling him what she had done. Matilda had intercepted it and the first Warren had known of it was when Boothroyd had stalked into his room, coldly furious, waving the sheet of paper and demanding to know what it was all about. He had held it in front of Warren's nose to be read, quivering with rage.

'Canada! The little minx has gone to Canada! I suppose this is your doing. Coming into my office, pretending you knew nothing—'

'I did know nothing,' Warren protested. They had freed his mouth of its gag and he was able to answer, though his voice was weak. 'I hardly knew she had gone away – *you* told me that. I missed her. I was worried about her.'

Alfred threw him a scathing glance. 'Missed her! Worried about her! Why, you never cared a jot for your daughter until after you'd lost her – '

'It's not true! She was everything to me.'

'She was *nothing* to you. You sold her to me without a moment's thought.'

'And you treated her so badly she ran away!' Warren

447

retorted. 'And now we've both lost her.'

Once again, Alfred raked him with that withering glance, but there was nothing further to say and he turned abruptly on his heel and left the room. Warren could hear him, instructing Godley that the patient – the *patient*! – should be kept extra quiet for the time being, and fed sparingly with a bland diet. Clearly, his blood had become overheated, and nobody who was getting so little exercise needed solid food.

It would achieve nothing. It was merely a punishment. But Warren was coming to understand that Alfred Boothroyd was a man who needed to punish. For a while, he had had Rowenna at his mercy. But now she had escaped and he must look about him for another scapegoat.

After that, Warren had few such coherent thoughts for some time. The meagre diet, the physical restrictions, the sheer tedium of his life in the bare room, all served to dull his mind until he found himself moving like a puppet through each day, waking when Godley came in with his breakfast, closing his eyes again obediently when told it was time to sleep. Eating when food was presented to his mouth, drinking when a glass was held to his lips, defecating when placed upon the commode. And eventually, when released from the stout linen in which they had bound him, walking stiffly and painfully wherever Godley took him, and sitting silently in the drawing room when Matilda wanted to show him off as an object of pity.

Now, as he sat on the rock, he knew that some of his mental strength was slowly returning. Humiliation, starvation and deprivation had eaten away at him, and he was, as Alfred had said, a wreck of the man he had been.

He stared up at the fells, rising above the river. Rocky outcrops made sharp, jagged ridges. Away to his left he could see the silhouette of the Langdale Pikes and the snub-nosed whaleback of Wetherlam. He had lived here all his life, brought up at Ashbank with the mill on his doorstep. He had hoped to pass it on to his son, as his father had passed it to him. And now it had all gone wrong, so bitterly wrong. Why? What had he done to deserve it? Surely he *didn't* deserve it. Surely no man deserved to be treated as he had been.

He thought of his wife, Dorothy. He had met her when old Jacob Tyson had brought his family back for a visit to Penrith. There had been relatives in Kendal too, and Warren had been invited to a party in their honour. Twenty-two years old, he had been, full of strength and vigour, and Dorothy just eighteen. Her accent had charmed him, and she had fallen in love with him. Old Jacob had taken some persuading, but eventually he had agreed to their marriage and gone back to Canada, leaving Dorothy as Mrs Mellor.

And they had been happy. Hadn't they? Happy enough, anyway, until old Martin Mellor had died and Warren took over the mill. And then he had become more and more absorbed in it – and wasn't that right, for a man with family responsibilities? And Dorothy had become pregnant, promising him the son he so ardently desired. And lost it at six months. And lost another, and another – until, when he'd almost given up, Haddon was born.

He'd almost forgiven her then, thinking that their family had started at last. But she'd gone on losing them, year after year, until after Rowenna was born she had refused to risk any more pregnancies. And then, ten years later, had died.

As Haddon had died. Leaving him with nothing more than a daughter to see him into old age. A daughter, moreover, with whom he had never been in accord.

Well, he had done his best by her. Kept her company of an evening. Married her to a man who should have looked after her. Kept her close at hand, so that she could spend as much time with him as she wanted. He'd thought that with marriage she would mellow and mature, be more understanding, and indeed it had seemed for a while that she was. He thought of the days when she slipped across the bridge to be with him, the comfort she had tried to offer.

And now she was gone. Driven away by that damned bastard who had stolen her from under his nose. She had been part of the price he had paid to save the mill, to save his own livelihood, but the price had been greater than he'd expected, and it had cost him not only his daughter but his sanity.

Warren lifted his head and stared across the river. Alfred Boothroyd, the man who had stripped him of everything, was standing on the opposite bank watching him. And as their eyes met, Warren knew what he must do.

He chose his time carefully. Godley was a vigilant nurse and rarely took his eyes off his charge, but since Warren had quietened down he had taken to leaving him in the care of one of the other manservants each morning at ten o'clock, to take tea in the kitchen with the rest of the staff. Normally the man who kept watch on him then was Billy, the boot-boy, a simple-minded fellow of about twenty who had been with the family since he was a child. He had been much attached to Haddon, following him about like a dog, and when Haddon had died he had transferred that affection to Warren. It was he who had run for the doctor on the occasion of Warren's first collapse. Now, his task in the mornings was simply to accompany his master into the garden, if that was where he wanted to go, and take care of him.

'How d'ye like to go down to the mill this morning?' Warren asked him. 'It's a long time since we've been down there. You like the mill, don't you, Billy?'

The boy nodded his tow-coloured head. He was big and

slow-moving, with a loose grin, the youngest of a family of twelve. Several of his brothers worked in the mill and he snatched every chance he could to go there and watch them at work. He followed Warren readily enough and was pleased to be allowed to stand and watch the great fourdriniers at work.

Alfred Boothroyd was not in his office and Warren wandered through the big paper mill, trying to look as if he were still the master. Steam rose all around him, and the noise of the machinery filled his head. He watched the huge, endless sheet of paper rolling its way to the end of the presses, and thought of the days when he had come here each morning with Haddon at his side, of the plans they had made, the future they had envisaged.

I should have let Rowenna come in with me, he thought. I should have let her help. She knew about the mill, and I turned her away, I blinded myself to what she was.

Bitter regret flooded his heart, a pain that he had never known until these past few weeks. Never before had he been able to see that his misery and frustration were consequences of his own actions. And now, unused to the pain, unable to tolerate it, he did what he had always done and turned it into anger – anger first with himself and then, because that was another emotion too uncomfortable to feel, with someone else.

Boothroyd.

The swine. The bastard. He had taken everything – everything. Like a vulture, he had swooped down when Warren was vulnerable and picked the very flesh from his bones. And left him to rot.

Warren stood very still. The steam was in his eyes, his nose, his mouth, and the scream and roar of the machinery filled his ears. It grew to a roar, a thunder, throbbing through his body, pounding its way into his veins. He

451

trembled with it, quivered, shook. He laid his hand on the wall to steady himself and looked up.

On the upper floor at the far end of the hall, where the pulp swirled in great vats before being passed through the fourdriniers, Alfred Boothroyd was leaning on the rail, watching him. Again, their eyes met. And Warren felt his rage swell and burst, a searing, red-hot fire of fury, a conflagration that must have outlet, a savage, burning pain that spread from his heart out to his fingertips, down into his loins and through his legs, and drove him, burning at every step, along the length of the hall and up the iron steps. He could see Boothroyd still standing there, watching as if frozen, his eyes two black marbles in a death-white face, his mouth open as if in a yell of fear. But nothing could be heard against the screech and rattle of the machinery, and when Boothroyd moved at last it was too late. Warren was upon him, his frenzy driving him through his anguish. In sudden panic, Boothroyd put out his hands, trying to ward off the man who had at last gone truly mad. He backed away, still screaming for help, but no one was near, no one watching, for at that moment the endless sheet of paper had split and the end struck Billy, slicing his arm clean from his body, and every man in the mill had rushed to the scene.

Alfred Boothroyd felt the rail of the open vats at his back. He leaned against them, watching in terror as Warren approached. Time seemed to slow down, but his body had slowed with it, as if paralysed. He could only shake his head and plead for his life as the man he had tormented for months bore down upon him, reached out both hands and pushed.

They found them soon after that, for the vats had to be stopped while Billy was taken away and the tangle of blood-stained paper removed. The remains of Alfred Boothroyd were lifted out and laid beside Warren's body, and the doctor came up the iron stairs and shook his head.

'He must have seen Boothroyd overbalance and tried to save him. And the shock brought on another attack. It's no surprise – he's been failing for some time.'

Their joint funeral was held a week later, at the church of St Oswald within sight of the fells. It was November, cold and blustery as it had been on the day of Haddon's funeral. But there were no spring flowers, no daffodils or primroses to lighten the scene. And the only family mourner was Matilda Mellor. Rowenna was far away in Canada and did not even know.

Chapter Twenty-Three

Rowenna did not hear of the deaths of her husband and father until mid-December, when she received a letter from James Abercrombie. She sat in the parlour, holding it in her hand, staring blankly at the words.

Alfred dead. Her father dead. And at the same time, in the same appalling accident. And Billy, poor silly Billy, whom she had known since she was twelve years old, with only one arm. How would he clean and polish boots now?

For a few minutes, that seemed to be the worst thing of all. Her father and Alfred were dead, but Billy must go on living, must somehow earn his meagre living with one hand. Was Matilda looking after him? Would she let him stay at Ashbank? There must be jobs a one-armed man could do. He could not be turned out, to wander the streets and end up in the workhouse.

The door opened and Serle came in. He took one look at her face and came instantly to her side.

'What is it? What's happened?'

She looked up at him as if he were a stranger, but did not shrink away. Since their return to Ottawa he had been all solicitude, taking every trouble to ensure her comfort, careful not to touch her in any way that might be misconstrued. He came to the house almost every day, ostensibly to meet Jacob but always managing at least a few minutes with her and Fay, who was now happily convinced again that he was courting her.

Racked as she was with anxiety over Kester, Rowenna could not but respond to his concern. Now she held the letter out to him, saying in broken tones, 'Poor Billy. Poor Billy,' as if that were all the news it contained.

'Billy?' he said in bewilderment. 'Who on earth is – ' He read the letter and she saw his face change.

'Boothroyd's dead,' he breathed, and stared down at her. 'Rowenna, Boothroyd is dead.' He dropped to his knees beside her. 'And your father, too. My dear, I'm sorry about your father – but *Boothroyd* . . . This must be tremendous news for you!'

She gazed at him. Her mind was still refusing to acknowledge the contents of the letter. 'But Billy – poor Billy . . .'

'*Billy*?' He looked at the letter again. 'The boot-boy you mean? The one who lost an arm. What of him? He was a simpleton by all accounts.'

'But he's lost an *arm*.'

'And you've lost a husband. And a father.' He touched her cheek with one finger. 'Rowenna, what's the matter with you? Don't you understand what has happened? My dear, your father has died, quite quickly and painlessly, I should imagine – and your husband, the man who caused you so much misery. You're free. Don't you realise? Free!'

Rowenna stared into his face. Then she reached out and took the letter back. She read it attentively, as if it were the first time she had seen it, took note of each word Mr Abercrombie had written in his flowing copperplate script, read it again.

Alfred dead. Her father dead. The words burned themselves into her brain.

'You're free to live your own life,' Serle repeated. 'He can't hurt you again, Rowenna. Neither of them can. You're free to do whatever you like.'

456

She turned her head, looked into his eyes. She still could not believe it. Both dead. Both at once. And Billy, poor Billy . . .

'It's come as a shock,' he said quietly. 'It was a terrible death. But it's over now – it's been over for almost a month. They're both at rest. But you – you have your life before you.'

My life, yes, she thought dully. But what use is that, without Kester?

Serle slipped his arm around her shoulders and held her, not tightly but warmly, as a father might hold a weeping child. He laid her head against his shoulder and stroked her hair.

'Grieve for them,' he murmured. 'Grieve for the way they died. But be glad for yourself, Rowenna, for you're now a free woman, and you can start your life at last, in the right place, with your own family around you.'

Jacob Tyson's sawmill was busy from early May until late November. All summer, logs had been coming down the Ottawa River, bound together in huge rafts. Each one had several log huts built upon it, and in these the river drivers ate and slept. Although there were still treacherous rapids to be negotiated, once the logs were in the main river there would be long, smooth stretches on the journey and the men had little to do but guide the raft's direction.

'It's like a party at times,' Jacob commented as he stood with Rowenna on the high promontory of Parliament Hill, looking down at the river. 'See 'em dancing the jig of an evening, floating down the river. I tell 'em, they don't need a holiday when they've been river-driving.'

Snow had fallen during the past fortnight, and was now piled in banks several feet deep beside the roads. The river had begun to freeze, not smooth and shiny as Rowenna had expected, but with large, uneven lumps as the ice formed,

457

broke away, massed together and froze again. The few rafts that had come down last were frozen where they had stopped, and John Booth's barges, normally kept busy loaded with timber around Booth's mills at Chaudiere Falls, were moored and still.

Rowenna smiled. In her grandfather's view, nobody ever needed a holiday. He enjoyed hard work himself and expected everyone else to feel the same way. Anyone who didn't, he would point out, could always get a job with someone who *liked* paying out money for nothing.

'What happens when the logs stop coming?' she asked.

'Oh, there's plenty to do. We try to get 'em all in, but river-driving's a long job – takes a coupla years sometimes to bring timber down from some of the tributaries. But hard as we go, we'd never get all the logs sawn into boards, so that keeps us occupied, and then they have to be carted to the piling yards and stacked.' He glanced proudly at the piling grounds, stretching away to their left. 'A hundred and fifty thousand pine logs a year, that's what we reckon to bring in. And saw 'em up into over twenty million board feet of lumber. Now, that's work, that is. And a lot of carting and stacking to be done.'

Rowenna nodded. She had seen her grandfather's wagons – several hundred of them, plying backwards and forwards through the streets, carrying lumber from the saw-mill to the big yards where it was stacked ready for shipment or use. Most of it, in previous years had been transported to America or overseas, to England. Now he was planning to build his own pulpmill and perhaps even start to manufacture paper.

At over ninety years old, she thought, gazing at him in wonder, he was planning to expand!

She thought of her own father, dead in his fifties, looking in the past year as old as Jacob himself and a good deal less fit. Why did some men keep their strength into great old age, while others failed before they had even reached their three-score years and ten? Why did some grow in stature with each year that passed, while others seemed to diminish?

Was it some inner strength, born in them, or something they developed through their own attitudes to life? She remembered Warren, taking each fresh blow – her mother's death and, even more, Haddon's – as if it had been a personal affront, as if God had singled him out for hardship. His answer had been to cloud his pain with brandy, to befuddle his mind so that he no longer felt the anguish. But had he succeeded? She remembered the look in his eyes, the torment that had kept her at his side. Had he died, still in that torment?

But Jacob, who had known his own tragedies, stood hale and straight beside her at almost twice Warren's age. How had he withstood the misfortunes that had beset him? She thought of the stories he had told her as they sat by the fire of an evening – the death of his beloved wife after twenty years of loving marriage, the fire that had raged through his timberyard fifteen years earlier, destroying almost two hundred thousand dollars' worth of wood. There had been other fires too, forest fires that had damaged more than ten times the amount of trees felled. All good timber, all lost for ever.

Yes, Jacob had had his tribulations, but where Warren had allowed them to crush him, he had risen above them. Was it because Warren had always seemed to believe that he was being deprived of something that should have been his by right – a fertile wife, sons, a life that proceeded smoothly – whereas Jacob believed that a man should have only what he earned by his own toil?

And Alfred – what of him? He had worked hard enough,

459

but he had taken no joy in it. He had married, but never shown love or tenderness. His pleasure seemed to have come from giving pain to others, like a small boy who delights in pulling the wings off flies or the legs from frogs.

What happened to men, to make them like that?

The wind was growing cold and more heavy clouds were massing to the north. More blizzards were on the way, and even now the snow was probably falling in the forests. The loggers would be in their camp, ready to sit it out until the clouds rolled away and they could resume their work.

The question that was always in her mind and in her heart returned to stab her again.

Where was Kester?

Rowenna stared northwards, willing the clouds to roll away. Somewhere up there, Kester was lost in the forest, wandering alone without food or shelter. Or was he, as Serle insisted and Jacob regretfully agreed, dead? For a long time, she had refused to acknowledge it, certain that he would survive, that somehow he would come back to her.

But how long could such certainty last?

The first of the blizzards had found Kester huddled in a hut, built with shards of wood and bark peelings, close to an old skidway. It must have been one of the earliest areas to be logged, he thought, for the hardwood trees that had been left had seeded themselves and the young saplings of maple and beech were already several feet tall. A skid road, much overgrown, led down to the lake but the road, coming in from whatever camp there had been, had disappeared long since under the jumble of broken earth and tangled growth that smothered it.

Kester had come to this place by making his way along the edge of a lake. Only here, where the sky could be seen unhindered by the thick growth of pine, was it possible to see the sun and so navigate oneself through the forest. His progress had been slow, for there was no path and the thickets tore at his clothes and skin. In places he had to skirt large areas of swamp, and when he climbed on a fallen log to keep his feet above the sucking mud, as often as not the log proved to be nothing more than a heap of rotting dust, giving way treacherously under his weight.

He slept wherever he could find a dry spot, lighting a fire for warmth and protection, but the ground was growing colder and daylight often found him stiff and aching. He would get up several times in the night, stretching and jumping to warm his limbs, and he was thankful for the warmth of the mackinaw coat and breeches, and the warm woollen underclothes he had been advised to buy.

After the first day, when he had begun to realise that Duffy had in truth left him to wander, he had looked for a way to catch food. Again, the lakes came to his aid. In his pockets, as he had learned to do years ago when travelling with his family, he carried a variety of useful items, including a fishing line and hook. With these, he caught several fish and roasted them. He sat eating them, looking out over the lake, and wondered what to do next.

Duffy had left him deliberately, of that he was certain. They had walked together for four days through the forest, leaving the noise of the lumber camp far behind. The only sounds to accompany them had been the twittering of the chickadees and the hammering of woodpeckers. At night they had camped, lighting a fire to cook their food, and Duffy had set Kester to gathering wood.

On the fourth night, when he returned to the camping place with his burden of sticks, the tent had gone.

Kester stood for a moment, staring at the space. There was nothing to show that anyone had ever been there, yet he was sure this was where they had been. Hadn't he hung

461

his spare jacket on that tree stump? Hadn't his haversack been dropped by that fallen log?

Perhaps he had mistaken his way. He called the other man's name and set half a dozen birds fluttering in panic from the branches, but there was no answer. He called again, more loudly, and listened to the sound of his voice ringing through the bush; but again there was no response. Thinking that perhaps he had mistaken the place, he retraced his steps, but he could still find no sign of the other man. It was as if he had evaporated.

Kester stood thinking. Duffy was an experienced woodsman. He knew all the tricks of surviving in the forest and he could walk as silently as an Indian. If he had wished, he could have gathered up all their belongings the moment Kester was out of sight and disappeared without making a sound, leaving no track at all through the leaves.

Perhaps he knew of some hiding place nearby, a cave perhaps under the rocky cliff that rose above them. Perhaps he was within earshot, or even watching from some hidden point, laughing to himself at Kester's dismay.

Kester came back to the original clearing and looked around again. There was the stump where Duffy had hung his pack. There was the log where Kester had dropped his own.

There was a tiny patch of fresh earth, scuffed up by the heel of a boot.

Kester walked across and stared at it. He had not crossed to that side of the clearing since returning to it. But someone had stood there, someone had turned sharply and dug his heel into the damp earth. Perhaps Duffy, perhaps himself. But it meant that this was the clearing where they had decided to make camp. It meant that Duffy had definitely and deliberately abandoned him.

And it's easy enough to guess why, Kester thought,

remembering Serle's face as they had walked out of camp four days ago.

He dropped the bundle of sticks. There was no point in pursuing Duffy now. The man probably knew a different route back to the camp and would be well ahead. In any case, he wasn't likely to make Kester welcome if he turned up again. He had probably been paid to get rid of Kester; he could not go back to the logging camp with him. He might even take more drastic steps to make sure the gypsy was out of the way.

He had chosen his time well, Kester thought, realising that the light was fading quickly. It would soon be dark, with no chance to search for a man who was determined to stay hidden. He had no choice but to stay where he was and make camp with the few possessions he carried in his pockets.

The first priority was a fire. He knelt down and picked up the pine root he had dug from a bank, slicing it into a fuzz of thin slivers, then shredded a piece of bark peeled from one of the paper birches and built them into a small pyramid. With the flint and steel he always carried, he set a spark to his tinder and blew it into a tiny flame. The flame licked along the bark and sputtered into life on the pine splinters. Kester reached out and dragged a few twigs on to the little blaze, and then drew in the larger branches until finally he had built around his little fire a mound of logs, each beginning to smoulder.

The flames brought a heartening light to the now dark clearing. He felt in his pockets and found a piece of jerky, cold meat compressed so tightly that it was almost like a stick itself. Enough to sustain him until he could find more food tomorrow. He sat chewing it, thinking over what had happened, and finally, making up the now white-hot ashes to a fresh blaze which would smoulder through the night, he

463

rolled himself up in his mackinaw and lay down to sleep.

Since then, he had walked doggedly each day through the desolate forest. He kept by the riverside as much as possible, navigating by the sun and catching fish to eat. There were a few berries as well, some clearly the blackberries he was accustomed to finding at home, others he did not know, a few that Duffy had told him were good to eat, others he dared not sample. But most of them were over now, and he did not have time to search too long for food. The days were growing short and he knew the blizzards were on their way.

He paused and looked up at the sky. The way to the logging camp was south, but he was still heading north. The temptation to turn and make his way back to safety – if he could find it – was strong. But he could not do that yet. He had a promise to fulfil – the promise he had made to Rowenna, that he would find her timber and look at it and tell her what he had seen.

Before leaving Penrith, Jacob Tyson had given him a map. It showed all the timber limits granted in the Ottawa valley, with the name of the owner of each limit printed clearly across the terrain. Lakes and tributaries were shown as well, and by taking note of the twisting path of the river as it cut its way through the forest, Kester was able to judge roughly where he was.

But it wasn't always easy to keep close to the stream. Rocky cliffs, deep valleys and swamps lay in his way, and often he had to make long detours to avoid a particularly icy marsh or undergrowth too thick to hack his way through. He blessed the axe that he had taken to collect wood; without it, his journey would have been impossible. Occasionally he had to cross one of the tributaries, and this could mean a long walk upstream to find a suitable place.

He looked at his map. Rowenna's timber stood on a

tributary which joined the main streams in a large pool, in itself as big as a lake, which reached long fingers into the forest. Each of these fingers must be either crossed or circumnavigated, and in places the banks were little more than swamps. With the crowns of the huge trees still blotting out the sky, it was difficult to tell where the sun was, and all too easy to wander in the wrong direction. And there seemed to be no one about. In spite of the fact that the whole of the Ottawa valley had been divided into timber limits, almost all of them owned by some lumberman – mostly, according to the map, either Jacob Tyson or J. R. Booth – the forest was strangely silent. No noise of chopping and sawing, no great crash as another monster tree fell to its death, no trumpet sounding its clear note through the air as the cook called the men in for supper.

It was this more than anything else which brought home to Kester the immensity of the Canadian forest. And this which gave him his first doubts as to whether he would ever escape.

Perhaps I should have gone back to the camp, he thought. Four days' walking . . . I could probably have found my way back without much difficulty. Now I'm twice as far away and might be going in a different direction altogether. I might be walking in circles . . .

And yet, if he had gone back, what kind of a welcome would he have received? Serle hated him. He had told – probably paid – Duffy to lose him. What might he do next, if Kester came strolling back into the camp, knowing that what Serle and Duffy had done was no better than attempted murder.

Murder.

They wouldn't, he thought. They wouldn't deliberately kill me. But accidents could happen anywhere. A tree falling. An axe slipping. A sledge running out of control down the skid road. An experienced man could find plenty of ways of ridding himself of someone who was being a nuisance.

Why was Kester a nuisance?

Because I came looking for Rowenna, he thought. He wants her for himself – even though she's married. He thinks if I'm out of the way she'll turn to him.

But there was more than that. He remembered Serle's face when Jacob had given him the map, showing him the plan of Rowenna's own timber limit. He hadn't wanted Kester to go there. And he hadn't wanted Abe to take him. Instead, he had manoeuvred things so that Abe could not go, and he had sent Duffy in his place to ensure that he never arrived.

What was there about those limits that he didn't want Kester to see?

Dusk was beginning to gather, and a cold wind ran through the forest. It was time to pitch camp. The sun had long gone, blotted out by sullen grey clouds that seemed to descend into the forest itself, creeping like a huge, soft-padded animal between the trees. But the ground was too swampy, and although it was now freezing over, there were still thin patches in the ice and Kester knew that he must get on to drier ground before he could rest. He moved inland, away from the water's edge, striking with his axe at the trees as he passed them to make a blaze that would lead him back in the morning.

And it was then that he found the skidway.

It was the first sign he had seen that these forests had ever been worked, but he realised now that the trees around him were mostly hardwood, with saplings growing between them, as if all the pine and hemlock had been taken out.

It was not always easy to tell that a particular spot had been harvested. Old stumps and fallen logs lay everywhere in the forest. Trees near the edge of lakes were felled by beavers. New growth was taking place all the time as the forest regenerated itself, giving rise to the widely held idea that it would last for ever, however much was taken out by man. But now that Kester looked more carefully, he could see that there was a pattern to the place, that there was more young growth than normal, that the stumps were all of the same height and did not have the conical shape left by the gnawing of a beaver.

And there was the skidway, a log platform built to pile timber on as it waited to be skidded down to the river. At some point in the past, men had been here, the forest had resounded to the noise of their operations. Somewhere nearby there was a camp – a camboose probably, where they slept, ate and cooked all in one big log shanty. If he walked inland from here, he would find it.

Kester hesitated. It was almost dark now, and the first flurries of snow were feathering his face. He could still see enough to light his fire, but in fifteen minutes even that much light would be gone. And here, by the skidway, was the bark that had been hacked from the logs, and the splinters of wood that had been taken off as the timber was squared. Plenty of material to build a rough shelter, plenty of kindling for his fire.

By the time the snow started in earnest, he was inside his hut, his fire smouldering safely just inside, listening to the wind surging through the trees above. And when he woke next morning, the forest was covered in a thick white blanket of snow and a tall man, with reddish skin, a nose like a hawk's beak and black eyes, was bending to peer in at him.

Kester lay still, rolled in his mackinaw, staring up at the dark silhouette of the man who stood at the opening of his rough shelter.

'Who are you?'

The man squatted down. He said nothing and Kester wondered if he had understood. Could wild Indians who lived in the woods speak English? They had, he knew, become much more civilised now; the days of the wagon trail, and the burning of farmsteads, were over. Many of them lived in reservations, but it wasn't easy for them to continue their tribal life and traditions, and he felt a kinship with the wanderers who would rather dwell beneath the stars than shut themselves up in houses, and lived in harmony with the land, instead of trying to force it to do their bidding.

But Indians, like everyone else, were being forced to take on the white man's ways. To fight for their land, they had needed guns and horses. And in the end they had been driven back, their vast stamping grounds taken from then, and even took European names.

Kester looked at the red man. He was the first he had seen at close quarters, and he felt a twinge of unease. Stories of white men being brutally murdered, their scalps removed and hung from the Indian's belt as a trophy, slunk into his mind. Where had this Indian come from? Were there more outside? What did they intend to do?

'Who are you?' he asked again, and then, pointing to himself, 'Kester.'

Suddenly, the man smiled. He showed teeth that were yellow with age, but strong and whole. He moved, so that he was no longer in silhouette, and Kester could see him more clearly. He wore ordinary working clothes, similar to Kester's – a mackinaw jacket and trousers, with moccasins on his feet. At his belt he carried a knife and a tomahawk. There was no sign of any scalps.

'You come from Wolf Lake,' he stated suddenly, and Kester breathed a sigh of relief. Grey Otter, he thought. The

Indian trapper who knew the forest like the back of his hand, who had rescued wandering lumbermen before.

He sat up, shrugging his arms into the sleeves of his jacket, and nodded.

'I'm looking for a timber limit.'

'Wolf Lake? Wolf Lake a long way from here.'

'I know,' Kester said ruefully.

The Indian stared at him thoughtfully. 'You should go south to Wolf Lake.'

'I know. But I'm not going back there.' How could he explain? 'I'm looking for – ' He fumbled in his pocket and drew out the map, wondering if it would mean anything to the red man. 'See, I want to get to this place – by Coon Lake. There's some trees there I want to see. D'you know where it is?'

The Indian took the paper and studied it, while Kester watched anxiously. Had he ever seen a map before? This one was specially complicated for, apart from the twisting river and its tributaries and the ragged shapes of the lakes, it was divided into numerous squares and rectangles, each one denoting a timber limit, together with the name of the man to whom it was assigned.

'Coon Lake,' the red man said, and pointed to the shape marked with that name.

'Yes, that's it,' Kester said, feeling encouraged. 'Do you know it?'

'Ugh. I know. One day walking from here.'

'A *day*? So I'm almost there!'

The tall man looked out at the snow. It was at least a foot deep, and piled up in huge drifts. 'In summer, a day. Now – two or three days.'

Kester sank back, gazing at him in dismay. Two or three days in deep snow, and then the long walk back to the camp – if he could find it – with the weather worsening all the time? And little food, apart from the fish he had been able to catch? And no more of them, in all probability, for the lakes were freezing fast and he had been forced to break the ice at the edges to do his fishing. Yesterday, he had caught nothing at all.

Would he starve to death first, or freeze?

And if he did make it, and found his way back to the camp – what then? He had no illusions now as to the welcome Serle would give him.

'I take you to Coon Lake,' Grey Otter said suddenly.

'*You'll* take me? But – why?'

The Indian shrugged. 'I go there sometimes. Why not now? I got skins anyway.'

Skins? What did he mean? Kester sat up again. He realised that the Indian must have replenished the fire, for it was burning brightly, a small, sturdy blaze that warmed the shelter. He felt suddenly hungry.

'You don't have to take me to Coon Lake,' he said. 'But I'd be glad if you could show me which way to go. And if you have any food you could sell . . .'

Grey Otter looked at him. For a few moments, he did not speak. His face was set in stern, almost forbidding lines, his dark eyes thoughtful. At last he shook his head.

'Red men don't sell food.' He straightened up and stood just outside the shelter, still within Kester's vision. 'I go to Coon Lake. You come too, if you want. But first, we eat.'

And he strode off through the snow, not even looking to see whether Kester were following or not.

Kester scrambled out of his shelter. He stamped out the fire and scattered the dead ashes – timber fires had been started before by careless loggers. The Indian's footprints marked a track through the snow, and he followed them, noticing that the sun was once more shining after the storms of the night, and the trees cast long blue shadows on the snow.

He found Grey Otter in the remains of the logging camp. As Kester had expected, it was an old camboose, with one large shanty, in a clearing that was rapidly becoming over-grown. But someone – the Indian? – had cleared away some of the saplings and stacked the wood under a bark shelter. And in the middle of the clearing was a wigwam.

The Indian was standing over a fire, stirring something in a metal pot. He glanced up as Kester hesitated, and beckoned him nearer.

'Food. We eat before we go.'

'Thank you.' Kester peered into the pot. A delicious aroma of meat and herbs rose into the air, good enough to eat in itself, and he realised suddenly how long it was since he had eaten meat. All at once ravenous, he was hard put to it not to wrench the pot from the fire and devour its con-tents instantly, but instead he sat down on a rock and waited while his host divided it between two birch-bark bowls and handed him one.

'What is it?'

'Snowshoe hare. Good white fur. I trap him.' He began to eat and Kester followed his example. The meat was tender and its juices rich and hot. He could feel them coursing down his body, heating his stomach. There were vegetables in there too of some kind – roots which he could chew, leaves with aromatic flavours. It was as good as anything he had ever eaten in gypsy camp, as good as anything he had cooked for himself. He ate three bowlfuls of the stew and then grinned at the red man.

'That was good. Put new life into me.'

The stern head inclined a little. Grey Otter got up and took his bowl, wiping both out with leaves and stowing them into a pack. Then he looked at the sky.

'We go to Coon Lake now.'

'Now?'

'Snow on the way again.' He pointed up at the blue sky,

visible through the swaying crowns of the trees. 'Soon we don't go anywhere.'

'But don't you want to stay here? This is your camp – your home. Why should you go traipsing off to Coon Lake?'

The Indian waved his hand. 'This is my home. Forest – all is my home. Here – Coon Lake—' he shrugged. 'Coon Lake is better for you, anyway.'

'Better for *me*? But – why?'

Grey Otter stared at him. Then he turned away and went into the wigwam. When he came out, a few minutes later, his pack was bulging. He laced up the canvas flap, making the wigwam secure against the weather, and then turned to Kester and jerked his head.

'Come. We go to Coon Lake.'

Kester looked at him. The man had obviously made up his mind. He was already turning away, moving off towards the edge of the old camp. It seemed that he was going to Coon Lake, whether Kester accompanied him or not.

But why? What was there in an unharvested timber limit to interest an Indian?

'They tell me you're known for rescuing men lost in the forest,' Kester observed as they walked in single file through the trees.

The Indian shrugged. 'Men get lost sometimes. If I find them, I guide them out. No more than that.'

'But you've rescued people from bears? From wolves?'

At this, the red man laughed outright, a sharp bark that could itself have been mistaken for a wolf's yap. 'Don't white men have any other stories to tell? No gods? Maybe the bush gets into their heads.'

It gets into their heads. Kester looked around at the tall trees that seemed to grow on for ever, stretching across thousands of miles. Perhaps it was natural that this

472

immensity should begin to play tricks with a man lost in its vastness. And the loggers, used as they were to living in the middle of the bush, were not necessarily accustomed to being alone there. A logging camp was a busy, noisy, gregarious place. The forest was silent and, especially as dusk fell, menacing.

Even he, who was happy to wander alone, who had lived in wild enough places for most of his life, found the sounds and silences of the forest unnerving, and was glad of the Indian's company.

They walked all day together, scarcely speaking. Grey Otter went first, apparently able to find a path through even the thickest of the trees. He trod lightly, making no sound in the snow even though there must have been twigs and branches out of sight under its white blanket. Kester followed, his admiration increasing. His own people were wild, like the Indians, but even their woodcraft was not of this quality.

After a while, Grey Otter turned suddenly aside. Kester stopped, watching him bend and examine something on the ground, then give a grunt of satisfaction. He stood up, with something dangling from his hand, and beckoned Kester to join him.

'Mink. Good for fur.' He was holding a steel trap, removing the dead animal from its jaws. He eased it free without damaging the pelt, then stowed it in his pack.

Kester looked at the trap. 'Is that yours? Did you set it?'

'Before the fall,' came the laconic reply.

'My traps all along this way. Get good furs. Mink, otter, muskrat, coon. Nearer the water, get beaver. All good furs.'

They set off again, Kester thinking deeply. Clearly, the Indian not only knew this part of the forest, he lived in and worked it regularly. He had been here during the summer and fall, setting his traps, making deadfalls, and now he was

473

on his rounds, collecting what animals had been caught and taking their pelts to be sold. But where would he take them, this far into the bush? Were there any townships, any settlements? Where did he trade?

That night they camped beside a lake. Together, they set up their shelter and Kester built a fire while the Indian skinned his catch for the day. He had stopped at several more traps after that first one and had a good bag of mink, otter and raccoon. He had also shot four red squirrels with his bow, and these were roasted over the fire. Kester thought he had never eaten anything as good.

'You know the way to live in woods,' Grey Otter said at last, as he sat smoking his pipe after the meal. 'But there are things you don't know. You don't come from these woods.'

Kester shook his head. 'I come from England,' he said, wondering if the name would mean anything to the Indian.

The black eyes widened. 'Over the big water?'

'Yes. But I didn't live in a house.' He explained about gypsies and travellers. 'We don't live as wild as you do – England's too small. And there aren't enough wild animals to live off the land. But we can snare rabbits and hares, and catch fish with our fingers. And make fires in the rain and the snow,' he added with a glance at the sky. The clouds were rolling in again and it looked ominously black.

For a while, they talked about their different cultures. Kester discovered that the red man's command of English was better than he had at first supposed; he spoke economically because he disliked waste, even of words. But his intelligence was sharp and quick, and he understood concepts and ideas. He nodded his head as Kester talked about the culture of his people, and as the two men realised that there was much in common between them, they were aware of a bond.

'White man don't go for tradition,' Grey Otter said. 'Thinks only about tomorrow. But today's the only day we got, and yesterday made today. Made us, too. Good magic.'

Kester gazed at him thoughtfully. 'You mean our past is important because it made us what we are?'

'Ugh. Must remember – not forget. Not let it die. Memory is important to all peoples. Makes a – a' – he waved his hand, indicating that he did not know the correct word – 'a string, a rope.'

'A link,' Kester suggested, but the Indian had never heard the word so could not tell whether it was right or not. 'You mean that our memories are a link between the past and the present.'

'Ugh.' The Indian looked around at the forest, at the frozen lake, hidden now beneath a smooth white blanket of snow. 'All this real – we can touch, see, smell. But also a world we can't see.' He tapped his head and then his heart. 'World in here. Part of that too. Two together make real – memories and tradition tell us meaning.'

'Meaning? What meaning?' The Indian was trying to tell him something important, something that lurked at the edge of his mind, just beyond his grasp. 'What meaning is it that's so important? What is it that tradition and history tells us?'

'Not by itself. All that too.' Grey Otter's hand waved again. 'All together.'

All together. Kester gazed out across the lake. The clouds had drifted apart and revealed a rising moon that lit the snow-covered lake with gleaming white. The reality that one could see and touch, together with the world that lived inside – both added to the traditions of one's own people, and the memories of a past that went back further than one, two or even three lifetimes. What did it all mean?

'Life,' Grey Otter said suddenly, and repeated the simple word. 'Life. People search. But it's here all the time. No need to search.'

The meaning of life. Could he be right?

Kester thought of his father's philosophy. *Take your chances when they come, and if they don't come, make them.* Was he right? Was Grey Otter right? Or were they both right?

He sighed and threw another log on the fire. The clouds, which had parted to reveal that brilliant, cold moon, had now drawn together again and an icy wind raced across the snow and splintered against his cheek. He rolled himself in his mackinaw and lay down.

It was mid-afternoon the next day when they finally arrived at Coon Lake and found Rowenna's timber limit.

They had walked steadily since dawn, stopping only to examine Grey Otter's traps and retrieve whatever had been caught in them. Not all the animals were worth keeping; some were old or sick, with poor or mangy pelts. Most were buried under the snow, and had to be dug out. The Indian showed Kester how he had marked the trees nearby with blazes, several feet above the ground, to indicate where the traps were. A few traps were still empty and some had been sprung without catching anything.

'Fisher weasel does that,' Grey Otter said. 'He's a devil creature, bad magic. He can even open a porcupine.'

They found some more mink, a couple of martens and two beaver. The beaver were big, heavy animals, and the Indian skinned them on the spot. Their meat was good to eat as well, and he wrapped it carefully in leaves and stowed it in his bag, to be roasted later.

'Not far now,' he said. 'Coon Lake not far from here.'

Kester felt his excitement rise. What he was expecting to see, he had no idea, but Coon Lake was his objective, the reason why he had embarked on this long and arduous journey, and now it was close. More than that, it seemed to be the Indian's objective too, and Kester was curious to see why. What was there that would interest an Indian, apart from a few more traps?

They crossed the last ragged finger of the big delta of tributaries running into the Ottawa River. The ground rose sharply in front of them in a long, rugged cliff. From the top of this ridge, they would be able to stand and look down on Rowenna's trees, and then perhaps he would understand . . .

A narrow path led up the face of the cliff. It was the first Kester had seen since leaving the logging camp. But he had no time to wonder, for within moments they were at the top, pushing their way through the last of the brushwood, and then the world opened out before them and he found himself standing on the edge of an escarpment, gazing northwards over thousands of miles of forest.

But it was not the forest that caught his attention now, not the trees that gripped him. For immediately below was a sight for which he had been totally unprepared. A sight he recognised at once, but knew should not have been here.

A logging camp. The clearings and shanties of a large logging camp. And to his ears there now came the sounds that went with it – the chopping, the sawing, the cries and shouts, the yell of 'Timber-r-r-r!' as yet another giant of the bush crashed to the forest floor.

Rowenna's timber stands, which were to have been kept until she decided for herself what to do with them, were being harvested. And with the sight, Kester understood everything.

Chapter Twenty-Four

'For pity's sake,' Serle said, 'the man's dead. You have to face it, my dear. It's no use hiding your head in the sand any longer.' He moved towards her, as if to take her in his arms. 'Forget him. You're a free woman. You can do anything you like.'

Rowenna stared at him. She moved away, shaking her head. 'I can't forget him. He went into the forest to find my trees. If it had not been for that, he would be here today.' Her voice broke. 'I can't believe he's dead. I *won't* believe it.'

'Rowenna, look out of the window.' Serle's voice was tinged with exasperation. 'The snow's piled up, six feet deep. If it's like that here, what do you suppose it's like further north? No man could survive alone in the forest, with no shelter or equipment. Not unless he were an Indian.'

'But Kester's a gypsy. He's used to living wild. He knows how to survive – '

'A gypsy! Why, they're no more than tramps. We have them here – vagrants, wandering from place to place looking for handouts. Put one of them in the bush and he'd die of fright before cold and starvation had a chance. A shifty, useless lot.'

'Kester's not like that! He's a fine human being – he's

479

brave and intelligent. And he would never, never go off and leave another man in the forest without searching for him.'

'And you think Duffy didn't search for him? He was exhausted when he got back to camp. Was it his fault your gypsy friend wandered off without making sure he knew the way back? If it was anybody's fault,' Serle continued, 'it was mine, for sending them out in the first place. I should have known something like that would happen. The man was a greenhorn, not fit to be let loose in the bush, and I could have lost one of my best men along with him.'

There was a short silence. Rowenna sank down on a chesterfield and covered her face with her hands. After a moment, she felt Serle at her side. This time, when he touched her, she did not move away.

'Rowenna, my dear,' he said gently, 'it really is time you faced the facts. It's five months now since Matthews disappeared. Five months of cruel winter, with temperatures of twenty below freezing. How *could* he have survived? The best you can hope for him is that he *didn't* survive too long – that his sufferings were over quickly.'

Rowenna lifted her face and searched his eyes. They were silver this morning, reflecting the cold light of the snow outside. They looked straight back at her, calm and direct, without fear or guile.

'You really do believe it, don't you?' she said slowly.

'Of course I do! Haven't I been telling you, all these months?' His arms were around her, holding her loosely, and she wondered how long they had been there, why she had not noticed their touch. 'My dear,' he went on gently, 'don't think I don't understand. You loved him. Of course you did. He was the first man ever to show you kindness, to let you see that there were men in the world who were not like your father or your husband. It was only natural that you should fall in love with him. And to lose him so soon, before you could really get to know each other, before you could really know whether it was a love that would last – believe me, I understand your pain.' He was silent for a moment, then added in a quiet voice, 'If anyone understands that, I should. Haven't I loved you from the first moment I saw you?'

'Serle – ' she began and he nodded quickly.

'I know. I promised never to mention it again. But that was when Kester was still alive. I knew it was useless – you told me so yourself. *Never while Kester Matthews walks this earth*, you said.' He paused and his voice was almost too quiet to hear as he said, 'Some time, you will have to recognise the truth and start looking to the future.'

She looked up at him, startled. But already he was moving away, as if afraid he had said too much, and a moment later Fay came into the room and stared at them suspiciously.

'Well, you two look as if you've been talking secrets! Why don't you share them with me? I love a secret.'

'No secret at all,' Serle said easily, turning from the window where he had been gazing out at the snow. 'I was just trying to persuade Rowenna to come skating. The ice is really good on the canal just now, but she thinks it's too cold for her.'

'Well, *I* don't think it's too cold,' Fay declared, going over to take his arm and hug it against her. 'I'll come skating with you, Serle.' She began to draw him towards the door. 'Why look, the sun's coming out – it's going to be a lovely day. You stay here by the fire if you'd rather, Rowenna – we're going to have fun!'

She gave Rowenna a triumphant look and swept Serle from the room. Rowenna smiled wryly to herself, then moved to the window and stared out, as Serle himself had done just a few minutes before.

Serle had made it quite clear that he still loved her, that if she turned to him he would be there. He believed that if Kester had lived and come back, she would have realised that their love was no more than a transitory thing, and turned to Serle anyway. Could he be right?

She gazed at the snow, piled so deeply outside. What was it really like up in the forest now? Could Kester have survived – or had he been killed that very first day, by the bear that must have torn his coat?

Must she give him up for lost? And if so, what should she do next?

The weather began to improve. Spring came quickly on the heels of winter and the snow piled in the streets, and still a thick white blanket over the Gatineau Hills, began to thaw and run down into the river. The ice melted, leaving lumps like small icebergs to float down to the seaway, and the river itself swelled with the meltwater coming down from the higher tributaries.

'The first rafts are starting to come,' Jacob Tyson observed, standing on his favourite vantage point on Parliament Hill. The scene was already busy, with barges plying to and fro and the rafts that had been caught in the ice last fall now being released. 'Now you'll see some action. The river's like a town, rafts from shore to shore – you could walk to Hull across 'em. And when the sawmills get started over on Chaudiere, you can't hear yourself speak for the noise.' He turned to walk back to the house on Elgin Street. 'I like it. I like to see the folk about, all got something to do, somewhere to go. I like to hear the place humming. Busy, that's the secret of a good life, being busy.'

'Yes,' Rowenna walked beside him. She hesitated for a moment and then said, 'Grandfather, I have to talk to you.' His sharp eyes turned towards her, the shaggy brows drawn down a little. 'I've been thinking – I think I shall have to go back to England.'

Jacob stopped dead in the middle of the sidewalk. 'Go *back?*'

'Yes.' Her face was filled with distress. 'I don't want to. I don't want to at all. But since my father and Alfred died – '

'You couldn't have gone back then,' he interrupted. 'They'd been dead a month before you knew it – and the weather wasn't fit – '

'I know. And there was nothing I could do. Mr Abercrombie had everything in hand, and the other lawyers – my father's and Alfred's – said there was much to be sorted out before I could be involved. And Grandison, my father's clerk, was keeping all in order at the mill. But now, I think I should go back. I still don't know how the property is all disposed – Matilda must have some inheritance – and as long as I stay here I shall never be quite sure what's happening. I shall have to go.'

Jacob took her hand. 'Does it really matter, my dear? Can't you simply let the lawyers sort it out? You don't have to involve yourself.'

Rowenna shook her head. 'I must. If I own the mill now – or any other part of the property – I must see that it's operated properly. Besides, it's my own income. What else do I have to live on?'

'You have the money your mother left for you. And the timber.'

Her eyes filled with tears. 'The timber. Do you know, Grandfather, I wish I had never heard of it. I know my mother meant it for the best – and so did you – and I was happy enough when I first heard of it. But now – what has it done for me? It's taken away the only man I could ever love! If it hadn't been for that timber, Kester would never have gone into the forest, he would never have been lost.'

483

She gazed up the river at the logs that were coming down, the huge rafts made up of fifty or a hundred cribs, all lashed together. 'Men are coming down now from the camps,' she said in a low voice. 'If Kester had come out of the forest, they would have heard of it. They would have known. Perhaps he would even have come down with them. But there's never been a word.'

Jacob held her hand between both of his. His eyes were tender as he said, 'There's still a chance. He may have made it to one of the more remote camps. He might be travelling even now. You've kept your hope so long. Rowenna. Are you going to give up now?'

She shook her head. 'I've hoped for too long, Grandfather. I seem to have spent all my life waiting for Kester and losing him. I'm beginning to think it was never meant to be. Or perhaps his father was right.'

'His father?'

'I met him once,' she said. 'At the Horse Fair at Appleby. He's a fine man – the sort of man Kester would be. Your sort of man, Grandfather.'

'And what did he say to you?'

'He said it to Kester, and Kester told me. He said we must take our chances when they come, or they might never come again. Kester and I didn't take our chance when we had it, and it's never come again.' She turned back to gaze at the crowded waters of the river. 'I didn't want to believe that Kester had really been lost, but what else could have happened? You aren't allowed a second chance. I should have known it from the beginning.'

They walked on in silence, crossing the Rideau Canal to visit Byward Market, one of Rowenna's favourite places. Jacob kept her hand tucked firmly into the crook of his arm. He could feel her sorrow, knew it in the echoes of his own life. He had lost his own wife too soon in their marriage, too soon in a long life that could only be filled now by keeping busy. Hard work, he thought, that's the only thing in life you can trust, the only thing that's constant.

But how could a woman fill her life in the same way as a man? Married, she would have a husband and children to look after, certainly – but there would be servants to help her. Women of Rowenna's class did not scrub floors and cook dinners. It wasn't like it had been for his Jemima, living the life of a settler's wife in the forest. That would have suited Rowenna, he knew, far more than sitting at home or paying calls on the neighbours as his daughter Ruth did, far more than the parties and balls that delighted Fay.

'I thought it would be different here,' Rowenna had said once, a little ruefully. 'I thought the Canadians would be freer – not so formal. But a lady is still expected to go calling in white kid gloves. It seems so strange, when people were living in log shanties only a short time ago.'

'I reckon that's why,' Jacob had replied. 'Their aim was to get out of the shanties and into homes as good as those back home. Or better! And it's like Serle says – folk only appreciate their homes when they've left 'em. So they try to make up for being homesick by building their home here, as near as they can get it, like what they left behind.'

You could see the proof of that wherever you looked, he thought now as they strolled slowly through the city streets. On Byward, the market was in full swing, with stalls set up and down the thoroughfare, loaded with spring vegetables, fish and craft goods. Women bustled about with their shopping bags, stopping to examine goods, considering the quality and prices before deciding which to buy. Horses and traps thronged the road, delivering more produce, and on every side they could hear the cries of the vendors, shouting their wares.

It was just like any market place back in England, he thought, and the flat-fronted redbrick shops and houses behind the stalls had been built in just the style of some prosperous industrial town. Even he had done the same thing in naming his own settlement Penrith, after the little country town where he had grown up in Cumberland.

'It's natural you should feel homesick,' he said as they crossed the canal again to return to Elgin Street. 'But I wish you wouldn't think of going back. I like having you here. I'd miss you. And you don't have to worry about what you'll live on. We're your family – we'll take care of you. And you do have some money of your own, even if your husband left you nothing.'

'I know. But I have responsibilities there. The house – the mill. Mr Abercrombie wrote to say it was all in hand and he would take care of things for me, but I need to know for myself. There are the people who work there – the servants.' They turned the corner of Lisgar and Elgin. 'I can't leave them to – '

'Hallo!' her grandfather interrupted. 'Who's that at our door? A cab? Were we expecting visitors?'

'I don't think so.' Rowenna gazed curiously at the cab which had stopped in front of her grandfather's house. Two people were standing on the sidewalk, and the driver was unloading luggage. A good deal of luggage, it seemed.

She stared, half recognising the figures, half disbelieving. And then she quickened her pace.

'Why, surely—' her grandfather began, but she had loosed her hand from his arm and was now running along the street.

A man and a woman. A short, almost round, little man with curling white hair, white whiskers and bright blue eyes in a rosy, cherubic face.

He turned and saw her coming, and Rowenna almost threw herself into his arms.

486

Spring came to the forest. Warblers began to sing in the conifers, grey jays, nesting earlier than any of the other birds, finished up last winter's hidden stores of berries and insects and began at once to amass food for the next. The maples and beeches began to put out soft, tender green leaves and as the snow melted a myriad of spring flowers transformed the forest floor to a carpet of colour.

Kester watched the ice begin to melt on the river. All winter he had stayed here in the logging camp, first learning to fell the giant trees and then working with the horses. Already at home with beasts, he took over when one of the teamsters was injured by the sleigh, and spent the next few months driving the timber down the ice road to the river.

It was hard, dangerous work. Each morning, he was up at four, feeding and harnessing the horses in the bitter cold. A quick breakfast of porridge and bacon in the shanty, and he was off to the skidway. Here, piled high, was the timber the skidders had brought in from the logging area and Kester would begin at once, loading the huge logs on to his sleigh, piling them as high as the horses could draw. He would sit on the top log, take the long reins in his hands, give them the chirrup that horses everywhere seemed to understand, and watch them move forward in the shafts, throwing their weight into the task until the sleigh began to move, sliding on the smooth ice road.

He soon learned the shape and contours of the track, the steep hills where the horses might need the assistance of a second team, the downhill runs where a sandpiper would stand on top of a hillock ready to throw sand under the feet of the horses to slow down the sleigh. Plenty of men and horses had been killed, he learned, by a sleigh suddenly going down at a run and overtaking the horses, crashing into them with its whole weight and running over them as it careered out of control through the trees. There were stories of miraculous escapes – horses tumbling into hollows in the ground, unscathed by the sleigh and logs rolling over them, men buried in snowdrifts and brought out alive. But there were many more tales of deaths and horrific injuries, and Kester had no wish to add to their number.

Grey Otter had left the camp. He stayed only long enough to sell his pelts and buy whatever equipment he needed from the store, then disappeared into the bush again, to go round his traps and call at other camps. He sought Kester out before he left and the two clasped hands for a moment, looking into each other's eyes and remembering the few days and nights they had shared in the bush. It was impossible, Kester thought, to express his thanks for what the Indian had done; he could only hope that the other man understood.

Now, with the spring suddenly burgeoning around him, he stared at the meltwater coming down and thought that soon he would be able to leave here. Only one more skill to master, one more journey to make, and he would be back in Ottawa, with Rowenna again. What would he find there? What would she say when he told her the truth?

Kester thought of the day when he and Grey Otter had come down from the ridge and walked into the camp. Dumbfounded by what he had seen from the ridge, he had asked the Indian why he had not said that the timber limit was being worked. But the red man had looked at him in surprise and answered simply, 'You not ask.' And he realised that he hadn't. Taking it for granted that the trees were still standing, such a question had never occurred to him. And the Indian, thinking that he already knew, hadn't bothered to mention it. Why should he?

'Tyson's,' he had answered when Kester asked him whose camp it was. 'Serle Tyson. He bin running this camp long time now – two, three years. Plenty timber taken out.'

Plenty timber taken out. *Rowenna's* timber. No wonder Serle hadn't wanted him to come up here. No wonder he had sent Duffy with instructions to lose him in the bush. For the past two or three years he had been stealing Rowenna's timber, and of course he would not want Kester to see it.

How was he getting rid of it when it reached Ottawa? Probably by selling it under a different name – perhaps he had an accomplice. But all that could be ascertained later. The main thing was for Kester to stay here, working, and then get out as soon as possible in the spring, to take the news back to Rowenna. Together, they could decide what to do.

And now spring had come and the logs were beginning to move. The meltwater was coming down fast and would soon sweep the seething, jostling crowd of timber with it into the main river. There, single logs would be lashed into cribs, and again into huge rafts which could house a dozen or more men on their way to Ottawa.

It was the quickest way to return. And Kester, watching as the river-drivers began to practise running on the first few logs, determined that this was the way in which he would come back to Rowenna.

It was a difficult and dangerous job, even more dangerous than sleighing. Riding the logs down the river was like riding a horse, but worse, Kester thought. It was all a matter of balance. He watched carefully as the other men demonstrated, leaping and dancing on the shifting logs as if they were dancing on a wooden floor, apparently unheeding of the water surging beneath. Now and then the logs rolled unexpectedly, and then the driver must keep his feet moving, flashing to and fro to maintain his position as the great timber bucked and tossed beneath him. Some of them had brought it to a fine art, performing acrobatic tricks from log to log as if they were in a circus.

One of the most popular tricks was birling. The river-driver, usually barefoot, would choose a log just large enough to hold him up – about sixteen feet long was the preferred size. With his pike pole to balance himself, he would stand in the middle and then start rolling it backwards with his feet. In a few moments it would be spinning with its own momentum, and the river-driver's feet would be racing in order to keep up. Most of them ended by falling into the river, but a few could keep it going as long as they liked, and then slow it down by their own strength.

'Step on every log you come to,' the best of them told Kester when he came ashore. 'Use the pike to help you keep your balance. And don't take long steps, just nice short ones. You see fellers take a long step and afore they know where they are, they've got one leg up and one trailing down, and they're on hands and knees. It don't take much to throw a man off balance.'

Kester practised and found that his natural litheness, together with his experience of riding horses and perhaps even his prowess at step-dancing, all helped him to master this new skill quickly. By the time the logs were going in full strength down the river he was ready to go with them.

He rode out of camp on a log, standing up to survey the forests that had been his home for the past six months. But his thoughts were no longer with timber and all the things he had learned during that time. Instead, his mind reached forward to the quaysides of Ottawa and the girl who waited for him there.

He thought of the cold, sleepless nights when she had invaded his imagination, of the memories that had tormented his mind. He thought of Rowenna in his arms in the forest near Penrith, of the kisses they had shared, the loving that had been theirs. How had she felt when she had heard the news that he had been lost in the bush? What had she thought? Had she waited, hoping to hear that he had returned, or had she been persuaded that he must have died, that no man could survive the bitter winter alone there?

Had Serle Tyson persuaded her? Had he won her, as he had been so determined to do?

She was still married, Kester thought, to that bastard Boothroyd. But that hadn't stopped Tyson from wanting her. And it was easy to see why. For Rowenna owned timber, valuable timber – timber that Serle Tyson had been stealing for the past three years. That was why he hadn't wanted Kester to go up into the forest; that was why he'd wanted him dead.

Had Duffy been paid actually to kill him? Serle would surely have wanted to be sure that the job was done. He wouldn't have wanted any chance of Kester's returning. He certainly wouldn't have wanted him to find his way to the limit and then come back to tell the tale.

Kester rode the logs, watching the river stretch its way down to the sea, and smiled. Next to seeing Rowenna's face when he returned to Ottawa, he was looking forward to seeing Serle's.

If only she'd waited for him, he thought, with a renewal of anxiety. If only the swine hadn't managed to talk her round . . .

'You mean you never received my letter?' Mr Abercrombie's face was crumpled with distress. 'Really, my dear Mr Tyson, I must apologise. I wrote as soon as I decided to come. Admittedly, I left before there was a chance of a reply – but I made it clear that I'd be happy to stay in a hotel, I wouldn't expect you to put us up.' He turned to his wife. 'My dear, we must leave at once, and find somewhere to stay. We can't put these good people out – '

'You'll do no such thing,' Jacob Tyson interrupted. 'Why, I'd be insulted if you didn't stay here with us. You helped my daughter, you've been good to Rowenna here – of course you'll stay as long as you like.'

'But why did you come?' Rowenna asked. She had been sitting on the edge of her chair ever since coming into the room. The Abercrombies had been welcomed, brought into the house, shown the bathroom and given tea. Now at last they were able to relax a little and she could ask the questions that had been crowding to her lips ever since she and her grandfather had turned the corner and seen the cab standing in front of the house. Why were they here? What had happened to make them journey all the way to Canada?

Her aunt Ruth, who had been busy arranging for a room to be prepared for the unexpected visitors, shook her head at her.

'Rowenna, you're too direct! Don't you know you should never ask visitors that question? Let them tell you in their own good time, child.'

James Abercrombie smiled and lifted one hand.

'No, no, dear lady, Rowenna's quite right to ask. Naturally she's surprised and anxious about why we've appeared so suddenly on the doorstep. It was all explained in the letter . . .' He turned to Rowenna, his rosy face kind. 'It does seem a little extreme, I daresay, to come all this way, and in normal circumstances I would rely on the postal service – not that it seems very reliable! – but in this case, I must confess that I – well, both my wife and I, to tell you the truth – '

'We wanted to see you,' Mary Abercrombie interrupted, cutting short her husband's uncharacteristic rambling.

492

'We've missed you, Rowenna, my dear.' She smiled at her husband and took his hand. 'You became like a daughter to us, you see. The worry over your marriage, seeing how unhappy you were. Helping you to escape – helping you to come to Canada. We just felt we had to see you again.'

Rowenna's eyes filled with tears. She reached out both her hands and the Abercrombies took one each. They sat for a moment, clasping each other's fingers, feeling the warmth of true affection flow from one to the other, and then Mr Abercrombie cleared his throat loudly and felt in his pocket for a large white handkerchief.

'Hrrmph! Well, there was also the little matter of explaining your inheritance to you – papers to sign – that sort of thing. These things can be complicated done through the post – it's especially difficult to send important documents. Always better done in person, I believe.'

'I think so too,' Rowenna said. 'I was going to come to England to see you. I should have come earlier, but the winter – '

'No, no, my dear, not necessary at all. It's taken all this time to sort out the affairs of the mill. There were other solicitors involved, you see – your father's and your husband's, and each one taking his own time. Nothing you could have done any earlier. Besides, we were glad of the excuse to make the journey.' He smiled at his wife and then at Rowenna. 'We've always wanted to travel,' he confided. 'It's been a promise made to ourselves for many years now – that one day we'd travel. And here we are at last.' His smile widened. 'I've handed over most of my business to my son-in-law and retired. This is my last task before we become gypsies!'

Gypsies. The word struck at Rowenna's heart and she caught her breath. How could she have forgotten Kester, even in the excitement of seeing her friends? How could she have forgotten that he had been lost in the Canadian forests, had wandered in the bitter cold, had probably starved to death? Her eyes filled once again with tears and her lips trembled.

'My dear!' Mary Abercrombie was all concern. 'What is it? What's upset you?'

Rowenna shook her head. 'Please – don't let's talk about it. Tell me what papers you have for me to sign, and what is happening to my father's and husband's property.'

Within a few weeks, the logs were crowding down the river into Ottawa and the quaysides were thick with ships loading timber to take overseas. The sawmills were busy day and night, the screech of their saws audible on both banks, and the city was filled with lumbermen fresh from the bush with money in their pockets.

The Abercrombies were out every day, exploring the city and walking beside the river or canal, marvelling at the strange sights and sounds, so different from Kendal. They crossed to Hull, amused to find themselves in what amounted to a foreign country, with French being spoken on all sides, and took trips up into the Gatineau Hills to wonder at their beauty. They listened to Rowenna's descriptions of her stay in Penrith and Jacob's tales of the forests and logging camps, and they gazed at the Rideau Canal, fascinated by stories of how in winter it was frozen, the ice crowded with skaters.

Serle had left for Penrith to make his next visit to the camp to see how work had progressed during the winter. Before leaving, he had tried once more to persuade Rowenna to forget Kester.

'He wasn't for you. He was a gypsy – rough, uneducated. He couldn't ever settle into our ways. You'd have lived to regret it, my dear, if you'd allowed yourself to become involved with him.' His voice softened. 'Marry me, Rowenna. Forget all that's happened to you in the past. I'll take care of you.'

She gazed at him. Since the night when he had thrust himself upon her in the farmhouse at Penrith, he had been careful never to touch her except in gentle affection. He had apologised over and over again for that incident, telling her that he had been overwhelmed by his love for her, that his passion had been too much for him. But now, he said, it was under control and he would never frighten her again.

'I understand you had some unhappy times with your husband,' he said, stroking her fingers gently. 'It wouldn't be like that with me, I promise you.'

'Serle – please – '

'It's all right,' he said. 'I don't want any answer now. I just want to know that I've a chance – I just want to know that while I'm in Penrith you'll remember me occasionally – write to me – and that you'll think about what I've asked you. Will you do that? Will you?'

She shook her head helplessly. 'Serle, I don't think I will ever marry again. I can't imagine – '

'Oh, now, that's foolish. of course you will. You're a young woman – still only twenty-two or -three. You're still feeling upset at the moment – it's not surprising. You've had enough happen to you in the past two or three years to last most people a lifetime. But that'll pass, believe me. And then you'll want what all women want most – a husband and home of their own. Children.' He touched her cheek with a delicate forefinger. 'You don't want to go through life without having children, do you?'

Rowenna thought of the months when she had thought herself to be carrying Alfred's child and shuddered a little. She had scarcely known what to feel during those months, knowing that if there was a child it had been conceived in hatred and brutality. What would she have felt if it had been a true pregnancy, if there had been a child born to her, a child of Alfred's blood? Would she have loved or hated it?

I want children, she thought, but there is only one man I want for their father.

'We won't talk about this any more now,' Serle said quietly. 'But promise me you'll think about it while I'm away. And then we'll talk again.'

Since then, the Abercrombies had arrived and now she knew what Alfred and her father had done with their property. She knew that it was all hers – the mill, both houses, the entire business. All that Matilda had been left by a husband who had increasingly hated her was the right to live in Ashbank for as long as she wished and sufficient income to keep her for the rest of her life.

Alfred had never changed his will. Perhaps he had been too proud to go to a lawyer and admit that she had left him, perhaps he had never stopped believing that she would return. Whatever his reasons, his will left everything he owned, apart from a few small bequests to his sister, to his 'dear wife, Rowenna'.

She was a woman of property. A woman who owned timber concessions in Canada, a stake in the family business here in Ottawa, and another thriving mill in England. By combining all interests, she could become almost as powerful a force in the timber industry as her grandfather, or perhaps even John Booth or Ezra Butler Eddy.

Was that what she wanted? She recalled the days when Haddie had taken her into the mill with him and shown her how the fourdriniers worked, how he had explained the ledgers and accounts. She remembered how she had begged her father to allow her to help him and how he had refused. Now the mill was hers, to do with as she pleased. Should she go back and settle down as a manufacturer, flouting convention, ignoring the fact that women did not do these things?

Why not? How had convention ever helped her? Wasn't it when she turned her back on it that she found what she had most wanted in her life?

Oh Kester, Kester, she thought, why are you not here, so that we can share this? Together, we could work the mill and build up the logging, together we could conquer the world . . . Kester, Kester . . .

But Kester was not here. Kester had been lost in the forest. And though she could still not accept the possibility that he might be dead, she was slowly coming to face the fact that she was not likely to see him again.

She stood at her bedroom window, gazing out across the city at the forest that spread away into the distance. The blazing colours of fall had been replaced by the green of summer. For a few weeks it would be like this, then the colours would begin to change, the blaze of autumn flame across the landscape and the logging year begin again.

She thought of the choices that lay before her. Leave this country and return to England, to a mill and home that held nothing but painful memories? Or – marry Serle? Or take a third choice, which was to do neither but make her own life, away from all that had gone before, abdicating all responsibilities and living only for herself.

'You're going back to England?' Jacob Tyson said, his brows bristling. 'Well, I'm disappointed. It's been a pleasure to have you here, a great pleasure. I'd hoped you'd stay longer.'

'Indeed, we've trespassed on your hospitality far too long as it is,' James Abercrombie answered. 'And it's been a wonderful experience for us. But there are things to see to at home – family affairs to be attended to, you understand

497

the kind of thing. And if we're to accompany Rowenna – '

'*Rowenna?*' Jacob turned and stared at his grand-daughter, who came quickly forward and laid her hand on his arm. 'Are you leaving me too? This is the first I've heard of this.'

'I'm so sorry – I'd no idea – ' James Abercrombie began, his face puckered like a baby's with distress, but Rowenna shook her head at him and he broke off.

'Grandfather, I have to go. I can't go on with my life, knowing that all that is there in England, going on without me. I'm responsible for it. I have to see for myself what's happening and decide what to do about it all. There are two houses to maintain, for a start – servants who must be wondering what's going to happen. I can't leave it all in the air. You understand that, don't you?'

Her eyes pleaded with him to understand much more. He gazed at her with his bright blue eyes, then sighed and patted her hand.

'Aye, I understand. You need to make your own decisions. You need to know your life is yours at last, and that you don't have to answer to anyone – man or woman. You need that freedom and independence you've never had.'

'Perhaps that's it,' she said slowly. 'Do you know, I hadn't thought it out for myself – but perhaps that's why I must go. I'd thought about it all in terms of other people – but perhaps it's really for myself that I want to make the journey.'

'And it's high time too,' her grandfather said. 'Live your life for yourself, Rowenna. Think of others, yes, take your responsibilities, but don't let them rule you. Take on the responsibilities *you* want – not those other people foist on to you. It's all I've ever done, and I'm a happy man.'

'Yes,' she said, and kissed his cheek. 'Oh, Grandfather, I was afraid you'd be upset. I almost decided not to go – '

'Because of me?' He shook his head. 'You've done

enough of that in your life, child. Letting your own chances go by while other people took theirs. Go now, and come back to me when you're ready. I'll be here. I've not lived this long to be snatched away by a puff of wind, like some people I've known!'

Rowenna left him to talk to the Abercrombies and went out. She walked through the city streets and up on to Parliament Hill, where she stood and gazed down at the crowded river.

What had she learned from all that had happened to her, all that she had seen and heard and done? What lessons had life taught her?

She thought of Kieran Matthews, the old gypsy with his black curling hair now white around his head, and his dark eyes so full of wisdom. It was his wisdom that had echoed in his son's heart and in hers, yet it seemed still that they must learn it for themselves. And what was wisdom, after all, but the learning of joy, lost or found?

How long, she wondered, did it take to learn wisdom? Time stretched before and behind her, all around, filled with the wisdom of others, like the endless forests, like a song that had no end.

Her grandfather had understood her better than she understood herself. But now her feelings were clear. Never before had she been permitted to live her own life, as herself. Always, she had been someone else's property – a daughter, a sister, a wife. Now she was her own person, her own woman, and could decide for herself what her life might be.

Jacob Tyson was not a possessive man. He loved her and wanted her – but he would not hold her back. With his love and understanding, he had set her free. And if she ever gave herself to another man, it must be one who would let her continue to be herself.

Kester would have done, she thought sadly. But Kester

was gone, and she must make her life without him.

The river was thronged with rafts. They had been coming down all summer and she had grown accustomed to the sight of them, to the little huts and shanties built upon them, to the sound of music and singing, the rap of dancing on their decks. They were still arriving, and she felt a sudden urge to go down to the quayside, to see them more closely. She began to descend the steep, wooded slope.

Halfway down, she began to hurry. It was almost as if some invisible cord were pulling her, as if something told her she must make haste. She ran down the path between the trees, her heart thumping, breathless, and came out on to the path at the very bottom of the hill, where the rafts passed close to the land and the men's faces could be seen as they steered their cumbersome craft to the docks.

Rowenna stopped. She gazed at the rafts, scanning the faces of the men aboard them. She scarcely knew what she was looking for, only that some instinct told her that she must. She clenched her hands into fists and lifted her head, stretching her body as if even those few extra inches would bring her the sight that must be there.

And then she saw him. Standing proudly at the head of the next raft to pass, his hands on his hips, his head held high. Tall and broad and strong from the months he had spent in the camp, tanned a deep brown, his black hair curling on his collar.

Kester . . .

Epilogue

The long white farmhouse at Penrith looked little different when Rowenna and her family arrived for the summer. It was as if, during all the years since her first sight of it, it had remained constant, unchanging, a symbol of all that was of most enduring value. A symbol of the love between Jacob Tyson and his wife Jemima, who had built it; of the love between Rowenna and Kester, whose home it was now.

Yet there had been many other changes in their lives. Rowenna watched the children scamper into the house, eager to make acquaintance again with old Mrs Hutty. Eleven-year-old Jacob, born just in time for his great-grandfather's blessing, for old Jacob Tyson had died quickly and easily in his sleep less than two years after Rowenna's wedding to Kester. Shy, serious Dorothy, nine years old; seven-year-old Christopher, named for his father; the twins, Mary and Louise, with their honey-cream hair so like their mother's. And in her arms, dark as any gypsy babe, Kieran, named for the grandfather who had died only a few months before.

Kester stepped down from the buggy and turned to take the baby from her arms. Together, they walked into the garden, always their first visit when they arrived from Ottawa, and stood at the edge of the forest. The trees rose high above them, their great crowns forming the rich canopy that would in a few months turn to a blaze of gold and crimson.

'Are you happy, sweetling?' Kester asked, as he always did, and she smiled at him and nodded.

'Always happy, as long as we're together. Whether it's here or in Ottawa, or back in England. It doesn't matter where – but I think I'm happiest of all at Penrith.'

'Aye,' he said, 'it's a good place. I reckon your grandfather built some happy memories in to this house, and they've lived on, for us to take care of.'

It was a thought to be cherished. Rowenna turned and looked again at the house, so different from the gloomy mill where she had grown up. Yet there had been happy moments too – in the garden with Haddon, in the bluebell grove with Kester. And when they went back now, to deal with matters concerning the mills which she still owned, the house was a different place, brightly furnished, the windows opened to let in light and air, the cheerful voices of young William Grandison's family ringing through the rooms.

William was the son of her father's clerk, who had now taken over the running of the mills in England. He had lived at Ashbank since Matilda's death, and had taken in Billy, the man who had lost his arm on the day that Warren Mellor and Alfred Boothroyd died, to be his manservant. John Richmond was now head gardener, and he and Molly had added four more children to their family, though little Jack was always their leader and talking now of going for a soldier. John had known long ago, Molly told Rowenna, that Jack was not his son, but with the generosity he had always shown, he had accepted him, for by then he loved the boy as his own, and saw no reason for that to change.

There was plenty for the English mills to do now. Rowenna had also inherited part of old Jacob's estate, which she and Kester had combined with the English business to supply paper to both British and American newspapers. New sawmills had been built in Ottawa too and soon, it was said, they would rival J. R. Booth as one of the most prominent timber businesses in Canada.

They had been good years, Rowenna thought, standing with Kester's arm about her waist. They had had their share of sadness, for Jacob's passing had left them all the poorer, old though he was. And there had been family upheavals too – Serle, his perfidy discovered when Kester had returned, had left Ottawa and gone west, where he was now working in the redwood lumber business, and Fay had been furious, first blaming Rowenna, then Kester, and eventually running away with a smooth-talking American who had promised her an easy life in California. She had returned a few years later with a baby and tales of being beaten and abused before she finally left her husband, and now lived with her parents again, subdued and bitter, devoting herself only to her son.

But for Rowenna and Kester, life had been sweet. And would continue so, she thought, for they shared a love that was rich and true and had never let them down. A love that would continue to the end of their lives without falter.

As long as Kester Matthews walks this earth, she thought, remembering those words. And remembered other words as well, words spoken long ago by Kieran Matthews in a gypsy caravan by a smouldering wood fire.

Take your chances when they come, for they may not come twice.

A selection of bestsellers
from Headline